Wall of Stone
By Nancy J. Farrier

Dedication

To Audrey, Dell, and Jeri,
who keep my writing on course;
my husband, John, who says, with good cause,
that writers starve because they forget to stop and cook;
my son, Adrian, and my daughters,
Anne, Abigail, Ardra, and Alyssa,
whose enthusiastic encouragement keeps me going.

"Afflicted city, lashed by storms and not comforted,
I will rebuild you with stones of turquoise,
your foundations with lapis lazuli.
I will make your battlements of rubies,
your gates of sparkling jewels,
and all your walls of precious stones."
ISAIAH 54:12

8 WEDDINGS
and a Miracle
Romance Collection

Janet Lee Barton, Lena Nelson Dooley, Nancy J. Farrier,
Pamela Griffin, Diann Hunt, Loree Lough, Tracie Peterson
Sandra Petit & Gail Sattler

BARBOUR BOOKS
An Imprint of Barbour Publishing, Inc.

Print ISBN 978-1-61626-546-5

eBook Editions:
Adobe Digital Edition (.epub) 978-1-63409-231-9
Kindle and MobiPocket Edition (.prc) 978-1-63409-232-6

Published by Barbour Books, an imprint of Barbour Publishing, Inc., P.O. Box 719, Uhrichsville, Ohio 44683, www.barbourbooks.com

Our mission is to publish and distribute inspirational products offering exceptional value and biblical encouragement to the masses.

ecpa Member of the
Evangelical Christian
Publishers Association

Printed in Canada.

Contents

Move a Mountain
By Lena Nelson Dooley

Dedication

This book is dedicated to my writing friends who have met in my home for several years to critique each other's work—Pamela Griffin, Candice (Candy) Speare, Beth Goddard, Lisa Harris, Jill Moore, Anne Green, Mary Ann Hayhurst, Carol Glindeman, Jeanette DeLoach, Erin Lackey, Linda Godsey, Lory and Joe May, Jamesetta Wyche, Marianne Robards, Ronnie Kendig, Susan Sleeman, Georgeanne Falstrom, Shauna Smith Duty, Dawn Morton Nelson, Rhonda Fields, and Gail Gallagher. We have been together at varying times, but you have all contributed to the author I am today. Donna Gilbert and Kaye Dacus have each visited this group, too.

I'm also dedicating it to the Wordpainters critique group—Candy Speare, Lisa Harris, and Laurie Alice Eakes—and Crit Group 9 at American Christian Fiction Writers—Pamela James, Cheryl Wyatt, Jeanie Smith Cash, Linda Rondeau, and Jenny Carlisle. We are all learning together.

As usual, I dedicate all my books to my wonderful husband, James. We've walked a long path together, often holding each other up in times of stress and sharing times of joy. My journey would be very lonely without you. I love you dearly.

Prologue

Mrs. Oleg Olson
and
Mr. and Mrs. Matthew Davis
request the honor of your presence
at the ceremony uniting
Christine Marie Dailey
and
Christopher Dean Davis
in holy matrimony
on Saturday, February 14
at 4:00 p.m.
in the chapel of
Wayzata Community Church.
Dinner reception to follow
in the Fellowship Hall.
R.S.V.P.

Chapter 1

The moon above Litchfield, Minnesota, poured liquid silver over Christine Dailey as she cuddled in the back of a horse-drawn carriage with Christopher Davis. The flirty skirt of her red satin dress blew toward her lap, and she pushed it back over her knees, hoping it would stay down. She wouldn't have worn such a short dress if she had known what would follow dinner.

She wondered if he knew that this had been her dream date. The meal at the out-of-the-way elegant restaurant had been a gourmet dream. Even though an autumn breeze nipped the air, this ride through tree-laden areas, where lovely homes with expansive lawns stood the test of time, made her feel like a princess in a fairy tale. Only one thing could make the night even better.

"Are you too cool?" Christopher's breath disturbed her hairdo, but she didn't mind.

"No." Tucked under his muscular arm, she felt anything but cold.

The *clip-clop* of the horses' hooves on the pavement matched the erratic thumping of her accelerated heartbeat. If she spent much more time so close to this man, she just might have a stroke.

Pulling from the comforting cocoon of his arms, Christine glanced up into his dark brown eyes, almost hidden in the shadows. She would never tire of looking at him. Unruly brown curls spilled across his high forehead, and she reached up and gently pushed them back, but to no avail. Christopher took the opportunity to shift her closer. His lips descended toward hers. Her eyes drifted shut, waiting for the wonderful sensations his kiss always brought her. Lost in the wonder of their embrace, she barely noticed when the forward movement of the carriage ceased. The jingling harness bells that sounded when the horses shuffled to a halt joined with the bells pealing through her head and heart.

Christopher slowly released her lips, and the love shining from his eyes went all the way through her. He pulled her arms down from around his neck and took her hands in his, rubbing his thumbs across the back of them and sending shooting shocks of sensations up her arms. "I can't get on my knees in this carriage, but I want you to spend the rest of your life with me."

Christine almost forgot to breathe. The moment she had dreamed of since the day she met this wonderful Christian man might be happening tonight. If so, this night would be perfect.

"I love you more than life itself." He paused, and she felt his hands tremble slightly. "Christine, will you marry me?"

She nodded, and her "yes" was swallowed in the soul-deep kiss that followed. Christine wished this moment could go on forever.

Much too soon, he leaned away from her. "I forgot this."

Christopher reached into the front pocket of his slacks to collect the small, midnight-blue velvet box. When he flipped it open, moonlight glittered off the most beautiful princess-cut diamond she had ever seen. He quickly removed the ring from its resting place and picked up her left hand. When he slid the cool metal onto her finger, it fit perfectly and quickly warmed to her body temperature.

She lifted her hand and turned it in the moonlight, noticing other gems that surrounded the large stone. "It's so beautiful." She glanced up at Christopher's smiling face. "How did you know I like princess-cut stones, and how did you find out my ring size?"

"Oh, I have my ways." Christopher urged her back under his protective arm and signaled the driver to go.

"I can't believe you planned all this." She was sure her smile stretched from ear to ear.

A laugh rumbled through his chest where her cheek rested. "I wanted everything to be perfect for you. I asked the driver to stop where the moonlight was brightest so you could see your engagement ring."

☙

Monday morning came too soon.

Christine stood behind the counter of her flower shop, halfway between Wayzata and Minneapolis, designing a centerpiece for one of her regular customers, when the bell over the front door tinkled announcing the entrance of her best friend and soon-to-be business partner.

"So how was the date last night?" Melissa Clark strode past the displays and hung her sweater on a hook right inside the back room while she kept talking. "Where did Christopher take you?"

Christine surveyed the almost-finished decoration and decided it needed a little more yellow. She took a deep breath to calm her excitement so Melissa wouldn't guess too soon. "Well, we went to Litchfield. Christopher knew about a new restaurant with good food and romantic ambience." As she stuck a long-stemmed flower into the design, she wiggled her left hand a little so her ring would catch the light.

Melissa came to look at her work. "Is that all you did?"

"No." Christine crossed her arms, making sure her left hand was on the outside. She wanted Melissa to notice for herself. It wouldn't be as much fun if Christine had to tell her about the ring. "We also went for a carriage ride."

After picking up a flower and gently rotating it in her fingers, Melissa placed it back with the others. "That sounds like fun."

"It was." Christine used her left hand to push a lock of hair behind her ear. "We stopped in the moonlight." The morning sun cast rainbows of color from her ring across the counter, rivaling the kaleidoscope of flowers scattered in profusion throughout the shop.

"Christine! Is that an engagement ring on your hand?" Melissa's long red corkscrew curls whipped straight out from her head when she swiveled. "Let me see it!"

After Melissa grabbed her hand, Christine gushed, "That's why we stopped in the moonlight. So he could propose. He wanted me to be able to see the ring."

Melissa grabbed Christine and danced around in the limited space behind the counter. "I'm so glad for you. When is the wedding?"

Christine carefully picked up the arrangement and started toward the display cooler. "Will you open the door for me?"

Melissa hurried around her.

After placing the design in the middle of the center shelf, Christine closed the door. "I've always dreamed of a Valentine's wedding. It sounds so romantic, pledging your undying love on the day everyone celebrates love."

"But this is Minnesota. It could be snowing." Melissa scanned through the order book then picked up a basket from behind the counter. "How about if I use this one for the Melsons' centerpiece?"

Christine pictured walking down the aisle with scattered, feathery snowflakes drifting to earth outside the windows that lined the sanctuary. Her bridesmaids, dressed in red velvet with white fur trim, preceded her down the aisle, slowly swaying to the time-honored music. "Snow would be a romantic touch—what did you say?"

❧

Nothing like the old man calling him in for a conference to dampen the start of a Monday morning. Chris wondered what had gone wrong. Dad had sounded gruff through the phone intercom. When Chris reached the double doors that led to the CEO's office, he took a deep breath and straightened his shoulders. Here he was almost thirty years old, and when he was called into his father's office, he felt like a little boy going to the principal's office. Maybe he would have felt more comfortable around him if his father had been home more while he was growing up. He had to get over this. Maybe he would just get a job somewhere else. He had good credentials. It shouldn't be too hard.

Chris lifted his fist and gave three quick raps on the solid walnut door. It was so sturdy, he wondered if his father even heard. Before he could decide whether to knock again, the door opened. The floor-to-ceiling windows that made up two connecting walls of the executive office outlined his father in warm sunshine.

"Come in, my boy." His father smiled and moved back to allow Chris to pass. Then the older man followed him and took a seat in the navy-blue Moroccan-leather chair behind his massive mahogany desk. "I have something important to discuss with you."

Chris dropped into a cushioned office chair made of the same materials as the one his father occupied. "Okay, shoot." He steepled his fingers under his chin.

"How are things going with you and Christine?" Matthew Davis sounded more like a CEO asking the question than a father.

"I proposed to her last night." Chris hadn't planned on telling him like this. He had hoped to wait until the whole family was together at their regular Friday night dinner and tell everyone at once. Of course, Chrissy would be with him, too, and the women could exclaim over her ring. Clasping his hands at his waist, he stared straight into the navy-blue eyes of his father, waiting for his reaction.

Matthew leaned forward. "Good show. I thought that should be happening soon. So when is the wedding?"

Chris shook his head. Not only at the new phrase his father had evidently picked up from one of his foreign clients, but also at the question. "I'm not sure. We're going to discuss that over dinner tonight. I'm hoping for a short engagement."

A quick laugh burst from his father. "I can see you have a lot to learn about women and weddings."

A pile of work waited on Chris's desk. This personal discussion was taking up valuable time. "Is that what you wanted to talk to me about?"

After placing his palms on the desktop, Matthew pushed to a standing position. "No, but it does concern your future here at Davis Enterprises."

Not wanting to be at a height disadvantage, Chris stood, too. "My future?"

His father turned and clasped his hands behind his back, looking out at the bright autumn sunlight bathing St. Paul. He stood there for several moments while Chris wondered what was coming.

When his father turned back toward him, a smile covered his face. "I'm going to retire. Your mother and I want to travel before we're too old to enjoy it."

"You're not getting old." Chris couldn't help interrupting.

His father beamed even more. "I know, but we have a lot of places we want to visit." He cleared his throat. "What I'm getting at is that I'm stepping down right away, and you'll be the new CEO. That has been the plan since your grandfather established the company in 1956. I took over in 1986. Now it's your turn."

Chris had to sit down. He didn't know what he expected, but it wasn't this. He was going to become CEO now, not when he was forty as his father had been. He glanced from the carpet up to his father's familiar face. "I don't know what to say."

His father sat on the desk corner nearest to Chris. "I know it's a lot to think about right now, but being CEO will give you a better salary for raising a family, won't it?" He stood up and clapped Chris on his shoulder. "I've been planning this for a while. That's why you've gradually been given more important assignments. You've earned the title. I think we'll announce it next week in the staff meeting. In the meantime, we can start the transition."

This promotion came much sooner than Chris expected it to, but he knew he could do the job. His father's decision felt like a compliment. Chris smiled all the way back to his office.

❧

Christine looked at her watch for the tenth time since she sat down at the white linen-covered table. The waiter had already brought her a refill of soda. She pulled her purse from the extra chair beside her and started digging through the contents for her cell phone. She couldn't find it until it started ringing, steering her under the empty, zippered bank bag that rested on the bottom of her tote. She glanced at the display.

"Hello, Christopher." Christine tried not to sound peeved. She really hated to wait on anyone for very long.

"Chrissy, I'm sorry. I didn't know the meeting would run so late." He did sound harried. "I'm running to the car, and it should take me less than ten minutes if the traffic isn't bad." Evidently he looked at his watch, because he whistled. "Wow, I didn't know it was this late. So okay, the traffic won't be bad. See you in a few minutes." Kissing sounds accompanied the slamming of his car door. "Maybe that'll hold you until I get there."

The smacking brought to Christine's mind the kisses they shared last night. She studied the ring on her left hand as she shut her phone and slipped it inside her oversized handbag. Warmth spread through her as she relived every moment of the kiss after he proposed. Even the memory caused her temperature to rise. She knew she couldn't stay mad at him. He was the man of her dreams. And tonight they would plan the wedding of her dreams.

The waiter came by to ask if she wanted a refill.

"No, thank you. I'll wait for my fiancé to get here."

Did the man's expression contain pity? Did he think she had been stood up? She hoped not.

When Christine came out of the ladies' room a few minutes later, Christopher sat at their table, talking to the waiter. She hurried toward him, and he stood. When she was close enough, he dropped a kiss on her cheek, but the expression in his eyes promised more when they were in a less public place. Shivers of anticipation traveled up and down her spine.

Christopher pulled out her chair, like the gentleman he always was around her. After she slipped into it, he sat down and put his hand over hers and squeezed it. His eyes said *that will have to do for now.* They discussed what they wanted to eat, and he placed the order with the waiter, who now acted more friendly than he had while she waited alone.

"So what took so long today?" Christine really wanted to know.

He leaned back in his chair. "You'll never believe what happened."

"Okay. Tell me." Her eyes traced his features. He looked tired but maybe a little elated.

Christopher took a deep breath. "It's hard to believe the day I've had. Dad called me into his office first thing this morning. I almost felt as if I were in trouble."

"Why would you feel like that?"

"I don't know. Maybe a flashback from one of my many trips to the principal's office."

Christine reached her hand toward him. He leaned forward and placed his palm against hers, intertwining their fingers.

"Dad is retiring, and I'm going to be the new CEO of Davis Enterprises."

The news astounded Christine. Christopher would be a very young chief executive officer. "Oh that's wonderful! You'll be as good or better than your father. When will it take place?"

"We're going through the transition right now. We'll announce it at next Monday's staff meeting. I'm not sure when Dad will actually leave. But we don't need to worry about that now. We have a wedding to plan. Tell me what you want."

Once more, Christine picked up her purse and dug through it until she found a small notebook. She held it up. "I'm not going to leave anything to chance. I'm writing down everything we decide."

Christopher laughed. She loved the musical sound as it enveloped her.

"So when do you want the wedding?" He scooted his chair closer to the table corner that separated them.

The look in his eyes mesmerized her, making her train of thought derail. She blinked and tried to remember what they were talking about. Oh yes, the date for the wedding. "I've always wanted to get married on Valentine's Day. What do you think?"

"It's all right with me, as long as it's this next one. I wouldn't want to wait for over a year." This time his gaze seared its way to her heart. "You can plan a wedding in four and a half months, can't you?"

After that look, she would do almost anything to please him. She had hoped to have more time.

"Of course I can."

Chapter 2

How was she ever going to get this wedding planned in four and a half months?

Christine couldn't believe she'd agreed. All her life, she looked forward to her wedding. The proposal was all she imagined and more, so she wanted the wedding to equal it. Now she wouldn't have time for anything at all to go wrong, as it often did. Of course, she and Melissa could take care of the flowers.

The wedding dress would take more time. The nearest large store that carried wedding attire was in Minneapolis. If she took the day off from the shop, maybe she could at least decide on a design. She wondered how much that would cost. Some dresses cost more than she paid for her economy car. Maybe she should talk to Sharon Thornton. Christine's friend from college worked in the marketing department of The Bridal Boutique. The headquarters for the business that supplied many high-end wedding shops across the country was outside Minneapolis. She was sure Sharon mentioned an outlet store there.

"Look what I have." Melissa's statement quickly followed the ringing of the bell above the door to Floral Haven, the shop Christine opened when Grandmother Dailey died and left her an inheritance.

Melissa hurried across the shop and plopped a stack of bridal magazines on the counter. "You know what I was thinking about?"

"What?"

"You will both be Chris Davis after you're married." She straightened her hair from the mess made by the wind. "That ought to get interesting."

"Don't you dare start calling me Chris! My name is Christine, and I always call him Christopher." *This shouldn't be a problem.* Christine started counting the magazines. "Did you really buy half a dozen?"

Melissa laughed. "More or less. The man from the supplier was there getting ready to pull them and put out the spring issues, so the storekeeper sold them to me for half price. We can look through them and see if you find anything you like."

"I thought we might go see Sharon."

"Your friend at the bridal factory?"

Christine nodded as she opened the first book. "You're going to be my maid of honor, aren't you?"

When Melissa gasped, Christine looked up at her. Melissa smiled. "I thought you would ask one of your cousins. You have a bunch of them."

"Yeah, fifteen first cousins. But only nine of them are girls."

Melissa giggled. "That's a lot. I can't imagine having so many. Both of mine are guys, and they weren't interested in spending time with a *gurrrl* cousin."

Christine put her elbows on the pages to keep them open and leaned her chin in her hands. "All of my female cousins lived close to me, and we were all within four years of age. I was in the middle, so none of them were more than two years older or younger than me. We had a lot of fun growing up."

"And you've kept in contact as adults, haven't you? I don't even know where those two knuckleheads are." Melissa opened the next magazine in the stack. "What are we looking for?"

While bright sunlight streamed into the shop, painting everything in a golden glow—even the magazines—Christine turned several pages. "I'm not sure what I want in a wedding dress, but I want my bridesmaids to wear red velvet. Maybe with a short cape trimmed in white fur."

"Well, that leaves me out. I'm not going to come down the aisle looking like something on fire. My red curls would be the top of the flames." Melissa shrugged. "Maybe you *should* ask a cousin." A saucy grin accompanied the last statement.

Christine stared at her. "We've been friends since first grade. You are going to be my maid of honor. Besides, we could have you wear the same kind of dress, but in a different color. The cousins can all be bridesmaids. The others might resent it if I choose one of them as maid of honor."

The bell announced the entrance of a few customers, and Melissa went to wait on them. Christine leafed through the pages of her magazine, but nothing caught her eye. She had just picked up a different one when the phone rang. She went in the office at the back of the shop so the call wouldn't disturb the customers.

"Floral Haven, Christine Dailey speaking. How may I help you?"

"Chrissy."

"Gram, how are you?" It had been too long since Christine had been to visit her only remaining grandparent. "I'm sorry I haven't been out to the farm in a while."

"I know a lot's going on with your new business." Gram didn't sound like an eighty-year-old woman on the phone. "I called for another reason."

"Do you need something? I could be out there in a few hours. Melissa can watch the shop." Christine picked up a pen and started doodling flowers on the pad by the phone.

"No, dear, I don't need anything. I want to do something for you." Gram giggled like a teenager. "I hear there's going to be a wedding in the family."

Christine dropped the pen. "So Mom already called you?"

"Why didn't you tell me yourself?"

"It only happened night before last. I wanted us to set the wedding date before I called you, and we did that last night. You were on my agenda for this evening. Christopher has a business meeting tonight."

Christine pictured Gram's smiling face and the twinkle in her eyes. "Now you don't have to call me. I'll get right to the point. I'm making your wedding dress."

After taking a deep breath, Christine declined. "I would like nothing better than that, but it would be too much for you."

"Now I don't want to hear anything like that. I made all of the other girls' dresses. Since you're the last to marry, this will be my last wedding dress." Gram sounded wistful. "You must let me do it."

Christine thought about how disappointed Gram would be if she said no, but she didn't want to take advantage of the older woman. Of course, she didn't look forward to being the only cousin who didn't have a Gram-original wedding dress. Christine had looked forward to it for years. She gazed at the calendar above the desk and tried to figure how much time she really had to plan the wedding.

"Christine, did you hear what I said?"

"Yes, Gram. We're getting married at Valentine's. That won't give you much time to make the dress."

"I don't have anything else I have to do, so it won't be a problem. It will be my number-one priority. So when are you coming out to show me what you like?"

If she didn't want to hurt her beloved grandmother, there was nothing else Christine could do. "Melissa and I will be there Sunday afternoon. Bye, Gram." The phone clicked as she rested the earpiece in its cradle. Maybe Christopher wouldn't mind her missing their regular Sunday night date.

"Hey, Christine." Melissa's call alerted Christine that the customers had gone. "Come here and see what I found."

After glancing in the mirror beside her desk to see if she needed lipstick, Christine walked through the doorway. "What did you find?"

Melissa held up one of the books. "These dresses."

A full-color page showed several different colors of a gown that fit the idea in Christine's head. Long flowing dresses with short trains and capes that hit halfway between the shoulder and elbows of the girls modeling them. Something white trimmed the cape and the hem of the skirt, even continuing up the front to meet at a deep vee below the waist. How could anything be more perfect? The jewel colors in the picture ran the whole spectrum, from black all the way to white.

"They're the ones." Christine took the book and studied the text. "These are manufactured right here, a product of The Bridal Boutique."

Melissa pulled on her right ear, a habit she'd had since they first met. "Maybe it's time to call Sharon. They could have some in stock, and we might get a good deal on them."

Christine laid the magazine on the counter. "That would be too much to hope for. You know one of my cousins is pregnant and some are tall and some short. They surely wouldn't have the right sizes for all of them without having to order some. I'll call Sharon tonight. Just tell me what color you want to wear. The others don't have a choice."

By the time Sunday arrived, Christine had found the perfect wedding dress. She marked the page in the magazine with a Floral Haven brochure. After going to the early service, she and Melissa would be on their way toward Litchfield. They should arrive in time to eat a late lunch before they drove out to the farm.

※

After she and Melissa were seated near the back of the sanctuary, Christopher slid into the pew beside Christine. "What are you doing here at this service? We always go to the one at eleven."

"You said last night that you were coming, so I decided to try it." He leaned over and dropped a quick kiss on her cheek. "Besides, I hear the new contemporary service is lively. We might want to start attending this one."

"Not me. Sundays I can sleep later than on other days." She put her arm through his, and he took her hand.

The service was different, but she liked it. Although the music was more upbeat, it resonated with a strong message of hope, and the sermon was just as powerful as the one she usually heard at the traditional service later in the day. Maybe they would try it again.

Christopher accompanied them to her tiny car. "How about letting me go with you? I love Gram, too."

"No way!" Melissa pushed between them. "Christine might be tempted to let you, but I'm not. You can't know anything about the wedding dress, and you might if you are with us. Go watch a football game or something."

Christopher laughed before kissing Christine good-bye. He did a thorough job of it. More than he had ever kissed her in front of anyone else. By the time he finished, Christine knew her face must be flaming red. She felt hot enough, and the knowing smile from Melissa didn't do anything to help her feel more comfortable.

"You be very careful." Christopher opened her door then dropped another quick kiss on her willing lips. "You're very important to me, you know." He shut the door and stood watching them until the car exited the parking lot.

Christine drove out of Wayzata floating on a cloud. That man did things to her she never had imagined. Her stomach fluttered so much, she didn't know if she would be able to eat when they arrived in Litchfield, and her pulse throbbed so loud, she was sure Melissa could hear it.

"That's a becoming shade of red." Melissa's comment sounded casual.

"I'm not wearing red." When Christine turned to glance at her friend, Melissa's smirk stopped her. "Just you wait. You'll fall for someone one of these days. Then it will be my turn."

They arrived at Gram's house without incident. She must have heard them coming down the lane, because she was waiting on the porch to pull them into big hugs. She had always treated Melissa like just one more grandchild.

When they showed her the picture of the dress Christine picked out, she studied it for a few minutes. After asking several questions, she started writing things on a lined pad. Then she took Christine's measurements.

"Gram, you'll have to tell me how much of each kind of fabric to buy." Christine put her arm across Gram's shoulders.

"I'll have to do some figuring before I know." She reached over and kissed Christine's cheek. "You'll be so beautiful in this dress. I'll call you tomorrow or the next day with the information. Now let's go to the kitchen for a snack. I made your favorite macaroon cookies."

Chapter 3

"**W**ow! I can't believe how well things are going for you." Melissa took out a glittery heart garland and handed it to Christine on the ladder. "I was worried when we had to work on the wedding *and* Thanksgiving and Christmas all at the same time."

Christine stretched as far as she could to either side to push in as many of the red tacks as she could without moving the ladder. "You know finding all ten bridesmaid dresses in the colors and sizes we need them is nothing short of miraculous."

Melissa started to bend down toward the box but quickly stood back up and took hold of the ladder. "Be careful. You don't want it to tip over. Can't have you walking down the aisle on crutches."

Christine carefully stepped down and moved the ladder. "Please hand me the end of that garland. I want to finish this. Christopher and I have a dinner date tonight."

"I'm glad Sharon got those dresses for us at clearance price."

"Me, too." Christine stuck the last tack in the end of the garland. She descended and stepped back.

Melissa walked over to the counter and ran her finger down the calendar page. "What else do you have to do for the wedding?"

"Christopher and I have an appointment on Friday with the caterer to make the final food choices. My cousin Maria bakes special cakes, so she's doing the wedding cakes as her present to us."

"That'll save a bundle." Melissa turned the page on the calendar. "Girl-friend, you are going to have an easy time. You can just coast these last few weeks. You'll be the most rested bride I've ever seen."

❧

Christopher took Christine back to the restaurant where they went the night he proposed. As the maître d' led them to their secluded table, Christine reveled in the ambience. Low lights in the room allowed the candles to turn the tables into isolated islands in a sea of soft music. The thick carpet swallowed any sound of footsteps as they moved across the floor. After they ordered the very same meal they had eaten the first time they were there, the waiter left them to their privacy.

Christopher reached across the corner of the table and picked up Christine's hand. He lifted it toward his lips and bestowed a quick kiss on her fingertips. Would she ever get over the tingles that shot through her at his slightest touch? She hoped not.

He put his palm against hers and intertwined their fingers, a favorite point of connection between them. "I'm leaving in the morning for Hong Kong."

Christine almost pulled her hand away. "Why?" Before he could answer that question, she asked another. "When will you be back?"

"It's a business meeting I can't miss." He smiled into her eyes. "I'll be home Thursday evening. In plenty of time for our meeting with the caterer."

Christine heaved a sigh of relief. "I really don't want to go without you being there. It's your wedding as well as mine."

"I'll be there." He glanced around before he leaned toward her to give her a gentle kiss.

When he finished, the waiter materialized beside them with their salads.

"Besides, isn't your final fitting for your tux on Saturday?"

He picked up his fork. "Relax, honey, everything will be all right. We're right on schedule. Remember, God is in control." He took a bite of his salad.

Christine wasn't at all sure Christopher understood the importance of this last month and all they needed to do together. "I guess I'll just miss you."

"That's why I bought us something." He reached into his pocket and pulled out a cell phone.

"I already have one." She started digging in her purse to find hers.

He placed a hand on hers to still her movements. "Not like this one. It's a satellite cell phone, and I bought myself one, too. We can talk while I'm gone, almost anywhere in the world. Like Dad said, being CEO has its perks."

⊗

After she took Chris to the airport, Chrissy stayed with him until he had to go through security. He waited as long as he could so they would have more time together. The pucker in her forehead told him that she wasn't happy about him leaving. When he picked up his luggage after it went through the scanner, he turned back to see her standing just outside the security area, watching him with a forlorn expression on her face. He blew her a kiss then started toward his gate.

Chrissy's forlorn face haunted Chris's thoughts for the first hour of the flight. If only he could assure her of the peace in his heart every time he thought about the wedding. She was a planner, and it bothered her when anything happened that wasn't on her schedule. Hopefully, the longer they lived together as man and wife, the better she would learn to trust God with everything more than she did now. Oh, she was a Christian, but her plans meant too much to her. He hoped it wouldn't be a problem later on. Chris leaned back against the headrest of his thickly padded leather seat in first class and closed his eyes. Maybe everyone else would think he was sleeping and leave him alone. He wanted to spend the next several minutes praying for Christine.

As soon as Chris was through customs, he hailed a cab to take him to his hotel. Since there were so many tourists and international businessmen who frequented Hong Kong, many of the hotels were world class. He had chosen one of them. After the porter accompanied him up the elevator with his bags, Chris tipped the man and closed the door. He walked to the floor-to-ceiling windows and opened the curtains. While looking over the bustling city, he pulled out his cell phone and punched the buttons that automatically dialed Christine's.

"Hello, Christopher." Her voice sounded sweet, even through the electronic gadget. "Are you already there?"

"Yes, in my hotel room."

"Is it nice?"

Was that a wistful note in her voice? He pictured her long blond hair framing her expression. He never tired of running his fingers through those curls. "After we're married, you can come with me when I have these meetings. I think you'll like the hotel. It's a five-star. Really top-notch."

"I'd like that."

He could hear her sigh, even over these thousands of miles. Her eyes usually darkened to a forest green when something bothered her. He rubbed the back of his neck with his free hand. It was always sore after such a long flight. "Honey, you know I love you with all my heart."

"Of course, and I love you just as much." Her voice softened on the words they often said to each other.

⌘

Melissa came through the door of the shop, accompanied by a sharp north wind. She wrestled with the packages she carried, trying to push the door shut against the strong gusts. "Boy, it's really getting cold out there." She plopped the packages and her purse on the counter. "Do you think it'll snow? Most of what fell last week is gone."

"I don't know. Does the wind feel wet?"

"Who can tell? It's really blowing hard."

It was almost time to close the shop for the day. They didn't get much walk-in traffic after six.

Christine opened one of the sacks Melissa had brought in and started toward the back room. "I think I'll turn on the TV back here and listen to the news while I put these away."

After she clicked it on, she turned around and pulled out supplies to stock. She wasn't paying much attention until a special announcement came on.

"An unusual tropical storm is headed for the island of Hong Kong."

Christine whirled to look at the pretty Asian woman making a special report for one of the national networks.

"It's too early for the typhoon season, but weather has been unseasonable in this part of the world. The reports are that the storm might reach typhoon strength before making landfall sometime today or tonight."

All Christine could think about was Christopher in Hong Kong. She grabbed her satellite cell and dialed his number, not even waiting to calculate the time difference. The phone rang and rang, then went to his voice mail. She left a message, clicked off her phone, and clutched it so hard her knuckles went numb. *Oh, God, please protect Christopher. I can't stand that he is so far away, Lord. I want him here with me.* Her grip loosened and blood circulated into her fingers once again. What did the scriptures say? Something about God moving mountains. She wished she could believe that He would just miraculously move Christopher from Hong Kong to Minnesota in an instant. She dropped into her desk chair and stared at the TV, not even noticing what else the local reporter was saying.

Lord, I need Christopher.

It seemed almost as if God was standing in the room talking to her, she heard His answer so strongly in her heart. *"Christine, you need to trust Me."*

◈

Chris stepped out of the steamy bathroom with a towel wrapped around his hips and one slung around his neck. He flipped on the TV and started drying his hair with the towel from his shoulders.

"An unusual tropical storm is headed for the island of Hong Kong."

Chris put the towel back around his neck and glanced at the woman giving the news report.

"It's months too early for the typhoon season, but reports are that the storm might reach typhoon strength before making landfall sometime today or tonight."

That really was unusual. He guessed he could cancel the meetings for today and try to get a ticket home on an earlier flight.

A frustrating hour later, he was glad he hadn't canceled the meetings yet. There wasn't a flight available anywhere. Everything was already overbooked.

He wasn't going anywhere before his regularly scheduled flight. He hoped Chrissy hadn't heard the report. It was from a local station, but he couldn't trust that it hadn't made international news. She would be frantic. He picked up his cell and saw that someone had called. After listening to his message, he punched in the numbers for Chrissy.

"Hello?" Her answer sounded tentative.

"Chrissy, I love you." Then he heard her sob. "Honey, it's okay. I'm going to be all right." He imagined tears slipping down her soft cheeks. Cheeks he wished he were touching right now. If he could just kiss the drops away and take her in his arms.

"I love you, too." She paused. "Do you think you'll be able to get home tonight?"

"I'm planning on it." When he bought these phones, they sounded like a good idea, but they would never take the place of cuddling her in his arms and holding her near his heart. "Have you penciled in on your schedule to meet me at the airport?"

"I'll be there."

"Honey, just imagine me with you right now. I would kiss you just the way I did when I asked you to marry me."

Her sigh sounded loud through the phone. "I don't want to have to make the decisions without you." He heard her words, but he also sensed the underlying worry for his safety she felt but was afraid to mention.

Chapter 4

After the meetings, Chris went back to his room to pack. He called the airport before he ordered a taxi. "Is flight 2991 to San Francisco on schedule?"

"I'm sorry, sir." The man sounded tired, making his singsong English hard to understand. "But because the storm is moving faster than anticipated, the airport is officially closed for now." The harried man hung up before Chris could ask anything else.

Chrissy would be upset. *That is an understatement.* Chris took the global cell out of his pocket. He glanced at it before dialing. The low-battery light blinked back at him. When was the last time he charged it? He should have plugged it in last night as a precaution. Quickly, he punched in Chrissy's numbers.

"Christopher, where are you?" A hint of anxiety laced her tone. "I've been watching CNN, and they've been giving terrible reports from the area of Hong Kong."

He rubbed the sides of his forehead with the thumb and fingers of his empty hand. "Chrissy, I'm in my hotel room."

"When does your plane leave?" Now she sounded a little frantic.

"Not today. They've already closed the airport."

Silence screamed across the line.

"Chrissy, are you still there?"

"Yes." The breathy answer told him that she was trying to control her emotions.

"Now listen really close. My cell phone battery is about to go dead, so I have to talk fast. I love you. I'm going to be all right. I will be home, just not today. And Chrissy, it wouldn't hurt to pray for me."

As soon as he finished talking, the whisper of an open phone line was gone. Chris dropped to his knees beside the bed, buried his head in his hands, and prayed for Christine while gale-force winds howled outside his room.

❦

Exactly a week after he left, Christine waited by the luggage carousel for

Christopher to deplane. She had chosen the food for the wedding. One more thing checked off her list. At the time, she didn't care what he wanted to eat, but she knew that wasn't the right attitude. With a thankful heart that he wasn't injured, she had changed his appointment for the final fitting of his tuxedo. He wasn't renting one. As the CEO of a major company, he'd need one fairly often.

Christine dropped her head into her hands and took a deep breath. She wanted him to see a smiling, loving face when he came through from the concourse.

A hand touched her shoulder and shivers of delight raced down her spine just before Christopher pulled her into his arms. "I'm so glad to be home, Chrissy. I missed you so much. Talking on the phone just doesn't take the place of a hug or kiss."

She looked into those chocolate-colored eyes and swam in the depths of the love she saw there. When his lips caught hers in a long-awaited kiss, she didn't even care that they were in the airport with hundreds of people milling around. Only three more weeks until they could show the complete depth of their love.

Christopher pulled back, and the expression in his eyes devoured her. "I've missed you so much."

After he picked his one suitcase from the moving carousel, they started toward the company limousine waiting outside the door. Christopher had sent the driver to pick up Christine at the flower shop and bring her to the airport. When they were nestled in the backseat, Christopher kissed her again, with even more fervency than before.

"I just needed to touch you." He snuggled her under his arm. "That week in a lonely hotel room seemed to take forever."

"I missed you, too. So what are we going to do tonight?" She felt him stiffen.

"Since I was gone so long, I may have to work until midnight. There are a lot of things that were left undone because I need to approve them."

"That's okay," she forced through gritted teeth.

"No, it's not, but it can't be helped." Christopher turned her around so he could look into her eyes. "That's why I had Alfred pick you up. I had to see you. After he leaves me at the office, he can take you back to the shop. I'll call you when I have a break."

She reached up and kissed him again. This week might be a lot like last week, with them talking on the phone instead of being together, so she wanted to make the most of their time.

❧

Chris returned her soul-stirring kiss. He wanted her to remember it if this week turned out to be like last week. He decided he had to make time for them to see each other face-to-face, even if it was only a few minutes a day.

That last thought must have been prophetic. Things were even more hectic than he anticipated. His schedule was filled with meetings. Executives from different branches of the company came to St. Paul with varying agendas. Chris was sure some of them only wanted to check him out. They'd probably push him as far as they could to see if he would be as in control as his dad had been. The added stress didn't help his frustration at not seeing Chrissy very often. He called her every chance he could, and he started stopping by her apartment for a few minutes before he had to get to bed, so he would be fresh in the next meeting. Those islands of connection kept him from being totally wiped out.

⤫

The phone rang, and Christine picked it up. "Floral Haven."

"Chrissy?" Gram's voice pulled Christine's attention from the papers on the desk in front of her.

She leaned back in the desk chair. "Yes."

"Honey, I need you to come for a final fitting of your dress. I only have two weeks to sew all the pearls and sequins on it, and I don't want to do that until everything else is finished. Didn't the dry cleaner say we needed to get it to them a week before the wedding so they could have it pressed and ready?"

Christine loved Gram, she really did. But she didn't really want to go right now. She had seen Christopher such a small amount of time this week. She didn't want to miss seeing him even the one night it would take for her to go to Gram's. But she did want a wedding dress.

"Chrissy, are you still there?" Gram sounded worried.

"Yes, I was just thinking." Christine pulled her appointment calendar forward and glanced through the entries. "I'm trying to see when would be the best time to come."

"I hope it can be pretty soon."

Christine made a couple of notes on the already crowded calendar. "I'm coming today. Melissa can take care of things here tomorrow morning. I should be back by noon."

"I'm fixing chicken and dumplings for supper. You always liked them."

Christine laughed. "If you keep feeding me like that, Gram, you might have to let the dress out."

After she hung up from talking to her grandmother, she dialed her direct line to Christopher's office. The call went to voice mail. "Christopher, I'm going to Gram's for the final fitting of my dress. Please call me on my cell when you hear this."

The drive to the farm provided a welcome break from the hectic pace of the past week at the shop. She and Melissa had worked on wedding flowers in between filling orders. Why did she ever want a Valentine's wedding? Especially since she opened Floral Haven. It seemed as though every man who lived all the way from Wayzata to St. Paul ordered flowers from Floral Haven for his sweetheart or wife.

Just yesterday she agreed to hire Melissa's friend to help. Karen did a good job the rest of the afternoon. Christine felt sure the two of them could handle everything while she was gone. After she turned north in Litchfield onto the road that went by Gram's farm, she had to take off her sunglasses. She wore them because even a wintry sun shone brightly on snow. But the sky had become overcast. She flipped the radio over to a news station, trying to pick up the weather forecast. She had watched the news last night and didn't remember anything about a storm. National news blared from the speakers, and she switched back to her favorite Christian music station. Singing along with the tunes helped the time pass quickly.

By midafternoon she pulled up the gravel road that led to the house, thankful that one of the men who leased Gram's acreage always kept her drive free from snow. She made a mental note to call him while she was here to thank him for that.

Gram didn't let her catch her breath before she had her in the dress. Gram put on her pincushion that looked like a tomato but had a cuff bracelet that fit on her wrist. She stepped back to get a better look of her granddaughter. "Oh, Chrissy, you're even more beautiful than I envisioned."

Christine touched the scrunchie that held her hair in a long ponytail. "I didn't take time to style my hair this morning. I was going to do it before Christopher came over tonight."

Gram pulled the scrunchie, and a riot of curls cascaded down Christine's back. "So, are you going to wear it down or up for the wedding?"

Christine pulled her hair up and turned her head from side to side as she looked in the mirror. "Up looks more elegant." *This gorgeous dress calls for elegance.*

"And it shows off your graceful neck."

"But Christopher likes it down. I want to please him. Besides, it might be pretty cold that day."

Gram smiled. "Good. I have enough tulle to make a nice long veil with a train if you want one to match the dress."

Christine pulled Gram into her arms. "You are so good to me. You've been my rock since Mom and Dad have been gone. What would I have done without you?"

The praise embarrassed Gram, as always. "You'd have done fine. God would have seen to that. I'm just glad I was here to take care of you. Have you found a headpiece you like? I can attach the veil to it and even add some seed pearls and sequins like the ones on your dress."

"Actually, I picked one up yesterday when I went to the fabric store for more netting to use in corsages for the wedding. It's still in the trunk of the car."

After Christine removed her dress and helped Gram replace it on the padded hanger on the back of the bedroom door, she went out to get the package. Dark clouds scudded across the sky, subduing the remaining daylight. Even in her down coat, Christine shivered.

She stomped the snow from her shoes onto the mat on the porch before she went back in. "Gram, have you heard a weather report? Those clouds look like they are carrying snow, and they might drop it at any time."

Chapter 5

After supper, Christine stood at the front window watching snow-flakes enter the circle of light on the ground that was cast by the lamp on the table beside her. Big fat flakes slowly drifted back and forth before settling upon the ones that hadn't melted from the last snowfall. What a pretty picture they made. What treachery they brought to the roadways. Maybe she should try to get home tonight.

Her cell phone rang, and she pulled it from her pocket. *Christopher.* "Hello. So this one night I'm gone, you get away from work early?"

"Not really." Papers rustled in the background. "I'm at my desk. I couldn't concentrate on my work. How'd it go today?"

"Fine. Traffic wasn't bad on the way out here." She waited for his next comment.

"Tell me what you look like in your dress. Do you like it?" Christine heard his chair squeak the way it did when he leaned back.

"It's beautiful." She was sure he smiled at that. "I'll look like a fairy-tale princess in it."

"That's all well and good, but I'm marrying a real flesh and blood woman, and I can hardly wait to watch you walking down that aisle toward me." His voice on the line sounded heavy with promise.

Christine glanced out at the flakes that had increased in the short time she had been talking to her fiancé. "I've been thinking maybe I ought to start home tonight. I should be able to get there before midnight."

Christopher's chair squeaked again. "Why would you want to do that? I don't like the idea of you driving so far alone at night. Tomorrow is soon enough."

She pictured him leaning his elbows on his desk. "It's snowing here, and it's coming down harder now."

"That's reason enough to stay. I really don't want you driving home in the snow. Some crazy trucker who doesn't know how to drive in this kind of weather might not be as careful as I know you are when you drive in bad weather."

She paused. Christopher was right. It wouldn't be wise, but what if it snowed a lot? "Okay. I'll come first thing in the morning."

⁂

Chris reached home at midnight from his exhausting day. His brain felt like mush, and tension had caused a cramp in his neck. The only bright point had been when he talked to Christine. He knew women really enjoyed all this wedding planning. He would just as soon stand before the pastor with only their families in attendance. They would be just as married without so much commotion. But Chris wanted a happy bride.

He was too keyed up to go directly to bed, so he trudged up the stairs of the new house he and Chrissy had purchased after he returned from Hong Kong. The furnishings were sparse, but he and Chrissy could take all the time they wanted after the wedding making it into the home where they would be glad to raise their children. At least the master bedroom was completely finished.

After loosening his tie and slipping out of his shoes, he dropped into the cushy recliner in the sitting area. He leaned back and tried to imagine Chrissy in her wedding dress, walking down the aisle toward him. Just thinking about it brought a lump to his throat. Maybe all this wedding stuff would be worth the time and effort. He smiled. *It won't hurt to check the Weather Channel.* He picked up the remote and clicked several times.

"Meteorologists are amazed at the blizzard that is blanketing more than the western half of central Minnesota. Although they had predicted snow, they didn't envision anything like what is going on out there." Footage of the storm scrolled across the screen behind the newscaster. "The highway department has released a bulletin stating that it might take quite awhile before they'll be able to clear some of the farm roads."

Chris sat forward and leaned his elbows on his knees. "Lord, I know Chrissy will be worried. Please keep her and Gram safe. And calm Chrissy's heart. Fill her with Your peace."

The peace Chris prayed about settled inside him. He knew everything would be all right. Quickly, he prepared for bed, knowing that he had to get up early, and he wanted to call Chrissy as soon as he could.

⁂

Christine walked down the aisle in cadence with the wedding march. The silk of her completed wedding gown swished with each step. At the front of the church her groom waited, but he was so far away she couldn't see his face. The longer she walked, the farther away he became. Tears pooled in her eyes. She might have to run to reach him in time.

The ringing of Christine's cell phone woke her. She blinked, glad to see her familiar room at Gram's house, and she grabbed the phone before it went to voice mail. "Hello?" Christine glanced at the clock while she answered. It was only six o'clock.

"Hi, honey." Christopher's smooth baritone voice sounded husky. Had he just gotten up or was it emotion? "I'm sorry to wake you so early, but you might not know what's been going on."

She sat up straight in her bed and glanced toward the window. Outside was a blur of white in the waning predawn darkness. "What are you talking about?" The fear of some impending disaster caused her hand that was holding the phone to shake so much it was difficult to keep it close to her ear, so she held it with both hands.

"Last night when I got home, the Weather Channel said this is one of the worst blizzards in years." He paused as if waiting for her reply. When none came, he continued, "You won't be able to come home today."

Tears welled up in her eyes, bringing with them a whisper of a memory. Oh yes, the dream. Using one hand, she dashed the tears away. "I have to go home. It's only two weeks until the wedding." She finished on a sob.

"Chrissy, it's going to be all right." His heavy breathing filled the silence. "I love you, and I have a peace about everything."

How could he have peace? Who would finish the last-minute details of the wedding?

She must have whispered the question, because he answered her. "Didn't you hire a helper? She and Melissa can take care of the flower shop and the wedding. Don't fret. Promise me."

How could she do that? She had planned a workable schedule for everything. If they got off schedule, she would lose her focus. Feel disconnected. Didn't he understand?

"Chrissy, I know you like to feel in control of your life." Could he read her mind? "Sometimes events are taken out of our hands. It's then we have to trust the most."

Platitudes. She hated platitudes.

"I've got to go to work. Will you be okay?"

"Yes." Her answer sounded weak in her own ears.

"I wish I were there so I could hold you in my arms. I'll call you later."

It wasn't fair. Christine clicked off her phone, pulled on her warm robe, and walked to the window. She wiped away the film of condensation caused by the heat in the room. Snowflakes filled the air, hiding everything else outside. Why could everyone in the metropolitan area move around in this, and she was stuck out here in Minnesota farmland for who knew how long?

"Today wasn't so bad, was it?" Gram sat in her rocker before the fireplace and sipped from her mug of hot chocolate.

Christine glanced over from where she was snuggled on the couch, one of Gram's knitted afghans pulled over her legs. After she set her mug on the table beside her, she smiled. "Not as bad as I thought it would be. Until you asked me to help you sew the pearls and sequins on the dress, I didn't feel useful."

Gram blew across her cup, trying to cool the liquid. Christine knew she liked hers lukewarm. Gramps had always teased her about it. "You perked up after you talked to Melissa."

Christine nodded. "She and Karen have everything right on schedule. And they're keeping up with all the customers' orders." Christine gazed at the dancing flames. "Melissa even told me she wished she could spend a few days snowed in somewhere. I don't think the storm hit as hard there. Or if it did, the highway department was out on the freeways and streets in force. She didn't have any trouble getting to the shop this morning. You know what the best part of today was, Gram?"

"Why, having you here with me, of course."

Christine laughed. "For me, it was being with you. I loved it when you talked about how you and Gramps courted and about your wedding and honeymoon. I just hope my marriage lasts as long as yours did."

"With God's help, it will. That's the only way we made it."

The melody of Christine's cell phone ringing interrupted the conversation. By the time she extricated her legs from the afghan and reached the device, it had gone to voice mail. She waited a couple of minutes, then hit speed dial for Christopher.

⟨❦⟩

Late afternoon of her third day at Gram's, Christine stood by the front window talking to her future husband. "You're right. This time with Gram has been wonderful. I'm not sorry we had this quality time together."

"That's good to hear." He paused, and she wondered if he had hung up. "Sorry, I had to put the phone down for a second. You're sounding more peaceful than you have in a long time. I'm glad to hear it."

She noticed movement at the end of the drive. "Something's out there."

"What?" Was that worry she heard in his voice?

"It looks like it might be the snowplow on the road. If that's what it is, Mr. Watson will probably be here before long and clean off Gram's drive. I can come home in the morning."

Christopher gave what sounded like a sigh of relief. "I'm glad. Be sure to call me and let me know when you start out."

Chapter 6

Soon after the snowplow moved down the road, Mr. Watson started working his way up Gram's drive, clearing a path in the snow as he came. Christine was glad to see him because she knew she couldn't clean off the long driveway. When he reached the house, she offered to pay him.

"No, Chrissy, I couldn't accept any money from you." He took his hat off and held it in both hands. "I just know I'd want someone to help my mother if she were still alive. It's what neighbors do." He put his hat back on. "Let me be sure that sidewalk is completely cleaned off. Can't have Mrs. Olson falling, now, can we?"

"Well, thank you again." Christine went back inside. "Gram, it looks like I'll be going home in the morning, and none too soon."

"Having you here this long has been a real blessing." Gram smiled. "Come help me get the dress in that garment bag you brought. Didn't the cleaners say they needed it a week before the wedding to guarantee they would have it pressed in time for you to wear it?"

The next morning, Gram insisted on cooking Christine a big breakfast. She didn't have the heart to tell her grandmother that she usually only ate yogurt and a bagel or maybe a toaster waffle before she went to work. Fortified with bacon, scrambled eggs, and biscuits so light and fluffy they almost floated off her plate, Christine started loading her luggage into the trunk of her car. She would bring the wedding dress out last.

"Chrissy," Gram called from the front porch, "I've made you a bag to take with you. Some biscuits with butter and that blueberry jam you like. . .and the rest of the bacon. You might get hungry on the road."

Not much chance of that happening. Christine would be home before noon. But she didn't want to hurt Gram's feelings. She started up the sidewalk toward the farmhouse. Evidently, Gram didn't want to wait for her, because she stepped onto the top step, and her feet flew out from under her.

With horror, Christine watched, as if in slow motion, her beloved grandparent fall, landing on the porch with a thud, the bag flying out of her hand and emptying its contents across the porch and snow-covered lawn.

"Gram!" Christine ran as fast as she could and knelt on the cold floor of the wooden structure, leaning over the fallen woman. Her grandmother was breathing, but her eyes were closed. "Are you all right? Of course not. Gram, can you hear me? Where are you hurt?"

She pulled her cell phone from her pocket. *How do you get emergency help out here?* At home, she would just dial 911 on her regular phone. Maybe she could call the operator. She punched the 0 then SEND and lifted the device to her ear.

Christine was thankful when a voice answered instead of a computerized answering system. "I don't know how to get help! My grandmother just fell on her porch! She's breathing, but she passed out! I'm afraid to move her, and it's very cold!"

"Just tell me where you are." The controlled voice soothed Christine a little.

After providing the information, Christine took a deep breath, hoping to calm herself some more. Hysteria would upset Gram if she woke up. "Do you think I should move her inside?"

"I wouldn't until the paramedics are there. Can you get blankets or quilts to cover her?"

Christine didn't want to leave Gram long enough to look, but she knew there were lots of afghans right inside. She rushed in, still holding the phone to her ear.

Soon the voice came over the line again. "I've contacted emergency help in Litchfield. One of their workers has an EMT vehicle at his farm, which isn't far from where you are. He keeps it there so he won't have to go to town before he heads out to help victims. Help should arrive in a few minutes."

"Thank you." Christine clicked off the phone and shoved it into her pocket. She grabbed every cover she could find and quickly returned to the porch, piling them on Gram. *Victim. She called Gram a victim. I don't want to think of her that way.*

Gram groaned. Then her eyes slowly blinked several times before she finally opened them, gazing up into Christine's face. No hint of recognition, just a blank stare.

Christine dropped to sit on the porch beside Gram. She noticed the signs of pain that lined her grandmother's face, pain that broke Christine's heart. It was all she could do to keep from sobbing. She blinked back the tears that threatened to overflow and cleared her throat before she spoke.

"Gram, I'm right here, and help is on the way." Christine wasn't sure Gram understood.

Gram wore a confused expression, her eyes roving all around as if trying to figure out where she was. She moved a little, then stopped with a loud moan. Finally her gaze settled on Christine's face.

"Chrissy, is that you?"

Christine leaned closer to Gram, hoping her presence would calm the older woman. "Yes, I'm here."

"I thought you went home this morning." Gram's voice sounded weak, and her eyes drifted closed once again. Her body began to shiver.

Tears made their way down Christine's cheeks. She dashed them away with one hand and held Gram's hand with the other, knowing the connection would comfort Gram. Then she tucked the covers closer around Gram to keep what body warmth she had from escaping.

In the distance, the wail of a siren became apparent, then quickly grew closer. *That didn't take long. Thank You, Lord, for getting them here so soon. Please take care of Gram.*

⌘

The morning meeting ran long. Chris didn't get back to his office until twelve thirty. He took his cell phone out of the holder at his waist and looked to see if somehow he had missed Christine's call since he had it on silent mode. He usually felt the vibration. *No, nothing.* He thought she would be home by now. He had hoped to have lunch with her. Punching her speed-dial number, he waited for it to ring. When the phone went immediately to voice mail, he hung up. Maybe she forgot to turn hers on.

He called Floral Haven. "Melissa, has Chrissy arrived yet?"

"Chris! No. I thought maybe this was her calling. This is the first day she's taken so long to call. Maybe the traffic was worse than she expected."

"Thanks." He flipped the phone closed, then buzzed his administrative assistant. "Marta, please have Chef's Touch downstairs send up the daily special."

"Don't you want to know what it is first?"

"No. Whatever they fix is fine. I just need to eat."

"I thought you were going out to lunch, boss."

He smiled at her impertinence. The lovely Chinese woman made an excellent administrative assistant, but she could be a little cheeky. "Christine hasn't gotten back yet."

His cell phone vibrated just as he clicked off the intercom. "Chrissy, I've been wondering about you."

"I knew you would." She sounded tired and something else he couldn't quite identify.

"Is everything all right?"

"I'm not sure." She took a deep breath. "When I was loading the car to leave, Gram fell on the porch steps."

"Oh no! Is she all right?" He quickly changed the phone to his other hand and picked up his pen.

"The doctor thinks so. Nothing is broken. But he wants to keep her overnight for observation."

He pulled his leather-covered memo pad close and flipped the cover open. "Where are you?"

"We're at the hospital in Litchfield. I'm going to stay here tonight, too." She blew out a deep sigh.

"You sound tired."

"I am."

Chris started writing on the pad as he talked. "I have a lighter load this afternoon. I'll be up there in time to eat dinner with you."

"Oh, Christopher." It sounded like a sob. "That would be wonderful."

❧

Although nothing was broken, Gram had many bruises. The doctor assured Christine that her grandmother was in wonderful shape for a woman her age. She would recover. He wanted to send her home as soon as possible. He explained that older patients often did better in familiar surroundings, especially after the sun went down. It concerned him that she lived alone. Gram was asleep probably from some of the medication they had given her.

Christine wandered out to the waiting room. She flipped open her cell phone and called her only cousin who had no children and a flexible job schedule.

"Mona."

"Chrissy, are you as excited as I was this close to my wedding?"

The wedding! Christine hadn't thought about it since Gram's accident. But she couldn't tell Mona that. "Actually, I'm calling about Gram."

"Is she all right?" Mona sounded as concerned as Christine felt.

"She's going to be." Christine walked toward the window. "She fell this morning before I left."

"Where are you?"

"At the hospital with Gram." She rubbed her neck and stretched it, trying to get the kinks out. "They want to send her home in the morning if she is okay. The doctor said she would do better in familiar surroundings, but she shouldn't be alone."

"I can't get there for a few days." Christine could almost hear the wheels turning in Mona's brain. "Is there any chance you can stay a little longer?"

"I'll do whatever I have to for Gram."

When Chris arrived at the hospital, he was directed to the waiting area near Gram's room. Walking down the hall, he wondered why hospital walls were always painted that horrible, muddy green. Surely there was a bucket somewhere labeled "Institutional Green." He arrived at the arrangement of couches with floral-embossed plastic upholstery to find Christine sitting in one with her feet pulled up under her. An open magazine lay in her lap, and her head rested against the top of her seat. A soft snore told Chris just how tired she was. He really didn't want to wake her.

He smiled and sat across from her. Thankfully, no one else shared the room with them. Chris could study her all he wanted to. Her hair was mussed and spread around her on the couch. She probably had makeup on this morning, but none remained. Her natural beauty overwhelmed him. In a week and a half, they would be man and wife. He was eagerly anticipating their wedding night—so much it almost scared him. Chris wanted to make the consummation of their vows wonderful. He had spent many hours in prayer asking the Lord to guide his every move that night.

More than that, he looked forward to spending the rest of their lives together. To grow accustomed to that soft snoring sound. To wake each morning with her sleep-mussed hair spread across the pillow beside his and her face painted with her deep love for him instead of makeup. Just thinking about it increased his breathing rate.

His eyes traced a path up and down, then across and back, covering every single inch of her face. The tiny brown dot beside her mouth that they laughingly called her beauty spot. Her perfectly shaped brows. The coal-black eyelashes that didn't match her naturally blond hair.

Chrissy must have felt his presence, because her eyes opened. She quickly sat up and smiled, smoothing her rumpled clothing. "Christopher, when did you get here?"

He moved over to sit beside her, pulling her into his arms. "Not long ago."

"Why didn't you wake me up?"

"You were tired." He pulled her even closer and captured her lips, savoring the feel and taste of them.

"I'm so glad you're here. I've missed you so much." This time, she kissed him. He could feel the longing she poured into it.

Only ten more days. Ten long days and nights.

Chapter 7

Morning sunlight slanted across the room, awakening Christine. She wondered why she wasn't stretched out in her bed instead of sleeping sitting up. She opened her eyes slowly so the brightness she could see even through her eyelids wouldn't blind her.

Of course. Christopher sat beside her, his arm holding her close, his head in an awkward position against the back of the couch. She hoped he didn't have a crick in his neck when he woke. She started to get up, trying not to disturb his sleep. His arm quickly tightened around her, pulling her even closer against his comfortable chest.

"Where are you going?" His sleep-deepened voice sounded sexy.

Was this what the rest of her life would be like? Hearing that voice first thing in the morning? Tingles ran up and down her spine. How wonderful!

Christine turned to look up at him. His face was so close with his eyes like melted dark chocolate, her favorite flavor. "I'm going to freshen up before I check on Gram."

"Good idea. I will, too, since she wasn't awake when I arrived last night." He dropped a kiss on her waiting lips. "I'll help you get her home before I head back." That merited another heart-stopping kiss.

❧

Chris washed his hands and face. Rubbing the stubble on his chin, he wished he had brought his electric razor. Of course, Chrissy hadn't seemed to mind. At least he had a razor in his private bathroom at the office.

Last night had been incredible. Yes, they were at a hospital, but spending the time with Chrissy and sharing their responsibilities as well as their love was what life was all about. His anticipation for their marriage increased by the second. Nine more days. Seemed like an eternity.

He quickly dried his hands and went to find his fiancée. Chrissy waited by the nurses' station outside Gram's door. "Can we go in now?"

"Yes, I was just waiting for you."

Christine could hardly believe that the wedding would take place in only five days, actually four since it was so late now. She was glad Mona would arrive at any time. Her cousin called from the airport saying she had rented a car. She wanted to be flexible to meet any of Gram's needs. A horn honked from in front of the house, and Christine made sure Gram was comfortable then rushed to the door.

When she opened it, Mona stood on the porch with a suitcase in each hand and her purse hanging on her shoulder. "Hi, Cuz, how are things?"

Christine stepped back to make room for her to enter. "Do you have anything else in the car?"

"No, I decided to bring everything in one trip." How like Mona. So efficient. No wonder she made good money teaching people time management. She wouldn't have any trouble taking care of Gram.

After all the greetings, the cousins sat near their grandmother in the living room to visit. Mona took the chair closest to the recliner where Gram rested with the veil in her lap. As they talked, she kept sewing on the decorations.

"Gram, are you sure you're okay?" Mona's eyes held concern.

"Of course I am." Gram gave a harrumph of indignation. "Chrissy has been hovering over me like a mother hen. I just have some interesting bruises. They're really colorful now."

"I was only trying to be sure you were all right." Christine was glad Gram didn't have any long-term damage.

Mona turned toward Christine. "You aren't going to try to leave tonight, are you?"

"I really want to, but when I talked to Christopher awhile ago, he insisted I wait until morning. He doesn't like me on the road at night." Christine shrugged. "I guess he's right, and after I talked to Melissa, I'm sure everything with the wedding will be fine. I'm surprised at how well she and Karen are getting along without me. I'm not sure I like it, either."

"Okay, Cuz, I challenge you to a game of Monopoly. No one will play with me in California because I always win."

Christine smiled. "Oh, you do, do you? Well, not tonight. But before we start playing, I want us to press the wedding dress. Even though I'm going home tomorrow, the cleaners won't be able to guarantee that they'll have it done in time. I think we can do it, don't you?"

Although she had wanted a skirt with yards and yards of fabric in it, after they worked on pressing it for a while, Christine wished she had chosen a sheath wedding dress. She was grateful that Mona was there to help move the dress around so they could press it without making wrinkles somewhere else.

"I can see why people let the cleaners do this." Mona swiped a lock of hair out of her eyes and pulled it behind her ear. "This is hard work."

"Yeah. Thanks for helping me."

"What are families for?"

✖

When Chris watched the Weather Channel this morning, the forecast was for another day or two without any snow. However, when he switched on the TV when he got home a little before midnight, the forecast was grim. *Why didn't I let Chrissy come home tonight like she wanted to? I thought it would be safer for her to drive in the daytime, and I wanted her to have some time with Mona before she left. Was that a mistake?*

He wondered if Chrissy was still awake. With Mona there, she might be, but if not, he didn't want to wake her. He dropped to his knees beside his bed. The familiar position welcomed him. He poured his heart out to the Lord. Somehow, he knew that Christine's tolerance had been stretched to the limit. He worried how she would take this new development.

When he tried to call Christine on Gram's phone the next morning, the lines were down. So he dialed the cell. Fortunately, it worked.

"Chrissy, how are you this morning?"

"Oh Christopher, I can't leave. The driveway is already impassable." Her statement ended on a sob.

"Honey, I'm so sorry. I wish I could be there with you. I'd pull you into my arms and kiss all your worries away." He made a soft smacking sound, hoping it would comfort her.

After a long silence, she answered, "I wish you *could* kiss them away."

Trying to take her mind off her troubles, he asked, "What did you and Mona do last night?"

"Would you believe we played Monopoly?"

Chris laughed. "So who won? I know you two are about equal in skill at the game."

"Equal? I don't think so. I beat her, of course."

"Honey, I'm proud of you."

✖

When Christine started to click the button to end the call, her low-battery light flashed a warning at her. Why didn't she check last night and plug the phone in for good measure? She would have needed it if she were on the road as planned. After going up to her bedroom on the second floor of the house, she pulled the charger out of her packed suitcase. She attached it to the phone and leaned down to plug it in. Before she reached the wall socket, everything went dim. Only the whiteout outside the window allowed her to find her way around the room.

"Chrissy, where are you?" Gram's voice drifted up the stairs.

"I'm in my room." She bumped into the edge of the footboard. The corner really hurt.

Mona shouted from below. "I thought you were going to help me fix breakfast."

After making her way across the hall, Christine started down the steps, feeling her way along the wall and banister. "I am. I went up to plug in my phone. It needs charging."

When she rounded the corner into the kitchen, her cousin stood hunched over, digging in one of the drawers. "What are you doing?"

Mona stood up. "Gram said the matches are in this drawer. She has lots of candles. She also has a couple of flashlights and three kerosene lamps. We'll have light."

"That's good to know. Where is Gram?"

"In the living room working on your veil."

Christine crossed to the sink to wash her hands, then she remembered that the pump wouldn't work. She turned around and leaned against the sink. "So what are we going to do for water?"

"That's easy," Mona quipped. "We'll melt snow on the stove."

"At least it runs on propane. Do you think the tank is full enough?"

Mona moved to look out the window, as if she could see through all the snow to where the tank stood. "I hope so. I don't want to ask her. If she needs more, she'll feel bad. I plan on only burning a few candles and one kerosene lamp at a time. That way they'll last longer."

What she left unsaid bothered Christine. They might be here until after the date for the wedding—snowed in. "And the furnace needs electricity to run the blower. How will we keep warm?" Christine knew there were a lot of things that could go wrong. A sense of dread dropped over her like an unwelcome cloak. So much had happened. Each time, it took more effort to deal with it. Christine didn't know if she had any resolve left, but she wanted to hide the fact from her grandmother and cousin. They didn't need any more to worry about.

"I've thought of that." Mona leaned closer to the window. "Have you been out on the back porch since you came?"

"No, even though I've been here several days." Christine shook her head for emphasis.

Mona moved to the back door then pulled it open. "There's lots of wood out here. It looks like we can burn the fireplace around the clock for a long time. We might have to sleep downstairs, though. I'm sure the upstairs will be too cool soon enough. It'll be like a slumber party." Her perky voice on that last statement did nothing to lift Christine's spirits.

Christine crossed her arms over her chest. "Well, at least something is going right."

Mona walked close and looked deep into her eyes. "Everything's going to be all right." She pulled Christine into a hug. "You'll see."

Yeah, we'll see. But what Christine saw looming on the horizon would definitely not be all right.

Chapter 8

When Christine went into the living room carrying a lighted lantern, Gram smiled at her. "Good thing I finished your veil last night. It would be hard to sew on those tiny seed pearls and sequins in this subdued light."

Christine didn't know what to say. She didn't want to discourage Gram, but she was afraid there wouldn't be a wedding. At least not four days from now. She went over and hugged her grandmother.

"You did a wonderful job on the dress and veil. Thank you." She dropped a kiss on Gram's soft, wrinkled forehead. "It's prettier than any wedding gown we saw at the Bridal Boutique when we went to get the bridesmaid dresses." She walked over to the couch and sat down, pulling a knitted afghan over her legs and tucking it in around them.

"Christine, I know why you're so glum. Want to talk about it?"

Gram's quiet inquiry brought tears to Christine's eyes. She didn't want to answer that question. She knew she couldn't do it without sobbing. Her nerves were stretched beyond their limit.

Gram's soothing voice continued, "Even though things seem grim right now, God is still in control."

Before Christine could think of anything to say, Mona came in with her arms full of firewood. Christine jumped up, letting her cover fall back on the couch. "Here, I'll help you. If you try to do it by yourself, you'll drop it all over the place. Don't want any of it hitting Gram."

Mona stood still while Christine took the pieces, two at a time, from her arms and placed them on the grate. While she arranged the split logs to her satisfaction, Mona went back out for kindling wood. Together they stuffed wadded newspaper under the grate, then placed kindling between the newspapers and grate.

"I'm surprised you remember how to build a fire, Mona." Christine liked to tease her cousin. "You don't have many fireplaces in Southern California, do you?"

Mona turned to smile at Gram then reached for the tall box of matches. "Gram taught me well. You remember all the times we spent holidays with her. Some skills you just don't forget."

When the lit match touched the newspapers, they quickly caught, flaring up and igniting the kindling. Before long, flames surrounded the larger pieces of wood, providing both warmth and a golden glow to the room.

"So. . ." Mona turned toward the back of the house. "Let's go gather snow for water. We can put it on the back burner of the stove."

Christine felt as if a large stone had lodged in her stomach. Four days from now, she should be getting ready to go to the church for her wedding. Instead, the snowstorm gave no indication of letting up anytime soon. The last time this happened, it took three days after the storm ceased for Gram's drive to be cleared. Three days that Christine didn't have if she wanted to get to the church on time.

A mountain of snow stood between herself and her wedding. She knew the Bible said that if you have faith equal to the size of a tiny mustard seed, you could move a mountain, but she wasn't sure she even had a mustard seed of faith. And this mountain of snow wouldn't be removed before the day of her wedding had passed. A terrible thought dropped into her mind, causing a rift to sink deep into her heart. Can a person have a "heartquake" the way the earth in California has earthquakes? *What if God doesn't want Christopher and me to get married?* Right now, she wasn't very sure. Maybe this was God's way of making her take another long look at everything.

Knowing how Gram could always read her expression, Christine turned toward the kitchen. "I'm going to help Mona." She rushed out before her grandmother said anything. She didn't want to talk to Gram about any of this. Especially about her doubts.

⚬⚬⚬

Chris held the phone tight against his ear while his chief accountant went over details of the latest acquisition. Chris couldn't help being proud of the progress he had made with the company in the months since his father left. At first, Chris had worried that he was too young to make the mature decisions needed to keep the company on track. A large number of people depended on this corporation for their livelihood, and he felt the enormous responsibility that entailed. With his rosewood pen, he scratched notes on the pad in front of him while listening to Mr. Jones.

Suddenly, some sort of strange, uncomfortable feeling sliced through him, almost like a stabbing pain. He couldn't hold back an audible gasp.

"Mr. Davis, sir, are you all right?" Herbert Jones had been with the company for more years than Chris knew. It felt funny when he called Chris "sir."

"Yes. I'm fine, Jones, but I'm afraid we'll have to continue this at another time."

"I'll wait for you to call me back." A loud click signaled the end of the conversation.

An ache spread throughout his chest, centering on his heart. Chris laid his watch on the desk so he could see the second hand. Then he counted his pulse for fifteen seconds. It was in a healthy range and beat strong and steady. Only three months ago he took a physical for the increased life insurance to protect his new family. He went to his own doctor and had Dr. Haddon do a thorough job of it. The doctor pronounced him as healthy as the proverbial horse. So where was this ache coming from?

With his hand pressing against his heart, Christ went into the private apartment behind his executive office, which he used when he needed seclusion from the workday world. When Chrissy was at Gram's overnight, he often just bedded down in the apartment instead of going home. Today he wanted privacy.

He dropped into the deeply cushioned leather chair and closed his eyes. *Lord, what is going on here? Is something the matter? What am I missing?* While he waited for an answer, a picture of Chrissy floated into his mind. An expression he had never seen on her face before held hopelessness and pain. "Lord, is it Chrissy?" Speaking the words aloud made God seem even closer, as if He were sitting in the chair across the room from him.

The unspeakable peace from Jesus settled in Chris's heart, and the ache subsided some. He closed his eyes and tried to imagine what could have caused her to look like that. *Of course!* So much had happened. Maybe she had all she could take and felt like giving up.

Chris poured his heart out to the Lord, asking Him to touch Chrissy in a way she had never been touched—to somehow let her know that He was still in control of their lives.

⤜∽⤛

"Chrissy. . ." Mona looked at her with a concerned frown wrinkling her brow. "What's the matter? You look like you've lost your last friend."

Christine couldn't stop the sobs that erupted. Mona pulled her into an embrace and rubbed her back while Christine poured an abundance of tears onto Mona's thick, layered sweaters. All the circumstances that had occurred in the last ten days formed an enormous reservoir of tears, which Christine kept bottled up, hoping they would go away. Instead, this final blow worked as a pump to send them gushing like a never-ending geyser. She cried until her whole body hurt from the effort, but finally the sobs subsided, and she moved back a pace.

"Maybe we should go into the kitchen. As wet as your sweater is, you'll freeze to death out here, even though the porch is enclosed." Christine swiped her cheeks with both hands, knowing that removing the wetness wouldn't erase the traces of all the crying she had done. What would Gram think?

Mona, always the mind reader, said quietly, "Gram knows something is bothering you. You can't hide it from her. Come on in the living room and we'll talk it out."

That was the last thing Christine wanted to do, but she knew there was no way around it. She followed her cousin through the kitchen and across the hall. When she glanced at Gram, the concern that cloaked her face hit Christine like a physical blow. Why couldn't she have been stronger and taken care of this by herself? She didn't want to hurt Gram. Not now, so soon after Gram's fall.

"Mona, why don't you put the kettle on for a pot of tea?" Gram pointed toward the couch. "Chrissy, sit down and tell me what's going on."

Christine glanced toward Mona a moment before her cousin exited the room. How could she not comply with Gram's wishes? So Christine took her place once again on the couch and pulled the afghan up around her shoulders, covering her body completely. Was she hoping it would shield her? It didn't work.

"Are you going to tell me what's going on, or do I have to get it out of you by asking pointed questions?" How like Gram to get right to the heart of the matter.

"You know what today is?"

Gram nodded. "It's four days before your wedding. And it's still snowing. Right?"

Christine shivered. "I can't believe this is happening to me. How could God let it? Everything was going according to plan, then all this—"

"According to whose plan, Chrissy?"

Why did that question hurt so much? Christine didn't want to face what Gram was bringing to the forefront. She had made the plans for her wedding. She really hadn't asked God what He wanted her to do. Except that at one time she felt it was God's will for her and Christopher to marry.

"Didn't God bring the two of you together?" Had Gram taken up Mona's mind reading habits?

"I thought so." Her answer, so soft that no one could hear it, didn't help. "I thought so," she said more forcefully.

"Don't you still believe that?"

Christine reached for a tissue from the box on the table at the end of the couch. Tears once again streamed down her cheeks. "I'm not sure. Look what He's allowed to happen. He could have stopped the storm."

Gram got up from the rocker-recliner and moved to sit beside Christine. "Shouldn't you stay in your chair?"

"Chrissy, I'm not an invalid. I just have some bruises." Gram settled two colorful throw pillows behind her back. "Now tell me why you aren't trusting God."

Christine sighed. "I'm not sure how to put it into words."

"You're just tired."

Mona came through the door carrying a tray with the teapot, three cups and saucers, and a plate of cookies. She set it on the coffee table in front of the couch. "Talk some sense into her, Gram." Mona began pouring cups of the fragrant, spicy brew.

"Chrissy has to work this out for herself."

⟡

When Chris finished praying, he lifted his cell phone. He punched in the speed-dial number for Chrissy. After a few rings, a disembodied voice told him that the phone was not currently in service. He could leave a voice message.

What had happened? He picked up the remote and turned on the large screen TV. The major report on the news station was about the snowstorm. Only a few flakes drifted in the air in St. Paul, but farther west the storm still raged.

"A large number of people in the center of the state have no electricity." The newscaster, wearing a stylish suit and an almost-fake smile, droned on. "The National Weather Service thinks the storm will abate later today. If it does, utility companies in other states have pledged to send workers to help restore power as quickly as possible. Maybe they will be able to reach the rural areas sooner than expected. There's even word that a team from Texas will be joining them. Sources believe the Texans probably have never seen the kind of storm that hit central Minnesota this last week. Some people wonder if they'll be prepared enough to really help."

Chris pushed the button to silence the man. *So, the electricity is off.* Evidently Chrissy didn't get to charge her phone before the power went out. He remembered how helpless he was in Hong Kong without being able to contact her. Probably she felt that way and more. Maybe that was why he had the pain. He knew God brought them together. Sometimes Chris knew that their souls were somehow connected. It would help him feel her agony, even at this great distance.

He dropped to his knees on the floor beside the huge chair and leaned his forearms on the cushioned seat, burying his head in his hands. "Father God, Christine needs You more than ever. Lord, show Yourself strong and in control so she can truly believe that she can trust You with anything, even the storm and our wedding."

After the first few spoken words, his prayer continued silently at length.

❧

Mona sat cross-legged on the floor across the table from Gram and Christine. She sipped her tea and stared into the depths of her cup.

At least she wasn't staring at Christine, who didn't want anyone else to see into her soul right now. Something was happening inside her. The heartquake had stopped, and the crevasse didn't feel as wide as it had before.

Gram patted Christine's hand. "I believe God has given me something for you. I'm not sure what it means, but here's what He's saying to tell you. 'If you can't trust God through the storms, how will you learn to hear His still, small voice during them?' Does that mean anything to you?"

Christine took a deep breath. Might as well get it all out in the open. "I was wondering if maybe this was God's way of telling me that Christopher and I shouldn't get married. There is no way the wedding will happen as planned."

"So, it will take place when you can get there." Gram's answer sounded emphatic. "It doesn't have to be in four—uh, three and a half days. What you need to do is understand that God is in control. Not you or your plans."

That much was crystal clear. What was it Gram said before? Trust Him through the storm. Christine knew she hadn't trusted Him for much of anything to do with the wedding. She wanted what she wanted—to follow her plans for the wedding of her dreams.

Mona looked up at her with a gleam in her eyes. "I don't think God is saying that it's wrong to plan, but schedules aren't what you should trust."

Wow! Christine was getting it from all sides. Most important, it was coming from the inside, too. The Lord's presence in her heart agreed with every word Gram and Mona spoke.

"And remember"—Gram waggled her index finger at Christine—"nothing is impossible with God."

Chapter 9

The morning of the third day before the wedding, Christopher clicked on the TV. The Weather Channel reported that the storm ended late yesterday evening.

"Most of the main roads were cleared by morning, but there is no estimate on when all the farm roads will be re-opened. It could take two or three days. And the electric company personnel can't get to some of the downed lines until the roads are cleared. Many people might not have power for several more days."

After taking his shower, Chris sat in the recliner in the bedroom and picked up his well-worn Bible from the table beside it. "Lord, I need a word from You." Talking out loud kept Chris from feeling so lonely. "I haven't done this very many times, but I'm going to close the Bible and hold it between my hands. When it drops open, Lord, please let it be a passage You want me to read."

When the book lay in his lap, Chris realized that the pages of Isaiah were open before him. What could Isaiah have for him? Chapter 30 started on the first page. He began to read, but nothing spoke to him specifically until he reached verse 21: "Whether you turn to the right or to the left, your ears will hear a voice behind you, saying, 'This is the way; walk in it.'"

"That's what I'm asking for, Lord. I want to hear Your clear voice speaking to me, telling me what to do right now."

A whisper as clear as if someone stood behind his shoulder sounded in Chris's spirit. With bowed head, he listened as the Holy Spirit spoke to his heart, giving him direction. With resolve, he thanked the Lord and reached for the phone.

❧

The morning of the third day before the wedding dawned bright. Christine stood at the front window where she had scraped a hole in the crystal frost that covered the pane. The wintry sun revealed all the diamond sparkles from the snow banked against the house and buildings. Both cars were almost covered.

"What are we going to do today?" Mona came into the living room, stretching and yawning. "I'm sure we won't be able to get out."

"Only if you want to shovel snow." Christine turned and smiled at her cousin. "I don't suppose you've done much of that in California."

"Naw, we let the servants do it."

Christine and Mona laughed at the joke.

"Well, we could play another Monopoly game." Christine leaned down to put more wood on the fire. "That is, if you want to lose again."

Gram started a pot of homemade soup while the girls set up the board. Just as Christine imagined, it lasted almost all day. They only broke for lunch. By early evening, Mona finally prevailed. At least each of them won a game while they were there. Soon they sat in front of the fireplace eating more of the delicious soup Gram made.

When she finished, Mona took her bowl to the kitchen and returned with a wrapped package in her hand. "Here. I bought this as a wedding gift, but you might need to use it now." She dropped it in Christine's lap.

Like a child, Christine tore the paper away, revealing a battery operated reading light. The package even contained extra batteries.

"I know how much you like to read in bed, and I didn't want you keeping your executive husband awake." Mona laughed. "Of course, the two of you might be otherwise occupied, and you might not even need this."

Christine felt the blush creep up her neck and cheeks. She hoped something else would keep Christopher occupied at night, but she didn't want to think about it right now. That was for after the wedding.

"Thanks, Mona. I tried to read my Bible after I got ready for bed last night, but it's hard to do by candlelight. I'll get to tonight."

❧

Christine pulled her warm plush robe close around her. Under it, she wore her sweats instead of pajamas. Because the floor was too hard, the cousins took turns on the couch. At least Gram's room, next to the living room, was warm enough when they left the door open. After the girls built the fire up, Mona went to sleep. She would have about four hours while Christine kept the fire going. Then Mona would take her turn and let Christine sleep.

Curled up in Gram's big rocker, Christine attached the reading lamp to her Bible, wondering where she should begin reading tonight. She had never done this before, but she prayed that God would open the Bible to the page where He had a message just for her. She ran her thumbs along the gold edge and flipped the book open. It had been a long time since she had read anything from Isaiah. She usually tried to do a chapter of Psalms, Proverbs, or the New Testament. Occasionally, she did one of those read-through-the-Bible-in-a-year things, but not recently.

Her gaze roved over the open pages, and an underlined verse jumped out at her. She wished she had noted when and why she highlighted it, but maybe that was what God wanted her to see again.

"Whether you turn to the right or to the left, your ears will hear a voice behind you, saying, 'This is the way; walk in it.'"

It must have been sometime when she wanted God to speak to her. That's what she needed tonight. *Lord, what are You saying to me?*

In the quietness, the still, small voice answered. *"Trust Me, child. Just trust Me."*

Christine bowed her head and felt the presence of the Holy Spirit hovering all around her. *I do, Lord.*

"Can you trust Me with your wedding?"

For a moment, panic seized Christine's heart. But only a moment. With resolution, she took a deep breath. *I trust You with the wedding. I think I always trusted You. I just let things get in the way. Forgive me, Lord. Whatever You want, I'm willing.*

For several minutes the heavy presence of the Lord filled the room in an almost tangible way. Christine basked in that presence, and peace like a soft blanket settled into her heart, covering everything there.

❦

Since both of the cousins were tired, they built up the fire one last time near morning and fell asleep. Later, the smell of brewing coffee and sizzling bacon pulled Christine from her slumbers. She sat up and stretched the kinks out of her body.

Mona, who had fallen asleep on the other end of the couch, began stirring. "What time is it?"

"I don't know." Christine stood up and started folding her blanket. "But it smells like Gram beat us to the kitchen. I could use some coffee."

She walked into the cozy kitchen. "Do I smell biscuits, too, Gram?"

Swaddled in a huge apron, her grandmother turned and smiled at her before taking the last slice of bacon out of the pan and placing it with the others on a paper towel–covered plate. "Yes, breakfast is almost ready, but it's more like brunch time."

Christine couldn't believe how much meat Gram had cooked. "We won't eat that much." She picked up a slice and took a bite.

"I just felt like fixing a big breakfast. Maybe we can have bacon sandwiches for lunch."

"Are we expecting anyone?" Mona's voice called from the other room. "Someone is coming up the drive in a horse-drawn sleigh."

"Must be Mr. Watson. He's probably checking to see if we're all right."

Gram poured some of the bacon grease into the old coffee can on the cabinet and started breaking eggs into the skillet. "I'll scramble enough for him, too. He probably ate breakfast early, so he should be hungry by now."

Mona came through the door. "I don't think it's your neighbor. I can't tell for sure, but it looks like a younger man. I'm going to put some clothes on before he comes in."

Christine rushed to the front of the house and pulled the door open a crack. She peered around the door into the brightness. Squinting her eyes against the glare, she shrieked, "It's Chris!"

Mona stopped on the stairs. "Who?"

"Christopher! He's driving the sleigh."

"Did you just call him Chris?" Mona smiled.

"I guess I did." She pulled the door farther open. At least she still was fully clothed beneath her robe.

"Chris!" She stepped out on the porch just as he stopped the sleigh near the front gate. She couldn't believe he guessed so accurately where it was under the snow. He had only been here a few times.

Bundled up in lots of layers, he looked almost Neanderthal, but Christine's heart beat in her throat as she looked at him. She couldn't remember when she had been so glad to see him. He took horse blankets from under the front seat of the sleigh and placed them on the animals. It looked like a really large sleigh.

When he turned, he pulled away the scarves that covered the lower part of his face and gave her a dazzling smile. With halting steps, he made his way through the snow up the completely hidden sidewalk toward her.

Her breathing accelerated. She didn't care what happened, or when. She and Chris were supposed to be together. Just looking at him made her quivery inside.

After he stepped onto the porch, he pulled her into a bear hug. His cold lips descended and covered hers. The heat of their passionate kiss soon warmed them.

"Come into the house," Gram called from the open doorway. "You can warm up before the fire while I finish scrambling the eggs."

They followed her into the house and closed the door. Christine helped Chris start to peel off his layers.

"God told me to fix lots of breakfast. Now we know why." Gram continued toward the kitchen.

❧

Seated across the table from his fiancée, Chris studied her face with amazement. Peace and contentment shone through the smile she gave him. He grinned, remembering the heart-stopping kiss they shared on the porch. Good thing he listened to the Lord.

"Are you girls ready to load up and go away with me?"

"Is that why you came? To take us back?" Chrissy sounded like an excited little girl, but no one looking at her would mistake her for a child.

"An interesting thing happened last night." Chris took the bowl of scrambled eggs Gram passed to him and piled them on his plate beside the biscuits and bacon. "I really wanted a word from the Lord, so I asked Him to open my Bible where He wanted me to read. It was in Isaiah 30." At Chrissy's gasp, he stopped.

"That's where He took me, too. The verse about the voice speaking from behind you telling you the way to go." She put her fork down and stared into his eyes. "This is so awesome."

Gram seemed to be unaffected by what was happening. After taking a bite and chewing it awhile, she spoke quietly. "I knew God had this all worked out."

Mona nodded and continued eating.

Chris laid his fork down and reached to take Chrissy's hand. "Did something happen day before yesterday? Late in the morning?"

Momentary sadness veiled her face. "It was the most horrible thing." She swallowed as if she had a lump in her throat. "I almost decided we weren't supposed to be getting married. It felt like my heart broke in two."

Everything in the room receded as though he and Chrissy were alone. "I felt your pain."

"Felt my pain?"

"I was on the phone with Mr. Jones and something shot through my chest, ending in my heart, making me gasp. I had to hang up." Just the memory was uncomfortable. "I went into my private suite and prayed for you."

With her other hand, Chrissy wiped at the tears on her cheeks. "How could that happen?"

He rubbed the back of her hand with his thumb. "God has tied our hearts and souls together. That's the only way to describe it."

Gram got up to refill the plate of biscuits. "That's when God gave me something for Chrissy."

Chris glanced at her. "What?"

Chrissy answered for her. "He said, 'If you can't trust Him through the storms, how will you learn to hear His still, small voice during them?' It helped me decide to trust Him. After that He was able to speak to me, and I heard Him."

Mona got up to take her plate to the sink. "God is awesome, isn't He?"

No one disagreed.

As soon as the dishes were washed and put away, Christine started packing her things. Chris was more than just her fiancé; he was her hero. She wondered how much trouble it had been for him to obtain a sleigh to come get them. Just the fact that he would go to so much trouble touched her heart.

When she went downstairs, Chris came into the house carrying a large, sort of flat box. "I got this from your friend at the wedding dress company. It's for shipping the gowns. There's just room for it under the backseat of the sleigh."

She dropped her overnight bag and took the carton. Soon the dress and veil were safely surrounded by tissue paper in the sealed container.

With Gram and Mona in the back seat and Christine beside Chris in the front, they started across the snow toward Litchfield.

"So what do we do when we get there?" Mona called from the back seat.

"We'll leave the sleigh at the edge of town. I have a car waiting for us there." Chris's breath caused puffs of steam in the cold air. "We'll have you to Chrissy's house before it's time to go to dinner."

"Dinner!" Chrissy grabbed his arm. "The rehearsal and rehearsal dinner were supposed to be tonight."

"They're still on." He dropped a kiss on her forehead. "Everything is right on schedule."

Right on schedule the next day, Christine started down the aisle clutching her soon-to-be father-in-law's arm with one hand. In the other she carried the beautiful bouquet Melissa and Karen created from her favorite flowers. Lazy white snowflakes drifted outside the windows of the church, but here in the sanctuary, the stained glass windows hid them from sight. Her bridesmaids lined the front in red velvet dresses trimmed with white fur. Melissa, as maid of honor, looked beautiful in a green dress.

Quickly Christine's eyes were drawn to the handsome man across the aisle from her attendants. The man of her dreams. Her hero who didn't move the mountain of snow to get her here. With God's help, he carried her across the mountain to get to this wedding of her dreams. She knew God smiled down from heaven with His blessing.

Chapter 1

Chandra Kirby stared a moment longer at shimmering hazel eyes flecked with bits of green and yellow, then slipped her mirror back in her purse as the plane taxied to a stop. She blinked back tears, dabbing at her eyes with a tissue. *Get ahold of yourself,* she admonished. *Some vacation this will be if you cry the whole time.*

"*You're running away.*" Her sister Clarissa's statement still hurt. *I am not running away.* Chandra's tears dried as her stomach churned. "*You ran away from love, you ran from facing death, and now, a year later, you're running away from the fact that our parents are still dead.*"

Clarissa's voice from their last phone conversation echoed through her head. Clarissa wanted Chandra to come back to Indiana for a week. *I already had plans. I am not running away,* Chandra defended herself fiercely as she edged her way into the center aisle of the plane.

Standing in the slow-moving line of people waiting to exit the plane, Chandra thought about the reason for her trip. All her life she'd dreamed of taking a bike tour through the English countryside. Then, after her parents' murder a year ago, she'd immersed herself in her work, trying to escape the anger and total abandonment she felt. As the anniversary of their deaths approached, Chandra knew she needed to get away in order to deal with it. A long dreamed of trip looked like a good answer to the problem.

Chandra followed the crowd through customs in Heathrow Airport and headed for the baggage claim area. Her body felt heavy from fatigue and stress. She walked slower than most of the people swarming past her. Without warning, she stumbled to the side, nearly landing on the floor as a man's body hurtled into hers.

"Excuse me," he said, his hand wrapping around her arm, steadying her. "I have to catch up to my party, and I'm sorry. Chandra? Chandra, is that you?"

Chandra tried to calm the thud of her heart, knowing who touched her from the sound of his voice. She looked up into the astonished face of Pierce Stillwell, childhood friend and, although unknown to him, the love of her life. "Hello, Pierce."

She almost sighed in relief at the even tone of her voice. It betrayed none of her inner turmoil.

"I can't believe we would run into each other in London of all places. What are you doing here?" Pierce's dark blue eyes sparkled, and his smile warmed the space around them. He glanced toward the exit doors. "Oh, sorry, Chandra. I've got to run. I'd love to stay and talk, but they're waiting for me, and I don't want to be too late. I'll call you sometime."

He leaned over, kissed her lightly on the cheek, and dashed away. The crowd eagerly swallowed him, and Chandra stood silently staring after him, her hand covering the place where his kiss burned into her skin. The longing to run after him, almost overpowering in its intensity, nearly caused her to forget he was the reason she'd left home in the first place. A lone tear slipped from her eye, wending its way slowly down her face. Chandra pulled her long french braid over her shoulder and twisted the ends through her fingers as she began to once more move with the crowd.

Approaching the luggage bay, Chandra noticed a young woman holding a placard with her name printed on it. She smoothed the skirt of her midnight-blue suit, trying in vain to wipe away the travel wrinkles. Weaving through the crowd, she slowly approached her. "Hello, I'm Chandra Kirby." She shifted her overnight case and held out her hand.

The petite brunette smiled, wrinkling her pert, freckled nose, and grasped Chandra's hand. "Glad to have you here, Chandra. I'm Leah, from Bikeway Tours. Let's collect your bags. Then we'll join the others in the van and motor to the inn."

❧

"Here we are," Leah said cheerfully as she set Chandra's bag next to a gray twelve-passenger van. "Go ahead and find a seat while we load your bags."

Chandra smiled at the young couple on the first bench seat behind the driver. She could hear other people talking in the back of the van, however the middle seat beckoned her with empty arms. She edged past the first seat, maneuvering through the narrow space and into her seat. Before fastening her seat belt, she glanced back at the couple seated behind her.

"Pierce!" Chandra's involuntary gasp reverberated in the quiet of the van.

"Chandra! I can't believe this." Pierce's husky voice brought back a rush of forgotten emotions. "I didn't know you were going on this bike tour. Do you remember Morgan Wilson?" Pierce indicated the gorgeous blond seated next to him.

How could I forget my worst nightmare? Chandra wanted to say as she watched Morgan snuggle closer to Pierce. "Of course, I remember Morgan. Who could forget our senior prom queen?" Chandra struggled to keep her tone light.

Pierce turned to Morgan. "Morgan, do you remember Chandra?"

Morgan's smile didn't reach her eyes. "Of course. She was the little shadow who followed you everywhere. I'm sure this will be fun, Chandra."

The look in Morgan's eyes chilled Chandra. She barely listened as Pierce introduced her to Kurt and Gina Holman, the young couple in front of her. She turned around as Leah and the driver of the van climbed in. Pulling a paperback novel out of her purse, she fastened her seat belt and pretended to read words she couldn't even focus on. *Oh God, I can't take this. I've always loved Pierce, and he's always loved Morgan.*

Chandra tried to ignore the soft murmuring from the seat behind her as the English countryside flashed by. Not wanting to picture Morgan with Pierce's arm around her, Chandra tried to concentrate on the emerald-green hills dotted with sheep, thinking how beautiful they were compared to the dry brown hills around Los Angeles. In the spring, L.A.'s hills were green but not like this. These rolling slopes blossoming with thatch-roofed cottages looked like something out of a fairy tale.

Leaning her head back against the seat, Chandra's thoughts filled with a warm smile and midnight-blue eyes. Pierce. Her childhood friend and confidant. When the other girls her age were giggling about boys, trying out makeup and perfume, and longing to meet the latest movie heartthrob, Chandra preferred bike rides and hiking with Pierce. They dreamed for hours on end of taking bike tours all over Europe when they grew up, planning each trip and the order in which they would take them.

Although to Pierce they were only friends, Chandra had always longed for a deeper relationship. She loved him for his easy smile, his wonderful sense of humor, and the fact that he put up with her constantly organizing his unorganized life. Only Pierce understood the hurt she felt from being continually rejected by the girls her age because she didn't share the same likes and dislikes.

Chandra turned to look out the window, blinking back tears as she recalled the last time she had been home. At her parents' funeral, only Pierce had understood her grief. She still remembered the comfort of his arms around her. The safe, protected feeling Pierce gave her turned out to be her only solace during that miserable time. They hadn't seen or spoken to each other since.

Anger bubbled up inside as Chandra thought about her parents and their needless deaths. They were such good people. Always ready to help anyone in need, Chandler and Darlene Kirby were well loved in Newbury. Serious crime rarely happened in rural Indiana, and the whole community suffered a shock over the cold-blooded murder of her parents.

It didn't take long for the authorities to track down the young men responsible, but that didn't bring back her parents. Drugs and alcohol were the contributing factors. It turned out her parents had helped these young men because they were needy. Then, high on drugs and alcohol, the two men decided to see if they could get some more money. Her parents refused, probably recognizing the disoriented state the young men were in. Thinking to ransack the house, the boys tied up her parents, and when they couldn't find any money, they shot them. Chandra clenched her fists, her stomach knotting.

Chandra hoped this trip would help her forget the anger and the pain. *God, I don't know why You allowed this to happen,* she thought bitterly as she did every day. *They loved You. You should have been there for them.*

"Well, we're almost to Winchester," Leah's cheery voice cut through the silence, startling Chandra. "The inn is only a couple of miles away."

In the distance, Chandra watched a windmill slowly circle its arms through the gray haze, as if beckoning her to come closer. She grimaced, thinking of Don Quixote trying to conquer windmills. Sometimes she thought her anger toward those young murderers was her windmill—a useless effort. Yet she couldn't seem to give it up, no matter how hard she prayed. *They deserve my anger,* she thought, clenching her teeth.

The van pulled to a stop close to the door of the quaint, country-style Green Meadow Inn. Chandra climbed stiffly from the van, watching the daffodils in the flowerbeds lining the walkway as they nodded their yellow heads at her. A light mist washed her face.

She tilted her head back and gazed up at the old limestone building, ivy snaking up the gray walls. The windows on the second floor opened out, and Chandra could visualize a young maiden leaning over the ledge, looking down the road, waiting for her favorite knight to ride by on his fiery steed.

After listening to instructions for meeting at the evening meal, Chandra followed the directions to her room. She opened a door to a small but neatly furnished bedroom complete with two twin beds. Chandra crossed to the window and, ignoring the weather, leaned out, wondering if her knight in shining armor would ride by.

Chandra sighed and sank down on the bed nearest the window. She couldn't remember being so tired. Before leaving on this trip, she'd spent a full day at the office tying up loose ends and preparing her staff for her absence. She didn't even have time to change clothes before catching her plane.

Groaning, she slid off the bed and opened her neatly packed suitcase to get some fresh clothes. They were to meet downstairs for dinner in an hour, and she wanted a shower first. Maybe then she would be able to stay awake during the meal.

After a long hot shower, Chandra undid her french braid and slowly brushed out her long hair. Her thick tresses hung in waves below her waist.

The door to the room suddenly burst open. Morgan stalked in and plunked her suitcase down in the middle of the floor. "It looks like we'll have plenty of time to reminisce, since we'll be sharing a room most of the trip." Her ice-covered words trickled bumps up and down Chandra's arms.

Chapter 2

Why did you choose cross bikes for your tours?" Pierce asked, looking up from the bicycle he knelt beside. Dale, the tour guide, glanced over from the Bikeway Tours bike he was examining. "Most of the trip is along back roads. A lot of them are fine for road bikes, but some are a little rough for those thin tires. Then we throw in a few paths for fun and a little off-the-road scenery. You don't necessarily need a mountain bike, but you need something sturdier than a road bike. These seemed to meet our needs, and we've never had a complaint about them."

"The components are good," Pierce admitted. "I like the Ultimate ones. I sell a lot of them in my bike shop."

Dale nodded and continued to check the bicycles's brakes, shifters, and gears, getting ready for the first day's ride. The sun, peeping over the rolling hills, bathed them in its warm glow.

"Good morning." Chandra stepped around the side of the inn. Pierce smiled at her, noting her black and purple paneled biking shorts and matching jersey top. Her purple and gray fingerless biking gloves and helmet dangled casually from one hand.

"Good morning to you." Pierce's husky voice broke the silence. Bikes forgotten, he found he couldn't take his eyes off of Chandra. The morning light made the auburn highlights in her hair stand out like a halo. The green of her hazel eyes glinted warmly. Her smile, fresh and open, beckoned him invitingly.

"Are you ready for the ride today?"

Pierce forced his gaze down and ran his hand once more over the bike frame before answering. "I'm ready. How about you? Have you kept up on your riding?"

"You bet." She stepped forward and ran her hand lovingly over the nearest bicycle seat. "I try to ride a little bit every day, and I do longer rides on the weekends. And you?"

"I started a bike club eight months ago." Pierce smiled at her and found himself trapped in her gaze again. "I guess I got tired of riding by myself. We do mostly road trips that are fairly short, but one weekend a month, part of the club gets together to do some off-road mountain biking."

"Are the others on the tour in your club or just from your church?"

Pierce nodded. "Morgan doesn't usually participate, but Kurt and Gina started the club with me. At first Gina ran the support team and wouldn't ride with us. Then after a couple of months she got tired of that and talked Kurt into buying her a bike." Pierce grinned. "She didn't have to talk much. Kurt and I were already discussing this tour, but he didn't want to do it if Gina wouldn't come with us. Now Gina rides every day and loves it."

"Oh, there you are." Morgan's sultry tone drew Pierce's attention like a magnet. Even in her one-piece bike suit and helmet, she looked breathtaking. Her blue eyes captured his, drawing him away from Chandra. "You disappeared after breakfast, and we wondered what happened to you."

Pierce noticed Kurt and Gina standing behind Morgan. "I wanted to check out the bikes we'll be using," he stated lamely. "You know I always have to give them a once over."

⊷∾⊷

A half hour later, Chandra swung her leg over her bike, flipped her long braid over her shoulder, and pushed off. The morning air, cool and moist, brushed against her skin like a damp washcloth. The village houses lined the road like a row of limestone checkers. A stream meandered alongside the trail, small footpaths crossing it at intervals.

Breathing deeply, Chandra relaxed, feeling her muscles tighten then gradually begin to loosen and adjust to the rhythm of her peddling. Once out of town, she would work up to the proper cadence, but just now she wanted to enjoy this quaint little village at a slower pace.

Chandra maneuvered to the front of the line at the town limits and picked up her pace a little. The clean country air almost made her lungs ache, as if they weren't used to such luxury. A click of bike gears alerted her that someone was catching up. Chandra glanced over her shoulder to see Pierce coming alongside.

"I see you're out front as usual." He grinned and slowed his peddling slightly to match hers. "I always did have to work to keep up with you."

Chandra laughed. "I seem to remember it the other way around. I think that's why I'm so competitive."

Pierce's deep blue eyes sparkled with laughter. "We sure had good times together. I think you were the best thing for me. You wouldn't believe how disorganized my life is without you around."

Groaning, Chandra rolled her eyes. "I can't bear the thought. I had to constantly keep after you. It's been ten years, so it might be impossible to get you organized after all that time," she teased. His warm smile lit up the morning, and Chandra felt her pulse quicken. Pierce always had this effect on her, yet she knew it was a one-sided attraction.

"Pierce!"

Pierce glanced back over his shoulder. "I'd better go," he said. "Morgan refused to take our advice on preparing for the trip. To her the thirty miles we're covering today will seem like a million. I'd better go see if I can encourage her." He gazed for a moment at Chandra. "Sometime this trip we'll have to find the time to catch up. I've missed having you around."

Chandra bit her lip as he slowed his pace and drifted back toward the others. He missed her? What did that mean? Did he possibly feel something for her just as she felt something for him? Or was it simply her friendship he wanted, not a deeper relationship? Obviously, he reserved that for Morgan.

Chandra slowed her pace while keeping an even cadence. Even though she'd prepared for this trip, she knew the first few days were designed to ease the group into the rhythm of steady biking without wearing them out. That's why the first days were the shortest distances. Despite the best training, any bike rider could be susceptible to fatigue, aching muscles, or sores where the bicycle seat rubbed the skin raw.

"Hi, Chandra." Kurt's cheerful voice cut through her reverie.

Chandra glanced over and once again felt warmed by Kurt's friendly brown eyes and welcoming smile. "Hi, Kurt."

"Isn't this the most beautiful country?" Kurt nodded his head toward a cottage near the road where two apple-cheeked girls waved excitedly, their brown braids bobbing with the motion. "I think this must be the best way to visit a new place. If we were in a car, we'd never see it in such a personal way."

Chandra nodded. "I hope we have time to look around. I wanted to examine the little village where we spent the night. I'd like to get to know some of the people, too. I love to travel and meet people."

"You work for a travel agency, don't you?"

"Yes. I enjoy working at Fantasy Travel and arranging people's dream vacations. It gives me the chance to visit places most people don't get to see." She paused a moment. "Tell me, how long have you known Pierce?"

"We moved to Newbury a year ago. I'm the assistant pastor at Pierce's church. We hit it off right away—you know how some people click? Well, Pierce and I were like that. Later we started the bike club, and that really cemented our friendship. How long have you known Pierce?"

Chandra frowned in thought. "I barely remember a time when I didn't know Pierce. Our parents were close friends, and we grew up together." She smiled as a fond memory surfaced. "As the tomboy of the neighborhood, I didn't get along with the other girls. Pierce always stepped in, and we spent hours together riding our bikes and talking. He was the slightly older brother I wanted but never had." *At least, that's what everyone thought.*

"Then you must be Chandler and Darlene Kirby's daughter." Kurt's casual comment struck deep. "I'm sorry about what happened to them."

"Did you know my parents?" Chandra tried to still the tremble in her voice.

"I met your dad and mom when I interviewed for the assistant pastor's position. They took Gina and me to dinner and made us feel so welcome. We were only in Newbury three weeks when they were murdered. I still can't believe it happened."

A tear trickled slowly down Chandra's cheek, and she angrily brushed it off. "I still miss them so much," she whispered. "I can't understand why God did this."

"But Chandra, God didn't do it." Kurt leaned forward to look at her. "We don't understand why God may have allowed it to happen, and I know this may sound trite, but He works out everything for good."

"Well, I can't imagine a loving God bringing some good out of this. Two wonderful people were murdered while the scum that killed them are allowed to live. Not only are they allowed to live, but they were barely punished because they were young and didn't know what they were doing." Chandra couldn't keep the sarcasm from her voice. "Now, please excuse me," she said as she pushed harder on her pedals and raced ahead of Kurt. Tears traced down her cheeks as she fought to control the anger and hatred that knotted her stomach.

❧

Pierce watched as Kurt dropped back beside Gina, and Chandra pushed ahead once more. Chandra's shoulders were hunched over her handlebars and her head bent low as if a great weight were on her. Pierce glanced over at Morgan, her face reddened with exertion, any attempt to be alluring momentarily forgotten.

What's wrong with me? Pierce thought. *Ever since high school I wanted to date Morgan. She's the most beautiful woman I've ever seen. I planned to ask her to marry me on this trip, yet now all I can think of is Chandra and how much I want to be with her.*

"Pierce, I think I need to stop for a while," Morgan panted as she slowed her bicycle. "I can't believe how hard this is."

"It's too bad you didn't make some of our longer trips."

"I rode my bike every day," Morgan snapped impatiently. "Some days I even rode through the trails in the park so I'd be ready for the off-road part of the tour."

"Morgan." Pierce took on the tone he used when instructing a group of children. "You didn't ride that far. And the trails at the park are only three miles long, so the most you ever rode is five or six miles at a time. That's a lot different than the thirty to fifty we're doing each day on this tour."

"Maybe you didn't explain how far we'd be riding." Morgan's voice began to emulate the whine of an airplane engine preparing for take off. "Not only are my legs dying, but I'm sure I'm getting sores from this bike seat."

"We'll stop for lunch before long. We can borrow a tool from Dale and check the slant of your seat. What kind of unitard did you get?"

"How should I know? I just picked one out of a magazine and bought it."

"I warned you to be careful to get clothing designed for women." Frustration crept into Pierce's voice. "The padding is different for us, Morgan. That might be why you're getting sore. We'll see what we can do at noon."

Pierce looked down the road to where Chandra and the others steadily pulled away from them.

"Oh, I see." He turned to see Morgan watching him. "You'd rather be riding with her—your old girlfriend. I suppose she trained properly for this tour."

"Chandra isn't my old girlfriend. We grew up together and have been friends for years. She's like a sister to me, and yes, I know she trained for this tour." Pierce stopped, wondering why he felt like he betrayed Chandra when he told Morgan she was like a sister. Hadn't they always been like brother and sister?

Morgan's cold tone jerked him back to the present. "Just remember, you invited me on this trip. I expect you to stay with me, not with your long-lost sister."

Chapter 3

Chandra hopped out of bed and stretched. Sharing a room with Morgan last night had been better than the first night. Morgan, too tired and sore to do or say much of anything, had climbed into bed early and fallen asleep instantly.

Crossing to the small window, Chandra peered out to see what the day would be like. The sun, playing peek-a-boo with gray clouds, promised possible showers and cool riding. Today they would see the famed Salisbury Cathedral and take a side trip, if they wanted, to Stonehenge.

A low moan from the bed adjoining hers alerted Chandra that Morgan had awakened. Chandra did her best to ignore Morgan's discomfort as she slowly pulled herself up in the bed. She and Morgan hadn't exactly hit it off, and Chandra didn't want to risk Morgan's anger this morning.

"Good morning," Chandra called over her shoulder, trying to sound cheerful. "Do you want to shower before breakfast?"

"I don't care," Morgan snapped. "You go ahead and I'll take mine later."

Chandra quickly grabbed a towel and washcloth and headed for the bathroom. *Why in the world did Morgan come on this bike tour?* she wondered as the warm water poured down on her, loosening her slightly stiffened muscles. *Surely it can't be for the sole purpose of being near Pierce. God, please help me see Morgan as You see her. I know You love her, so help me at least tolerate her presence.*

"How are your saddle sores this morning, Morgan?" Chandra asked after her shower.

"I don't know that it's any of your business," she snapped. "They hurt like crazy, if you must know. I don't have any idea how I'll ride that stupid bicycle today."

"Did you bring some salve?" Chandra held up a small tube of her favorite salve. "If not, you can borrow some of mine."

Morgan stared at her, looking surprised, then nodded and reached for the tube. Slowly, she pushed herself off the bed and hobbled toward the shower. Chandra pulled the hairbrush through her wet hair, staring at the closed door thoughtfully, wondering how Morgan would manage.

Chandra stared in awe at the towering Salisbury Cathedral. The cathedral, bearing the tallest spire in England, definitely displayed the mastery of medieval architecture.

"Marvelous, isn't it?" Chandra jumped as Pierce's husky voice sounded close to her ear. Her pulse quickened, and she felt a blush warm her cheeks as she looked into his deep blue eyes. "No wonder so many people thought God lived in these buildings. They hold a presence that reminds one of God," Pierce said softly.

For a moment they stood in companionable silence, gazing at the rows of arched windows and alcoves lining the sides of the buildings. Suddenly, Pierce began to chuckle, and Chandra glanced at him.

"Care to let me in on the joke?"

Pierce grinned at her. "Do you remember Pastor Robinson? He led our youth group for a while."

"I remember him," Chandra said, a smile tugging the corners of her mouth. "We were so mean back then. We used to refer to him as our favorite horse, because he had such a long face."

"That's him. I don't think I'll ever forget his face and the way he talked so slow." Pierce laughed. "I used to watch old Jimmy Stewart movies and wonder if Pastor Robinson did the voice parts for him."

Chandra giggled. "So what reminded you of him?"

Pierce gestured toward the cathedral wall. "See that alcove, the second one from the end? The figure in there could easily pass for Pastor Robinson, don't you think?"

Chandra strained to pick out the stone figure Pierce pointed out.

"You're looking at the wrong row," he said, leaning closer and lifting her chin with his hand. Chandra bit her lip as his light touch set her pulse pounding. She could feel the warmth of his nearness and fought a longing to lean against him.

"You're right," she gasped, pulling away from his disturbing touch. "Do you suppose his great-great-great-grandfather posed for that statue?" Chandra looked up at Pierce as his husky laugh drifted toward the imposing structure containing the statue in question. As she turned, she glimpsed Morgan watching from the edge of the grounds, her blue eyes blazing daggers even at that distance.

Quickly, Chandra moved away from Pierce. "I think I'll go inside and look around for a while. If the outside is this magnificent, I can't wait to see the inside. I'll see you later, Pierce." Chandra walked away, denying the look of hurt she'd seen in Pierce's eyes at her abrupt departure.

~~~

Pierce watched in shock as Chandra crossed the lawn and disappeared into the depths of the church. *What did I say?* he wondered. *Why did she leave like that?* The memory of those almond-shaped hazel eyes flecked with gold and green stayed with him. *She's always been special to me, Lord, but she just thinks of me as a brother. Help me get rid of these strange feelings. I plan to ask Morgan to marry me.*

Slowly, Pierce wandered over to the walled-in garden area of the church and slipped in through a doorway. For the next hour he wandered through the building and the grounds, admiring the medieval stonework and architecture.

Pierce paused to admire a particularly intricate piece of stonework, and the silence of the huge building closed in around him. It felt as if he were the only person in the whole world. The sound of quick footsteps and voices echoed down the hallway.

"Chandra." Morgan's sharp command echoed through the hall. "I want to talk to you."

Pierce glanced down the hall, wondering what he should do. He wasn't an eavesdropper, but this hall dead-ended, and the only other way out would be to pass them. As he stepped quietly down the hall, the conversation got louder, and he paused, not wanting to intrude.

"Hi, Morgan, isn't this a magnificent place?"

"You can quit with the concerned goody-two-shoes routine, Chandra. I saw you outside with Pierce, and I want it to stop."

"You want what to stop?"

"I know what you're doing. You're doing your best to take him away from me. Well, it won't work. I won't give him up."

"I don't know what you're talking about. Pierce walked up to me outside, not the other way around."

"She's right, Morgan." Pierce said.

Morgan's mouth dropped open and then closed. For a moment she stared at him then turned to walk away.

"I want to talk about this later, Morgan," Pierce called after her.

Pierce reached over and pulled Chandra close for a moment. "I'm sorry, Chandra. Morgan is usually so sweet," he murmured.

How could she have changed so suddenly? Have I just been blind? Pierce wondered. *Oh God, help me know the right thing to do,* he prayed.

"Everybody ready to set off?" Dale asked as Chandra stuffed the last bite of her sandwich in her mouth. "For those who want to, you can take a side trip to visit Stonehenge this afternoon. It's on the way to your lodgings tonight." He glanced at the overcast sky. "In case of rain, you have rain slickers in your pack."

Nearing the turn to Stonehenge, Chandra slowed, noticing the sluggishness of her bicycle. She looked down and groaned. "I hate changing flats."

"You hate what?" Pierce's voice so close startled her, and she nearly swerved off the road.

"Pierce, how do you manage that?" Chandra gave him an exasperated look. "You are always sneaking up beside me. I think you like to scare me like you did when we were kids."

Pierce laughed. "I didn't try to scare you. You just didn't hear me coming. Now, tell me what you hate."

Chandra gestured to the back tire on her bicycle. "Changing flats, especially on a back tire. Oh well," she sighed. "I guess it can't be helped."

After removing the tools and spare tube, Chandra flipped the bicycle upside down, balancing it carefully on its seat and handlebars. Pierce laid his bike down in the grass at the side of the road and stepped over to help her remove the tire.

"Pierce." The sugary sweetness in Morgan's tone turned Chandra's stomach. *What does he see in this woman?* she wondered.

"Pierce, I need you to ride with me." Morgan moaned slightly as she stopped and rubbed at her sore legs. "I don't think I can make it without your encouragement."

Chandra watched as Morgan widened her blue eyes and pursed her pink lips in a deliberate pout. Chandra remembered that same expression from high school days.

Pierce stirred beside her then slowly stood up. "Here comes Dale, Chandra. He can help you with this flat."

"That's fine, Pierce. Thanks anyway." Chandra bit her lip as Morgan flashed her a triumphant look. Pierce and Morgan pedaled slowly down the road as Dale stopped beside Chandra and hopped off his bike.

"Looks like you could use a bit of help here," Dale stated. He deftly turned the wheel around, searching for a nail or thorn that might have punctured the tire. He frowned up at Chandra. "You know, we use these tires because they're so hard to ruin. They rarely ever go flat, and when they do it's usually something obvious. Do you remember running over anything?"

"Nothing big enough to hurt one of these thick tires." Chandra leaned over to join in the search for the offending object.

"Well, I don't see a thing," Dale admitted finally.

Dale slipped the tire tool between the tire and the rim and expertly slipped the tire off. Unscrewing the cap, he pulled the tube out and slowly checked it over. Chandra peered at the flattened tube, unable to see anything wrong with it.

"Maybe a rock got in the tire." Dale pulled the tire apart and ran his fingers around the inside of the rubber. "No, I can't feel a thing." He sat back and stared at the tire, a puzzled look on his face. Dale shrugged and picked up the new tube Chandra had already laid out.

As Dale began to install the new tube, Chandra carefully inspected the flat, running it slowly through her hands. She couldn't find a single puncture or even a worn place. Slowly she examined the valve stem, knowing this could be a problem area. As she turned it around, something caught her eye, and she peered down into the stem.

"Look at this." Chandra held out the valve stem. "I think I found the culprit."

Dale reached for the flattened tube and looked down in the valve stem. "You're right," he said. "How do you suppose that got in there?" He pulled a pocketknife from his pouch and carefully dug the tiny pebble from the stem. "Did you take the valve cover off when we stopped for lunch?"

"I haven't taken it off at all. There hasn't been a need to."

"I can't imagine this rock getting in there all by itself." Dale held up the offending piece of rubble. "It's possible this was placed there on purpose." Dale looked at Chandra grimly. "I'll have to keep a better watch over the bikes. Now, let's get this tire pumped up, and we'll be back on the road."

Gritting her teeth, Chandra thought of how much she hated people who resorted to treachery. A picture of the young men who'd murdered her parents flashed through her mind. *Is this the way they started?* she wondered. *Did they begin with seemingly innocent pranks?*

The trip to Stonehenge passed without incident. When she arrived, Kurt, Gina, and Pierce were already strolling around the towering rocks. Visitors were not allowed to actually walk up to the rocks, but they could get a good view of them nonetheless. A rain-laden breeze brushed across Chandra's cheeks, sending a shiver down her spine. She didn't see Morgan or her bicycle.

"I see you got your flat fixed," Kurt called. "Come, look at these rocks. I'm trying to convince Pierce he should sneak in and pick one of them up."

Chandra laughed and warmed herself in Pierce's intense gaze. "I'd like a ringside seat for that. When we were growing up I used to think Pierce could do anything, but this might be stretching his abilities some."

They all laughed, and Kurt and Gina wandered off together. Chandra wished she could touch one of the rough pebbly rocks. "I wonder how they did move these rocks," she mused.

"I haven't any idea," Pierce answered, moving to stand beside her.

His nearness unsettled her, and Chandra thought about putting some distance between them. "Where's Morgan? I didn't see her bicycle with the rest."

"She didn't want to do the extra ride, so I sent her on to the inn."

Chandra leaned back and looked at Pierce. His closeness took her breath away. As he leaned toward her, Chandra's heart began to pound. For the first time, she wished she had never moved away from Newbury or from Pierce.

Chapter 4

A huge drop of rain splattered on the tip of Chandra's nose, dribbling down the side. Pierce could not help laughing at the shocked look on her face.

"Pierce, Chandra!" Kurt's voice echoed off the rocks. "I think we're about to get an impromptu shower. We're heading on to the inn. You coming?"

"Right behind you," Pierce called back. He gave Chandra a crooked grin. "Looks like we'll be needing those rain slickers after all."

Once they reached the inn, Pierce hurried through the front door. He hoped to get to his room with a minimum of dripping on the carpet.

"I'm sure you had a wonderful time without me."

Morgan's acid tone chilled Pierce's already cold body. The ride to the inn had been chilly, as the rain turned from a light smattering of cold drops to a deluge. The foursome had stayed together, riding slowly at the edge of the road. Pierce felt at times as if he needed a windshield wiper, even though he didn't have a windshield. Now, before he even had time to dry off, Morgan wanted a confrontation.

"You're right, I did have a wonderful time," he retorted. "I even enjoyed riding in the rain. For once on this trip, no one complained about anything, even though they had plenty of reason to complain." Pierce brushed past Morgan. She stood with her mouth hanging open, her beautiful face flushed, her eyes flashing angry darts in his direction.

Pierce climbed the stairs to his room, each step getting harder and heavier. He stopped and turned to look at Morgan, still watching him. What was happening here? All he'd ever wanted was to have Morgan's love. He had insisted she accompany him, yet now he resented her being here.

Despite the shivering in his limbs and the primal urge for a warm shower, Pierce retraced his steps until he stood face to face with Morgan. "I'm sorry," he said. "I'm half frozen and tired. I shouldn't have snapped at you like that."

Morgan's smile warmed the room. She raised her hand to touch his cheek then, as if thinking better of it, gestured toward the stairs. "Why don't you go get a shower and warm clothes? Then we'll snuggle up down here and make up."

A few minutes later, Pierce sighed as the warm water beat away the chill. *God, I'm so confused. I thought I knew exactly what was right for me when I invited Morgan on this trip. Now, I find I'm irritated with her most of the time. Is this Your way of showing me that Morgan isn't the wife You have for me? Please, help me see clearly. And why am I so attracted to Chandra? I can't get her out of my mind.*

The dark blue, baggy sweatshirt momentarily shut out the already dim light as Chandra pulled the shirt down over her head. She shook out the folds, letting it drop easily over her slim hips, ending half way to her knees. She traced the picture of two cats on the front of the shirt, right above the saying, "You're purrrrfectly wonderful." The shirt reminded her of her favorite things—Fluffy and Tinker, her cats, and Pierce's midnight-blue eyes.

She ran a brush through her still-damp hair, slipped on some shoes, grabbed her book, and headed downstairs. On the way up, she had noticed a crackling fire in the common room. Sitting in front of that warm fireplace looked like the perfect way to get completely warm and cozy.

The common room was larger than a living room in most houses but furnished much the same. Variegated blue carpet rippled across the floor, the colors emulating the swell of ocean waves. Blue and brown easy chairs held out inviting arms, beckoning all visitors to sit and relax. A high-backed, over-stuffed couch and love seat rested in the middle of the floor near the fireplace. Everything in the room whispered comfort and peace.

Chandra headed for the smaller love seat. She sank into its softness and curled her feet underneath her before she realized she wasn't alone in the room. Pierce stared at her from the couch while Morgan, seeing she had Chandra's attention, snuggled close to him, a look of triumph in her eyes.

"Excuse me." Chandra jumped up. "I didn't mean to interrupt."

"No, please stay." Pierce struggled to sit up straighter, obviously trying to move Morgan farther away. She wasn't cooperating. "We certainly don't have dibs on the room. Besides, I'm sure you'll enjoy the warmth of the fire. I know I do."

Morgan sat up slightly and then ran her hand up and down Pierce's arm, her eyes never leaving Chandra's. "Please do stay, Chandra. Perhaps we can reminisce a little."

Chandra hesitated. She knew who would come out looking good if they talked about old times. It would be the ever-popular Morgan, not Chandra, the little nobody. The sound of the rain drumming on the roof echoed in the tense silence. For a moment, Chandra pictured Morgan tossed out in the wet night while she snuggled on the couch with Pierce. A thrill of satisfaction raced through her.

God, forgive me. I know You want me to see Morgan as You do. She sank back down on the couch and tried to smile. "Of course, I'd love to talk about old times. Or perhaps we could just sit here and enjoy the fire." She held up her book. "I brought my own entertainment, so you needn't worry about me."

"How quaint." Morgan's mocking voice cut through the air. "You still have a thing for sticking your nose in a book."

Chandra bit back a sharp retort. What did Pierce see in this woman?

"I, for one, am glad you're still reading." Pierce grinned at her, warming her clear through. "I've even started reading more than I used to. It's a good way to relax."

Chandra smiled back, ignoring the daggers shooting from Morgan's eyes. Before a fight commenced, she opened her book and began to read, effectively ending the conversation. She didn't know how long she could keep up the pretense, but she didn't want to appear cowardly, running every time Morgan said something hateful. She had to stand her ground—without stooping to Morgan's level.

⥀⥀

The next morning dawned bright and beautiful. Everything had a fresh-washed look to it. The grass sparkled with dew. Flowers eagerly reached toward the warm sun. Even the air smelled crisp and clean, a wholesome earthy scent permeating everything.

Pierce stepped out of the inn and stretched. He could not wait to start the day's ride. They would be taking a side path part of the way, weaving through countryside rarely seen from a car. *Someday I'd like to have a bike tour business in Indiana,* he thought. *Maybe Chandra could give me some tips on arranging tours.*

He smiled thinking of Chandra and her interest in his business. Morgan rarely asked him about anything. She always talked about her little boutique that carried pricey, name-brand clothing and accessories. He frowned. Come to think of it, Morgan knew nothing about his likes and dislikes, even though they'd been dating for months. Chandra, whom he hadn't spent much time with in years, knew more about him than Morgan.

"Hey, Pierce, ready to go?" Kurt's words and hearty slap on the back startled Pierce back to reality.

"Yeah, I'm ready." Pierce tried to force a smile.

Kurt, ever the pastor, halted in midstep. "Looks to me like you lost your best friend. Something I can help you with?"

Pierce shrugged, not wanting to talk just yet. "Maybe later. Right now I need to sort some things out."

Kurt squeezed his shoulder. "Whenever you're ready, we'll talk. Okay?"

That evening, after a long day of listening to Morgan's complaints about the bike trip, the food, the company, and a myriad of other woes, Pierce needed to get out. He slipped through a side door of the inn, wandering down a well-worn path to a little stream. It would be a couple of hours before dinner. He hoped a little prayer would help.

He'd barely settled on a smooth rock when he heard cracking sounds coming from the brush. *Oh Lord, please don't let it be Morgan. I can't take any more of her complaints right now.*

"Pierce?"

Kurt's deep voice sent a feeling of relief sweeping through Pierce. "Over here, Kurt."

Kurt sank down next to the rock, sitting cross-legged on the grass. The stream gurgled a soothing melody. For a few minutes they contemplated it in quiet.

"I need to talk, Kurt, but I don't know exactly how to begin."

Kurt picked a blade of grass and ran it through his fingers. "Why don't you just start. If it doesn't come out right, we'll work on sorting through it together."

Pierce sighed. "When I came on this trip I knew exactly what I wanted. I had it all planned out, and I thought it was right. Now, I'm not so sure."

"You said you knew what you wanted. What about what God wanted?"

An arrow of pain arced through Pierce. "I guess that's the problem. I always thought I knew what God wanted, so I forgot to ask Him about it." He bent to pick up a stick, rubbing the bark from it. "Ever since I can remember, Chandra has been my best friend and Morgan has been the one I wanted to marry. I've always seen Morgan as beautiful and sweet. I know they say love is blind, but I'm beginning to wonder how I could have been so blind. She hasn't been so sweet on this trip."

"What about Chandra? Is she still your best friend?"

"That's the thing. Suddenly, I find I don't want Chandra just as a best friend. I want more from her or, maybe, I should say, with her. But when I think like that, I feel as if I'm betraying Morgan. I planned to ask her to be my wife."

Kurt looked up at Pierce, his brown eyes probing. "A wise mother once told her son that finding a virtuous woman isn't easy, but when you do, she's worth more than rubies."

Pierce grinned. "That sounds like some sort of scripture, Pastor."

Kurt laughed. "You're right. I can't seem to get away from it. You might try reading what Lemuel's mother tells him about a wife in Proverbs thirty-one. Maybe you can use that to discern what woman God has for you. Meanwhile, I'll be praying about your decision. It's easy to fall into the rut of assuming we know what God wants and forgetting to consult Him on the matter."

"I've heard you tell the teenagers over and over how God will stir things up if we're not listening. Well, I do believe there's some stirring going on here, and it sure is uncomfortable for me."

Kurt stood and stretched. "That's all right. We all need stirring up now and then. If everything was easy and went our way all the time, we would have a tendency to forget our need for God."

"Thanks, Kurt. I appreciate the talk."

Patting Pierce's shoulder, Kurt replied, "Anytime, you need me, I'm there."

Pierce watched Kurt walk back up the path to the inn then bowed his head. *God, please show me Your will here. I'm not so sure about Morgan anymore. In fact, I'm beginning to wonder why I ever liked her in the first place. Help me make the right choice.*

Pierce walked slowly, his footsteps silent on the hard dirt track. Twilight deepened and stars were peeking through the leaves overhead. He rounded the corner of the inn and stopped. Someone was by the bicycles. The slight figure wasn't Dale. In the dim light he leaned forward, straining to see what was going on. The inky shadow bent over, and a slight clink carried on the still night air.

Before Pierce could call out, the ethereal shape straightened and darted off into the darkness.

Chapter 5

The next morning, Pierce stepped outside early. Plants still dripped tears of water from the night's rain.

"Dale, I looked all over for you last night." Pierce's voice sounded loud in the quiet of the dawn.

"Don't tell me you wanted a moonlit ride." Dale grinned. "This is the one stop where I don't stay with the team. I have family living here, and I spend the night with them. What did you need?"

"I took a walk last night, and when I came back, I saw someone messing with the bikes." Pierce gestured toward the row of bicycles at the side of the inn.

Dale frowned. "Who was it? What did they do?"

Pierce followed him across the drive. "It was too dark, and I couldn't see much. I did hear a metallic sort of clink, but I couldn't figure out what would cause it." He hesitated. "I have an idea that it might pay to check Chandra's bike."

Dale stopped and gave him a sharp questioning look. "Why is that?"

"I. . .uh," Pierce stammered, "I don't know if I can explain it."

Leaning over Chandra's bike, Dale squeezed the tires and ran his hands over the gearshifts. "Any idea what part of the bike they touched?"

"I remember the person leaning over the front of it and then straightening."

Picking up the bicycle, Dale moved it away from the others then flipped it upside down to rest on the seat and handlebars. Pierce moved up beside him, and they both studied the gears and chain.

"I don't see anything wrong here." Dale set the bike back on its tires.

"Let me see if I can remember exactly where and how the person was leaning on the bicycle." Pierce moved to the bike as if he were going to mount it and bent forward. Looking down, he frowned as something caught his eye. "Look at this. There's a scratch mark on this bolt. Was this here before?"

Dale ran his finger over the gouge in the metal. "No. I go over these machines every day." He pulled a wrench from a pouch at his waist. "Someone loosened the handlebars just enough to cause an accident."

Pierce gritted his teeth in anger. "The bike would have worked fine until a downhill or rough stretch of road, then the wheels would go one way and the steering another. Chandra would have had no control."

"That's right," Dale agreed. "If you know who did this, I want you to tell me. I don't like anyone sabotaging my equipment."

"Like I said, I didn't get a good look. They ran off before I could even get close."

After breakfast Dale stood and faced the tour group, his face grim. He held up the wrench, twirling it between his fingers. "I want you to know that someone tried to impair one of the bicycles last night. I don't know who did it, but I wanted to tell you that I check those bikes daily. If I find out who did this and it was one of you, that person will be asked to leave this tour immediately. Understand?"

Pierce watched Morgan's face as Dale made his announcement. Her eyes narrowed and a faint flush crept into her cheeks. Had she been the one? Did she hate Chandra so much that she would try to hurt her by wrecking her bike?

❧

Chandra stopped at the side of the road and straddled her bike, looking at the idyllic scene before her, glad that she always rode ahead of the others for the quiet. A hill rose gently, terraced by stone walls and dotted with sheep contentedly munching on the emerald grass. A small stream wended its way along the bottom of the hill, and she could hear the soothing melody of the water tripping over the rocks.

"That's a beautiful sight."

Pierce's voice startled her out of her reverie. She looked into his laughing blue eyes and wondered briefly if he were referring to her or the vista before them.

"I didn't hear you," she blurted out. Looking back at the lambs frolicking through the grass, she took a deep breath, trying to calm her nerves. Every time Pierce came near, she felt like a silly schoolgirl with a crush.

"I can't believe we're finally here." Pierce spoke in a hushed voice. "I remember how often we used to talk about and plan the trips we would take. I didn't dream we would really be able to do it."

Chandra chuckled. "Do you recall some of the stupid things we decided on?"

Pierce managed to look wounded despite the grin on his face. "Now, what would we have done that was stupid?"

"I seem to remember wanting a basket on the front of my bike so I could carry my cats in it. And you wanted to bring your parakeet and have it ride on your shoulder."

"Well, pirates always walk around with parrots on their shoulders. I don't know why cyclists can't have parakeets."

"Did you ever try it?" Chandra asked.

Pierce lifted his foot onto his pedal. "I think it's time to get going."

"Not so fast, buster." Chandra grabbed his handlebars. "I think you're avoiding my question. Come on, fess up. Did you try to ride a bike with your parakeet?"

"Do you know how fast a parakeet can fly when it's outside?" Pierce's laugh echoed off the hills. "I never did see the poor thing again. And I thought we were best of friends sharing an experience."

Chandra doubled over with laughter. "I can't believe you really tried it."

"Okay, Miss Smartie, how about you? Did you ever take your cat for a ride?"

"I think you're right. We should be going." Chandra pushed on her pedal, but Pierce was faster. He grabbed her bike before she could even get started.

"Oh no you don't. This is true confession time. Let's hear it."

Chandra felt the heat rising to her cheeks. She grabbed her braid that had fallen over her shoulder and twisted the end. "I suppose I could tell you that my cats don't appreciate moving faster than their four legs will carry them. Now, they walk a wide circle around my bikes."

Pierce leaned closer, his fingers running softly down her cheek. "Why did you leave, Chandra?" he asked softly. "I've missed you so much."

She opened her mouth, searching for the words to say, but his nearness stole her breath. She closed her eyes, trying to think of one reason why she had moved away. Nothing came to mind.

"I wish you would move back, Chandra. I have some plans I'd like to tell you about and see what you think. Maybe you could help me." Before Pierce could say any more, the staccato click of a bicycle changing gears alerted them that the others had caught up.

"You took so long to catch up, I was beginning to think we'd have to send a search party for you." Pierce grinned as Kurt and Gina rode up beside them.

Morgan, red-faced, forced her bike the rest of the way up the hill and stopped at the rise next to Pierce. Chandra bit her lip. Did Pierce really want her to move back because he liked her? Wouldn't he always be attracted to Morgan? Even with a flaming face, sweat dripping down her cheeks, and a helmet squashing her bouncy hair, she looked devastatingly beautiful.

"What a gorgeous view," Kurt exclaimed. "No wonder the two of you stopped here."

For a few minutes, Chandra saw the vista afresh. The brilliant blue sky, white clouds scudding past, the sun bathing the hills with warmth, and the sheep, now resting in the grass in a contented group, tugged at her heart.

"This reminds me of your parents' farm, Chandra," Morgan spoke up. "Every time we drove by there were sheep in the fields. I wonder what ever happened to all those sheep."

Although the scene hadn't changed, Chandra felt as if the sun had dropped from the sky, leaving her chilled inside and out. Pain flared fresh inside, and she wanted to cry out. One glance at Morgan's face told her that the hurt was intentional. Her gloating look was unmistakable. A heavy silence descended over the group.

"My sister and her family live at the farm now." Chandra's throat closed painfully as she choked out the words. "I think they sold the sheep."

Anger welled up inside at the unfairness of it all. Her parents should still be alive and would be if God had taken care of them. Why hadn't He protected them and watched over them? Weren't they His sheep and He the Shepherd? A shepherd should watch over his sheep and keep them from being harmed by wild animals, and that was just what those two kids were—wild animals.

"Chandra?" Pierce's soft voice captured her attention. "Are you all right?"

She nodded, fighting back tears of anger and frustration. She looked at him, begging him silently to leave her alone.

Pierce knew her so well. He turned to the others and motioned down the hill. "I, for one, would like to cool my feet in the little brook down there. Anyone care to join me?"

"You're on," Kurt agreed.

Chandra closed her eyes and listened to the click and whir of the bikes racing down the path. She needed a moment alone to pull herself together.

"I know what you're trying to do," Morgan hissed close to her ear, making Chandra jump. "You're trying to get Pierce not to like me anymore. Well, it won't work, and I'm telling you right now to stay away from him. Do you understand?"

Anger and revulsion fought a battle within. Chandra tried to hold her temper, but it didn't work. "I'm not the one turning Pierce away from you, Morgan. It's you and your whiny, attention-demanding ways. Why don't you start thinking of someone else for a change?"

"I think of Pierce all the time," Morgan spat out.

"You only think of how you can trap him. He's a conquest to you, just like all the other boys were at school. Having one worship at your feet wasn't enough. You had to get them all to bask in adoration of you."

"You're just jealous because I'm prettier and more popular than you." Morgan's eyes flashed fire.

Chandra shook her head, realizing how foolish it was to argue about this. "Morgan, don't you think I've seen the little notes you've left in our room? Mrs. Pierce Stillwell. Morgan Stillwell. They're all over. That's something girls did back in high school. I don't care about being popular. I'm content with who I am and with the job I do. Maybe you should try to be the same."

Pushing against the ground, Chandra shoved off, heading down the hill. She heard a low growl from Morgan and glanced back. Morgan, her whitened fingers gripping the handlebars and her teeth clenched like a growling dog, bore down on Chandra's bike.

Swinging back around, she could see the others at the bottom of the hill, removing their shoes and dipping their toes in the stream. Pierce and Kurt were laughing. Even Dale seemed more relaxed than he had been all day. She tried to ignore Morgan's furious pedaling beside her.

"You think I'm a baby. I'll have you know I could have any man I wanted, including most of the so-called happily married ones. I won't have you taking the man I've decided to marry." Morgan's voice carried more than a hint of a threat.

A sharp jolt caught Chandra off guard. Before she could react, her bicycle jerked to the side. She slipped off the path and on to the rocky hillside. Her bike bounded crazily across the grass. Chandra fought to bring it under control. She squeezed the brakes tight, trying to stop. A huge rock, hidden in a patch of long grass, loomed before her. The front tire hit it, and Chandra flew into the air, bike and all.

She thudded to the ground and rolled toward the brook at the bottom. For an instant she caught the look of horror on his face as Pierce ran toward her. A sharp pain radiated through her body as she came to a stop near the edge of the stream. Something sharp jabbed at her cheek. She turned her head to see a sharp rock. Broken pieces of her helmet littered the ground around it.

"Chandra, are you hurt?"

Chandra looked up. Morgan knelt over her in pretend concern. Only Chandra could see the victorious smile spreading across her face.

Chapter 6

Chandra." Pierce knelt on the other side of her, holding her hand in his. "Don't try to move until we check you over. Thank God your helmet protected your head."

Morgan backed away as Dale knelt on the other side of her. "I want you to move a little at a time as we tell you to," Dale spoke softly.

Chandra tried to smile. Her leg ached. Her whole body felt bruised. "I think I'll be fine. Let me sit up."

Dale started to object, but Pierce held up a hand. "It's okay. She's been biking for years, and I know she's had some nasty spills. She'll tell us if it's serious."

The warmth from Pierce's hand holding hers gave Chandra incentive to move. With a moan she sat up. Her left leg stung, and she leaned forward to get a closer look. A rock had gouged a cut down the side. Bright red blood stained the green grass. "What happened?" she asked softly. "Did I hit a rock?"

"You hit your head on one." Pierce bent over her leg, his fingers probing gently. "Do you have a first aid kit, Dale?"

Dale nodded and ran to the bikes.

"Pierce, I think he can handle this," Morgan called in a soft voice. "Why don't we go on? I don't want to get in too late."

Pierce gazed at Morgan for a long moment. A hush fell over the group. "I'm staying here with Chandra, Morgan. Why don't you go on without me?"

Morgan's blue eyes welled with tears. She bit her lip as if trying to hold back a sob. "If that's the way you want to be, then it's okay. Stay with her. Maybe you should have invited Chandra to come with you rather than me."

No one spoke as they watched Morgan climb on her bike and head down the road. Finally, Kurt broke the silence. "Do you want me to ride ahead and have someone come with a car?"

"No, please," Chandra said. "I've been in plenty of accidents. I'll be fine. As long as the bike works, I'd rather ride and loosen up the sore muscles."

Dale smiled as he finished taping a bandage on her leg. "I'll check the bicycle for damage. The good news is that we'll be staying two days in this town. There are some great antique shops to browse through. Also, you'll have a room of your own tonight."

"That will be a treat," Chandra admitted.

When Kurt and Gina followed Dale to see about the bike, Chandra suddenly realized she was holding Pierce's hand again. Or was he holding hers? She couldn't really tell, but it felt wonderful. She looked up into his dark blue eyes and serious face.

"What did happen?" he asked. "How did you wreck on such an easy hill?"

Chandra looked down and rubbed her finger lightly over the bandage on her leg, trying to decide what to say. "I'm not sure," she replied. "I felt a jolt, and the next thing I knew, I was flying down the wrong side of the hill."

As he wrapped his arm around her and pulled her close, she could hear the deep breath he let out. "Just be careful," he cautioned. "I can't stand the thought of you really being hurt."

Chandra relaxed, listening to the steady thump of his heartbeat. Her aching muscles, the pain in her leg, and the world around faded away. It would be utter delight to stay here in Pierce's arms forever.

Before evening, Chandra already regretted her eagerness to have a room to herself. Even though sharing a small room with Morgan proved difficult, it was better than being left alone with her thoughts. For the whole trip she had managed to keep herself busy or around other people so that the upcoming anniversary of her parents' deaths wouldn't bother her so much. Now she found she couldn't erase the hurt and anger from her mind.

She closed her eyes, surrendering to the awful memory and accompanying sense of panic when her sister, Clarissa, called to tell her of her parents' murder. She recalled with absolute clarity exactly where she'd been at that moment. Snuggled in bed, the red clock numerals blinking 5:30 in the morning, Fluffy still curled in a warm ball at her feet, and Tinker rubbing against her arm, purring his reminder that it was nearly breakfast time. She could still feel the coldness of the phone pressed against her ear and the unreality of the message being relayed.

Shock. She knew it must be shock. She hadn't cried. There must be a mistake. Her parents were going to live long lives serving God. They loved Him. He protected them. It was that simple. There must be a mistake.

It wasn't until she looked at the empty shells of her mother and father lying cold and still in their caskets that the truth finally sank in. They were dead. God had failed. He had allowed a stupid crime to happen to those who loved Him most.

A sob wrenched its way from deep inside. Chandra turned her face to her pillow, drowning the sound. *Why, God? Why did You do this? I needed them. I need them now.*

Only as her sobs quieted did she hear the small voice whisper, *"You need Me, My child. Only Me."* Oh, how she wanted to believe that. She longed to surrender all her hurt to God, but the thought of the two young men pushed to the front. All she could see was them being allowed to virtually go free because of their youth. Yes, they'd gotten a prison sentence, but it was such a short one, it was like nothing at all. How could the jury have been so gullible?

The soft whisper of God's voice fell farther away as bitterness pushed its ugly face into view. Soon the voice was only a faint memory. Self-righteous anger once again filled her.

⁂

Pierce strolled through the countryside. He loved England. It seemed so quiet and peaceful compared to the hectic lifestyle in the States. He felt like he had journeyed back in time when he came here. The old houses with stone walls and thatch roofs reminded him of tales in storybooks. The people were quaint, the children ran barefoot in their yards. Life was definitely slower here.

He lengthened his stride, enjoying the feel of stretching his muscles. From his second-story window at the bed and breakfast where they were staying for two days, he had noticed a stream that meandered through this pasture. Hoping the owner didn't mind, he crossed the stone wall surrounding the field and looked for a place to relax next to the water.

He sank onto the grassy bank, the cool of the ground seeping into his legs. Leaning back on his elbows, he watched the puffy clouds float across the sky. Smiling, he remembered when he and Chandra used to see who could find the best shapes in the clouds. It was never a contest. She always won. She had the best imagination and could pick out outlines he never would have thought of looking for. Now, as he gazed heavenward, he only saw a sweet smiling face with hazel eyes staring back at him.

Pierce shook his head and sat back up. He picked up the King James Bible he had brought with him and turned to the book of Proverbs. *Okay, God, I really need some help here. I need You to show me Your will. I don't want to just follow what I think You want. When I do that, I seem to just do my will, not Yours. Please, show me what You have in store for me in a wife.*

Bending over so his body would shade the words, Pierce began to read: "The words of king Lemuel, the prophecy that his mother taught him."

Pierce smiled. *I remember my mother teaching me wise things, too. Of course, at the time I didn't think they were so wise. Now, though, I can recall her telling me what to look for in a wife. Why didn't I think of that?*

He noticed a title heading at verse ten, "The Capable Wife." Skipping several verses, he began to read once more. "Who can find a virtuous woman? For her price is far above rubies. The heart of her husband doth safely trust in her, so that he shall have no need of spoil. She will do him good and not evil all the days of her life."

Pierce looked up again and chewed his lip. "She will do him good," he whispered to himself. "What good has Morgan ever done for me? She doesn't even know what I like or what interests me. All we ever talk about is what she likes and wants. All we ever do is what she suggests we do. This trip is the first time she's ever done something I wanted. I think the only reason she came is because she expects me to ask her to marry her.

"I don't think I could ever trust in her. When we're at home, I find I'm constantly watching other men, jealous if they so much as look at her." Frowning, Pierce realized that was because Morgan usually took advantage of those looks. She enjoyed attention from other men. In fact, she thrived on it. He didn't know if he could ever be content with that type of threat to his marriage.

Reading on through the wise words of Lemuel's mother, he marveled at the work that this wife did. She cared about every aspect of her family's life. "She openeth her mouth with wisdom; and in her tongue is the law of kindness."

He shook his head. Morgan certainly didn't fit very many of the verses here. Her words could be honeyed and sweet when she wanted them to be, but now that he thought about it, she didn't speak with a lot of wisdom or kindness.

"Favour is deceitful, and beauty is vain: but a woman that feareth the Lord, she shall be praised."

The words jumped off the page and grabbed him. Hadn't his mother said that more than once? She had told him over and over that beauty was only skin deep and you have to look farther than that.

God, is this what You're trying to show me? Is Morgan only something beautiful and vain? For long moments he thought about the years he chased after Morgan, hoping that someday she would be his. Now, he saw the truth. That had been a fruitless chase after a vain and empty woman.

Who can find a virtuous woman? God, forgive me for not seeking Your will earlier. Help me to set things right. I can see Chandra in these verses, Lord. I believe I've always loved her but was too blind to see it. Help her return my love. Give me the right words to say to Morgan, too, Lord. I don't want to hurt her.

Evening shadows stretched across the field before Pierce was finished praying. He knew dinner would be ready soon and hurried as quickly as he could without stumbling in the growing darkness. Anticipation of seeing Chandra made his heart pound. He could still feel her snuggled up against him. It felt so right to hold her. He wanted to be there for her every time she needed him. Maybe tonight he would get the chance to talk about it with her.

The smell of roasting meat and potatoes wafted through the air when Pierce swung the front door open. He breathed deeply, his stomach rumbling a protest at being empty. He bounded up the stairs to put away his Bible and change for the meal. Chandra, because of her hurt leg, had a room on the ground floor. He couldn't wait to see how she was and walk with her to the dining room.

A few minutes later, he stood outside her door. He ran a hand over his damp hair, smiling at the giddy feeling that made him so antsy. He had checked in the dining room, and Chandra hadn't been seated around the table with the others. He knocked, trying to calm his pounding heart.

"Yes?" The muffled reply barely sounded through the solid door.

"Chandra? I came to see if you're ready for dinner." He slid the door open slightly so he could be sure she heard him.

"Go away."

"Are you okay?" Pierce leaned farther into the room and could see her huddled in bed.

Chandra turned to him, and even in the dim light he could see the redness around her eyes. "Just go away and leave me alone. I'm not hungry and I don't want to see anyone."

Chapter 7

Taking the steps slowly, Pierce rubbed his sleep-laden eyes as he came downstairs the next morning. Rest had been an elusive companion after the brush-off Chandra had given him. He stayed awake most of the night wondering if it was something he had done that caused her to cry so much. He thought she'd enjoyed it when he held her after she was hurt. She seemed content to lean against him. Had he said something then or later that caused such a negative reaction?

Then, last night, as he turned away from Chandra's room, he saw Morgan with her inviting smile. For once, he hadn't wanted to spend any time with her. He wanted to tell her it was over between them, but he had been so upset because of Chandra that he couldn't even think straight. He spent much of dinner and the evening trying to act normal when his heart was breaking in two.

Only Kurt seemed to sense something was amiss. He and Gina stayed with Pierce and Morgan, talking and laughing as if trying to make up for Pierce's quiet. Pierce knew Kurt wanted to talk. It hadn't been easy to avoid him all evening. What happened was between him and Chandra, though. Perhaps later he could talk to Kurt about it.

Sunlight streamed through the windows next to the front door, highlighting the gleam of the polished oak floor. Pierce paused to look out at the tree-lined avenue passing by the bed and breakfast. Situated on a hill at the edge of town, it would only be a short walk to the streets that were lined with antique shops. Dale had pointed them out yesterday.

Heavy hearted, Pierce stepped toward the dining room. He had looked forward to spending the day combing those shops with Chandra. Now, he didn't know if she even wanted to see him again. And he still hadn't been able to say anything to Morgan. She would be expecting him to go with her. Well, first things first. He would have breakfast and then talk to Morgan.

The spicy smell of sausages drew him toward the table. Chandra was seated across from Kurt and Gina, laughing at something Kurt must have said. Morgan wasn't anywhere around.

"Good morning." Pierce slipped into the chair next to Chandra's. He could see a slight puffiness around her eyes, but other than that there were no traces of last night's tears. "Did I miss something?"

Chandra grinned. "Kurt was just telling me about some of your mountain biking experiences."

Pierce groaned and pretended to glare. "I thought pastors could be trusted to keep things in confidence."

"I believe that's only when they are things told in confidence." Kurt chuckled and Gina laughed. "Besides, half the congregation was there—or at least the half that rides bikes with us."

"So what deep, dark secret did he tell you?" Pierce tried to put on a wounded martyr look. Chandra's entrancing smile nearly undid him.

"Oh, I just heard about the time you decided to try a new trail. When you went over the hill, you landed in a big mud bog that was being prepared for a dirt bike race." She leaned closer, and he could see the green and yellow flecks in her hazel eyes. In a loud whisper she continued, "I have it in strictest confidence that even your very blue eyes turned brown."

Laughter rumbled up as Pierce remembered the very humbling incident. "I do believe God brought me down a peg or two that time. I know I needed it. I had mud everywhere—in my hair, my ears, up my nose. I was a mess."

"Pierce."

Morgan's hoarse call interrupted the fun. They all looked at where she leaned on the door of the dining room, her hand pressed to her forehead in a dramatic pose. Her legs wobbled, and Pierce and Kurt both jumped up to help her.

"What is it?" Pierce asked. He and Kurt helped her to a chair.

"I'm not feeling so well this morning. I think that maybe it's something they fed us yesterday. I should complain to the management."

"None of us is sick," Kurt said, "and we ate the same food. Do you need to see a doctor?"

"No, I think I'll just stay here today. Maybe by tonight I'll feel better."

Pierce brushed her forehead with his hand. She didn't feel exceptionally warm. He didn't think she had a fever. "I hate to see you miss out on the shopping. I thought you might be able to find something to take back for a souvenir."

Morgan put her hand on his arm and gave a pleading, puppy-dog gaze. "Please stay with me today, Pierce. I don't want to be by myself in a strange place."

Pierce forced a smile. How could he possibly give Morgan the news that it was over between them when she was sick? "Let me help you back to your room."

"No." Morgan pushed him away. "I'll let Gina help me. You go ahead and have breakfast. After I rest a little longer I'll come down and we can spend time together here."

Watching Morgan lean on Gina as they left the room, Pierce felt some of the carefree joy leave as well. *God, nothing is working out. What do I do now?* As if the Lord spoke directly to his heart, Pierce knew he had made his decision last night and he would stand by it. He had seen enough of Morgan's manipulations to recognize her "illness" for what it was. He would send Gina back up to tell her he was going shopping, and then he and Chandra would have some time together. Maybe he could even find out what had been bothering Chandra last night.

Chandra watched Kurt and Gina stroll arm in arm down the narrow roadway toward a bakery. She could still hear Kurt's words. "With all this biking, I'm wasting away. I'm sure I need a sweet pastry to get me through the shopping." Gina had laughed and asked what his excuse was all the other times he wanted something sweet in the morning. Chandra didn't know how he could even think of food after the huge breakfast they'd been served earlier.

"So, I'm ready to look in some of these shops. How about you?" Pierce's dark blue gaze captured and held hers. "You sure your leg is up to this?"

"Positive. But before we start, I have something to say." She took a deep breath. "I'm sorry about last night. I didn't mean to be churlish. I just miss my parents." She looked away, fighting against the lump in her throat.

"Hey." Pierce tilted her chin up with his fingers and planted a soft kiss on her forehead. "Enough said. It's forgotten."

She smiled, relieved to have the apology over. "Well then, where shall we start?" She hoped her wobbly voice went unnoticed. She didn't want Pierce to know how his nearness set her heart racing.

Placing his hand under her elbow, Pierce propelled her forward. "I think the best way to do this is to start with the closest shop and work our way through the whole bunch."

Chandra gasped in mock astonishment. "You mean you brought that much money with you? How will you carry everything on one little bicycle?"

"It's easy, my dear." Pierce wiggled his eyebrows at her. "Did you ever see Mary Poppins? All I have to do is buy a bag like hers and stuff everything in it."

For the next three hours, Pierce and Chandra wandered through the shops, exclaiming over their various finds. Everything was charming in an Old World way. Chandra spent a long time looking at the assortment of beautiful dishes. Clarissa collected antique dishes, and she wanted to get something special for her. Finally, she settled on a white cream pitcher, exquisitely decorated with blue flowers and trimmed in gold. The graceful handle and tilt of the pitcher spout reminded her of a pitcher her mother had given to Clarissa for a wedding present.

Pierce spent much of his time browsing through old books and tools. Chandra stepped into another room, waiting for him to finish. The musty smell of old dust made her sneeze. The walls were covered with artwork of various sorts. A ship tossed on restless waves. The wind whipping through its sails caught her eye. She shuddered. Sailing had never appealed to her, and she didn't want to imagine how frightened she would be in a storm like that.

Moving on, she stopped to look at pictures of the English countryside. Leaning forward, she gasped. One of the smaller pictures looked exactly like the scene she had stopped to look at yesterday. There were the rock walls terracing the hillside, the grazing sheep, and the small brook. She could almost hear the bubbly melody it had played. Even the clouds looked the same.

"That looks familiar." Pierce's low voice next to her ear startled her.

"I can't believe it, but it looks like the same place." She glanced up at him and found herself unable to drag her gaze away.

"It looks the same to me."

He spoke so softly she had to lean closer to hear the words. Pierce tucked a strand of hair behind her ear then trailed a finger across her cheek. A tingle of excitement coursed through her.

"Why don't you buy the picture?" he asked. "You could have a memento of the trip that will remind you of a place you actually saw."

"It could remind me of why I have the scar on my leg." She grinned. Tearing her gaze from his, she looked back at the idyllic scene. "I don't know why I like this picture so much. I love the walls and the sheep. It's something about them, but I don't understand what it is." She shrugged. "I think I'll look around some more."

They wandered out of the shop. Pierce slipped his hand around hers. "Look. There's Kurt and Gina. Shall we see if they're ready for some lunch? Shopping always makes me hungry."

Chandra smiled and nodded, not trusting her voice. She wondered if Pierce felt any of the electricity that raced up her arm from the contact with his hand. This day was so perfect. Nagging thoughts of her agony last night tried to intrude, but she pushed them away. She didn't want anything to spoil this closeness with Pierce.

By late afternoon they had visited nearly every little shop in town. Chandra's leg ached as they headed back to the inn. She tried to keep from limping, but Pierce must have noticed.

"Are you okay?" The concern in his eyes warmed her.

"I think my leg's had enough walking for one day," she admitted. "Maybe we could sit somewhere and rest before we climb the hill to the bed and breakfast."

"That's what I like about England." Pierce grinned and gestured to the side of the road. "There's always a wall to sit on when you need it. Imagine back home. You'd have to sit on a barbed-wire fence."

"Ouch!" Chandra grimaced. "I think I'd rather put up with an aching leg."

Pierce sat close to her, his arm brushing against hers. As if reading her thoughts and knowing how she longed to rest her head against his shoulder, he put his arm around her and pulled her close.

"Do you know how much I've missed having you around?"

She could only shake her head in answer. His hand cupped her chin and pulled her close. He ran his thumb gently over her lip, and she thrilled to his touch. Slowly he bent his head and lightly brushed her lips with his.

"I can see you're worried to death about me being sick."

At the sound of Morgan's voice they both jumped. Chandra started to pull away, but Pierce pulled her closer, his arm tightening protectively around her shoulders.

"I'm glad to see you're feeling better Morgan." Pierce didn't look too happy. He let his arm drop. "If you'll excuse us, Chandra, Morgan and I need to talk."

He stepped toward the beautiful blond, and Chandra shivered as his warmth left her. Morgan shot her a look of victory as Pierce took her arm and turned her toward town. Chandra watched them walk away, the lump in her throat nearly shutting off her air. How could he do this? One minute he was kissing her and the next he was walking off with Morgan.

Chapter 8

You're dumping me for that skinny little nobody?" Morgan's voice carried such a threat that Pierce actually stepped back a pace.

"I'm not dumping you for anyone," Pierce tried to explain. "I can see it won't work out for us. You aren't interested in the things that interest me. We don't have anything in common."

Morgan flipped her blond hair over her shoulder and pointed a purple-nailed finger at him. "What do you mean I'm not interested in things you're interested in? How many boring church services did I sit through for you? All the time I would smile and act like I loved it, yet I only did it for you."

Pierce felt as if someone had knocked the air from him. He floundered for an answer. "Do you mean you don't believe in Jesus?" he choked out.

Looking annoyed, Morgan answered tartly, "Of course I believe in Jesus. Even when we weren't dating, I went to church at Christmas. I always enjoy watching the manger scene reenacted."

"But, Morgan, it's more than just believing in a baby in a manger. What about Jesus dying on the cross? What about His resurrection? You have to repent of your sins and ask Jesus into your heart as Savior. Have you ever done that?"

"I don't need to be fanatical about religion like you," she retorted.

Morgan's words wrenched at his insides. Pierce watched helplessly as she stalked off toward the inn.

By midmorning the next day, Pierce thought he might freeze to death despite the warm sunshine blazing through a partially clouded sky. After last night, both Morgan, who rode behind him, and Chandra, who rode ahead of him, were giving him decidedly chilling glances.

I guess I shouldn't have gone off with Morgan like that without an explanation to Chandra, he thought for the millionth time. *I only wanted to set things right. I wanted Morgan to know our relationship is off. I can't continue with her after finally seeing that she is self-centered and not even interested in following God.*

Recalling the confrontation with Morgan, Pierce nearly groaned aloud. She hadn't taken rejection well. Morgan apparently was used to attracting any man she wanted and then casting him off when she finished with him, not the other way around. As if his eyes were opened suddenly after years of blindness, he could see how she had left a string of broken hearts and affected lives behind her.

Even now, he felt utterly incapable of reaching her. *God, I don't know what to do to help Morgan understand her need for You. Please work on her heart and give me the opportunity to talk to her. If not me, then send someone who can speak to her, Lord. I believe under all her sophisticated veneer, she's lonely and lost. She needs to know You.*

As for Chandra, Lord, I don't know what I've done to alienate her. She was so wonderful yesterday. I'm sure she feels something for me, too. I know I should have explained why I was leaving with Morgan, but all I could think of was getting it over with. Help Chandra forgive me. I know I've offended her.

Yesterday evening, after his talk with Morgan, Pierce couldn't wait to see Chandra and talk to her about his feelings for her. When he returned to the inn, he found that she'd gone to her room and didn't want to be disturbed. She didn't come for the evening meal, and this morning she had already eaten before he got down to breakfast. She barely returned his greeting before hopping on her bicycle and heading off for the day's ride. Now he rode a few yards—what felt to be several miles—behind her, hoping she would give him a sign of some sort to let him know she wanted to talk.

Chandra steadied her bike with one hand and reached up to rub her eyes with the other. If someone had thrown a handful of sand in her eyes, they couldn't have felt worse. Dry and gritty, they burned from lack of sleep and too much crying. Last night, every time she closed her eyes, a picture of Morgan walking off with Pierce drifted across her eyelids. Of course, that was better than the few times she managed to get some sleep. Then the dreams of Morgan in Pierce's arms, wearing a gorgeous wedding dress, made her wake in a cold sweat.

This morning she had been unable to face Pierce. Why had he kissed her and then walked off with Morgan? Did he think he could just toy with her affections? Had he meant it as a brotherly kiss? It sure hadn't felt like one. Even now, she could remember the feel of his fingers tracing a path down her cheek.

To make matters worse, this was the anniversary of her parents' murders. Oh, how she longed to have Pierce hold her and comfort her. Instead, she found herself pulling away, estranged by his feelings for Morgan and her own hesitancy to trust anyone.

By late afternoon when they stopped for the day, Chandra was ready to quit. Her leg ached a little, although the cut was healing nicely. Thanks to being in good shape, her bruises were fast disappearing. She hadn't spoken more than two words to anyone all day, and all she wanted was time alone. With that in mind, she headed down a narrow path that meandered through a small grove of trees.

Birds twittered overhead. The rich, moist smell of freshly watered woods filled the air. Chandra bent down to push her finger into a piece of moss at the base of a tree. She smiled as water welled up around her finger. She had loved doing that as a child, admiring the moss's ability to store water. It had been years since she had seen such succulent plants growing wild.

The path turned and ran alongside a low rock wall. Chandra climbed up and sat cross-legged on the top, gazing at the valley stretched out before her. She didn't think she would ever tire of the green hills.

A small scuffing noise on the path behind her set her heart thumping. She swivelled around and saw Pierce, his hands stuffed in his pockets. His blue eyes studied her with a pleading little-boy look. She couldn't help but smile.

"I hope I'm not disturbing you," he said.

She shrugged, not sure what to say. She didn't really want company, but she just couldn't turn him away.

"Are you sure you won't offend Morgan?" She hadn't meant to sound so catty.

"I need to talk to you, Chandra." He climbed up on the wall and settled down beside her. "I've tried to talk to you all day, but you wouldn't let me. I know this is the anniversary of your parents' death. Is that what's bothering you?"

Tears welled up in her eyes. She thought after the last few days she wouldn't have a single drop left to shed, but they still rose to the surface all too readily. "I'm sorry I haven't been good company. You could have talked to Morgan." *Oh God, I sound like some bitter old shrew. Please help me.*

"That's who I wanted to talk to you about."

"No, I can't talk about you and Morgan right now." Chandra looked away so he wouldn't see the pain she knew was showing in her eyes.

"Would it help to talk about your dad and mom?" he offered. She could hear his desire to help.

"I don't know." Her voice caught. She bit her lip, trying to control her wayward emotions. One minute she didn't want to ever see him again, and now she couldn't bear to have him walk away.

Pierce scooted closer. He slipped his arm around her and pulled her against his side. For a minute she resisted, then she relaxed against him, feeling his strength as a comfort seeping through her.

"For as long as I can remember, I loved your dad and mom." Pierce spoke softly, almost as if he were afraid of saying the wrong thing. "I used to watch your dad as he worked on the farm. He always whistled a hymn or sang while he worked. He told me more than once that when you give your all to Jesus, He gives you more blessings than you know what to do with."

Pierce paused and Chandra wanted to ask him to continue, but she knew she couldn't say a word right now without crying.

"Your mom always treated me like a son. She fed me every time I came over. She even chewed me out when we would ride through the mud and get our clothes filthy. If you remember, I got yelled at right along with you." A low rumble of laughter echoed through Pierce's chest.

Chandra couldn't keep the chuckle inside. Pierce was right. Her parents never treated him as a friend; he was always family to them.

"Do you remember the time we decided to round up the sheep on our bicycles?" Chandra asked. She could feel the vibration of Pierce's laughter as he squeezed her tight against him. "We thought we were sheep dogs," she said, "and the sheep thought we were monsters. It's a wonder the poor things lived through it."

Pierce's laughter rang across the hills. "It's a wonder we lived through it. I don't think I'd ever seen your dad quite that shade of red."

"That's true," Chandra agreed. "I don't think he whistled the rest of the day. That's what showed me how mad he was."

"But, you know," Pierce spoke thoughtfully, "the best thing about your dad was his ability to forgive. He certainly let us know we were in the wrong and we never were to do that again. But as soon as it was over, he'd forgotten it. Oh, maybe not forgotten, but he never brought it up again, and he treated us with the same love and respect he always did."

"You're right," she agreed. "My dad and mom were both that way. I remember Dad saying if Jesus forgave him, then who was he to hold anything against anyone else?"

For several long minutes, Chandra and Pierce sat quietly. She could feel the soft rise and fall of his chest and the slight pressure of his fingers on her arm. She tried to concentrate on him, but other thoughts pushed insistently to the surface.

What about you, child? Can you forgive as I have forgiven you?

Chandra shivered at the words spoken to her soul. "Cold?" Pierce asked. She shook her head no, and the quiet settled over them again.

God, maybe I should forgive, but I don't know how. I can't even feel You there most of the time. Why did You let this happen? My parents loved You. Why are they dead and those animals that killed them still alive?

Once again, anger welled up inside. Chandra wished she could face those two boys. How would they feel tied to a chair with someone threatening them with a gun? They wouldn't be so cocky then. How would they like it if someone they loved were brutally murdered? Forgive them? Not likely. They didn't deserve it.

Chandra pulled away from Pierce, ignoring the cold that settled over her when she did. She swung her legs over the side of the wall, kicking the rocks as if the aggressive act would allay some of her feelings of hatred.

"Are you okay?" Pierce's soft question irritated her.

"I just need to be alone for a while. If you want to talk, you have friends back at the inn." Chandra glanced at Pierce and hated the hurt look that crossed his face. Why did she always hurt people she loved? She wanted to reach out and stop him from leaving, but the bitterness welling up inside forced her to turn away. She pulled her knees up and buried her face in them, trying to ignore the sound of Pierce's receding footsteps.

Chapter 9

Scraping up a few pebbles from the top of the wall, Chandra plunked them one at a time into the green grass beyond. She was glad Pierce had left. Now she could just spend time thinking. Maybe if she thought the hurt through a few more times it would ease some, and the hatred she felt toward her parents' murderers would ease also.

"Chandra?"

She threw the pebbles in the air and let out a screech. Pitching forward she nearly fell off the wall.

"I'm sorry." Kurt appeared genuinely concerned. "I didn't mean to startle you like that. Pierce reminded me that this is a hard day for you. I thought you might like someone to pray with you."

Chandra felt like a fool staring at this pastor as if he were some sort of freak. She couldn't think what to say. "I. . .I think I just need to be alone." She felt her face warming with embarrassment. What would Kurt think of her hatred and anger?

As if reading her mind he asked, "Are you able to deal with the anger that generally follows an act of violence like your parents' death?"

She stared, groping for words, hoping he would just leave.

"I didn't know your father very well, but I've heard a lot about him. I know he loved Jesus, and he is remembered in the church for his ability to forgive no matter what." Kurt paused and rubbed his hand over the back of his neck. "I don't know why, but I feel I need to tell you that when we are unwilling to forgive others, it becomes a root of bitterness. Pretty soon, that root grows into a wall that comes between us and God."

"I know," Chandra heard herself whisper. "I can't even feel God out there anymore. I've tried to tear down the wall, but I can't."

Kurt smiled, and she felt he truly understood. "Of course, you can't. Only God can do that."

Chandra closed her eyes and thought of the voice earlier that had asked her about forgiving. "I suppose in order for Him to tear down the wall, I have to forgive those boys who murdered my parents. Well, I don't think I can do it. I don't even want to try."

"Chandra, I remember being really hurt. I didn't want to forgive either. Sometimes, I've had to ask God to help me want to forgive someone."

She studied him for a moment then nodded. Kurt bent his head and prayed, "Father, You know how Chandra's hurting. It's hard to lose someone you love, especially to an act of violence. Please help her turn all her hurt and anger over to You. Heal her, Lord."

It was such a simple prayer that Chandra ached inside. *Oh God, help me have that kind of relationship with You.*

After Kurt left, Chandra watched the light grow dim as the sun set behind her. The shadows lengthened, and still she sat, thinking about the wall that stood between her and the Lord. Had she built the wall? Was her bitterness keeping her from having the joy God intended?

She bowed her head, resting it on her upraised knee. *God, I don't want to live like this. I remember how my father forgave. I know You've forgiven me, but Lord, I don't know how I can forgive those young men.*

She sat for a moment lost in thought. *God, I guess I need to forgive You, too. I've felt all along that all You had to do was intervene and my parents would have been okay. I blamed You for their deaths. I forgot that Satan still causes evil to happen, and that You can redeem such horrible things by bringing good from them. Help me, Lord, to forgive.*

Cleansing tears flowed down her cheeks as, for the first time in a year, peace swept through her. Stars began to twinkle in the darkened sky. It still hurt to think of her parents' death, but for once, there was no bitterness and hatred accompanying that hurt.

Chandra made her way slowly back to the inn. As she let herself in through a side door, she saw Kurt, Gina, Morgan, and Pierce relaxing in the front room. They were laughing about some funny story Kurt must have told. Chandra smiled and quietly made her way up to her room. Tonight, she wanted to spend time in prayer, relishing the complete contentment she now had.

⁓⧉⁓

Early the next morning, Chandra brushed out her hair and braided it, trying not to disturb Morgan. Morgan had come up late last night, mumbling about Pierce and how she wouldn't let some little nobody like Chandra take him away from her. Chandra had pretended to be asleep, yet she couldn't help wondering why Morgan thought she was losing Pierce. Had something happened between them?

Now, as she prepared to leave the room, Chandra glanced over at Morgan. Eyes narrowed to slits, Morgan looked at her with such an expression of hatred that Chandra shuddered. She quickly slipped out of the room and downstairs. She might miss an evening meal, but never a breakfast. It was her favorite meal of the day.

❦

"Pierce?"

Morgan's cloying whine made his hair stand on end. They'd only been on the road for about an hour, having done a little sightseeing before they set out. All Pierce wanted to think about was Chandra. He didn't know why she wanted to be rid of him last night. This morning she seemed fine. In fact, she appeared happier than he had seen her for the whole trip. Now Morgan was back in her demanding mode again. He thought he'd taken care of that when they'd talked the other night.

"Yes?" He tried not to be short with her.

"I know you're sorry for talking to me like that the other night." Morgan gave him her most dazzling smile—the one she usually reserved for getting her own way. "I want you to know I forgive you completely. You don't have to be so moody. I know you've been upset about our talk."

Pierce just stared at her, not believing what he was hearing. "Morgan, I was serious when I talked to you the other night. I haven't changed my mind."

The scrunch of bike tires and the whir of the wheels turning grew loud in the silence that followed. Morgan's face whitened, and then a red flush crept up her neck into her cheeks.

"I can't believe you would really choose Chandra over me. She'll never be able to help you like I will."

"And just how will you help me?" Pierce tried to keep the aggravation from his voice.

"I am a business woman. I can help with your image as a business owner. Together we can make a name for ourselves." She almost sounded as if she were pleading.

"Morgan, I don't want to make a name for myself. I never have. I enjoy my bike shop and would like to expand a little, but my main desire is to have a wife and family. I want a wife who believes in Jesus Christ as her Savior and Lord. You've made it clear that you don't have the same beliefs I do."

"Fine," Morgan hissed. "Have your little family and go to church every Sunday. If those are your ambitions, I'm sure Little Miss Nobody will do fine. As far as I'm concerned, our relationship is over."

She threw her weight onto the pedals and pulled ahead. Pierce stopped in the middle of the road, totally dumbfounded. "I do believe she just wanted to feel like she's the one who ended it," he said aloud, startling himself. "I cannot believe it. She just couldn't let me have the final word."

Pushing off, he started down the road after Morgan and Chandra, the only ones ahead of him. *God, please touch Morgan. I think she is really lonely, but she's afraid to admit it. And, Lord, help me get things right with Chandra.*

⌘

Chandra breathed deeply. The fresh air of the country couldn't be compared with the smog-laden fumes in Los Angeles. Here, it rained so often that everything always had a newly washed appearance. She smiled. No wonder the story of Camelot, the perfect kingdom, had been born here. Then again, maybe it was just her outlook that was different today. She hadn't noticed everything looking so bright and pretty any of the other days. She laughed at the antics of a pack of dogs cavorting over rock walls in the distance. Even the animals were excited.

Yesterday she'd felt like the weight of the world sat on her shoulders. The feelings from her parents' deaths and her confusion over her love for Pierce and his love for Morgan all weighed heavily. After her hours of prayer and healing, she felt like a new person. She wanted to sing and dance. She was more carefree than she could ever remember being. God was in charge of her life and it felt good.

Slowing her bike, Chandra noticed for the first time that she didn't have the insistent urge to always be in the lead. She wanted to take it easy. Maybe it would be fun to slow down and spend some time talking with the others. She was even looking forward to talking to Morgan. She wanted a chance to heal the rift that had always been between them.

A crunch of gravel alerted her to the bicycle pulling up beside her before she saw it in her mirror. Morgan, pushing hard on her pedals, gradually closed the distance between them. Chandra glanced over at her and flashed what she hoped was a friendly smile.

"Hi," Chandra called. "You've really improved your riding on this trip."

Morgan glared back. "I didn't ride up here to chitchat with you."

"Did you have something you wanted to talk about?"

"Yes." Morgan glanced over her shoulder. "Pierce."

"What about Pierce?" Chandra couldn't imagine what Morgan wanted this time.

"I just wanted to warn you about what happened the other night," she said, her voice gloating. "Pierce proposed to me. Of course, I had to turn him down. He begged me to marry him, saying if I didn't, he would be stuck asking you to be his wife."

The breath left Chandra, and she forced her feet to push the pedals, hoping the familiar motion would calm her. *God, help me understand this,* she cried. In that instant she knew Morgan was lying. Pierce wouldn't say that about her.

If he had proposed, Morgan would be flashing a diamond at her, not telling her how she'd turned him down.

Chandra glanced in her rearview mirror. Pierce was catching up to them. She could hear the barking dogs getting closer. Stopping the forward motion of her feet, she began to coast. She looked up and met Morgan's eyes, noting the challenge sparking from them.

"Maybe, I'll just wait and ask Pierce about that." Chandra tried to steady her quivering voice.

"You wouldn't dare."

Was that fear Chandra detected in Morgan's voice? Tightening her hands around the brake levers, Chandra let her bike drop behind Morgan's. A hoarse yell sounded faint above the din of the dogs. Suddenly a mass of bodies flowed over the wall beside the road. Tails wagged and tongues hung from panting mouths. Chandra braked hard.

The pile of dogs hit Morgan's bicycle full force. Morgan screamed. Her bike wobbled as she shifted her weight, trying desperately to stay upright. Then one last dog raced over the wall, hitting her front wheel on its way through. Morgan flipped, smashing into the rocks at the side of the road. She lay there, her leg tangled in the bike frame at an awkward angle, her face white as chalk.

Chapter 10

C handra gathered with the others around the stretcher Morgan was strapped to. She had broken her leg in the fall, and the ambulance attendants were waiting to take her to the hospital to have it set. Morgan's blue eyes, glazed slightly from the pain and medication, narrowed when she saw Chandra.

"Pierce has always loved you, even though he was too stupid to see it," she murmured as the pain medication began to take effect. "I tried to get rid of you. I loosened the handlebars on your bike, but they found it. Then I kicked your bicycle so you would wreck. I hoped you'd be hurt so badly you'd have to leave the tour. I said hurtful things whenever no one else could hear. But no matter what I said or how I treated you, you never took revenge." She shook her head as if to clear her thoughts. "Maybe there's something to your God after all." Her last words were barely audible as she drifted off into a drug-induced sleep.

The small group stood in stunned silence as Morgan was loaded into the ambulance. Dale pulled Pierce off to the side to talk with him. Chandra hurt for him, knowing how Morgan's admissions must have been a blow. She watched silently as the van carrying Morgan's bicycle headed down the road toward their next stop.

"Chandra, are you okay?" Kurt asked.

"I'm fine," she whispered in a voice that sounded hoarse. She knew that learning the depth of Morgan's hatred for her should hurt, but instead it seemed as if a protective shield were in front of her the whole time.

Thank You, Lord. I know this state of calm must be Your doing. It must be the peace that passes all understanding Mom used to talk about. Thank You.

She looked over to where Pierce stood talking with Dale. His eyes met hers. He smiled and a tingle raced down her spine. How she longed to have him hold her. How did he feel about Morgan now? Would he still want to marry her?

A subdued group climbed back on their bikes for the remainder of the day's trip. Chandra hoped a hot shower would wash away the cold that seeped into her bones, knowing all the while that it wouldn't really help.

⟨⟩

Pierce stopped in the open doorway of the den, clutching the small package tightly in his hand. Chandra stood across the room talking to Kurt and Gina. Her light brown hair swung in loose, shimmering waves to below her waist. He longed to run his fingers through it. *Oh God, how I love her. Morgan was right. I've always loved Chandra. I was only enamored with Morgan, and I couldn't see the difference. Thank You for showing me the right qualities to look for in a wife, Lord. And Father, please help Morgan come to know You.*

Earlier, Pierce had learned that Morgan had asked Kurt and Gina to visit her in the hospital. Maybe at last she was willing to admit her need for God.

Kurt glanced up and beckoned Pierce to join them. Chandra turned and gave him a half-smile. He could see the uncertainty in her eyes. He crossed the room in three long strides. Taking Chandra's hand in his, he pulled her close to him.

"If you'll excuse us, I'd like to speak to Chandra outside." Pierce barely waited to see Kurt's answering grin before he headed for the door. He had to slow his eager steps so Chandra wouldn't have to run to keep up.

"Pierce, where are we going?" Chandra gazed up at him with her gorgeous hazel eyes. For a moment he almost forgot the reason he wanted to talk. All he wanted to do was stroke her honey-colored cheek and kiss her upturned lips.

Taking a deep breath, he tugged on her hand, leading her toward a copse of trees down the road where they could talk in privacy. "I need to talk, Chandra. There's too much that's gone unsaid between us lately. I also have some plans I've been trying to share with you for several days."

She smiled and his heart skipped a beat. He wanted to draw her into his arms and forget all about talking.

"Well, what's so important?" she asked as they entered the shelter of the trees. The hesitant look on her face told him how unsure she felt.

"I've been wanting to talk to you," Pierce repeated. He took a deep breath, praying for the right words. "It seems like every time I try to talk to you lately something interferes. A couple of times I've been sure you were mad at me."

"I'm sorry." Her sad expression reminded him of a forlorn puppy dog, admonished for some misbehavior.

She looked up at him and explained. "It's just that for the last year I've been struggling with the senselessness of my parents' deaths. Kurt showed me I needed to forgive before I could go on with my life, how bitterness was building a wall between me and God. Last night I finally turned all those feelings over to God. I can't believe how free and clean I feel today. I'm sorry

I was so difficult."

Pierce wanted to leap for joy. Instead he gave her a quick hug then gestured at an open grassy knoll. When she sat down, he dropped down beside her, once more picking up her hand. He ran his thumb over the palm of her hand, trying to think where to start.

"First of all, I have something for you." He handed her the small package wrapped in brown paper.

"What is it?" Chandra looked like a child with a gift. Excitement sparkled in her eyes as she tore the wrapper off. She gasped. "It's the painting. I thought about this last night while I was praying. I know why it's so special." She slowly ran her fingers around the frame. "It reminds me of how I need to be the sheep in God's pasture and let Him put a wall of protection around me. For a long time I've been on the outside with a wall of bitterness separating me from Him."

A tear of joy traced a path down her cheek. Pierce gently wiped it away. Chandra gulped in air, fighting her swirling emotions as Pierce slowly touched her cheek and then smoothed her hair. How could he do this to her if he still cared about Morgan?

He looked into her eyes, and she nearly drowned in his midnight gaze. "Chandra, Morgan was right."

She hesitated. "Right about what?" she finally asked.

"I've always been enamored with Morgan, the beautiful prom queen, but until the last few days I didn't realize that's not what I should look for in a woman—particularly one I want for a wife."

She pulled her hand away. "Are you telling me you're planning to ask Morgan to be your wife?"

"No." He grabbed her hand again. "I'm trying to say that Morgan isn't right for me. I don't love her. I never have. I've always loved you. Since you left, part of me has been missing. I didn't know what was wrong until God hit me over the head. I love you, Chandra. I have ever since I can remember." He leaned forward and cupped her cheek with his hand.

Chandra sat very still, relishing the feel of his warm fingers on her cheek. Had she heard right? Did he say he loved her?

"But, Morgan said you proposed to her."

"I didn't." Pierce drew her even closer, slipping an arm around her shoulders. "I told her there was nothing between us because she doesn't share my interests or my beliefs. I hope these experiences will lead her to God, but even then, we are too different to ever be able to share a life together."

"But I live in LA and you live in Indiana. This will never work."

"I've been thinking about that, too." Pierce smiled and leaned so close she could feel his breath brush across her cheek. "I would like to start a tour business to go along with my bike shop. You could move back to Newbury and help me with arranging the tours."

Her heart pounded. She needed to gasp for air but couldn't. "And would we be partners in business?"

"I'm hoping we'll be more than that." Pierce's lips were only inches from hers. "Will you marry me, Chandra?"

She gazed up at him, not sure she could even answer. Slowly she reached up and traced her finger down his jaw, smiling at the rough, stubbly feel of him. Slipping her hand behind his head she pulled him to her. The kiss lasted for a long moment of ecstasy.

He lifted his head and looked at her. "I don't believe you answered me, Miss Kirby."

She giggled and threw her arms around his neck. "Yes," she almost shouted. "The answer is yes, Mr. Stillwell." Looking into his eyes, she could hardly wait for the adventure of life together to begin.

Blown Away by Love
By Pamela Griffin

Dedication

To my crit buds, and especially to Mom, a big thank-you for helping me at a moment's notice. To my Lord, my Deliverer, who saved me and my sons from the whirling jaws of a tornado once-upon-a-spring, and proved I could always put my confidence and trust in Him during any storm—natural or emotional—this is for You.

Prologue

The favor of your attendance is requested
at the celebration of marriage between
Dale Michael Endicott
and
Marie Elisabeth Barrett
On the twenty-third day of April, at twelve noon
at Good Shepherd Christian Church in
Sunnydale, Texas.
Reception immediately following
at Sunnydale Reception Hall.
R.S.V.P.
(Three times is the charm.)

Chapter 1

Okay, Marie, correct me if I'm wrong, but you're getting married to-morrow, right? This has been your dream since senior year. So, mind telling me why you're acting as if someone just put itching powder in your bridal bouquet?"

Marie scratched her arm, a nervous habit she'd had since childhood. "You really need to ask, Shalimar?" Her laugh came out a bit high-strung as she eyed her maid of honor, then tossed the silk bouquet to the counter of the recreation hall lobby where the rehearsal dinner was under way. "I just know Dale's go-ing to back out again. I just know it. Why I'm even going through with this is anybody's guess. Do I have some inborn brutal desire for everyone to look at me as the town laughingstock again?"

"No one thought that about you. And Dale didn't back out either of those two times the wedding was postponed. You know that."

"Sometimes I feel as if my entire life is being postponed." Marie shot a brooding glance at the discarded bouquet. "I know that first time couldn't be helped, since he's a doctor's son and a paramedic, and that woman was parked in her van and having a baby. But the second time—"

"Dale's no liar. He missed the flight."

Marie let out a heavy sigh. "I suppose you're right. Sometimes, though, I think he's just hunting up excuses not to marry me."

"Do you love him?"

Marie looked up in surprise that her friend would ask such a thing. "Of course. Would I be here if I didn't?"

"Right. And he loves you. You're both Christians, you share the same in-terests. Girl—any fool with eyes can see you're crazy about each other. So what gives?"

"Nothing. I'm just being silly. Maybe it's just a bad case of nerves."

Marie attempted a smile, but in the back of her mind lurked her mother's frequent cautions to her during childhood. "If someone really cares, they'll be on time, and they won't make a habit of being late." Mom should know, since Dad had done the same. He'd missed Marie's tenth birthday party because he had been putting in overtime, and the fur began to fly between her parents once he'd arrived home that night. When he left for good, Marie had thought for a short time that she might have been the reason for the breakup, but the fights between her parents had been continual long before that, part of a daily routine.

"Speaking of our topic of conversation," Shalimar said, "here he comes now."

Marie looked toward the entrance. Her heart gave a little zinging leap at the sight of Dale. With his thick, wheat-colored waves tamed as much as was possible with the comb he carried in his back pocket, the sparkle in his hazel-green eyes, and the lopsided grin on his face that never failed to make her smile in return, he was just the person she needed to see right now.

"I wasn't sure you were going to make it," Marie quipped lightly, though a pall of heaviness lay in her tone.

"Ben had to stop and get gas, and then we got to talking to an old friend who dropped by," Dale explained as he came up beside Marie and dropped a kiss near her mouth. "Sorry I'm late. Hi, Shalimar."

Marie's maid of honor nodded with a bright smile that enhanced her exotic African American features. Marie had always thought her friend should have been a model. "I'll let you two talk things out. It's high time you did." With that, Shalimar headed back into the dining room.

Dale's brows drew together in question. "What did she mean by that? Something wrong?"

Marie wished Shalimar hadn't spoken. This didn't seem like the time or place to unload any of her qualms, but then again, maybe it was. She needed to be sure of his motives before they proceeded any further.

"Do you love me, Dale?"

Surprised confusion filled his eyes. "Of course." He dropped a swift kiss to her lips as if to prove it.

"And you really do want to marry me?"

A trace of realization sobered his gaze and made his smile slip. "This is about what happened two months ago, right?"

For some reason his response needled her. "If you mean by that the second time we had to cancel our wedding, yes, it is."

He looked around, and Marie saw that they'd drawn attention from Dale's two young teenage cousins—Donna and Jillian—who'd just left the dinner area chattering and giggling. They gave carefree waves, and he nodded in return, but his smile was masklike. He slipped his arm around her waist, steering her toward the double glass doors.

"Let's talk about this outside."

Marie allowed him to escort her to a bowl-shaped stone fountain, but once they reached it, she broke a short distance away from him. Avoiding his gaze, hands clutching her elbows, she looked inside the fountain. Lack of rain had made the water evaporate a few inches, but the tiny goldfish still had enough of a home to survive. Orange-gold flashes of light darted here and there. Fleeting, rushing around the ring, as if bored with where they were swimming. Trapped inside a bowl, never able to get free from it.

"Mind telling me what brought this all up?" Dale asked.

Marie shrugged, blew out a breath, then tore her focus from the fish and swung her gaze sideways to her fiancé. "Twice now there's been an excuse for why you didn't show. I'm just a little leery of what'll happen tomorrow. It's no fun having to address a church full of guests that the wedding's been postponed—again."

"I'll be there." He moved toward her and laid his hands on her shoulders. "I promise."

"That's what you said last time. And, Dale, I mean it. If you stand me up a third time, that's it. There won't be a fourth chance."

She could see she'd stung him, but her emotions ran topsy-turvy. Her mother always told her she wore them on her sleeve for all the world to see. She scratched her arm.

"That's not fair, Marie." He drew back, his brows angled in a frown. "I couldn't help it that a major wreck on the highway made me late to the air-port—or that the next flight was booked. At least I did try, and I got a red-eye flight to get back to you as soon as I could."

Marie hung her head, hateful tears clouding her eyes. She despised her-self when she acted like this. She knew that second time, months ago, a small family emergency involving his stepgrandfather had necessitated him flying out of town and missing the rehearsal dinner; it really wasn't his fault. She offered to postpone then, but Dale had told her the danger with his grandpa had passed and to go ahead as planned. She didn't want to start another fight with him now. But once again her tongue worked against her, uttering words she'd rather not say, words she'd kept buried for a long time.

"Maybe that's not all it was. Maybe you're just afraid of marriage. I mean, think about it. You never really proposed to me. One day we just found our-selves at that point, talking marriage. But maybe what it all boils down to is that you're trying to find an escape hatch because you don't want to commit. And those two unavoidable incidents became more like golden opportunities."

She scratched her arm harder. He stilled her movements with one hand. "Let's not argue. Not on the night before our wedding." His voice was gentle, putting a lump in her throat. She looked up.

"I know past circumstances can hardly speak for themselves," he contin-ued. "If the shoe were on the other foot, I might feel the same way. But please believe me when I tell you I love you, Marie Barrett. And for me there's no other woman I'd rather marry."

A tremulous smile caught the edges of her mouth. "I want to believe you, Dale. I honestly do. But like my mom always told me, seeing is believing." Why did she keep saying things she didn't want to say? She tried for a more peaceable remark. "Promise me tomorrow will be different. That you *will* be there no matter what. I love you so much and want everything to work out right for us. For once."

"Wild horses galloping through a hailstorm on my front lawn won't keep me away."

With that promise, she allowed Dale to draw her close. The feel of his warm lips lingering on hers made her heart beat and feel whole again. But it didn't erase all the doubt from her mind.

❧

A hand roughly shook Dale's shoulder, rousing him from sleep. Groggy, he opened his eyes a slit. The image of his brother, Ben, dressed and wearing a windbreaker, didn't connect with the dream he'd just had about chasing wild horses.

"Get up!" Ben threw Dale's shirt onto his bare chest. "We've gotta hurry if we're going to make it on time."

Hurry? The words roused the memory of what this day meant to him, and Dale shot up on Ben's couch, his gaze whizzing to the black deco clock on the wall. "We're not late for the wedding?" No, it was only twelve minutes past eight according to the tall digital numbers. The wedding was scheduled for noon.

With a groan he fell back on the plaid cushions and closed his eyes, intent on getting more shut-eye. Last night Ben had kidnapped him and brought him to his apartment, where a bunch of Dale's friends had thrown a good-bye-to-bachelorhood party—his third one. He'd endured a lot of ribbing because of that fact, but at least the guys had kept the event clean. They hadn't gotten any sleep until the early hours of morning, though, after the others left, and Dale was tired.

"Come on," Ben urged. "I need your help." Dale's jeans landed with a hard thump against his unprotected stomach.

"What's with you?" Dale growled, knocking the jeans aside and glaring at his big brother. "Can't a guy get some sleep around here?"

"Not with a storm brewing in Millbury, you can't. Alarm went off a few minutes ago. I need your help."

"Go without me," Dale mumbled into the pillow.

How many times in the past five years had he helped his storm-chasing brother by handing him equipment, driving while Ben videotaped, or engaging in whatever other tasks Ben ordered of him as they approached a funnel or thunderstorm to observe the raging weather and take pictures? Some of which had earned Ben spots in newspapers and magazines, since he was a professional photographer. Well, he wouldn't rope Dale into working with him this time—not today. Memory again pushed its way through his foggy mind, and Dale lifted his head from the pillow. "Hey, what about my wedding? You're supposed to take pictures, remember."

"Wedding is hours away." Ben had turned his back and was grabbing boxes of snack foods and a large bag of chips from the kitchen cabinet. "We'll be back in plenty of time since Millbury isn't far." He held out the potato chips toward Dale. "Breakfast?"

"No thanks." Realizing any notion of additional sleep was only a hopeless delusion, Dale slowly rose to a sitting position, swung his feet to the flat carpet, and looked down. Trying to get his bearings, he rubbed the back of his neck where a crick had started.

"Grayson called this morning and told me about the storm. He's been tracking it for two days."

Grayson—a meteorologist at a local news station who went to school with Ben.

"But why today of all days?" Dale asked.

"Hey, I don't pick when storms happen—they just do. And I want to be in on every one of them, especially a local one like this. You never know when you'll get that perfect shot." He rolled up the paper sack of food; breakfast, Dale assumed. "Like I said, there's a boatload of time before the wedding. I'll get us both to the church in plenty of time for you to take your stand in front of that altar and manacle yourself in marriage. I'm bringing the cameras with me, as well as my tux. You bring yours, too."

"If I wasn't here, you'd go by yourself, right?"

"Yeah. So?"

"So can't we just pretend like I'm really not here? I'll find my own way home." He sounded like an idiot, but his mind wasn't clearly functioning yet. Coffee. He needed coffee.

"I was never that great at playacting when we were kids. So I guess it's a good thing for me that you really are here. Some might even call it Providence."

Dale didn't respond, realizing he was getting nowhere fast. He pulled his T-shirt over his head. Knowing his brother, once he set off on the track of a storm he wouldn't want to detour, but Dale couldn't afford a taxi to take him back to his apartment and his car, not with the two bills in his wallet. Then again, maybe Ben was right. Millbury was only fifteen minutes away. They should be back in plenty of time before the wedding.

Chapter 2

W ake up, sleepyhead bride-to-be!" Shalimar's teasing broke through Marie's dreams of Dale riding a white horse, with her pressed up against her fiancé's back, arms circled around his waist. "You've got less than four hours left to prepare for the big day."

A little miffed at being snatched from such a delightful vision, Marie sat up in bed. Her illusionary dream metamorphosed into today's reality—she was getting married this afternoon! Yawning, she stretched her arms high above her head and rubbed the sleep from her eyes. A contented smile took over her lips when she remembered her parting with Dale last night. He'd held her a long time, murmuring reassurances that he would be there before noon, come hell or high water. Their parting kiss on her doorstep erased all lingering worries.

"Mmmmm. I'm hungry. Do I smell muffins—and bacon?"

Shalimar laughed. "Well, it's good to see you feeling better. Lynette made breakfast. All the girls are here and eager to start getting ready for the big event. Nervous?"

Marie shook her head. "I've had a lot of time to get used to the idea," she said wryly, but in fun. She looked at the alarm clock. "I think I'll call Dale first."

"I wouldn't do that if I were you. I heard the guys gave him a party last night."

"Yeah, I know. He told me it was in Ben's plans. But it's nine o'clock. Surely he'd be up by now, since there's so much to do before the wedding."

"Newsflash—it takes a guy ten minutes to do what it takes a woman two hours to accomplish. Didn't anyone ever tell you about the difference between the sexes?"

Marie ignored Shalimar's teasing and picked up the phone. "Dale won't mind. He's not the type to sleep in late. I've called him in the mornings before."

"Well, it's your funeral." Shalimar struck a melodramatic pose, a far-off look in her eyes. "And the bride wore black, a bouquet of withered crimson roses in her hand."

Laughing, Marie threw a pillow at her maid of honor. "Oh, will you just get out of here?"

"Humph. Fine way to treat a former roommate." Shalimar smiled as she left.

A touch of melancholy trickled through Marie. She and Shalimar had been roommates for three years, but everything must change at some time or other. It was inevitable. At least Lynette was moving in to take Marie's place. All three women had been good friends since their junior year in high school, when Marie moved back to Sunnydale, Texas. That had also been the year she met Dale.

Smiling secretly with pleasure of what their future might bring, she dialed Dale's cell phone number but got his voice mail instead of a personal greeting. She left a brief message, considered, looked at the clock again, then dialed Ben's.

The phone rang and rang.

⧉

"Will you relax already?"

Dale fidgeted in the passenger seat of Ben's black Bronco, tightening his lips over his teeth in a grimace. "I can't help it. I still don't like this." He slugged down the last swallow of coffee, welcoming the heat burning his throat.

"I told you, I'll get you there in plenty of time. Do me a favor and check the videocam battery. It might be low. If it is, there's a new one in that plastic black case on the backseat."

Dale reached behind him to grab the camera from its case and turned it on. "She said that if I'm not there this time, it's over between us. I don't want to risk losing her."

"You won't."

The battery light registered strong, so he shut it off. "It's good to go."

"Great. Just put it down by your feet, in case we need to grab it fast."

Dale did so, then crossed his arms over his chest. He stared out the windshield ahead to the flat gray sky they were approaching.

Ben looked his way and let out a grunt. "Man, you're pathetic. Now you're sulking like a kid? If you're so worried, give her a call. Let her know what's up and that you'll be there."

Dale nodded. "Good idea. About calling her, I mean. Not about telling her what's up." That would only make her nervous, and Dale didn't want to cause Marie any anguish on her big day. *Their* big day.

With a sigh, he reached to the backseat for his jean jacket. How had he let his brother corral him into this? He blamed his foolishness on lack of sleep. Two and a half hours wasn't enough shut-eye for anyone to engage in rational thinking. His mind had been too fuzzy to really put one and one together, and Ben had herded him to the SUV fast, eager to get on the road for his storm-chasing jaunt. Already the vehicle had been packed with gear, and, at the time, Dale wondered why Ben had waited until the last minute to wake him. Now that Dale *was* awake, he realized Ben had done so purposely, knowing Dale was never alert enough in the mornings until he'd had a cup of black coffee and at least a twenty-minute start into the day.

Of course, it was too late to backtrack, but Dale regretted his sleepy decision to tag along like an obedient puppy with his master. Ben had always been the leader, since they were kids, but if he didn't get Dale back to Sunnydale in time, Dale would be the one demoted to a life in the doghouse—not Ben.

A search of Dale's pockets produced no cell phone. He twisted around to look on the floorboard and the seat, but his studied observation didn't yield the silver device.

He groaned.

"*Now* what's wrong?"

"My phone's gone. It must have fallen on the floor in your apartment. Or maybe it's in the couch." He'd tossed his jacket aside before he'd lain down in the early hours of morning. "Got yours on you?"

Ben shook his head and pulled his cell from his shirt pocket. "Here."

"Thanks." Dale punched in the numbers for Marie's apartment.

"Hello?" Her roommate came on the line.

"Hey, Shalimar. Can I speak to Marie?"

"She's in the shower. Try back in ten minutes."

"Okay." Disappointment twisted his gut. "Could you just tell her I called?"

"Sure. She'll be glad to hear you did. She tried calling you earlier at Ben's but didn't get an answer."

"Yeah." Dale fidgeted at the information. She must have tried calling after they'd already left. Or maybe Ben had turned the ringer off on his phone last night; he was notorious for doing that when he wanted undisturbed sleep. "If I don't call back, could you just let her know I'll see her in a few hours? At the church."

A pause. "Everything okay?"

"Sure, sure. No problems." He forced a laugh.

"So why don't I feel reassured?" Shalimar dropped her voice a notch. "Listen, Dale, just do me a favor. Stay away from any pregnant women or traffic jams. Take the back roads if you have to, but be there. Don't put Marie through a third trial run."

Her take-charge attitude irritated him. "I already told Marie that wild horses wouldn't keep me away, and they won't." He felt the sudden need to end the call before Shalimar unearthed the truth. "Look, I gotta go. Just tell her. And thanks."

Shutting off the phone and slipping it into the console, he looked toward the eerie boiling mass of clouds on the horizon fronting the empty highway. Cumulonimbus clouds—the kind that bred tornadoes. A funnel did appear to be forming, and while that thought reached his mind, the Bronco accelerated in speed as Ben floored it, muttering under his breath about needing to get closer.

Dale clutched the dashboard. He'd thought wild horses weren't anything to worry about—but what about this stampeding Bronco with his brother in charge?

"Will you slow down before you get us pulled over or killed?" Dale muttered.

The red speedometer needle moved a fraction to the left, but not enough, and the car sped farther away from home and closer toward the angry sky.

Dale winced. If he didn't make it back in time, a twister would seem like a mild stirring of dust compared to the maelstrom that was in store for him.

Chapter 3

B en, I'm telling you, this is just another bust," Dale muttered, glancing at his watch one more time. "No tornado's going to hit today. It's time to turn around and head for home." The tail of the funnel they'd seen had been sucked back into the cloud bank before it even formed. Maybe it had all been a shared illusion fostered by lack of sleep.

"You never know what the future holds. If a storm chaser gave up that easy, we'd never get a decent shot." Relentlessly Ben kept his foot on the gas and continued past Millbury to the next town. While he drove he searched the skies ahead, as if to get a bearing on the storm and its movements.

Dale glanced at his watch again. Of the past eight storm chases Ben had gone on, he hadn't spotted a single tornado, though there'd been some great shots he'd taken of a baseball-sized hailstorm while he took shelter under the cover of a metal awning in a park. Tornadoes just weren't all that common. In the five years his brother had been a storm chaser, he'd viewed a sum total of six, often needing to drive for a day or more to reach the location. Some who'd taken up the pastime for as many as ten years had yet to view their first twister. It helped to live in "tornado alley," as one of the locals called their area of Northeast Texas.

On their first sighting of a tornado, Dale had been along for the ride. Neither of them had been looking to chase any storm, and it had caught them unawares. The funnel had been an F-5—a 318-mph monster. Since Ben was a professional photographer, he'd pulled his gear from the back of his SUV. The shots he'd taken of the mammoth twister earned him a spot in the local newspaper, and other photographs he'd sent to a nature magazine. From that day on, Ben was bitten by the storm bug.

"Turn the weather radio on," Ben ordered, "and let's find out where this baby's headed."

"You said we were only going through Millbury. Now we're in Canton." As they stopped at a red light, Dale looked around him at the buildings of the small town. Ben impatiently drummed his thumbs on the steering wheel.

"It's only about an hour's drive back."

"An hour's drive?" Dale shook his head. "Ben, I'm getting married in less than three hours."

"Yeah, yeah. I know, I know."

His mind clearly lay elsewhere.

"All right, let me get this straight. You're not giving up this storm chase—again, no more than a bust—and turning the car around to take me back, right?"

"Soon, soon." Ben's eyes searched the dark mass of clouds ahead.

"That's what I thought."

Dale unhooked his seat belt, reached around for his tux laid across the backseat, and opened his car door.

"What the. . .what do you think you're doing?" Ben asked incredulously. "Are you nuts? Get back in here before the light turns green."

"No can do." Dale surveyed his brother. "I'm not about to jeopardize a future with the woman I love just so you can go chase over hill and yon to find a storm."

"I told you, I'll get you back in time."

"There are no guarantees of that, and you've already driven me thirty miles past the point you said we'd go." Dale shot a look behind the Bronco. A beige car had pulled up, though the stoplight remained red. "I better head out. Hopefully, you will remember that you're my best man and be at the church at the right time. If not, I'll get Todd to take your place."

"Have I ever failed you before?" Ben slapped his palm on the steering wheel. "You're being unreasonable. I'll probably be there long before you show. I mean, just how are you planning on getting back home?"

"I'll call someone if I have to, but I *will* be there on time." He slammed the door before Ben could respond. The light turned green, and Dale stepped backward onto the curb. The SUV drove on. Dale noticed Ben shake his head and give him a look in the rearview mirror as if he'd flipped his lid.

Now what?

Studying the nearby buildings, Dale eyed the sleepy little town where he'd made his escape. A rusty white pickup sat in front of a truck stop diner on the side of the street where he stood. Not far from that was a four-pump gas station, the hinged sign offering cut-rate prices in gasoline. It creaked as the wind swayed it back and forth.

Trying to decide on the best course of action, Dale inhaled a deep breath. Maybe Ben wasn't far off the mark; maybe Dale had flipped. But he'd made a promise to his sweet Marie, and nothing was going to stop him from seeing it through. Not a tornado, not a crazed brother, nothing.

"Lynette, that was the best omelet I've had in ages." Marie set her plate on the sink counter and headed back to her chair at the table. "I can't believe I ate so much. I just hope I fit into my dress." She giggled a bit ruefully, eyeing the remnants of food on the platters that she and all four of her bridesmaids and two cousins had devoured. Both cousins possessed angelic voices and were singing a duet before the ceremony.

"Ha, with the way your body seems to absorb the food instead of the fat, I doubt it'll matter much anyway." Stacey, her seventeen-year-old cousin, had been upset about not making progress on her battle of the bulge. Marie noticed she'd just picked at fruit for breakfast and felt sympathetic toward the teenager. The teen years were some of the hardest ones; how well she remembered.

"Has Ricky asked you to the homecoming dance yet?" she prodded gently.

The girl's face flushed but her lips turned up. "He mentioned it."

"Well, good for him!" Marie shared in the girl's triumph. "He's a lot like Dale in that he sometimes needs a push, doesn't he?"

"You can say that again!"

"Oh, speaking of Dale, he called while you were in the shower."

At Shalimar's calm words, Marie whipped around. "How come you didn't tell me then?"

"Guess I forgot." Leaning against the kitchen counter, Shalimar lifted her shoulders in a careless shrug, but her tense expression caused apprehension to puddle in Marie's stomach. Suddenly she wished she hadn't eaten a full plate.

"Something's wrong, isn't it?"

"He didn't say that. He only said to tell you he'd see you at the church."

Still, her friend wouldn't look her in the eye and, instead, drained her full glass of pineapple juice.

"Did he say he'd stop by the florist and pick up the boutonnieres and mothers' corsages? He offered to do that since he lives so close." Bogged down with her wedding to-do list, Marie had been grateful for Dale's offer last night. Her own bouquet was silk, something she could cherish for a lifetime, and she'd picked it up last week. Everything had been planned down to the last minor detail. She wanted her wedding to be perfect; anything less wasn't an option.

"Maybe I'd better call the florist and make sure." Shalimar left the kitchen.

Not liking the sound of that, Marie rose from her chair and followed.

Shalimar was already talking to whoever was on the other end of the line, so Marie waited but didn't need to be on the other extension to understand, especially when Shalimar said she'd be there in fifteen minutes. She hung up and turned to see Marie.

Shalimar slapped her hand to her heart. "Girl, you've got to go put shoes on so you can be heard. I had no idea you were behind me."

"He didn't show, did he?"

The fake smile Shalimar gave didn't reassure Marie one bit. "Well, hey, you know he's still got a few hours to go."

"If that's the case, then why did you just tell Dorothy you'd come and pick up the flowers?"

"I just want to be on the safe side. In case he forgets. The man's probably got a lot on his mind."

Marie crossed her arms, determined to act as a human barricade until she got some answers. "Shalimar, what aren't you telling me?"

"It's nothing. Really." She acted even more nervous, and as Marie continued to eye her, she fiddled with the belt around her top. "Anyway, I didn't want to upset you, especially since it probably is only nothing."

"So why not tell me and let me be the judge?"

"The flowers—"

"Can wait another few minutes until you spill what you know."

Shalimar expelled a heavy sigh. "Marie, I want your wedding day experience to be a happy one, from start to finish. Why bother giving you information that is probably conjecture in any case and, at best, inconclusive?"

"Okay, that does it. When you start talking like you've already passed the bar, I know something's up. You only sound like a lawyer when you're trying to hide something."

Shalimar rolled her gaze toward the ceiling. "Like I said, it's probably nothing."

"If it's nothing, then it's no big deal. And I want to hear what this 'nothing' is."

The breath that hissed from Shalimar's lips was one of resigned disgust. "Okay, okay. You win. It's just that when Dale phoned, it sounded as if he was making the call from inside a car. There's a distinctive sound—like a whirring—that only a car makes."

Marie pulled her brows together. "I don't think we're on the same wavelength. Why should that worry me?"

"Because he's with Ben. And there's a tornado watch thirty miles north of here."

"A tornado. . .I had no idea." Marie closed her eyes, the truth smacking her a shaky blow. Ben, the incurable storm chaser. Ben, who never could take no for an answer when crossed. Ben, who still treated Dale like his little brother, using whatever method was at his disposal to get Dale to come along on one of his jaunts.

Ben, a confirmed bachelor who'd once announced at a dinner party that any man who chose marriage over his freedom was absent a few screws and bolts.

And then there was Dale, who'd missed two weddings already.

Shalimar touched Marie's arm. "Hey, don't look like that. Like I said, it's probably just my overblown imagination at work. I wish now I hadn't said anything, though from the looks of you earlier, you wouldn't have let me out of here until I did."

"You're right about that, and I am glad you told me." Despite her calm words, Marie's thoughts flew in all directions. The next step seemed paramount. "I'm calling Dale. Right now."

Yet once she tried, she got the same response as last time. Ben's phone rang off the wall. Dale's voice mail answered.

Shalimar's grin tried to soothe. "He's probably just running around like a decapitated chicken, busy getting ready for the big event. You need to start getting ready yourself. It's not that much longer till showtime." She picked up a long strand of Marie's newly washed hair. "I can't wait to see what wonders Cynthia will perform with this, especially since she has so much that's good to work with. What I'd give for your curly hair. While she works her miracles, I'll make you a cup of hot chamomile mint tea. That should soothe your bridal nerves."

Marie forced a smile. If events were going the way she assumed, it would take a whole lot more than chamomile mint tea to give her any peace of mind.

Chapter 4

Dale wondered again if he was out of his mind for ditching Ben. But what other choice did he have? He still couldn't believe his brother would do something like this to him on the day of his wedding. Then again, maybe he could.

Ben avoided weddings—marriage in general, for that matter. Dale felt he'd owed it to his brother to make him best man since Ben was his only sibling and had helped him a lot in quizzing him on the manuals while he trained to be an EMT. Also, Dale suspected that making Ben his best man might be the only way to ensure his brother would even attend the wedding.

The four occupants of the diner regarded Dale as if he were an extraterrestrial—probably because of the black tuxedo slung over his shoulder on its hanger and his otherwise sloppy appearance. Dale directed a smile to the rosy-cheeked older woman behind the counter. The other three men sitting at a table nearby, all who looked like truckers, eyed him suspiciously.

"Mornin'," Dale said. "I was wondering if I could borrow your phone to call a taxi." Mouthwatering aromas of eggs, bacon, and sweetbreads made Dale's stomach pitch from hunger, and he looked at a mammoth platter laden with those items nearest him. As pressed for time as he was, he didn't dare take the opportunity to sit down and enjoy a meal.

The platter's owner, a man with a scruffy beard and plaid shirt, let out a laughing snort. "A taxi? In Canton?" The scrawny young man sitting next to him also got in on the laugh.

"Sorry," the woman said. "No taxi service in town, and I can't let you use the phone for long distance, neither. Only taxi service I know of is in Sunnydale, and that's a different area code." Her eyes were kind, though her news did little to cheer him. "Want breakfast?"

"No time." Dale blew out a long breath. Ironic that the only known cab company was located in the very place he needed to be. He estimated the time from here to there. It had taken Ben over an hour's drive to reach this point.

Calling a cab to come all the way from Sunnydale might work, but then he remembered the lousy six dollars in his wallet. Even if the taxi company did take credit cards, he'd left that piece of plastic sitting by his computer.

"If you could just direct me to the restroom, I'd appreciate it." He felt he should at least put on his tux. Once already the slacks had slid from the hanger and landed on the street. Probably because the material was so silky. At least if he wore the thing, he could try to protect it from getting any dirtier.

She pressed her lips together in a sympathetic gesture. "Restroom's out of order. You can use the one at the gas station next door."

He wondered about that. "Is the area, uh, big enough to change clothes in?"

"You want to change clothes?" She eyed his tux.

"I'm supposed to be at a wedding in a few hours and this thing won't stay on its hanger. I don't want it getting dirty."

"Oh?" she asked, interested. "Who's getting married?"

"I am."

All three men twisted around on their chairs to stare.

"You?" the waitress asked, brows lifting.

"Yeah. And I need to get to Sunnydale before noon. Any chance one of you could give me a lift?" he hopefully asked the table of men.

"Sorry," the bearded guy said. "We're headed in the opposite direction. My boss wouldn't like it if we detoured. I'm on a tight schedule."

"Same goes for me," added the third man, who wore a Rangers baseball cap. "You could check with Jake at the gas station. His nephew is there and might take you where you want to go."

"Okay, thanks." Relief tinged Dale's words and he turned away.

"Wait just a minute," the waitress stalled him. She lifted the plastic cover off a pedestal tray of sweet buns next to the register and, taking a filmy piece of paper, selected one. "For the road. Consider it a wedding present. You look as if you could be hungry." She grinned.

Smiling wide, Dale accepted her generous offer. She was right. Half a bag of salty potato chips and a cup of bitter coffee hadn't done much to stave off his waking hunger. "Thanks, ma'am. I really appreciate it."

"Good luck to you," she called out before the door closed.

In the gas station restroom, he changed into the tuxedo, but left the black dress shoes for later. If he had to do any walking, he preferred his comfortable white sneakers. He got a number of double-take glances from two customers and the attendant as he opened the glass door of the main part of the station and approached the register.

"Any chance anyone here could take me into Sunnydale? I'll pay twenty dollars to whoever can. I have six on me, but I'm good for the other fourteen once we get there."

The attendant, a man wearing grease-stained clothes, eyed his ruffled shirt. "I can't take off work, and my nephew's already left or he could've given ya a lift."

An old man in dungarees and a straw cowboy hat approached from the mini-mart food section of the store. He laid a loaf of bread on the counter, all the while eyeing Dale from head to toe. The man stared at him as if he were wearing a space suit instead of a tuxedo, but Dale decided to give it a try. "Sir, is there any chance you can drive me into Sunnydale? I'd gladly pay for the gas and time lost."

"Only going to Millbury," the man said, pulling out a bill to pay. "Got to take my Myrtle on home."

"Millbury's good." At least it was halfway. "Anything helps. I need to get back for my wedding," Dale explained.

"How's that?" The old man took the sack with his purchase from the attendant. "You say you're getting married?"

"Yes, sir. And I've found myself in a jam, without transportation. My brother took off chasing a tornado."

"That a fact? Well now. . ." He took another long look at Dale. "I reckon you must be tellin' the truth. Cain't see no other reason you'd be all doodaded up like that this early of a mornin'. You'll have to ride in the back with Myrtle, though. I got grease on the seat earlier, and it's sure to ruin them fancy pants o' yours. Upholstery's all tore up, too."

"That's fine, wherever you want me to sit." Dale was just so relieved to find a ride, he wouldn't mind being roped to the roof of the car. "Can I have a sack for my clothes?" he asked the gas station attendant.

The man reached down for one. Dale stuffed his casual everyday wear and nice shoes into the paper sack, then followed the old man outdoors. A green pickup sat near one of the gas pumps.

"Daddy's back, Myrtle." The old man pulled the bread sack from the bag, ripped off the plastic tie, and laid the whole thing in the rear of the pickup. "And I brought you some of that nice white bread you like, for being such a good girl at the vet's."

"Mmaaaaahhhhh!"

In stunned unease, Dale looked past the old man's shoulder and toward the root of the sound. In the back of the pickup stood a live goat.

❦

With two hours and fifteen minutes to go before the wedding, and no sign or word from Dale, Marie constantly battled a whirlwind of conflicting emotions. She'd called Ben's apartment, still getting no answer, then tried Dale's groomsmen. No one had heard from him all morning. One of the guys mentioned that Ben talked about a tornado last night, the words driving home to Marie what she felt must be the truth of the matter.

Dale had gone storm chasing with Ben.

Shalimar and the other bridesmaids tried to reassure her, but Marie wouldn't be comforted. She'd scratched her arms so much that dark pink streaks scaled both of them, and Shalimar gently rebuked her and put cream on them. At least her wedding gown had long lace sleeves so no one could see the damage she'd done.

If there was even going to be a wedding.

"Stop it," Shalimar said, disrupting Marie's black thought. "He'll show."

"How'd you know what I was thinking?"

"Because we've been friends and roommates for years and I know how your mind works. We should get to the church now. There's a lot to do before the big hour hits. Come on."

Marie followed Shalimar to collect her things. She wrapped a bandanna around the soft twist curlers that Cynthia had put in her hair and insisted stay there until the dress was donned once they were at the church. "What if he doesn't show, Shalimar? What if this time is just like the last two times?"

"I don't think that'll be the case."

"But what if it is?"

"Then you'll deal with it as graciously as you did before, with the strength of all your friends to support you." She grabbed her purse off the end table and pulled out the car keys.

Marie pondered Shalimar's words. Yes, she could pretend. Her mother had taught her well how to keep up appearances when the world was falling down. Appearances were always so important to Mother. And Daddy never had met any of Mother's expectations.

"Why borrow trouble, Marie?" Shalimar interrupted her dismal train of thought. "Instead of wasting elite brain cells worrying about what could happen or might happen, I think you just need to forget all that and concentrate on what's happening right now."

"Wasting elite brain cells?" Marie repeated with an amused quirk of her mouth.

"Yeah. An odd sort of phrase I picked up from my nephew. And I have to tell you, he's excited to play the bass for the reception. His band hasn't had that many gigs."

"The pleasure is all ours. Dale and I liked their sound."

At the memory of that audition, when Dale had stood behind her, his arms wrapped around her middle, his cheek pressed against her hair as they'd swayed from side to side while listening to The Sizzling Cats play their blues/jazzy sound, Marie felt a tear start behind her eye and quickly averted her head. She brushed at her lashes.

"Now then, none of that. Give me your hand."

"Why?" Marie asked, even as she held it out.

Shalimar clasped it in hers. "Because I'm willing to bet you haven't had any kind of spiritual fuel to start your morning. Am I right?"

Ashamed, Marie nodded. She knew better, but from the second she'd woken up, Dale had been uppermost in her thoughts, and time had skied on a downhill course from then on and gotten away from her.

Shalimar bowed her head. "Father, we come to You in the name of our Lord Jesus and thank You for this wonderful day of promise that belongs to Marie and Dale. Please reassure Marie and give her the peace she needs. Help her through this anxious time, and wherever Dale is, help him, too. And please, Lord, just get him to the church on time."

⁂

With his eyes closed and the back of his head against the cab of the truck, Dale let his sluggish thoughts slide to Marie, slipping from image to image. Her sunny smile. . .the way the light hit her hair. . .her dark eyes brightening when they focused on him. . .the feel of her in his arms.

A smile on his lips, the mental image of her so vivid, he could almost imagine her warmth now and feel her nuzzling his neck.

Whaaa. . .?

His eyes flew open. Inches from his, a fuzzy white face loomed, its mouth delicately feasting on one end of his unraveled black tie.

"Ah!" He let out a cry and pushed at the goat, at the same time trying to wrest the black ribbon from its teeth. A struggle followed, but Dale arose the victor. At least he thought he'd triumphed, until he studied the damage done. The wet strip of black was now in shreds.

"Stupid goat," he muttered, giving it a malevolent look.

"Maaaaaaahhhhhhh!" The white bearded lady had the audacity to mock him. And was that a goat smile? It nosed the empty bread sack and began to chew on it.

All through the remainder of the ride, Dale crossed his arms high on his chest and kept his gaze fastened on the goat. He wasn't about to make the mistake of closing his eyes again.

Knowing how important appearances were to Marie, Dale decided he could switch ties with one of his groomsmen. At least the farmer had given him a clean blanket on which to sit, so as not to get his tuxedo dirty. Dale wondered why the blanket couldn't have been used on the passenger seat and guessed the farmer didn't trust a stranger to ride inside. Not that Dale blamed him. It had been a mistake to change clothes, but he was stuck now. If he changed back into his jeans and T-shirt somewhere along the way and folded his tuxedo into the sack, it would get wrinkled. He'd left the slippery metal hanger in the gas station restroom, and it wouldn't do to go to his own wedding looking like a six-foot-one-inch raisin.

Within minutes, Dale saw the sign for Millbury, and the farmer pulled off the road at a crossroads. After exiting his truck, he moved around to Dale. "This is as far as I can take you." His gaze lowered to the damaged tie as Dale fished for his wallet. "Myrtle do that?"

"Yeah, seems she ran out of bread. I appreciate the lift."

He held out the six dollars, but the man shook his head. "Don't seem right to take your money since Myrtle did that." He eyed the goat. "For shame, Myrtle. That wasn't a nice thing to do."

"Maaaahhhhhhh."

The man looked back to Dale. "Shoulda warned you she likes ribbons and shiny things. Let's just call it even. I was goin' this a-way anyways."

"Thanks," Dale muttered as he replaced the bills and crawled from the back of the pickup. As his feet hit the ground he was glad he'd decided to wear his sneakers.

"Good luck with your weddin'. Hope all goes well for ya."

If I ever get there. "I appreciate the well-wishes, sir."

The truck pulled onto a long dirt road opposite the highway. Dale was sure the goat had a gloating expression on its fuzzy face as it turned to look at him and gave one parting, faint, *"Maaaaaaaahhh!"*

"Stupid goat," he muttered before looking both directions down the empty highway. Nothing but grass and trees and sky. At least the sun wasn't blazing down on him, wasn't apparent behind the ash-gray clouds at all.

Hoping it wouldn't rain as it had done earlier, Dale puffed his cheeks, blew out a huge breath, and set off on foot for home.

Chapter 5

Marie arrived at the church at the same time her uncle brought her mother, who'd made a special trip from West Texas just for the wedding. Hurrying across the parking lot, Marie approached her mother and the two women hugged.

"I apologize that I couldn't come earlier," her mother said, "but Henry had a business trip, and I had to help him prepare for it."

"It's okay. You're here now." No mention of Henry wanting to come, though she doubted her mother's husband would care to see Marie married. He'd made his excuses during the last two failed attempts also. They'd never gotten along, ever since Marie was fifteen. She'd always hoped Daddy would return to take his rightful place in the family, but after years elapsed, she put that childish fantasy behind her. He'd left because he hadn't cared. It still hurt, but she'd come to accept it, and the ache was now only a dull memory.

Everyone had left her in one way or another. When she was six, her beloved grandmother was taken suddenly, struck by a car. As a child, she could only reason that Grandma had left her. Then her father left. And later, in a sense her mother left—to marry another man and move them all to another town. Neglecting Marie, her mom doted on her new family. So on her seventeenth birthday, Marie left West Texas and moved back to Sunnydale and in with Shalimar. It had been difficult finishing high school and holding down a job to help pay rent, but she'd done it. Just as she was paying for this wedding, she and Dale both.

"Why the gloomy face?" her mother asked.

Marie forced a smile, not wanting to discuss her fears, knowing Mom would begin to harp on the reason for Dale's tardiness yesterday and apparent absence today as a sign that he didn't care and that Marie was about to be stood up a third time. Instead she aired another thought that had been worrying her. "It looks as if it might storm."

Her mother studied the sky. "I noticed. Not a good sign. Unhappy is the bride whose wedding day is filled with showers."

A superstition Marie didn't need to hear now or at any time. She moved to her uncle and smiled, giving him a quick hug. "Uncle Joe. Thanks for bringing Mom and for taking off work to come today. It means a lot to me."

Red flushed his face when she pulled away, and he averted his gaze. He'd always been so shy. "Aw, weren't nothin' any other red-blooded American boy couldn't do."

Marie smiled at the familiar phrase her grandfather also had used. Of all her family, she wished she could have gotten to know her uncle better.

"Excuse me for interrupting," Shalimar said from behind Marie, "but we need to get you inside and ready for the big event. Hello, Mrs. O'Brien."

"Hello, Shalimar." Marie's mother coolly studied the tall, slim brunette in a disapproving manner.

Wanting to smooth the waters before they roughened further, Marie quickly spoke. "You're right. I wouldn't want anyone to drive by and spot me in my curlers." She tried for a light laugh but it came out tense.

"Why you didn't go to a salon and get it professionally styled is what I can't understand," her mother said. "But I guess working at that computer store you don't make all that much money, do you?"

That stung, though Marie would never admit it. She had never asked her mother's husband for a penny. He'd made it clear years ago that he didn't give handouts. Yes, she and Dale had needed to scrimp in areas while planning their big day, but the results satisfied Marie. And at least they didn't lose anything from the last two failed attempts, except for the deposits.

"Cynthia just graduated from beauty school. She has loads of talent, and I like her style." Marie took Shalimar's arm and hurried up the walk with her. At the moment, she didn't need one of Mom's critical remarks. Not when her mind and heart were in such turmoil over Dale.

She wondered what he was doing right now.

❧

One foot in front of the other. That was the only way he was going to get there. And each step brought him closer to home.

That's what Dale kept telling himself as he continued walking the deserted stretch of highway. Three cows in a field to his left stood close to the wire fence and chewed their cuds, watching him as his sneakers thudded across the damp pavement.

Great, an audience.

Feeling their brown eyes never leave him, he turned in irritation. "Don't you have anything else better to do?"

They continued to stare, as if he were some unfortunate creature to be pitied. He shook his head in disbelief. Now he was talking to the cattle, imagining what was going through their heads?

He really did love animals. He and Marie even had discussed getting a dog from the animal shelter. But today any four-footed variety of beast was getting on his nerves. These were no pre-wedding jitters. These jitters were more of the "Will there even be a wedding?" shakes.

If he had to move heaven and earth, sod or roadway, he would get there on time. He wouldn't disappoint Marie again. He looked up at the sky. "I sure could use some help down here," he said. "A private plane landing on the highway maybe?" By the calculations on his wristwatch, he'd need to fly if he was going to get there by noon. "Or how about bringing a race car driver down from the local speedway to give me a lift?"

He let out a self-disgusted laugh, knowing he was to blame for everything. Unwise decisions made for unexpected problems. He'd brought this all on himself and now would have to deal with it. He couldn't expect God to bail him out of his own mess.

It began to sprinkle.

Terrific. That was all he needed.

About the same time that thought slammed across his mind, he heard a faraway motor and the whishing of tires on pavement. Looking over his shoulder, he caught sight of a blue sedan coming his way and felt a moment's relief.

That is, if the driver stopped.

He understood the dangers of hitchhiking. But desperate times called for desperate measures, so he held out his thumb.

The car whizzed past, then came to an abrupt halt, brakes squealing, about twenty yards ahead. It reversed until it came alongside Dale. The passenger window went down, and Dale found himself face-to-face with a young woman, her hair in a long red ponytail.

"Whatcha doin' all the way out here in the boondocks dressed like that?" she asked in greeting.

"Trying to get to Sunnydale. Can you give me a lift? I'll pay you." He repeated the situation with his funds.

"Sure, hop on in. I'm going that way, too."

Relieved, Dale did so. Before he could buckle his seat belt, she took off with another squeal of tires.

"I'm Janie, by the way," she offered as an introduction. "So what takes you to Sunnydale?"

"My wedding."

"No joke? You're getting married today?" Her head turned his way as a pink bubble expanded from her mouth. She popped the chewing gum and faced front again. "That's really cool. So, like, what's your name? I guess since I'm giving you a ride, I should at least know that."

"Dale." Now that he sat inside her car, he studied her closer. Not the young woman he'd thought, the remnant of baby fat on her face placed her more at sixteen. Suddenly he wasn't so sure about this arrangement. *He* was safe, of course, but still felt uncomfortable by how the situation could be perceived, not that anyone was around to do any looking. But he was a stranger— a man—riding with a kid.

"Janie, just how old are you?"

She hesitated. "Eighteen."

Eighteen wasn't so bad, he guessed. Dale stared out the windshield and at the spots of rain clouding the glass, then studied the speedometer. "Don't you think you're going a little fast? Speed limit's sixty, and it's started to rain again. You don't want to hydroplane or anything—skid."

"Aw, don't worry. These tires are good. Poppy just put brand-new ones on." She picked up a large paper cup that Dale now noticed was propped between her jean-clad thighs. Taking a hefty slurp from a straw, she grimaced. "Man, they make these things so thick you can't get anything out of them. Would you take the lid off for me?"

"Sure." He took the cup at the same time she began to search on the dashboard for something.

"You like rock?"

"Not really. I'm more into jazz."

"Jazz, huh?" She didn't sound impressed. "Well, you'll like this. It's sorta got a jazzy, pop, rock sound." She slid a cassette into the tape deck. Out of the speakers boomed raucous sounds of stacatto drums and squealing guitars. Dale jumped back at the sudden onslaught.

"You think you could turn that down some?" he raised his voice to be heard over the noise.

"Sure, whatever." Frowning, she turned the volume about a half decibel lower.

His eyes darted to a bend in the road ahead and then to the speedometer again. "Janie, if you want to make that turn you're going to have to slow down." One hand still on the shake, he slapped his other to the dashboard, "Janie. . ." His grip went white-knuckled. He'd seen too many accidents caused by negligent driving in his years as an EMT. "Slow down!"

"Yeaaaaahhhh!" she squealed like a maniacal speedster as they took the turn too fast. "We're flyin' now!"

Frozen in dread, Dale stared, eyes wide, mouth hanging open. Somehow they made the turn on all four wheels, but half of her chocolate shake spilled over onto his trouser leg.

A siren wailed behind them, red lights flashing. Glancing in the side view mirror, Dale spotted a police car racing after them from its hiding place behind a billboard, where it was probably set up as a speed trap.

Dale felt his stomach bottom out.

❧

Marie felt literally sick to her stomach with nerves. She loved her mother, but Mom had put on her "critical hat," criticizing the bridesmaid's dresses, the decorations in the church, everything. Worse, Dale still hadn't called. No one had even heard from him. Not the groomsmen, not the florist, not anyone. And failing to get in touch with Dale by phone only upped the level of her anxiety.

From the other side of the room, two of her bridesmaids, Rachel and Lena, avidly watched as Cynthia unrolled the curlers from one side of Marie's head. Marie frowned at her reflection in the mirror. She couldn't help thinking history was repeating itself again. Despite her warning to Dale, he'd obviously stood her up yet again to go chase a storm with his brother. Well, she wouldn't be foolish enough to go through with this wedding fiasco a fourth time! If Dale didn't want to share a life with her, she could take a hint. She wondered if she should call the whole thing off right now. At least if it came from her, it would be less humiliating. Still. . .the thought of canceling the wedding made her heart crack like aged concrete; she just couldn't do such a thing. She loved him too much, insensitive jerk though he was.

Peering into the mirror's reflection of the window, she noticed how the sky had taken on a greenish-gray cast. Evidently, no sun would make an appearance, though normally she didn't mind overcast days.

She again looked at her face, her memory tripping back to last year. She'd gone along on one of Ben's and Dale's storm chases, all the way to Dallas, but there'd been no tornado, only a "bust" as Ben had called it. However, later they'd seen a small dust funnel on the side of the road, and Dale asked Ben to pull over. Dale had given her a pair of goggles to protect her eyes, also donning a pair, and the jacket she'd worn protected her arms from getting stung from the miniature whirlwind. Holding hands, they approached the swirling dirt that ended a few feet over their heads and stepped through the dust devil, hair flying every which way. Marie had been amazed to look from inside the funnel at the whirling brown walls, while standing safe inside its center. Just enough room for both of them to stand, face-to-face, in each other's arms. Dale had even kissed her, a slow, tender kiss that added to the fantastical moment she'd shared with him.

Would there be other moments like that? The togetherness, the oneness, the sharing of dreams? Her shoulders slumped and she shut her eyes.

Someone knocked at the entrance to the bride's room. "Excuse me. . ."

Her uncle again tapped on the door that stood ajar and pushed it open another notch. "Don't mean to bother no one none but, Marie, your purse has been singing quite a tune out here. Sounds like one of them TV show reruns."

Marie stood and approached him as he held out her tote bag. She'd forgotten that she'd dropped it on a chair in the foyer, just outside the bridal room. "My cell phone." Dale had programmed it to play the theme from *Mission Impossible*. What their wedding was proving to be.

Glad the mechanical tune continued to play, she fished in the inside pocket for her phone and flicked it open and on. "Hello?"

"Marie, it's Ben."

Her throat constricted. "What have you done with my fiancé, Ben?" She managed to keep a civil tone, her words coming out both light and ominous.

"You mean he's not there yet? I would have thought he would've gotten there by now. It's him I was hoping to talk to. He left his cell at my apartment, and I couldn't remember the church's number, so I called yours."

The tightening worsened until she could barely breathe. "He's not with you?"

"He was. But he insisted we'd be late if I didn't turn around, so he got out when we were in Canton. I'm heading back now."

"Got out? What do you mean he 'got out'?" She tried to stay calm but he wasn't making sense.

"He said he'd find a way back home. He hoofed it, I guess."

Stunned, she could only stare ahead, though she had no idea what she looked at. "You mean he *walked* back?"

"Unless he hitched a ride." When she didn't answer, he added, "Don't worry. He's a big boy and has been in worse situations. I'm sure he's fine."

A hundred thoughts went flying through her head, half of them curt responses she'd like to hurl at Ben right now. The foremost reply in her mind being what she thought of a man who would go storm chasing on the day of his brother's wedding.

Closing her eyes, she pressed her fingers to her forehead, rubbing the taut skin there. Somehow she managed to rein in her tongue before she accused him of planning the whole thing to prevent their marriage. Hysterically she wondered if he'd also planned the traffic jam in Missouri two months ago. Or had stationed the pregnant woman in her van off the side of the road last year.

"You still there?"

Hanging by a thread.

"Thanks for letting me know what happened. I have to go now." She flicked off the phone without a good-bye. The man didn't deserve one.

"Trouble?" her uncle asked from the doorway where he still stood.

Marie told him, though she kept her words low since she heard her mother's voice in the next room, talking to someone.

"You want I should go look for him?"

"You'd do that?" Hope flared inside her.

"Sure. It's the least I could do for my favorite niece."

"Thanks, Uncle Joe. I'd really appreciate it." Moved by his kindness, she stepped forward to kiss his cheek, which turned tomato red, as did his whole face. Making a decision, she pulled the straps of her tote over her shoulder. "And I'm coming with you."

His gaze went over her hair, half of it still in curlers, half of it springing around her shoulders. "Uh, you sure you should? You look like you have some more fixin' up to do."

"But you don't know what he looks like, do you? You've only seen him once."

"Can't say I remember him all that well."

"I'll go with him," Cynthia volunteered.

"You have to finish fixing her hair," Lena said suddenly from the other side of the room. "And we're running short on time. I'll go with him."

"Thanks, Lena." Marie felt relieved. "Not a word to Mother, please." She switched her focus to her uncle. "Neither of you."

Her uncle nodded in understanding and left the room with Lena following.

Marie understood the logic about her not going but wished she'd been the one to go with Uncle Joe. Yet she did need all the prep time she could get, or she would be the one arriving late to the altar. And she'd never been late a day in her life. Assuming they would find her absent fiancé in time, and there would even be a wedding, that is.

Oh, Dale. Where are you?

Chapter 6

O ne phone call."

Dale nodded at the officer and followed him to a wall with two pay phones, muttering his thanks when he gave Dale the coins needed.

He hesitated before sliding them into the slot and punching buttons. What would he say to Marie? How could he ever face her? More importantly—would she believe him? Three questions that settled what felt like the weight of a two-ton truck on his shoulders.

There was no answer at her place. She must already be at the church. Where he should be. Sighing, he studied his wristwatch. It would take a miracle to get him out of this fix and at the altar in time for his wedding. Maybe it was better Marie hadn't answered. Thinking fast, he called one of his groomsmen.

"Yeah?" A male voice came over the line loud and clear.

"Todd," Dale said in relief. "Listen, I need you to do me a favor. Where are you?"

"At the church, where you should be. Where are you, anyway?"

"It's a long story. Is Marie there?"

"Yeah, she's in the back getting ready with all the other girls. Wanna talk to her?"

"No! I mean, not yet."

"You okay, dude?"

"Yeah, great." Dale released the air through his teeth. "No, not great. I'm in jail."

"Jail! You've gotta be kidding."

"Shh! Don't let anyone hear you."

"No one knows who I'm talking to," Todd's voice came back, and Dale heard the creak of a door opening then closing with a click. "Okay, I'm outside now where no one's listening. How'd you land in jail?"

"I hitched a ride with a wannabe speed racer who not only didn't have her license, but was also underage and shouldn't have been behind the wheel. She was taking her poppy's car out joyriding."

Silence lengthened on the other side.

"You there?" Dale asked impatiently.

"Yeah. Not that I don't think this story sounds like it has great possibilities for one of the most interesting tales I've ever heard in my entire lifetime, but why'd they put you in jail for that? Especially if you weren't the one behind the wheel."

"She had a shotgun in her trunk."

Dale could hear the sound of Todd's breathing.

"For hunting possum. She told the police it was her brother's. Of course the fact that she's the mayor's granddaughter isn't helping *me* much. I think they assume I'm some sort of depraved psycho for jumping in the car with a fifteen-year-old. Or that we'd hatched plans to become a modern-day Bonnie and Clyde." The last he said sarcastically; his wit came to the forefront at the oddest times.

Todd whistled through his teeth. "Man, when you find trouble, you really know how to dig yourself in deep."

"Yeah, yeah." Dale didn't need this right now. "So can you come get me?"

"Marie's uncle Joe is already heading that way, though I don't suppose he'd know to stop at the jailhouse."

"Marie's uncle is coming here?" Dale softly knocked his head against the wall three times. "Then Marie knows I took off storm chasing with Ben this morning and that I left him in Canton."

"She knows. Ben called her."

Great. The one thing he'd hoped she would never find out. "Whatever you do, don't tell her I'm in jail. I'll never live it down if you do. Especially if her mother hears."

"You know me better than that, buddy. Hold on a sec. Someone's coming."

Dale waited several seconds then heard a clicking sound, followed by a buzz.

No! He'd been cut off. And he hadn't even told Todd what police station he was in. With no money to make another call, he pulled the receiver away from his ear, stared at it, then hung up and looked toward the sergeant's desk where Janie had been sitting earlier.

The sergeant crooked his finger at Dale, motioning him forward. Dale swallowed hard. At least they weren't escorting him back to that cheerless cell. And the handcuffs were off his wrists now, too.

Abuzz with activity, the station looked small, with few officers present. The sergeant leaned back in his chair and narrowly eyed Dale as if he had all the hours in the day to kill. Dale's eyes flicked over the wanted posters plastered on a nearby bulletin board, and he could almost imagine his mug up there. The sergeant eyed him as if he were the evil Pied Piper, luring children away from the safety of their homes with his pipes.

"Janie tells me you were walking on the highway and she gave you a lift." The officer eyed Dale's tuxedo, with its goat-chewed ribbon, chocolate-splotched pants, and scuffed, not-so-white sneakers. "I'm not even going to ask why you're dressed up like that, because what I really want to know"—here he leaned forward—"is what you were doing tagging along with someone who's barely more than a child."

"Hers was the only car that drove by." Dale shifted and muttered the rest, "And I didn't want to be late for my wedding."

"Excuse me?" The officer lifted shaggy brows. "Did you just say your wedding?"

"Yeah. I'm supposed to be married at noon." And with that admission, the whole story came tumbling out, from the start of Ben's storm chase until the police handcuffed him and put him in the back of their car, along with Janie.

The officer's expression lightened considerably during the retelling, and Dale could see his mouth twitch a few times as if he tried to contain a laugh or two.

"Well, now. . ." He thought a moment, staring at his desk blotter before looking up at Dale. "Janie pretty much cleared you, had nothing but good to say about you. And we ran a check on your license. You're clean."

Dale could have told him that, but only nodded.

The officer stood and shrugged into his jacket. "I can't see holding a man in custody on the day of his wedding." He chuckled as if unable to control himself. "Fact is, we've got nothing to hold you on here."

"So I'm free to go?" Dale asked, hardly daring to believe it.

"You're free."

"And Janie?" He couldn't help but wonder about the poor kid's fate, even if she had brought it all on herself.

The officer frowned at Dale's interest. "Her grandfather'll take care of her. It's not the first time she's had a brush with the law." He slipped on his cap. "I can take you as far as the city limits if you want a ride."

"That would be great." And more than Dale ever hoped for.

⚭

Marie stood by the window, staring out at the stormy landscape. Nearby trees rustled with the wind, the sound of which Marie could hear even inside the building. A couple of boys pedaled past on their bicycles, struggling against the swift current of air. The grass had browned and could use a good rain-storm, but why today of all days? Marie sighed, hoping Dale wasn't fighting the elements like those two boys were. She no longer felt angry about his absence; instead she was fearful for his safety.

She couldn't understand what had compelled him to leave Ben's car and walk back to town. Surely if he had asked, Ben would've taken him home. Marie tilted her head to the glass in thought. Then again, maybe not. Storms were Ben's first love. He and Dale shared similar traits in that they were both stubborn, and when they each wanted something, they did all in their power to get it. Remembering the first time she and Dale met, Marie felt her lips turn upward in a wistful smile.

A junior in high school, she'd been waitressing at the local steak house and had approached the table where Dale sat.

"Have you decided what you'd like?" she'd asked him.

"Yes, I have." He'd folded the menu closed and looked her straight in the eye. "You."

"Excuse me?"

"I'd like to take you out on a date. To the movies. Friday night. Seven o'clock."

She gave him an openmouthed stare. The guy was drop-dead gorgeous, with his wheat-blond hair, heart-stopping green eyes, and slim, athletic build. Though she'd seen him in the school halls and noticed him, his delivery wasn't the type to win any awards with her. They'd never been introduced, though she knew his name.

"Sorry, I'm not on the menu." She tried to say it coolly, hoping he didn't notice the catch in her throat or the whispery way her words came out in a rush. "If you'd like something—on the menu—please let me know so I can take your order. Otherwise, I have other tables to wait on if you're not ready yet."

He raised his dark brows in half amusement, half interest, obviously not deterred. Once he made his order, she hurried away, almost asking another girl to switch tables with her. But something had prevented her from doing so. Dale intrigued her, even if his come-on had been a bit on the arrogant side. He hadn't pushed her when she'd brought his steak burger to the table, only asking her if she liked her classes and what teachers she had, but she'd been so nervous she almost let his glass of soda slip from her hand while setting it before him. At school, she'd heard only good comments about him and his family, newly moved to the area. A lot of the girls wanted to date him.

After that first encounter at the restaurant, when Marie later caught sight of Dale, she stared long and hard, intrigued, until he glanced her way. Then she abruptly fixed her gaze elsewhere. The next time he asked her out, after a youth meeting at this very church, she didn't hesitate to accept. And from their first date on, they'd been inseparable.

She had emotionally supported him as he'd trained to be an EMT, and he'd done the same for her when she went to night school to learn computer design. Two years after graduation, their talk evolved into marriage, as if it was the natural course to take. Yet, had she pushed him into something he didn't really want since he'd never proposed to her?

"Marie, I just have to tell you again, I love this necklace, though you didn't have to buy us another gift since you gave us the bracelet the first time the wedding was on." Talking all the while, Lynette came through the door and stopped suddenly. "Are you crying?"

Shalimar came in behind her and darted a look at Marie.

Marie swiped at the telltale tear. "Just taking a stroll down memory lane." She looked at Lynette and smiled. "I'm glad you like it. I knew they'd be darling with your lilac dresses, and really, you gals have stood by me through so much and been through this three times now. I wanted you to have something more to show my appreciation." When she'd seen the teardrop pearl necklaces on a spring sale, she'd splurged a little and grabbed four of them up for her three bridesmaids and maid of honor.

Shalimar put a supportive arm around her shoulders. "He'll be here, Marie."

Marie let her eyes close for a second. There was no fooling her best friend. "I want to believe that. . .I need to believe that. But I've been thinking, and maybe I pushed him too hard. Maybe he wasn't ready to commit but didn't want to hurt my feelings."

"A guy who'd leave his brother's car and set out on foot over thirty miles to get back to you sounds ready to me."

Hope flickered. "You think so?"

"Yes. Dale's one of a kind." Her gaze searched Marie's face. "I think the devil's playing mind games with you, and with your history of being hurt by others, you're listening to every lie he's throwing your way."

Shalimar could be right about that. Almost everyone close to her had left in some way—her grandmother through physical death, her father through abandonment, her mother through emotional detachment.

"Let's pray about this. You can never have too much prayer." Shalimar looked over at the other bridesmaids. "Lynette, Rachel, want to come join us?"

"Of course," Rachel said and both girls followed. All of them clasped hands and bowed heads.

"Father, we come to You in the name of our Lord Jesus," Shalimar said. "Please protect Dale, wherever he is, and bring him safely back to Marie. And, Lord, give her the assurance she needs. She's been hurt by so many people in her lifetime. All of those who were close to her have hurt her so much, and she's lost the ability to trust. Help her to grasp just how much Dale really does love her, and heal the hurts of the past so she can go on to fully enjoy the present. Amen."

"Amen," three echoes came.

Her heart already lighter, Marie looked up to thank Shalimar and caught sight of her mother standing in the doorway watching them.

"Mom?"

An expression of hurt on her face, her mother turned and hurried away.

Chapter 7

The sergeant dropped Dale off at a fast-food restaurant near the boundary line of Sunnydale with a parting line of, "Next time be more careful who you catch a ride with."

At his tongue-in-cheek statement, Dale gave a wry nod. "Yeah, you can bet I'll do just that, sir."

"Congratulations on your wedding. Hope you make it home in time."

"Thanks for giving me that chance. I hope so, too."

As the squad car pulled away, the sergeant lifted his hand in a casual wave, which Dale returned. Well, that went better than he'd expected. Now what?

Frustrations of the day had taken a toll on his stomach, creating a gnawing emptiness. He needed a quick bite before he could figure out the next step. He decided to buy a hot dog for the road. With the change, maybe he could hunt up a pay phone and call Todd again to come and get him. He wasn't taking any more chances at accepting rides from strangers, that was for sure.

The restaurant was empty of customers, and in no time, he returned outside, cradling his hot dog while bringing it to his mouth and taking a bite as he walked. He loved mustard but didn't want to risk spilling any on his crisp white shirt, so he ate it plain.

A horn honked not ten feet behind him. He almost choked on the bite he'd just swallowed and nearly dropped his soda.

"Hey, Dale—that you?"

Relief whistled through him when he turned and saw Mac Avery. Dale often took his car to Mac's garage for repairs.

"I can't tell you how good it is to see you." Dale strode toward the driver's side. Mac had just exited the drive-thru and regarded Dale through his rolled down window.

"Pretty spiffy duds you got on there."

"Yeah. Listen, can you give me a ride to my church?"

"Sure thing. I came into Millbury for some parts, but I'm headed back home now."

"Great. Those are some of the best words I've heard all day." Dale hurried around to the passenger side and slid into the car.

"That wind sure is picking up speed," Mac said, popping a french fry into his mouth.

"Yeah." Dale smoothed the hair out of his eyes, glad to be out of the gust, which had picked up velocity in the past ten minutes.

"So what brings you way out here, dressed like that, and why're you on foot?"

Dale couldn't blame Mac for being curious. Once more the story of his morning came out, between his polishing off his hot dog and drink.

"Wheeeeww." Mac let out a long whistle. "Sounds like one of them cornball romance movies my girlfriend likes to watch. The kind where reality takes a loooong vacation," he added with a grin.

Dale couldn't agree more. The day seemed like one never-ending Technicolor nightmare, even if it had been studded with its strange, almost comical moments.

Minutes of relaxed silence passed. Beneath the hood, a sudden *clunkety-clunk* rattled the car.

"Uh-oh." Mac studied the gauges. "I need to pull over."

They had left all buildings far behind, and Dale looked along the deserted stretch of road they were on now. "What's wrong?"

"She just needs a little fixin' up. I spend so much time working on other people's cars, I'm afraid I haven't paid the attention I should to my own."

"You're kidding." Dale couldn't believe this was happening.

"Not to worry. I can fix 'er up so she'll get us home. Carburetor just probably needs a whack or two."

A *whack* or two? This was the man he'd entrusted with his car?

"I plan to spend all Saturday working on her."

Which didn't help matters now; still, if Mac hadn't been in Millbury for parts, Dale wouldn't have gotten this far. That is, if they both didn't end up needing to hoof it.

God, please, please, please. . .I know I said on the road earlier that I made mistakes from the moment I opened my eyes this morning, and I probably deserve this whole miserable day. But Marie doesn't. I love her and don't want her to suffer for my stupidity. Please, God, just get me to the church before it's time for her to walk down the aisle. That's all I ask.

❧

With twenty minutes till curtain time, Marie felt restless. If Dale didn't show, it would be curtains for him. No. . .she took a deep breath and let it out slowly, ousting the thought with it. Knowing Ben as she did, she doubted Dale was to blame for the present set of circumstances. Though maybe an *n*th of the blame was his. Still, after Shalimar's prayer, Marie had calmed somewhat and was ready to forgive, even if his actions didn't make sense. Ben, too, though forgiving him would prove harder. What was important was that she knew Dale had tried to reach her, even leaving Ben's vehicle in an attempt to get home.

Her gaze traveled around the parking lot full of cars. Hearing a distant rumble, she looked to the sky and frowned. Deciding she wanted a closer view, even if she was decked out in her wedding gown and veil and someone might see her, she left the window and bypassed her bridesmaids, who were finishing up last-minute preps to hair and face. She headed toward the hallway that led to the rear door.

"Where are you going?" Shalimar asked.

"I just want to check on something."

She sensed her bridesmaids behind her as she opened the door that led to the back parking lot. The hot, sticky air held an electric sort of waiting current, as unusual as the yellow and grayish-green cast to the dark clouds.

"Whoa," Rachel said. "I've seen that kind of sky before."

So had Marie. She hadn't heard Sunnydale was supposed to get hit with inclement weather, but then she hadn't listened to the forecast this morning in her rush to get to the church.

"Whose car is that, the one driving into the parking lot?" Rachel asked.

"I don't know, but it sure is a clunker," Shalimar said. "Just listen to the rattling of that engine."

Marie turned her head to look. As the car came closer, her heart jolted to a stop, then beat with a frenzy. "It's Dale!"

Without thinking twice, she grabbed the sides of her skirt and flew down the two steps to meet him as he exited the passenger side of the car and waved thanks to whoever sat inside. The car drove off.

"I'm so glad to see you!" Marie threw herself into Dale's arms, holding him tightly. She buried her face against his coat, then wrinkled her nose and pulled her head away. "You smell like a barnyard." Her words were curious, but she didn't release her hold from around him now that she finally had him there with her.

"Probably because of Myrtle." His own arms tightened around her waist and he dropped a kiss to her lips. "I can't tell you how good it is to be with you again. I never thought I'd make it."

Marie's mind remained stuck on the first track. "Myrtle?"

"The goat I rode with. My first ride." The expression in his eyes softened. "You sure look beautiful."

She blinked at his answer of a goat and dropped her gaze to his tuxedo.

Her eyes widened. "What happened to your tie—it's in shreds!"

"Myrtle got hungry. I already plan to get another tie from one of my groomsmen. For me to go without one might not look so good since I'm the groom, but I think it would be okay for Todd." He looked beyond her and nodded. "Hello, Mrs. O'Brien."

Marie barely noticed that her mom now stood in the doorway, she was so busy taking inventory of his appearance. "Your shirt!" She looked agape at what seemed to be a splotch of black grease covering the ruffles on his chest, near the buttons.

"Mac—the guy who brought me here—had car trouble. I helped him so we could get here faster. See, I did make it in time, Marie. I promised you I would, though for a while there I gotta admit I wasn't sure it was gonna happen."

A smile colored his voice, but she had pulled away to look down even farther. Her eyes widened. "And what happened to your slacks?" A huge brown stain covered one pant leg.

He looked down, too. "Oh, that. Janie—my second ride—was speeding and took a turn too fast. Her shake dumped all over me. I guess I should have cleaned up in jail, but they didn't give me a chance."

"Jail!" Dazed, she shook her head. "You were in *jail?*"

"Oops. I wasn't going to admit that one, at least not yet. It's kind of a long story, and I'll tell you the whole thing after the wedding. Promise. It'll be my third time to tell it today." His mouth suddenly dropped open. "My shoes! Oh, man, I left my good shoes and my other clothes in Mac's car." He darted a look toward the church entrance, where Mac had long since driven off, and groaned. His eyes reminded her of a hopeful little boy as he turned back to face her.

"Would you mind too much if I married you in my white sneakers?"

With a slight disbelieving shake of her head, Marie smiled. Once, his question would have made her upset, but now she was just so glad to see him she didn't care if he wore neon orange flip-flops.

Before she could open her mouth to tell him so, a warning siren shrieked through the air, startling them. They both shot a look to a heavy cloud a few miles away, its dark bottom boiling and writhing, and saw a vortex had formed. With an eerie, loud hissing, the funnel crooked a gray finger toward the earth in their direction. Standing as if she'd been turned to a statue, Marie could only stare in horror.

Chapter 8

Take cover—everyone!" Dale called, at the same time grabbing Marie's wrist and running with her. About fifty yards away, the storm shelter entrance stood behind the church, a basement with no windows. They followed the others over the spongy lawn toward it. But Dale could see that with Marie's awkward dress and high heels, they weren't going to make it in time. A shallow ditch lay to the side, near the fringe of trees flanking the property. He pulled her along with him, then pushed her down into the ditch at the same time throwing himself on top of her, to protect her as much as he could.

Crazed lightning flashed across the sky like continuous flashbulbs popping. Thunder rumbled and the rain beat down hard. What sounded like a thousand freight trains approaching at full speed invaded his ears. Still he could hear Marie softly cry beneath him, "Please, God. Save us!"

Silently Dale added his own petition, turning his face to her neck and hair, covering the back of her head with his hand and arm as much as he was able. Small sticks and papers flew in a crazy dance all around them. A soda can shot high into the air, lifting, lifting. Something hard struck his leg, bruising it, but he didn't think the injury was major. The wind stung his eyes, and he shut them tight. His ears, however, couldn't be protected from the cacophony. Glass shattered. Metal groaned. Wood creaked and gave. Marie let out a yelp of pain, and Dale assumed the only reason he could hear it was because his ear was so close to her mouth.

Please, God, protect Marie. Don't let any harm come to her. Let us have a chance at a life together. Please. God, she means the world to me. He'd never realized just how true that was until today.

Dale wasn't sure if seconds or minutes passed—all measure of time seemed to be sucked up in the maelstrom—but as suddenly as it started, the wind died down to nothing and calm returned. Opening his eyes, Dale sucked a breath into his lungs then crawled off Marie. The tornado had sped off in a northeasterly course through a cornfield, now miles away from them.

"You okay?" His gaze assessed and took inventory as he helped pull her

149

to a sitting position. A smudge of dirt covered her cheek, and an angry red scratch raced across her neck. Her face was almost white, her eyes huge, like dark smudges, but she moved easily and Dale didn't think he'd done any real damage.

"Just a little bruised, I think," she whispered.

"Sorry for tackling you."

"Are you kidding?" She pressed her fingers against his jaw. "You saved my life."

He helped her climb out of the ditch, and together they surveyed the damage. Torn-up earth to their right showed where the twister had touched down and run a path not fifty feet from where they stood. Cars in the parking lot had been pushed against each other by the force of the mighty wind. About a hundred feet away, a yellow rocking chair stood upright in the middle of the field. A tree was missing, and others had been uprooted and lay on their sides.

With relief, Dale noticed that the church stood like a harbor, rock solid and strong, with only a back window broken. He moved with Marie toward the building. Guests filtered into the parking lot, some acknowledging the wedding couple, all going to check out the damage to their cars and town or observe the retreating tornado, which, as Dale watched, was suddenly sucked back up into the clouds. *Thank God.*

Marie's mom came hurrying out the storm shelter door, her gaze spinning frantically around. When she saw Marie, she took off at a run toward her and pulled her into her arms.

"Oh, my baby," she softly cried, repeatedly sweeping her hand down Marie's wet veil as though it were her hair. "I was so worried."

"I'm okay, Mom. Really."

Dale heard the surprise in Marie's voice. He knew she'd never thought her mother loved her all that much. Not wanting to spend a moment away from his fiancée's side, but deciding the women needed time alone, he laid his hand upon Marie's shoulder and gently squeezed.

"I'm going to join the others and check out the damage," he said. "There might be some who need my help. I need to find Mom, too. I saw her head for the shelter, so I'm sure she's okay. But I'm not leaving the immediate area without telling you first, just so you know."

Still cradled in her mother's arms, Marie gave him a sideways glance of gratitude, her eyes shining with love for him, her smile trembling, soft.

Dale forced himself to leave her and walked off, then stopped in his tracks. His brother approached from across the street, waving his video camera in his hand. Dale walked faster to close the distance between them.

"You look like you've been through it," Ben said in greeting. "Should have stuck with me. I told you I'd get you back in time."

Dale thought it best not to answer.

"Got some great footage. Who woulda thought I'd capture a tornado practically in my own backyard? An F-2 unless I miss my guess."

"Yeah, who woulda thought? Guess we never would have had to leave Sunnydale after all." Dale's tone came across borderline curt. Catching sight of his petite mom gathered in a circle with some other women, he felt a moment's relief to see she was okay.

Ben hung his head, sheepishly. A character trait that didn't fit his devil-may-care brother at all. "Listen, I'm sorry about this morning. I really didn't think you'd bail on me like you did. You must love her a lot to do something that crazy."

"Yeah, I do." Dale regarded his brother. Ben had never experienced true love with a woman, the heart-bonding kind, so he couldn't understand what Dale felt for Marie. Dedicated to bachelorhood, Ben often told Dale he'd rather go through the years as a hermit than be chained to one woman for eternity. Yet now a wistful sound edged his words, leading Dale to believe that all was not as it appeared and Ben's former declarations didn't match what he really wanted.

"So, am I still your best man?" Ben spoke the words in jest, but his expression remained serious.

Ben had put him through a lot of misery today, but he was still family. Dale clapped a hand to Ben's far shoulder and gave him a quick one-armed hug. "Sure, but the tornado might make us have to postpone again. I just don't know right now what's what."

"You've had to do that a lot, haven't you? Postpone."

"Yeah. More's the pity."

Ben nodded twice, as if preoccupied, then looked Dale straight in the eye. "Truth is, I thought maybe those other times you got cold feet and were looking for ways out."

"Nothing doing. I don't want a way out." Ben's admission shocked Dale. If his own brother who'd known him a lifetime thought that, then it wasn't so surprising Marie also had doubts concerning Dale's feelings. "I love Marie so much, sometimes it hurts. This may sound corny, but she's what makes my world go round."

"I think I'm actually beginning to envy you." Ben's eyes were dead serious.

"Someday you'll find the right woman. You just have to keep your eyes open. And now and then it's better keeping your mouth shut, too," he added, only half joking.

Ben shrugged and the two men continued to walk across the parking lot strewn with branches and other debris. The tornado siren had quit, only to be replaced by other sirens of emergency vehicles in the distance. They met up with a few wedding guests, and Dale was surprised to see one of the bridesmaids, Rachel, on the opposite side of the street, squatting down to offer aid to a young girl. A thin line of blood marred the girl's pale forehead, against which Rachel blotted a handkerchief. Dale approached, his brother in tow. Rachel looked up, glad to see him.

"Dale! Good. Can you take over?"

"Sure." Dale dropped down on one knee in front of the wounded teen and quickly surmised that she was in emotional shock, evidenced by her dilated pupils, irregular breathing, and the pallor of her face. Her hair dripped with rain; her eyes dripped with tears. She looked no more than fourteen years old.

"I w—was just out riding my bike," the girl said in shuddering monotone, "when I heard the tornado come. I jumped off my bike and h—hid behind that tree. My bike's gone. I coulda been on it." Her voice rose, trembled.

Hiding behind a tree wasn't a good safety measure, but Dale knew it was more important to keep the girl calm rather than give her constructive criticism. "You're okay. Soon I'll have you fixed up and you'll feel even better. This is what I do for a living. Fixing up people. So you're in good hands."

A smidgen of relief touched the girl's eyes and the weak smile she gave him.

"What's your name?" Dale asked.

"M—Monica."

"And are your parents home, Monica?"

"No, they're both at work."

Rachel stood. "Anything more I can do to help?"

"Yeah. Go ask Pastor if he has a first aid kit. And call this in while you're at it. Right now the emergency team will have their hands full meeting the needs of the community, but we should still report this. Also, be sure and tell them an EMT is at the scene but without equipment. Bring back plenty of water and cups. You can pass those out to anyone who needs it."

"Gotcha." Rachel turned to go.

"I'll come with you," Ben offered. "You'll need help carrying all that."

Surprised, Dale glanced at his brother. He couldn't help but notice the spark of interest between the bridesmaid and the bachelor, and smiled, then turned to the wounded teenager, all the while speaking to her in light, reassuring tones as he did his job.

"He's a good man."

Marie turned from studying the damage to the property, knowing she needed to go help, too, but not sure where her efforts could best be used. She stared at her mother in surprise, noting her expression looked both sincere and uneasy.

"I mean it, Marie. Any man who'd go through all Dale did to be here today deserves an award. You're blessed to have him." She lowered her gaze to her polished nails, running her thumb along their edges. "I wasn't always a perfect mother. I'm not sure I was even a good one. I'm often hypercritical of people and the way they do things."

Flabbergasted by her mom's confession, Marie scrunched her brow in uncertainty. "Why are you saying all this?"

"I heard that prayer Shalimar prayed over you, and I know your friends must feel the same way you do."

"Mom—"

"No, let me finish." Her stance grew more fixed, bolder. "When your father walked out on us, I was hurt, barely able to cope. But I was wrong to speak of him the way I did—and in front of you. After hearing Shalimar's prayer, I realize now the mistakes I made."

"I'm not sure I understand."

"Honey." Her mother took gentle hold of her upper arms then dropped her hands back to her sides as if unsure. "Trust is earned, and Dale has more than done that by his actions today. But people still make mistakes—he'll make mistakes. I'll make mistakes. You'll make mistakes. No one's perfect. You can't judge others' love for you by one failure, or even two. I guess you're not really supposed to judge them at all." She gave a careless little sniffle, blowing air through her nose. "I'll admit, I was hurt when I heard Shalimar and your friends talk about how all those closest to you have hurt you. I suppose I never cared for Shalimar because you left home to move in with her, despite my objections. And I've made no bones about that. But I can see she's a good friend for you. I'm glad you have her."

"Thanks, that means a lot to me." Marie had never heard her mother unload like this.

"I'm just sorry that you don't feel you can trust me now, that you're afraid I'll pounce on you or put Dale down. Otherwise you wouldn't have felt the need to withhold from me the information about Dale's problems in getting here today." At Marie's gasp of surprise, her mom explained. "I overheard two girls talking in the restroom about your uncle going to look for Dale, and one warned the other not to let me know. When I really thought about what they'd said, I saw Shalimar was right. In my own pain, I wounded you and made you an enemy. And for that I'm sorry."

"Never an enemy, Mom." Not sure how else to respond, Marie gave a helpless shrug. "But it's okay. I know you had a hard time of it in those days."

"No, it's not okay, and I shouldn't have excluded you after I married Henry, either. I never meant to; it was just such a new life, being a lawyer's wife, with new responsibilities. Everything had to be so perfect, entertaining his friends, throwing parties, and I didn't have the time I used to have—"

"Mom, it's okay. Really." Marie wasn't sure how much more she could handle before she collapsed into a pool of tears filled by hurts of the past.

"You're right." Mom sighed. "Today's your wedding day. I shouldn't be dumping all this on you."

"I sincerely doubt the wedding's still on." Marie wondered how her mom could even think such a thing, in the wake of what just happened.

Her mother looked around as if just noticing the area had been hit by a tornado approximately ten minutes ago. "Oh, right. I guess this does put a damper on things. Maybe tomorrow will work out better for you."

Marie couldn't help but smile. Mom might be overcritical at times and somewhat unrealistic, but she did have a good heart. Moving forward, Marie gave her a quick hug.

"What was that for?" Astonishment widened her mom's eyes.

"Just because." Her smile matched her mom's. "I'm really glad you're my mother." She sobered. "But now I guess I should pitch in and see what I can do to help. I'll need to change clothes first. Can you help me out of this dress?"

"Of course." Her mom looked pleased that Marie had asked, and Marie felt a twinge of remorse for excluding her from helping to plan the wedding. At the time, Marie had thought her mom wouldn't be interested.

In the bridal room, Marie went through the cumbersome task of removing all her finery, soaked and heavy from the rain, then dried off and donned her casual clothes. Five minutes later, as her mom hung up the wedding gown, Marie headed to the door. A tap sounded on the outside before she reached it.

"Marie? You in there?"

At the sound of Dale's voice, she opened the door, a smile rising to her lips. Even with his tuxedo grimy, his tie a tattered mess, and his whole appearance more rumpled than when he'd arrived at the church, he was candy to her eyes.

"Can I talk to you alone for a minute?" He pointedly looked at her mom, smiled.

She returned it. "You two go on. I just want to hang these things up so they don't wrinkle any more than they already are. And I'd like to try to see what I can do about getting those dirt stains out. You both have a lot to discuss, I'm sure."

Marie silently agreed. Today's entire experience had taught her a hard lesson. She needed to say what had been running through her mind while she'd changed clothes, no matter how difficult it was for her. For Dale, she must do what was right.

Chapter 9

As they walked to the rear door, Dale looked at Marie. "We do have a lot to discuss, don't we?" They stepped outside. The sun made a weak entrance through the gray clouds, as if struggling to regain its throne. The faint shimmering rays felt welcome.

"Yes. I'm so grateful for the man you are and for your love. I love you so much, Dale."

His brows arched. "Then you're not mad about earlier? About all this?" He waved a hand around the area.

"Well, of course I'm not happy we got hit with a tornado, but it's helped me to see things a lot more clearly. Blew away some of the cobwebs, so to speak."

"Oh? How's that?"

She faced him and took hold of both his hands. "I realize now that sometimes I've blown things out of proportion and been too structured, believing everything has to go a certain way for it to succeed or hold any special meaning. I've learned today that outside influences can and do interfere, and anything less than my expectations doesn't necessarily mean a person is unworthy of my trust. Or my love."

"Wow. You learned all that through a twister?"

She laughed. "You bet." Despite the circumstances, she felt strangely lighthearted, as if removed from what was happening around her. For the first time she understood the term about being at peace even in the midst of a storm, or in this case, the aftermath of one.

"Know what I learned?"

She lifted her brows expectantly.

"Never wear a tuxedo till you get to the church. Never ride with hungry farm animals, and never, under any circumstances, get in a car that has speedway racing stickers plastered all over the back bumper."

She chuckled. "I can't wait to hear about your morning, and I know we need to talk, but shouldn't we go help the others?" Marie wanted to avoid what she had to say as long as possible.

"No need to. Except for that girl I just bandaged up, no one else was hurt in the area. Damage is minimal—not counting that big field over there, which apparently is the main path the twister took. Only a farmhouse and barn got smashed, a few roofs got ripped off, but from what we and others have learned, all other buildings are standing and there are no fatalities."

"Oh Dale, that's wonderful. Praise the Lord for that!"

"I also talked to Pastor Carmichael. He's eager to go ahead with the ceremony. Truth is, now that he's finally got us here, I don't think he wants to let the opportunity slip by again, tornado or no tornado." One side of Dale's mouth crooked upward. "Since the church is still standing, and the guests for the most part have stayed, I second the motion. Let's get married."

She blinked, stared. "You're kidding, right?"

"I've never been more serious in my life."

"But our clothes!" She thought about the dirt and grass staining her skirt. Her veil was also torn. Cynthia did have a blow dryer, which could dry the material, as well as her ruined hairstyle, but surely Dale was joking.

"We can get cleaned up, and what we can't clean we'll ignore. I'll trade ties with Todd. Or we can switch to our street clothes. I really don't care what we wear, so long as I get to spend the rest of my days with you. When I thought I wouldn't be here in time, I felt sick inside, since you'd told me this was my final chance at tying the knot."

His words made her prickle with guilt and reminded her of what needed to be said. "Dale, about that. I'm sorry. I was just upset. I didn't mean it. I'll wait, as long as you need me to. I was wrong to give you an ultimatum, and I feel we should postpone the wedding to a day when you're ready, too. The last thing I want is to make you feel pushed into doing this."

"But I am ready, and I don't want to wait." His eyes twinkled, and Marie's heart gave a little lurch. Whenever he got that look, she knew to prepare herself for a shock.

He took hold of her left hand—and dropped to one knee, staring up at her.

"Dale, what are you doing?" She tried to pull her hand from his, but he tightened his hold. She looked around self-consciously, glad to see everyone was too busy to pay attention to them.

"Something I should've done long ago, and you reminded me I never did do." With his other hand, he gently covered hers that he clasped. "Marie, you're the wind beneath me and what keeps me going when I want to give up and quit. You're the reason I get up in the morning, hoping to spend time with you, to see your face. I've loved you ever since high school, and I'll go on loving you until all our hair goes gray or falls out or both."

Shyness gone, she bit back a smile. His poetic words touched her, and his inborn, inadvertent humor drew her to him all the more.

He shook his head slightly. "You know what I mean. Marie, if I have to go through another day like this without you, I'll go nuts. But with you beside me, as a part of me, I can tackle anything. Say you'll marry me. Today. Now."

She studied the sincere hopefulness shining from his clear eyes, the slackness of his expression as he waited, his faint smile. His wasn't the most eloquent of proposals, but it was all she desired and a symphony to her ears. Time schedules, a myriad of details to be met, flawless attire—none of that seemed to matter anymore. She, like most other women, had always longed for the perfect wedding, but how better to describe perfection than it being all about true love? The joining of two hearts and souls as one, in and through Christ Jesus—that was all that truly mattered. The rest were just little extras, here one day, gone the next. But their love was big and would last a lifetime. She no longer had any doubts about that.

"Yes," Marie whispered. "I'll marry you whenever you'd like."

Dale quickly stood to his feet and enfolded her in his arms. From behind, they heard Dale's twelve-year-old cousin say to someone, "Um, am I missing something here? Isn't that why we came today, 'cause they're gettin' married?"

Dale laughed, Marie with him, and both turned to look at his two young cousins who'd come up behind them. "Right you are, Donna," Dale enthusiastically agreed. "And thank God He got me to the church on time!"

⋙⋘

Reception in full swing, Marie heard Dale groan when Ben approached the microphone. He aimed a few jokes about the "three-times-is-a-charm wedding" at his younger brother, who took them well. He then spoke of what a great guy Dale was and how blessed he was to have Marie, wishing both of them a good life. Before Marie had a chance to recover from that shock, Ben dedicated the next song to his "newly-wed, but never-thought-we'd-get-there brother," a look of mischief on his face. The musicians grinned the wedding couple's way and began playing the rousing old show tune from *My Fair Lady*, "Get Me to the Church on Time."

"Why are you smiling like that?" Dale asked Marie, his smile just as wide.

"Am I smiling?" She slid a forkful of bridal cake between his lips and chuckled when the white and lilac frosting smeared the corner of his mouth. With her cake napkin, she brushed it away. "Your brother really isn't such a bad guy. I noticed Rachel seems to think so, too." She glanced to where the couple was dancing in a comical way. Ben was no dancer like Rachel, who'd taken both tap and ballet, but she was laughing at his antics, going along with all the awkward spins and fast twirls he led her into.

"Yeah, pretty amazing how fast they honed in on one another."

Marie studied Dale. "But to answer your question, I've been replaying those words we spoke: 'to love and to honor, in sickness and health, forsaking all others as long as we both shall live.'"

"I do."

"So do I." She didn't think she could be any happier than right at that moment. A third of the guests had needed to leave, to check on their homes and families, but those out-of-towners who hadn't been personally affected by the tornado had stayed. As well as those who'd called their homes and neighbors to learn all was well. And all was well.

Despite the storms that blew their way, she had finally married the man of her dreams. The third time really was the charm. And so much more had happened in these past hours, as if God was mending the tears in Marie's life, just as the people would soon clear away the debris and put their town in order again.

Before the ceremony, which had taken place a little less than an hour ago, her mom fixed Marie's torn veil with her handy travel sewing kit. As she'd sewn the gauzy strips back together, both women talked as if they were old friends. In those twenty minutes, Marie felt closer to her mom than ever before. Even Henry called on her mom's cell to wish her a happy wedding, a gesture that stunned Marie. And strangely enough, though the women were different in personality, Dale's mom and Marie's mom were getting along as if they'd been best friends for life. Marie looked over the reception hall to the far table where they, along with another interested guest, pored over childhood photographs of the bride and groom from the albums they'd each brought from home.

"I cringe to think what pictures Mom might have put in there," Dale said, following Marie's gaze. "I guess I should've checked to see if they passed inspection first."

"You were a beautiful baby," she soothed. "I loved the picture of you all muddy from the creek with only your Snoopy boxers on."

Dale groaned. "She put that in there?" He looked at his tux, which he'd cleaned up as best he could but which still bore faint traces of grease on the shirt. "Guess I haven't changed all that much," he said wryly. "I'm still a mess."

Marie thought him the most handsome man at the reception. "To tell the truth, I hardly noticed."

They stared deeply into one another's eyes, a message that couldn't be vocalized linking them, heart to heart. The band switched to a slower song, and Marie smiled. "They're playing what they did when we first auditioned them."

"So, beautiful, you wanna dance?"

"With my favorite guy in the whole world? I'd love to."

On the ballroom floor, Marie linked her arms around Dale's neck while he did the same to her waist. Slowly they swayed as one and stared at one another, nearly oblivious of the other couples dancing around them.

"I still can't believe you went through so much to get back here today," Marie said softly. "What made you keep it up and not quit, Dale? Even if it was just about what I said last night, that was a lot for one person to go through. I probably would've given up after the goat ate my tie."

"I almost did give up, in jail, but I just couldn't do it. This was too important. You're too important." He snuggled her closer, pressing his forehead to hers. "You never pushed me into marriage, Marie. I went into it with my eyes wide open." He grinned. "I guess you could say I was blown away by love."

His words made her feel alive, yet at the same time cosseted in dreamlike softness, and she looked up at him in adoration.

The sudden sound of the guests' spoons clinking against crystal glasses in unison made Marie's face warm as she realized what this particular wedding custom meant. The ringing continued, other spoons joining in the clinking, as everyone there eyed them in expectation.

Dale smiled. "They're asking us to do something."

"Yes."

Anticipating the moment, Marie turned her face upward as Dale lowered his mouth to hers in a warm, tender kiss. The guests applauded and a few whistled through their teeth. Yet, lost in each other, neither Marie nor Dale paid the slightest bit of attention to them.

Wrong Church, Wrong Wedding
By Loree Lough

Chapter 1

B reena winced as her heels click-clacked against the polished marble. If she had arrived on time, her footsteps would have blended with the rest of the pre-wedding din. Grabbing the first available seat—on the aisle, second pew from the back—she heaved a relieved sigh and sat. *This is the lumpiest cushion I've ever. . .*

" 'Scuse me, miss," drawled the tall stranger beside her, "but you're sittin' on my Stetson."

As the flush of embarrassment heated her cheeks, Breena handed the flattened black felt hat to him.

"Well," he said, turning it this way and that, "it used to be my Stetson. . . ."

"I-I'm so sorry. I never even saw it. I. . ."

He shot her a playful half grin. "It's all right." As if to prove it, the cowboy winked. "I was thinkin' of gettin' me a new one, anyway."

A white-gloved hand reached up from behind and tapped his shoulder. "You're a guest in the house of the Lord, for goodness' sake," an elderly woman warned. "Show some respect and *be quiet!* "

Like a little boy caught with his hand in the cookie jar, he shot Breena an "uh-oh, we're in trouble now!" expression and dutifully faced forward. She did the same as her seatmate tried unsuccessfully to reshape his mangled headpiece.

This has definitely not *been your day, Breena Pavan!*

First, her hair dryer's motor blew up, forcing her to let her short dark curls air dry. Then the power went out altogether, and she had to apply her makeup by the light of the tiny bathroom window.

She was halfway to the church when she realized she'd left the wedding gift on the hall table, and on the way home to get it, her right front tire decided to go flat.

She had managed to get the spare on without incident, but as she tucked the jack back into the trunk, her knee brushed the license plate, snagging her panty hose. She might have made it to the church on time. . .if that *first* drugstore had carried anything other than leotards.

Unfortunately, things had started going wrong long before she got out of bed this morning. Take yesterday, for example, when she realized she'd misplaced the invitation to Todd and Sandra's wedding. It had taken several phone calls to find someone who knew when and where her old school chums would be getting married. "One o'clock, St. John's," Todd's harried sister had said.

Breena glanced at her watch. Unless it had suddenly gone the way of her hair dryer, she was only ten minutes late. No one seemed to have noticed her tardiness, and once she had a chance to replace the cowboy's hat, all would be right with the world again.

At least, as right as *her* world could be. . . .

She settled back and listened to the preacher's clear voice, reverberating from every rafter in the cavernous wood and marbled space as he read from Genesis: " '. . .she shall be called Woman, because she was taken out of Man. Therefore shall a man leave his father and his mother, and shall cleave unto his wife: and they shall be one flesh. . . .' "

The bride and groom exchanged vows, shared their first kiss as man and wife, and turned to face the congregation. She hadn't realized Todd was so tall. *And when did Sandra put on all that weight around her middle?* The church had been decorated with white roses and daisies, and gigantic pink satin bows hung from the end of each pew. *If I ever have a wedding*, Breena thought dreamily, *I hope it's as pretty as this one.*

As the congregation stood, the newlyweds linked arms and proceeded up the aisle toward the back of the church. It wasn't until they drew near that Breena realized. . .

. . .they weren't Todd and Sandra!

It had never occurred to her to ask Todd's sister *which* St. John's. . . .

She hung her head and closed her eyes. *Only* you *could end up at the wrong wedding.*

But why should she be surprised? Ever since she'd attended that faith rally with her college roommate, it seemed that nothing concerning religion had gone right for Breena. She slumped onto the seat and hid her face in her hands.

The cowboy sat down beside her. "Are you all right?"

Breena shook her head. *No*, she answered silently, *I most certainly am not all right. In fact, there's so much wrong with me, it'd take a ream of paper to list everything that. . .*

"Can I get you anything? Tissue? Water, maybe?"

Again, she shook her head.

"Please," she heard him tell the folks on his other side, "feel free to step around us; seems the lady's feelin' a mite dizzy. . . ."

She felt humiliated, embarrassed. . .but dizzy? *Well, going to the wrong church* was *a dizzy thing to do. . . .*

"I noticed you came in alone," the cowboy said. "Same here. Something came up, and my date had to cancel at the last minute."

If she didn't know better, Breena would have said he was gearing up to ask *her* to replace his date! But why would he do that, when she'd mashed his hat and gotten him scolded?

"We could go in my car, pick yours up afterward. Or I could follow you, if you'd rather. . . ."

She'd never seen bigger, greener, longer-lashed eyes on a man in her life. A thin streak of bright white gleamed in his coal-black hair. And that mischievous, slanting smile made him *GQ* material, for sure.

"So what do you say?"

Still focused on the dark mustache arching over his lips, Breena licked her own lips. "Um, say? To what?"

Chuckling, he repeated, "To joining me at the reception."

Again the warmth of a blush colored her cheeks. "I, uh, I'm afraid I can't."

Tucking in one corner of his mouth, he shook his head. "Figures."

Blinking, she raised her eyebrows.

"Ain't it just my luck to have a li'l gal who's prettier than the bride sit down next to me. . .and she's already spoken for."

"It isn't that, it's just. . ." *Be quiet, Breena; you sound like a little ninny!* She'd ended up at the wrong place at the wrong time *again,* and now she was gearing up to ramble like a raving lunatic.

She had no business even considering his invitation. He was obviously a devout Christian. She could tell by the way he'd closed his eyes during the ceremony, nodding and whispering "Amen" and "Praise Jesus" when the minister's words touched his heart. With her history, Breena knew better than to involve herself with a man like that.

"I shouldn't be here," she blurted. And for the next five minutes, Breena held his attention as she told him about her erratic, unlucky, unbelievable morning.

"Sounds like my afternoon. . .I suffered a hat-mashing and a tongue-lashing in a five-minute stretch." He grinned. "You look smashing, by the way. . . ."

Breena returned the smile. "So you see," she concluded as if he'd never interrupted, "I'm supposed to be at a different wedding, at a different St. John's."

"Which one?"

It was a simple question that ought to be followed by a simple answer. Breena sighed, knowing full well she had no idea which St. John's Todd and Sandra had been married in. She cast a forlorn glance at her watch. *And they're definitely married by now!* She shrugged one shoulder. "If I knew, I'd. . ."

He tucked in one corner of his mouth and frowned, thoughtfully stroking his thick mustache with thumb and forefinger.

He's probably thinking up a good excuse to make a quick getaway, Breena told herself.

His laughter began gradually, quietly, then bubbled up and boiled over like stew in an unwatched kettle. The delicious sound echoed through the now-empty church, bouncing back to wrap around her like a warm, friendly hug.

"That's some sense of humor you've got there. Ever consider becoming a stand-up comic?"

What would you think if you knew I wasn't joking, Mr. Perfect? she wondered, smiling wryly.

"Sorry," he said, extending a hand. "Forgive my bad manners. The name's Keegan. Keegan Neil."

The way he was pumping her arm up and down, she wouldn't have been at all surprised if water started trickling from her fingertips.

"And you are. . . ?"

"Oh. Um. Breena." She wriggled free of his grasp. "It's nice to. . ."

"Breena," he repeated. "Interesting name. Sounds Irish."

Smiling slightly, she nodded. "My mother was born on the Burren."

"And my ancestors hail from Edinburgh. Breena," he said again.

He had the deep, rich voice of a Galveston radio disc jockey. She'd always been partial to baritones. . .and Southern accents. . . .

"Is it a nickname for Sabrina?"

She shook her head. "Nope. It says 'Breena' on my birth certificate."

"Short and sweet and to the point. Just like its owner." He gave an approving nod. "I like that."

Breena either had a fever or she was blushing.

"This other wedding," he said, interrupting her thoughts, "did the invitation say you could bring a guest?"

"Well, yes, as a matter of fact, it did."

"So the *other* bride and groom are expecting you to show up with an escort?"

Another nod. "I invited a friend, but he woke up with an ingrown toenail."

Keegan's eyes and smile widened. "He. . .*what?*"

She shrugged the other shoulder. "An ingrown toenai—" The merriment on his face told Breena he'd heard her just fine the first time. He couldn't believe such a thing could waylay a man.

"No, really. His toe is all swollen up—twice its normal size," she explained, "and every step is torture. He didn't think he'd be much fun if. . ."

By now, Keegan was wiping tears of mirth from his eyes. Without warning, he placed both hands on her shoulders. "Breena, go with me to the reception. Doesn't matter one whit which one. You choose." Another chuckle popped from his lips. " 'Cause you're the most fascinatin' woman I've met since I left Texas." He paused. "That ain't entirely true, and I can't tell a lie, 'specially not in church." His left eyebrow rose. "You're the most fascinatin' woman I've ever met, *period*."

Before she knew what was happening, Keegan had sandwiched her hands between his.

"Say you'll spend the rest of the day with me. I'll promise not to bite."

If you knew the truth about me, Mr. Good Christian, you wouldn't be so interested in spending one more minute with. . .

Grinning, he jammed the now lopsided Stetson onto his head and poked out his elbow, inviting her to take his arm. "Shall we?"

Breena hesitated, because in truth, she *wanted* to spend more time with him. She tucked her hand into her pocket. He appeared to be a good man, a kind man. She guessed him to be twenty-nine or thirty; his eagerness to get to know her better told her he was probably looking to settle down, raise a family. He needed a good and kind woman, a *Christian* woman to help him accomplish that. And after what happened to her all those years ago in college, well, Breena knew for certain *she* wasn't that woman.

He was still standing there, arm extended, waiting patiently for her response. *He deserves an answer. Deserves far more than that.* "I can't," she said, regretfully.

His tantalizing smile disappeared and both brows dipped low in the center of his forehead. "Why?"

She lifted her chin. "Are you 'born again,' Keegan?"

"Yeah, of course. . . ."

"A steadfast believer?"

He frowned. "I reckon you could put it that way, but I still don't understa—"

"Then you don't belong with the likes of me."

His eyes narrowed. So did his lips. "I hate to repeat myself, but *why?*"

"Because. . ." *Oh, just spit it out, Breena!* "Because a man like you has no business hanging around with someone who's been rejected by God, that's why!" Snatching her purse from where she'd laid it on the pew, Breena left the way she'd entered. . .heels click-clacking across the shining marble floor.

"Breena. Breena, wait. . . ."

Keegan watched helplessly as the door closed behind her.

Rejected, he repeated, scratching his chin, *by God?*

It was a concept he simply couldn't comprehend. He'd been involved in the church for as long as he could remember, and never had anyone said such a thing.

During his elementary school years, Keegan had organized the collection of food to feed needy families at Thanksgiving and Christmas. In high school, he'd helped build a homeless shelter. As a college student, he'd worked with inmates at the state penitentiary. If those men—some of whom had committed murder, rape, armed robbery—could be forgiven their sins, *what in tarnation gives* her *the idea she had been rejected by God?*

Keegan headed for the door, the heels of his boots resounding in the unoccupied chapel. The noise reminded him of the sound her skinny-heeled shoes had made as she'd run away. She had such pretty little feet, such curvy calves. *And the biggest, brownest eyes I ever did see. . . .*

He'd looked evil in the eye enough times in that Texas prison to know a sinner—repentant or otherwise—when he saw one, and—Keegan snorted to himself—*It's not like she killed somebody or somethin'.* Her eyes reflected the bright, sweet soul of a child. Yet there was more. . .something faraway, something sad. . . *Wonder what that's all about?*

Why not ask her? He could look her up in the phone book, give her a call, convince her that no one with eyes like hers could have done anything to cause God to reject her. He could ask her. . .if he'd thought to get her last name.

Still, there was one way he knew he could help her: prayer. Again he pictured her lovely face, her friendly smile, her sparkling eyes, and knew he'd be praying for more than her well being and peace of mind. . .he'd be praying for God to help him find her.

Breena. . . Even her name was lovely. . . .

Something in her had called to Keegan, and something in him had answered. Breena had been in his life for thirty minutes, at best; she'd been gone for perhaps thirty *seconds. . .*

. . .and already he missed her.

Chapter 2

God must have wanted Breena to attend Todd and Sandra's reception. She took a left turn out of the parking lot of the *wrong* St. John's when she should have taken a right, but she didn't realize her mistake until she'd gone about a mile. By now thoroughly frustrated, she tried to take the expressway as a shortcut home, only to get caught in a huge traffic snarl behind an accident. Exasperated, she pulled off at the next exit, and while she was trying to establish her bearings she looked down the street. . . and spied the Chapel of St. John just a few blocks away.

She arrived at the banquet hall a few minutes before the newlyweds, found a seat at a big round table, and did her best to join in the conversation with Todd's neighbors and co-workers. As she pushed a piece of wedding cake— the awful kind, with an unidentified fruit filling and that frosting that leaves a coating of lard on the roof of your mouth—around her plate, her thoughts persistently drifted to Keegan Neil.

❧

Keegan Neil was on her mind again as she climbed the spiral staircase leading from her workshop to the apartment above. Sighing, she hung her purse on a peg in the hall closet and flipped the switch beside the front door. Soft light flooded the room, puddling on pale oak tabletops and washing over the cushiony brown sofas that flanked her floor-to-ceiling fireplace. Breena loved everything about her home, from the panoramic view visible through a row of arched windows to the rough adobe walls where she'd hung her collection of antique lutes and mandolins.

Before she'd rented the property, the upstairs space had been an artist's studio, complete with kaleidoscopic paint spatters dotting the warm hardwood floors. She hadn't scraped them up because she liked the way the multi-hued splashes brightened the otherwise dull boards. Using those drips and drops as her color palette, Breena had matched scatter rugs and throw pillows to the bright shades, giving the open area a lively, eclectic look.

She'd carried the cheery look downstairs and into her workshop, too, coating the trim boards, doors, and windowsills with brilliant enamels.

Breena enjoyed her home, but she relished her work even more. Music—and anything to do with it—had always been her heart's desire. Her love of music had, at the age of ten, inspired her to take apart the battered old piano in her grandmother's back room. Hours after closing the door to that oversized closet, she emerged, eyes shining with victory at having turned an out-of-tune beast into a beautifully singing instrument. Fingers swollen and bruised from struggling with stiff wire and rough wood, she'd placed both hands on her hips and announced her plans for the future to her family: "I'm going to be a piano tuner when I grow up!"

Her parents had exchanged patronizing glances. "Only Breena could say a thing like that," her mother had said. And because of it, Breena had made up her mind right then and there to prove she could do it. She studied hard to reach her goal. The job, her research taught her, involved more than a talent for the keyboard. It required a good ear, physical strength, dexterity. . .and a slightly reclusive nature, since the best tuning work is done in solitude. Not that Breena didn't like chatting with her customers, but in her opinion, the real fun began when the interview ended. She likened being alone with the instruments—and the music they made—to visiting heaven several times a day.

She'd always liked her lifestyle, free to come and go as she pleased, unencumbered by the tethers of a nine-to-five office job, or family, or beaus. Her only responsibilities were to her customers. . .and Hershey.

As usual, the cat leapt from his cozy bed—a threadbare afghan piled on the seat of a bentwood rocker—and padded toward her. The brown-striped tabby wove a figure eight around her ankles, alternately chirping and purring his affectionate greeting. "It's good to see you, too," Breena said, scooping him into her arms.

Digging a fish-shaped treat from a foil-lined pouch, she let him nibble it from her open palm, then stooped to put him back on the floor. "Don't look at me like that," she said, wagging a finger in his direction. "You know the rule: More than one a day and you'll get fat and lazy. And we don't want that, now do we?"

Hershey's hollow-sounding *meow* told her that was *exactly* what he wanted. He looked up at her with big green eyes. . .which reminded her of Keegan.

Keegan Neil. It was a fine, strong name that fit the man well, she thought. But why does the name sound so familiar?

Breena headed for her bedroom, slipped off her heels, and put them on the shoe shelf in her closet. *No point straining your brain trying to remember, because even if he is everything you've ever wanted in a man, you can't have him. Not with your past.*

Breena hung her dress on a padded hanger, shrugged into jeans shorts and a T-shirt, and climbed down the spiral staircase that led to her workshop.

A mahogany baby grand, Breena's pride and joy, dominated the center space. Someday, she hoped to own a home of her own. She could see it in her mind's eye—a two-story Victorian with a covered, wrap-around porch. Through the tall, narrow windows to the right of the red-painted door, folks would be able to view her grandmother's oak dining room table and matching claw-footed chairs.

And the baby grand, placed at an angle, would be visible through the living room windows to the left of the door.

Mind on your work! Breena scolded herself. She turned on the overhead lights with one hand and grabbed her tool bucket with the other. She'd promised to have the little spinet repaired and ready by midweek. *No way you'll make that deadline if you don't get cracking!* The piano needed new wires and hammers before it could be returned to the customer's home for its final tuning.

Pulling on a pair of well-worn leather gloves, she hunkered down and began the arduous task of removing the old strings. The last one hit the floor as the grandfather clock struck twelve. Glancing around her as she got to her feet, Breena chuckled. *You look like some kind of weird bird sitting in a wire nest.*

Yawning and working the kinks from her neck, she put away her tools and headed back upstairs. *First thing tomorrow,* she told herself, *you'll finish that job.*

She wanted to get on to rebuilding the old player piano she'd bought for a hundred dollars at an estate sale a month ago. It would take time to get it up to playing speed. Time, and a myriad of new innards. Patience, she knew, and hard work would turn the miserable old clunker into a sweet-singing instrument that would easily fetch ten times what she'd paid for it. . . .

She stuffed her shorts and shirt in the hamper and, after a quick shower, stepped into her favorite sleepshirt—white cotton and covered with thousands of little black Zs.

Hershey made himself comfortable at the foot of the bed as Breena pulled back the covers. He knew the routine and curled into a comfy ball, blinking as she got onto her knees and folded her hands.

"Dear Lord, I know it must be hard, listening to my petty wishes and concerns. . .feeling as You do about me. . . ." Breena paused, for this had always been the hardest part of her nighttime prayers: Should she continue in the hope that the Lord would accept her as He'd accepted her roommate, as He'd accepted all those other kids that night at the rally, or say a final "Amen" and let God have some peace? Tears filled her eyes as she fluffed her pillow and cuddled into it. *Why am I so inept when it comes to praying!*

Her parents had taken good care of her. Thanks to their tutelage, she knew which fork to use at dinner, how to introduce adults to adolescents, when to speak. . .and when not to. . . . The Pavans had been upstanding members of the community and taught her to be a responsible citizen as well.

But though they'd done themselves proud, feeding and clothing and educating their daughter, they had not seen to her spiritual needs.

Until Breena went away to college, she hadn't been aware she *had* spiritual needs. By contrast, her roommate Melissa seemed filled to overflowing with unbridled Christian joy. When Breena asked her *why* she was always so happy, Melissa had said, in what Breena would soon recognize as her matter-of-fact way, "Because God loves me, of course."

Hope had simmered in young Breena's heart: Could God love her the same way He loved Melissa? But always on the heels of that hope came despair: Why *would* God love her that much? After all, Melissa hadn't been responsible for her own mother's death. . . .

Everyone (except her father) had said it wasn't Breena's fault. But she knew better. It didn't matter that immediately after the funeral, she'd turned her life around. Her mother was still just as dead as if she had continued pulling the adolescent pranks that had distressed her so.

Besides, what had she done lately to earn God's love? She hadn't worked to help feed the poor, or babysat toddlers so their parents could attend Sunday services, or visited people confined to nursing homes, as Melissa had. Why, until her roommate dragged her to Good Faith, Breena had never even set foot in a church!

"Better late than never," had been her new friend's advice.

Cliché or not, it made sense, and Breena began helping as Melissa went about her Christian duties. But even after months of volunteering, Breena sensed something was missing, and she shared her concerns with Melissa.

"Do you pray?" Melissa had asked. "Because the more you pray, the closer you'll feel to God. . . ."

For Breena, talking to the Almighty—even alone in a room—had seemed painfully awkward. He knew better than anyone what she was. . . .

"There's a faith rally this weekend," Melissa had said. "*Dozens* of people are saved every week. I can't believe I didn't think of this before!"

With that memory still bright in her mind's eye, Breena punched her pillow. "Saved, indeed," she muttered. "The only thing 'born again' in me that day was the knowledge that God doesn't want me."

Hershey, confused by Breena's tossing and turning, walked to the head of the bed and touched his nose to hers.

"Good heavens, Hersh, your schnoz is as cold as ice!" she said, grinning despite herself. "Here it is only June, and already I know what to get you for

Christmas: a nose warmer!"

He butted his forehead against hers.

Scratching under his chin, she chuckled. "You sound like a chain saw when you purr like that."

Hershey peered into her eyes, his big green orbs reminding her again of Keegan Neil.

Taking a deep breath, Breena kissed the top of the cat's head. Why Keegan had chosen that moment to pop into her mind, she didn't know. He hadn't even tried to hide his interest in her, a fact that both thrilled and depressed her. "I should have let him come with me to the reception," she told the cat. "One afternoon, watching me in action, and he'd know how wrong we are for each other."

She rolled onto her side and scrunched the pillow under her neck. "Keegan Neil. . .Keegan Neil," she chanted. "Why *does* that name sound so familiar?"

Turning to her other side, Breena began reciting the twenty-third Psalm, hoping it would calm her enough to induce sleep, as it had so often in the past.

But something told her that even after she'd whispered, " 'and I will dwell in the house of the Lord forever,' " the name Keegan Neil—and the man—would still be very much on her mind.

⁂

A shard of bright sunlight seeped under the window shade, angled across the burgundy peonies decorating the rug beneath her bed, and slanted across Breena's face. Throwing an arm over her eyes, she slapped the alarm's snooze button for the second time. "It can't be seven o'clock already," she groaned. Monday mornings were always the worst. She had spent Sunday in her normal routine of reading the paper and drinking coffee, followed by the usual awkward phone call to her father, and then laundry and trying to straighten up to get ready for the week ahead. Occasionally she would think about going to church, but the thought of all those happy faces only made her sad.

Rear end high in the air, Hershey walked his front paws forward and indulged himself in a long, luxurious stretch. After an equally expansive yawn, he sat up straight and stared until Breena said, "Quit lookin' at me like that." Ruffling his fur, she tossed the top sheet aside. "It isn't like you're gonna starve if I don't feed you at the stroke of seven. . . ."

But the stubborn look on his furry face clearly said, "That's what you think!"

Rolling her eyes, Breena gathered him close. "You're good training, Hersh," she added, kissing the top of his head. "If I ever have kids, I'll have the patience of a saint!"

Gently depositing him on the black and white tiled kitchen floor, she started a pot of coffee, and as it brewed, opened a can of cat food for the tabby. "Now,

I have lots to do this morning, so I don't want you pestering me for treats till at least noon. Got it?"

Noisy chomping was his reply. Smiling crookedly, Breena headed back to her room. "If I ever have those kids," she tossed teasingly over her shoulder, "I hope they're more grateful for their meals than you are!"

Half an hour later, showered and wearing capri-length stretch pants and a baggy T-shirt that read "Everyone Wants to Save the Dolphins. . .Who's Gonna Save the *Tuner?*" Breena grabbed her purse and headed for the garden center across town. Ordinarily, she shopped at Papa's Nursery and Crafts just up the road, but the ad in Sunday's paper claimed that the Grand Re-Opening of the newly refurbished That's the Way It Grows was going on from seven a.m. to seven p.m. Any establishment that offered those hours *and* a sale deserved her business.

Leaving her mini-pickup in the gravel lot, Breena headed straight for the hothouse, determined to find something that would thrive in the raised gardens she'd built on her deck. *No petunias!* she cautioned herself; *the ones you planted two weeks ago have already wilted.* Walking up and down the aisles of colorful blooms, Breena stooped now and then to read the care-and-feeding directions of each variety.

It was as she studied the instructions for growing impatiens that a deep Texas drawl said, "I'd invite you to set a spell, but there's not a Stetson in sight. . . ."

Chapter 3

Breena quickly straightened from the impatiens table, wide-eyed and clutching a small pot of pink flowers to her chest.

"Sorry," Keegan drawled, "didn't mean to scare you."

Brushing potting soil from her T-shirt, she put the plastic container back where she'd found it. "It's okay; I'm wearing my sneakers."

His brow furrowed with confusion as his mustache slanted above a half-grin. "Um. . ."

She matched his smile, dimple for dimple. "Well," she explained, "if my shoes hadn't been laced up good and tight, you'd have scared me right out of them."

He chuckled softly. "Sorry," he said again. And then, "You're up and about bright and early. Guess you didn't go to that reception yesterday. . . ."

I could say the same for you, she thought, taking note of his faded jeans, scuffed cowboy boots, and red T-shirt. "Oh, I went. I just didn't stay till the bitter end is all." Sighing, she added, "I have a million deadlines. Seems 'bright and early' is the only time I have to run errands."

His intense scrutiny unnerved her. Tapping a fingertip to her lips, she added, "I wonder where they keep the marigolds?"

He quirked an eyebrow. "*They* keep 'em in the next greenhouse. . ." He pointed to the airplane hangar–shaped building beside them. ". . .with the rest of the sun lovers."

One brow rose on her forehead. "Sun lovers?"

He nodded. "You know. . .plants that need a minimum of six hours of unfiltered sunlight a day?" Gesturing toward the vine-covered ceiling above them, Keegan told her, "These guys in here need plenty of natural light, but no direct sun."

Breena wondered how he knew so much about the subject. *Seems more the cattle branding type to me,* she thought, her gaze traveling from his pointy-toed boots to his callused hands.

Nonchalantly, Keegan plucked a wilting bud from a nearby stem, tossed it onto the bark chip-covered floor, then pressed two fingertips into the pot. Frowning, he called to the teenage girl, stacking wood pallets near the door.

175

"Billie, let that go for now. These guys need water."

"Have hose, will spray," the chubby redhead replied as Keegan returned his attention to Breena.

"You. . .you *work* here? Isn't it a little—"

"Sissified for a cowpoke to trifle with flowers?" The grin above his mustache slanted slightly as his eyebrows twitched once again.

Breena blushed. "I didn't mean—"

"Yes," he said, rescuing her, "I guess you could say I work here."

The redhead stood beside him, with a dripping hose nozzle in one hand and the hose itself in the other. "You want I should water the sun lovers when I'm through in here, Mr. Neil?"

Keegan nodded. "And tell Marcellus to unload that shipment of azaleas the tree farm delivered yesterday. That 'half price' ad ran in this morning's paper, and I have a feeling we're gonna be swamped in a couple hours."

That's where Breena had seen his name. . .in the newspaper advertisement. . . .

Grinning, Billie saluted smartly. "Yessir, Mr. Neil, sir. I'll get right on it, sir."

"You forgot to click your heels," he teased, winking. "Don't let it happen again, or I'll have to dock your pay." Then, "Did Agnes get the checks written?"

"Yessir," the teen said around a giggle, "put the stamps on the envelopes myself, first thing this morning."

"Good." He nodded approvingly. "What about the new schedule?"

"Me an' Agnes worked—"

"Agnes and I. . ."

Breena noted that the girl accepted his correction good-naturedly.

"Agnes and I worked on that after we stuffed the pay envelopes. Agnes thinks you'll probably need to hire two more kids to round out the summer staff."

He raised an eyebrow. "But I thought Marcellus had signed up for a whole slew of summer school courses."

"He did. But he's mostly goin' nights and weekends, remember?" Adjusting the water spray, she turned and began showering the plants behind them. Giggling again, she called over her shoulder, "He loves this place so much, he can't stay away."

From the easygoing atmosphere, it appeared Marcellus wasn't the only one who loved this place.

With a hand on Breena's elbow, Keegan led her farther down the aisle. He tucked in one corner of his mouth. "Kids," he said, shaking his head, "you've just gotta love 'em."

Breena could tell by his easy rapport with Billie that he meant what he said, and she added another item to her quickly growing "Reasons to Like Keegan" register. She noticed the shards of a broken clay pot, lying beneath the flower table. *If you have a lick of sense,* she warned herself, *you'll toss that list before your heart ends up like that. . . .*

"They'll behave responsibly," he continued, "if you give them a chance to prove what they can do, that is. My whole staff is made up of folks under the age of eighteen. . .kids who have had minor altercations with the law, mostly, or whose folks don't do their jobs. . ." Smiling, he nodded toward the office, where Agnes's white-haired head was visible through the opened window. ". . . and kids over sixty-five, of course."

His staff? Breena pictured him the way she'd seen him yesterday in the church, crisp white shirt tucked into sharply-creased trousers that exactly matched the dark flecks in his camel-colored sports coat, highly-polished brown boots, a gold-banded watch on his left wrist. Dressed as he was now, he could easily have been a customer buying petunias for his wife on his way to the hardware store. Though he'd changed his wedding attire for a more casual look, he still stood tall, his broad shoulders and wide stance telling anyone who took the time to look that this was a man who had every reason to feel confident.

Breena took the time to look. . .

. . .at his long, muscular legs and thick upper arms.

. . .at his square jaw and piercing green eyes.

. . .at the streak of snow-white that flashed through his shiny dark hair. *He's too young to be going gray; it's almost like he got hit with a shot of bleach. . . .*

As though he could read her mind, Keegan ran a self-conscious hand through his hair. Feeling a twinge of guilt, Breena bit her lower lip. She hadn't meant to stare.

She turned her attention to the basket of ivy hanging above them. "So tell me," she began, trying to sound nonchalant, "how long have you owned this place?"

He plucked a brown leaf from the plant. Breena frowned inwardly, wondering how he'd spotted it amid the mass of glossy leaves.

"Nearly a year." He glanced around, pocketed both hands, loosed a satisfied sigh. "Inherited it when my granddaddy died. He practically ran it single-handedly and didn't pay much attention to the details those last couple of years. I've been dotting i's and crossing t's and doing *a lot* of clean-up ever since he passed on."

"Your grandfather wasn't from Texas?"

"He was born there. Lived in Lubbock till World War II." Keegan's eyes brightened with a memory. "My grandma was an army nurse and he was a fighter pilot. He got himself shot down, and, well, as they say, 'the rest is history.'" Keegan shrugged as a smile of remembrance tugged at the corners of his mouth. "Nonna's people owned a restaurant in Baltimore, and after the war, the whole Citerony clan settled in Little Italy. Grampa worked hard, saved his money, bought himself a couple dozen acres here in Howard County."

With a jerk of his thumb he indicated a farmhouse in the distance. "Built it himself while he readied the land for planting. Grew Christmas trees, mostly, but he farmed all the usual stuff, too."

Everything about Keegan fascinated her, from his family tree to that streak of white in his dark hair. "The usual stuff?" she asked, pretending to be engrossed in the velvety ruffled leaves of a red-flowering geranium.

"Corn, wheat, soy. . . Had himself a vegetable stand during the summer months and sold salad fixin's to the neighbors."

Breena was beginning to feel like a parrot. "Salad fixin's?"

Trapping its stem between thumb and forefinger, Keegan nipped off a purple and yellow pansy. "Tomatoes, bell peppers, zucchini. . ."

"Oh," she said, fingering the waxy green stalks of a pink begonia, "salad fixin's."

He took a step nearer and tucked the flower behind her ear. "So tell me, Breena, what kind of plants are you in the market for today?"

Was it the perfume of the thousands of blossoms surrounding her, or his nearness that made her head spin? Breena looked into the face so near her own. *It isn't the flowers,* she admitted. *It definitely isn't the. . .*

"Earth to Breena. . .earth to Breena. . . ."

She mirrored his grin. "I need to replace the petunias I bought two weeks ago."

His inquisitive stare prompted her to quickly add, "They died."

"In just two weeks? What'd you do to the poor things?"

Shrugging, she sighed. Not once had she kept a houseplant or a goldfish for more than a few weeks. When she was still living at home, her father had often teased her about it, saying "Some folks have green thumbs; yours must be black, 'cause everything you touch dies!" His nervous chuckle hadn't hidden the fact that his joke wasn't a joke at all. . . .

"I honestly don't know," Breena defended. She didn't like it, but her father's opinion of her was one she'd more or less learned to live with. And why not? After what she'd done, Breena believed she deserved every cutting barb that came out of his mouth! "I watered them every day. Fed them. Made sure. . ."

He crossed both arms over his chest. "Did you stick 'em in the ground, or in a planter?"

"I built a raised bed for them. On my deck. So they'd get plenty of sunshine, and. . ."

He adjusted the pansy he'd stuck behind her ear, reminding her of a doctor, investigating his patient's symptoms during an examination. "Did the blossoms wilt before they fell off?"

"Yes. . ."

"And the greenery turned kinda yellow?" he asked, wrapping his finger with a lock of her hair.

Nodding, Breena wondered if he could hear her heart hammering. *He's certainly standing close enough. . . .*

The same finger gently brushed a wayward curl from her forehead. "Sounds to me like you pampered the poor things to death."

You must look like one of those dashboard doggies, the way you keep nodding.

"I know they don't look it, but petunias are hardy li'l things. A small dose of fertilizer when you put 'em in the ground, water when the soil is almost dry. . .that's all they really need."

She watched as he ran that very busy fingertip across his mustache. There had been just one romantic relationship in her past, and he had been clean-shaven. *I wonder what it would feel like to be kissed by a man with—*

Keegan licked his lips, a prankish grin playing on his face. *Had* it been a thought? Or had she spoken the words aloud? If she *hadn't* said what she'd been thinking, how was she to explain the fact that he seemed to be considering the same idea?

His face loomed nearer and, one hand on her shoulder, whispered in her ear: "Shhh. . .don't move."

Breena's joints locked involuntarily at his soft command.

"Don't be scared. . . ."

Her muscles tightened in response to his warning. Why would she be afraid of a little old kiss?

". . .but there's a spider in your hair. . . ."

Long, thick fingers combed through her locks, and then he said, "Gotcha!"

He stepped back, holding a daddy longlegs between thumb and forefinger. Both brows rose on his forehead as he studied her reaction. "You're not scared of bugs." It was more a statement than a question, and Keegan's admiration was apparent in his voice, his eyes, his smile.

"You act like you expected me to leap onto that bench over there, wringing my hands and squealing like a piglet." Breena laughed at the picture her comment conjured. "Bugs are okay. . .in their own environment." She narrowed one eye and held a fist in the air. "But let one drag its woolly li'l tail into my house, and. . ." With an affirmative nod, she shook the fist, warning any would-be eight-legged intruder what might happen if it dared venture into her world. She pocketed the threatening hand and added in a tiny voice, "I've never been stung, so I'm leery of bees and wasps and things. . . ."

Keegan chuckled quietly. "And mice?"

She furrowed her brow. "What about them?"

"Are you scared of 'em?"

Breena shrugged. "Nah." One brow arched in suspicion. "Why," she asked, grinning, "is there a mouse in my hair?"

"No, but there's one on the floor, right behind you. . . ."

Peering over her shoulder, Breena saw it, wee and white, pink tail flicking, whiskered nose wriggling, front feet pawing at the bark mulch. She got onto her hands and knees for a better look, held out her hand. "What a cutie you are," she cooed. "Whatcha diggin' for?"

From the corner of her eye, Breena spied a calico cat, golden eyes glowing, hunched to pounce.

"Gus," Keegan admonished, "don't even think about it."

The cat sat, flat-eyed and ears back, watching as the minuscule rodent disappeared behind a stack of bagged pea gravel.

Breena scrambled to her feet, dusted the knees of her stretch pants. "Why'd you name her Gus?"

"Because she was a gift from an old girlfriend whose name was Augusta."

There was no explaining the hot flash of jealousy that coursed through Breena's veins. She'd only met this man the other day. And there could never be anything between them, what with him being such a devout Christian and her being. . .

"How'd you know Gus was a girl?" he asked, interrupting her thought.

"Because, male calicos are very rare."

Eyes narrowed, Keegan regarded her carefully.

"I learned it on a cable station dedicated to teaching kids about animals; this veterinarian in Australia did a whole segment on calicos."

The thick mustache tilted above a rakish grin. "Is that right?"

He hadn't tried to hide his interest yesterday, and there was no mistaking the admiration glowing in his green eyes now. Breena took a deep breath—to stave off another blush and keep her curiosity under control—because cats and mice and spiders and plants were the last things on her mind. *Whatever happened to dear, sweet* Augusta? was her sarcastic, silent question. Breena waved a hand in the direction of the flower-laden table. "So what do you recommend?" she asked instead.

Keegan leaned his backside against the table, where hundreds of impatiens bloomed, and crossed both arms over his chest. "Dinner. Tonight. My place."

Chapter 4

The moment Keegan opened the door, his massive bulk was illumined by the glow of candles. They were everywhere. . .on the mantle and hearth, on the coffee table, lining the windowsills. The scent of freshly-struck matches wafted on an air current, tickling her nostrils.

"Bless you," he said when she sneezed. Stepping aside, he gave a grand, welcoming gesture with a sweep of his muscular arm. "C'mon in and set a spell. Help yourself to the cheese and crackers. How 'bout some iced tea?"

"Sounds nice," she said.

As he rummaged in the kitchen, Breena surveyed his living room. She'd more or less expected to find his tastes leaning toward Western decor—big buttery leather sofas and chairs, dark wood, brass lanterns rather than lamps, statues of cowboys on rearing stallions, framed prints of dusty cattle drives. . . Instead, well-worn books lined the ceiling-to-floor shelves flanking a flagstone fireplace, and vases of fresh flowers decorated the tables. Potted plants with shiny green leaves, illuminated by strategically placed spotlights, stood in each corner of the room. There were gauzy white curtains at the windows, topped off with valances that matched the upholstery of the two wingbacks facing the woodstove insert. And beneath it all, thick-piled cream carpeting.

From where she stood, Breena could see into the dining room, bathed in its own shimmering candlelight. He'd set the claw-footed oak table for two, complete with a five-piece service of china, crystal water goblets, and enough flatware to serve a small army.

The scents drifting in from the kitchen inspired her to lift her chin and close her eyes. She took a deep, lingering breath. Just as Keegan entered the room, a tall tumbler of iced tea in each hand, her stomach rumbled loudly.

"I think I can hold out a little while longer," she said in response to his teasing grin.

Their fingers touched when she accepted the offered glass, and Breena shivered involuntarily in response to the warmth of his skin as it grazed hers.

Gently, Keegan grasped her elbow and guided her through the dining room. "I thought it'd be nice to sit outside till the grub's ready." Throwing open the french doors, he stepped onto the sunporch.

Here, as in the living room, Breena was stunned by the cleanliness. Apparently, he'd been married, and "the little woman" hadn't vacated the premises very long ago. The evidence was everywhere—in the artistic placement of every knickknack, in the positioning of each article of furniture, from the perfect blend of color and texture and style to the use of lights and shadows to enhance every item's shape. She shrugged one shoulder and sighed, feeling a pang of pity for the woman who had let a man like Keegan Neil go!

"Pull up a chair," he instructed, opening several tall sliding windows, "and take a load off."

She sat in the wicker rocker nearest the door and nodded at the hat rack in the corner. "You have quite a collection. . . ."

"Yeah," he teased, "and I plan to keep 'em right there when you're around."

Breena laughed as the ceiling fan overhead whirred softly, and the breeze it roused caused the candle flames to dance, reminding her of the tiny ballerina that twirled and turned in the little pink jewelry box her father had given her for her tenth birthday. She still had that box, still kept trinkets and baubles inside it.

"Say, why the long face?" Keegan asked, sitting in the chair beside hers.

Sighing, she shook her head, then stared into her glass, as if the answers to all her problems swam among the sparkling ice cubes. "No reason," she said, resuming her former smiling demeanor. "Just remembering. . ."

"An old beau?"

Had she been mistaken? Did she hear a tinge of envy in his deep voice?

"No. . .nothing like that." She should be more careful with her responses, pretend there was a long line of old beaus in her past. Isn't that what the women's magazines would advise?

But Breena saw no point in playing hard to get with Keegan Neil. He wasn't going to "get" her, period, because once he found out about her wretched past, he wouldn't want her. He deserved better, far better than the likes of her, and she knew it.

It had been fourteen years since her mother's death, and Breena had taken over the role of doting on her grouchy, emotionally distant father. Even though he never appreciated anything she did, looking after him was the least she could do. After all, it was her rotten behavior that had caused the stress that induced her mother's heart attack. If she'd been a good girl, her father would still have the love of his life to look out for him. . .instead of a penitent, guilt-ridden daughter. . .and Breena would still have her beautiful, loving mother. . . .

It happened this way sometimes. . .shame and regret building up and building up until it had nowhere to go but down her cheeks. Before she even realized she was crying, Keegan was down on one knee, enclosing all of her fingertips in one big hand. "Hey," he whispered, wiping a tear from her lashes, "don't do that. . . you'll smear your mascara."

Scolding herself for exposing him to her weak-willed display, Breena stiffened her back. Sniffing, she blotted her eyes with the tissue he'd handed her and pulled herself together. "I-I'm not wearing any mascara."

One hand on each of the rocker's arms, he squinted in the dim light, then ran a fingertip across her lashes. "Well, I'll be a donkey's uncle. They're soft as my old granny's rabbit fur coat."

She opened her mouth to apologize, to thank him for the compliment, to tell him she'd never seen bigger, greener eyes in her life. . .

. . .and a loud groan issued up from her stomach instead.

Breena covered her face with both hands. "I'm so embarrassed," she admitted, voice muffled by her palms. "Blubbering like a baby, then growling like an old lion." Peeking between two fingers, she added, "What must you think of me?"

"I think," he began, his voice thick and unsteady, his gaze unwavering, "you're the most gorgeous thing on two feet." He stood, pulled her to him, and wrapped her in a warm embrace. "And I think," he tacked on, "we'd better get some food in that belly of yours before you drop over in a dead faint."

Despite the warm June night, Breena was cold when he let her go. Hugging herself to fend off the unexpected chill, she watched him head back inside.

"I hope you like spaghetti," he said over his shoulder, " 'cause that's the main course." Stopping dead in his tracks, he faced her. "Hey. . .you're not one of those vegetarian types, are you?"

Breena's eyes widened and she blinked. "Who? Me? Give me steak over tofu any day!"

He gave an approving nod and started for the kitchen. "Good. 'Cause there're meatballs, too. Now, c'mon in here, and help me put the vittles on the table."

⤙✬⤚

They chatted amiably over Caesar salad, spaghetti and meatballs, and the spumoni he'd made for dessert. It took some convincing, but Keegan finally agreed to let Breena help him do the dishes. She washed, he dried. "Makes more sense," she explained, "since you know where everything goes. . . ."

Keegan chuckled. "That's what I like. . .a sensible woman."

Afterward, they returned to his sunporch. The night breeze had intensified, blowing out all the candles. "Are you cold?"

"A little," she admitted, settling onto the rattan sofa, "but it's so pretty out here, what with these big windows giving us a view of the sky and all, that I hate to go back inside, even though it's warmer."

Keegan tore the long-fringed afghan from the back of the matching easy chair and gently draped it around her shoulders. Sitting beside her, he slid an arm around her waist and pulled her closer. "Warmer now?"

Nodding, Breena stared straight ahead, into the star-studded inky sky. The heat from his side seeped into her, warming not only her body, but her spirit, too. Self-recrimination for her mother's death had haunted her for so long, she hadn't felt worthy to let good and decent people close, for fear of contaminating them with her tainted past. Consequently, Breena had been cold and lonely for so long that being near him made her yearn for more.

Unconsciously, she rested her head on his shoulder and sighed. Eyes closed, she relaxed and smiled from her heart for the first time in a long time.

It began gradually. . .his fingers playing in her short dark curls, then softly stroking the back of her neck. Next, his lips found her temple, her cheek. Clasping her waist, Keegan drew her nearer. She knew he was going to kiss her; *wanted* him to kiss her. Logic reminded her they'd met only the day before yesterday. Still, there was no explaining it, but Breena felt as though she'd known him most of her adult life. *He deserves better than you,* she thought. *When he finds out what you did. . .*

She pictured the look of disappointment, of revulsion, that had so often been painted on her father's face. Would Keegan's kindly smile turn down at the corners, his merrily twinkling eyes dim with indignation when he learned the truth about her? She'd known him barely more than forty-eight hours. . . more than long enough to know for certain that she'd rather die than see that. . . .

Far smarter—and safer—to leave now. Breena made a move to sit up, but Keegan's embrace tightened. "No," he murmured, "don't leave me. . .at least, not yet."

Did he realize what he was doing? Could he have known that she'd been thirsting for attention, for affection, such a long, lonely time? The answer eluded her, and the question faded as his lips found hers. Breena drank hungrily, needily. Something inside her seemed to erupt; was she lost. . .or found?

Keegan inhaled a ragged breath and said, "I never meant for that to happen. . . ."

"Well," she interrupted, "it did." Breena ran a trembling hand through her hair, breaking the intense eye contact.

"Aw, don't look so sad, darlin'," he said, giving the tip of her nose an affectionate touch. "You didn't let me finish. I may not have meant for it to happen, but I'm glad it did."

Her heartbeat quickened in response to the sweet smile that slanted his burnished mustache. She had no right to feel utter relief at his words. *You're making mountains out of molehills,* she scolded herself, *dreaming like some silly school girl lost in the throes of her first crush.* Something told her that if she hadn't lived such a deliberately solitary life, this evening wouldn't seem like such a big deal.

But she had lived alone, and this evening *was* a big deal. The biggest in her life. If she were smart, she'd get to her feet right now, leave, and not look back. If she stayed, she'd be hurt. Maybe not right away, but sooner or later. *Better never to have loved and lost,* she rearranged the age-old cliché, *than to love. . .and lose.*

When she pressed her palms against his hard, broad chest for leverage to stand, he wrapped each slender wrist with his thick, callused fingers. His coarse whisper sliced the silence. "You're lovely."

She looked deep into eyes that gleamed with a blend of affection and passion. *You'd sing a different tune if you knew the truth about me.* The thought reverberated in her head a time or two. What better way to test his intentions, than by putting it all out there?

"I killed my mother."

Chapter 5

Keegan's brows dipped low in the center of his forehead as his gentle smile settled somewhere between bemused disbelief and cautious concern. "You. . .*what?*"

"She had a heart condition, and I wasn't exactly the best daughter." Shaking her head, Breena said, "But I'm putting the cart before the horse."

Breena stood and began pacing in the space between the glass-topped coffee table and the sofa, repeatedly squeezing first one hand, then the other. "It all started," she went on, feigning a light, nonchalant tone, "when my parents separated. I was fourteen at the time, and it scared me half to death. As an only child, I'd always been number one in their lives. I couldn't believe they were actually considering putting their needs and wants ahead of mine. I mean," she rolled her eyes, emulating her fourteen-year-old self, " 'how dare they mess up my perfect, happy life with talk of divorce.' "

Keegan got to his feet, slid an arm around her waist. "Breena. . .please, sit down." He chucked her under the chin. "They say this indoor-outdoor stuff wears like iron, but I hate to put it to the test with your pacin'. . . ."

She read the gentle smile in his eyes and allowed him to walk her to the sofa. Hands tightly clasped on her knees, Breena continued. "They'd always been so proud of my achievements—academic, athletic, volunteer—and constantly boasted about their sweet, smart little girl." Her lips thinned as her gaze found his. "When they split up, I wanted to hurt them, the way they'd hurt me. I didn't think I had any ammunition except—" She took a deep breath. "Something told me the best way to accomplish that was to take their bragging rights away from them."

Keegan nodded understandingly. "Got yourself involved with a rough crowd, did you?" he asked.

She answered in a voice heavy with sarcasm. "That's putting it mildly; I rode home from school in a squad car almost as often as I took the bus." She shook her head. "Eventually, my folks worked out their problems and got back together, but by that time, I was in so deep with my low-life friends, I didn't have the courage to get out. I became—"

"The kids who work for me used to get into trouble regularly, too," Keegan interrupted, patting her hand. "That doesn't mean they are—or ever were—bad." Tenderly, he tucked a lock of hair behind her ear.

"—I became incorrigible," she rattled on. "My behavior worried my mother to distraction. She was under constant stress, a lot of it, because of me." Tears filled Breena's eyes, and she bit her lip to stifle a sob.

Seeming not to notice, Keegan quirked an eyebrow as his mustache tilted above a mischievous grin. "So what sort of weapon did you use to do her in?"

Breena scowled at him in disbelief. "That isn't funny, Keegan."

"Sorry. . .I was only trying to—"

"I know what you were trying to do. You were trying to make a joke because you don't think I killed my mom." She tucked in one corner of her mouth. "Well, thanks for the attempt, but it won't work." She went on as if there hadn't been an interruption. "The only weapon I needed was my—"

He held up a hand to silence her. "Don't tell me. . . your *behavior?*"

Breena, appearing not to hear the gentle sarcasm in his voice, focused instead on something beyond his left shoulder. "One question has always plagued me, though," she said, more to herself than to Keegan.

Balancing both elbows on his knees now, he peered into her face. "And what would that be, darlin'?"

She met his eyes, and in a small fluttery voice said, "My parents never told me Mom had a heart condition. If—" Breena lowered her eyes, then her head.

With a wave of his hand, Keegan prompted her to continue.

"But if they had, would it have made any difference? If I'd known how sick she was, would *that* have given me the courage to break away from those kids, to walk the straight and narrow again, *for her?*"

For a long while, neither Keegan nor Breena spoke. Finally, she broke the silence. "Well," she said, rising, "there you have it. My horrible history in a nutshell." Hurriedly, she walked toward the front door and grabbed her sweater from the hall tree.

"What are you *really* hiding from?" His voice was stern, his face impassive as she opened the oak door.

She stood in the open entry. "Hiding?" she repeated. "I'm not—"

Keegan emitted a dry, cynical chuckle that silenced her. "You didn't kill your mama, darlin'." He jabbed the air with a forefinger. "Her heart condition did."

Standing taller, she lifted her chin. "Technically, that's true, but it was my behavior that—"

Keegan groaned under his breath, one hand in the air like a traffic cop, and said, "If you were still sixteen, I'd understand such an immature mindset. But we both know that you're not sixteen." He narrowed his eyes to add, "Let me get this straight: You want to be guilty of causing your mother's death?"

Blanching, Breena stammered, "Well, well, no. No, of course I don't. I don't *want* to—"

"Then don't be," he said emphatically. Then in a calmer voice, Keegan added, "God hasn't judged you as harshly as you've judged yourself."

Breena remembered that day in college, when she'd gone to the front of the big tent and accepted Jesus as her Lord and Savior. *If God hasn't judged me, then why did He—*

"I'll tell you what I think," Keegan said, breaking into her thoughts, "I think you're using this 'guilt trip' to keep people from getting too close. What's the matter. . .afraid you'll fall in love with somebody. . . and let them down?"

Breena began to tell him about the day when she had tried to give her life to God, but as she stumbled through the story, Keegan lay a silencing finger against her lips. "Hush, darlin'." His voice and demeanor softened even more, "You've already said too much."

He wrapped her in his arms and held her tight. "I said it before, I'll say it again: You're a fine woman, Breena. Your so-called shocking confession didn't change my opinion of you one iota." He winked mischievously and grinned. "You seem to have all the answers; what's your answer to *that?*"

"I-I never pretended to have all the answers." Rolling her eyes in vexation, Breena snapped, "For your information, I didn't make my 'so-called shocking confession' to change your opinion of me. I told you because—" Breena stopped short of completing her sentence, because she knew he was exactly right.

He lifted her chin with a bent forefinger, then pressed both warm palms against her cheeks. Whether she deserved it or not, he seemed to like her, and his acceptance was like a healing salve on her lonely, aching heart.

Her heart turned over as his gaze slid across her face, a tingling sensation began in the pit of her stomach as his thumbs drew lazy circles on her jaw. The draft of air that sighed through the open front door swirled around them in cool, electrifying currents. Trapped in the invisible warmth of his welcoming arms, she silently urged, *Do it! Kiss me, already, so I can gather what's left of my dignity and leave!*

As if he'd read her mind, Keegan's face moved nearer, until she could feel his faint breaths upon her face.

Breena closed her eyes to savor the moment, and like a giddy girl caught up in her own emotions, she waited. . . .

The soft touch of his mustache against her mouth put her on her toes, and what had begun as a feathery caress became an almost-timid kiss that sang through her. Breena ran her fingers through his soft, dark waves, hoping to imprint the feel of the satiny strands upon her brain. She wanted to remember the sound of his voice, his tender touch, the compassion that had glittered in his green eyes. This innocently provocative kiss in particular would be something Breena would treasure when she returned to her stark and solitary world.

Slowly, Keegan stepped back and, hands on her shoulders, turned her around and gently shoved her onto the front porch. He reached onto the hall table and picked up a huge bouquet of roses and baby's breath, wrapped in green tissue paper.

"What. . .what's this?" she stammered.

"Forty-eight flowers for forty-eight hours. . .but none as beautiful as you." He smiled broadly. "Of course, that's not exact. I wrapped these this afternoon. It's more like fifty-six and a half hours by now."

She cradled the roses as if they were a newborn child. Had it really been so few hours? Though Breena was in no emotional condition to calculate it, she had a strong suspicion that Keegan knew precisely how long it had been.

"Call me when you grow up," he said as the door swung shut, "and we'll pick up where we left off."

For a moment, Breena stood squinting into the bright glow of the porch light. There would be a pinprick of light shining through the peep hole unless it had been blocked by something. . .or someone. . . .

Smiling ever so slightly, Breena lifted the flowers a bit. "Thank you, Mr. Maturity," she said, and turned to leave.

❧

He'd been pretty hard on her, but Keegan believed he had no choice. Working with troubled kids had taught him that pity was never good medicine.

The truth of the matter was, he did feel sorry for Breena, mighty sorry. But he'd seen the same sad, self-punishing expression on the face of every adolescent he'd ever hired at the greenhouse. Each had responded to his version of "tough love" because, as Marcellus had put it, "You ain't no phony, man; you say what you mean and you mean what you say."

Marcellus had been Keegan's first "case," and there had been dozens since. Several, like Marcellus, had come to work at That's the Way It Grows, when Keegan took over and began to clean the place up. He didn't have any formal counseling training, which he liked to think set him yards apart from specialists in child psychology. He believed God had called him to this task, because he surely had not asked for the assignment! Keegan had always relied upon the Almighty to provide whatever he might need, whenever he might need it, to help kids in crisis. The Lord had seen fit to bless him with an ability to get the kids to open up, to reveal pertinent facts about themselves that would help Keegan get to the root of their problems.

Other than what she had said at dinner, Keegan knew virtually nothing about Breena.

Well, that wasn't entirely true. When Breena paid for the flat of marigolds, she'd filled out one of the "May We Send You A Catalog?" forms that sat beside the greenhouse cash register, so he knew her name and address. He knew by the condition of her hands that she wasn't afraid of hard work. He knew she had an amazing sense of humor, and that she was beautiful and sweet as cotton candy.

And her kisses were warm and genuine. *Mmmm-mmmm-mmmm*, Keegan said to himself, smiling at the memory. Something told him it meant every bit as much to her as it had to him.

The most striking thing he knew was that Breena actually thought she'd killed her mother. Why, he didn't know; certainly not for the far-fetched reason she'd given him. And for some off-the-wall reason she thought that God had rejected her. *Probably the two things are connected in her beautiful, mixed-up head. . . .*

Keegan pictured her, more beautiful than any woman he'd ever known, especially with tears shimmering in her big brown eyes, and heard the incredible sadness that dulled her otherwise musical voice. He had no earthly idea what could have put a cockeyed notion like that into her pretty head and kept it there all these years, but if it was the last thing he did, he sure as shootin' aimed to find out!

⌘

Breena was up all night thinking about Keegan. He'd been a doting host; dinner was delicious, dessert spectacular! From the time she'd arrived to the time they'd returned to the sunporch, she and Keegan had talked and laughed and genuinely enjoyed one another's company.

But all that changed the moment she began telling him about her past. Keegan's lighthearted mood had contrasted with her own dark disposition as he tried to convince her she hadn't been responsible for her mother's death.

Of *course* it had been her fault!

For the first time in fourteen years, Breena wasn't so certain of the answer.

She *hadn't* known about the heart condition, after all, a condition that had plagued her mother since shortly after Breena was born. Because of the ailment, her parents hadn't added to their family.

But there was still the matter of the unanswered question: If she had known about her mother's illness, would she have become the good, obedient daughter again her mother had boasted about?

Until Breena could be sure, she'd continue to believe that her mother had died, long before her time, because of her,

What if the answer to the question is "no"? Breena asked herself. What if, after all this time, she discovered that something else had caused her mother to overreact, and hyperventilate, and. . .

Breena slumped onto the chair nearest the telephone and glanced around her apartment. She'd been punishing herself for so long that if the answer was no, her entire life would change. She'd have a chance at a real, loving relationship with her father, at a complete life of her own, maybe even with a devoted husband and children who would think she'd hung the moon.

She shook her head and got to her feet. Much as she wanted to be set free from the shackles of guilt and shame, it was simply too much to hope for.

It hadn't been pleasant, taking the blame for what had happened, but Breena had lived with it for so long that she had grown to accept, if not be comfortable, with it.

Too bad, she thought, because she liked Keegan. Right up to and including the way he got all gruff and tough with her at the end of their dinner. Breena understood that he'd been trying to give her another viewpoint to think about. Oh, she hadn't understood it at first, that much was certain! At first, she'd been furious with Keegan for his paternal demeanor.

But he'd been so sweet, so funny, so forgiving earlier that, once back on familiar turf, she couldn't help but wonder *why* he'd so suddenly changed.

She walked over to the snack bar that separated the kitchen from the living room. It had taken two vases and a jelly jar to hold the roses Keegan had given her. The entire apartment was alive with their honeyed scent. Breena withdrew one of the long-stemmed beauties from the water and, eyes closed, reveled in the feel of its velvety petals against her cheek. "Forty-eight flowers for forty-eight hours," she said in a singsong voice.

Suddenly she remembered how Keegan had taken her to task about her mother, and she jammed the rose back into the vase.

Like an actress in a 1940s B-movie, Breena paced the width and breadth of her loft apartment, asking the seemingly unanswerable question, "Who does he think he is, expelling me like an unruly schoolgirl!"

Chapter 6

The frantic elderly woman paced back and forth like a nervous delivery room daddy-to-be as Breena tightened strings and adjusted the hammers of the ancient player piano. The instrument had been a tenth anniversary gift from the lady's dear departed husband.

Breena had always been glad for extra tuning or repair jobs. Mrs. Barber was a talker, and that was good, because the chatter would take Breena's mind off Keegan.

"It got out of tune once, back in '79 I believe it was," Mrs. Barber said, squinting one eye as she strained to remember, "but I never much minded the sour notes; they kind of reminded me of my Henry." She clasped thin-skinned, wrinkled hands beneath her double chins and smiled wistfully. The smile diminished, and she added, "Then this morning, I sat down to peck out a tune, and nothing!" The girlish pout erased ten years off her face. "You can fix it, can't you?"

Certain people and their pianos, Breena had discovered, forged relationships that would put some marriages to shame. *If folks gave this kind of care and attention to their spouses,* she'd often thought, *the divorce rate would plummet!*

"I'll do what I can," she promised. It was a bit like being in front of the tiger cage at the zoo, watching Mrs. Barber walk to and fro, back and forth. She seemed fit. . . for an older woman, but what if, like Breena's mother, she had a weak heart? Surely all this fussing and pacing around wouldn't be good for her. . . .

"So tell me, what's your favorite piano solo?"

Mrs. Barber's face lit up like she was standing in the spotlights on stage. She perched on the edge of the piano bench and crossed both arms over her ample bosom. "Hmmm. . ." She tapped an arthritic finger against her chin. "Guess I'd have to say 'Amazing Grace.' Umm-hmm. Definitely 'Amazing Grace.' Why, just a couple bars of that one can lift my spirits for hours, especially when I'm at work!"

This adorable senior citizen still has a job? "What kind of work do you do, Mrs. Barber?"

"Well, I retired last year, y'see. Hit the old seven-oh and decided it was time to slow down. Those first few weeks were fun, but then I started to *hate* havin' nothin' to do." Raising her chin and grinning with pride, she continued, "I'd been working for the same man nearly quarter of a century. When his grandson took over, I wasn't so sure I'd like the job, don'cha know. Turned out he's a better boss than his grandpa, and that's sayin' a mouthful, let me tell you!"

Crossing one knee over the other, Mrs. Barber smiled. "I asked the boss if he'd let me come back. . . cut my hours, and—"

As long as Breena kept her talking, Mrs. Barber seemed content to sit still, which took some pressure off of Breena,

"What sort of work do you do?"

"I'm an accountant. I may have lost my figure, but I'm mighty good at mindin' other folks' figures," she laughed. "Best thing about this job," she whispered conspiratorially, one hand beside her mouth, "I found out I'm pretty good with things that grow. And long as I don't get greedy, the boss says I'm welcome to a freebie now and then."

Atta girl, Mrs. Barber, keep talking. . .and sitting. . . . "What sort of freebies?"

"House plants, vegetable plants, border plants for the outside gardens. . ."

There had been a white-haired woman in the window of Keegan's office, and if Breena's memory served correctly, he'd called her Agnes. *Didn't Mrs. Barber say, "I'm Agnes Barber, and my player piano isn't playing."? Oh, come on, Breena. What are the chances Mrs. Barber is Keegan's Agnes?*

"Mr. Neil is the most generous boss I've ever worked for."

"Mr. Neil?" Breena swallowed hard.

"He lets me set my own hours. Long as the bills and the payroll checks get cut on time, I'm free to come and go as I please." Another gravelly giggle. "He's got me covered, let me tell you! Health care, pension, profit sharing. . . why, the man's generous to a fault."

Pension? Profit sharing? Full health care benefits. . . for a part-time, semi-retired employee? Breena had never heard of such a thing. Mrs. Barber was a fortunate woman to have such a concerned, caring boss.

Could Keegan have set up this piano house call? She'd never told him where she lived or what she did for a living. Breena couldn't remember ever telling him her last name!

Suddenly, her cheeks burned with a blush. *How ridiculous to think that a busy man like Keegan would be plotting to send me business.* Still, he did seem interested. They had shared a peaceful, pleasant dinner; four dozen aromatic red roses filling vases in her apartment proved his thoughtful, romantic nature. He had kissed her—on the first date—and she had kissed him back. All this and they'd only known each other for three days! She was falling feet over forehead for a virtual stranger.

". . .and what a handsome young fella," Mrs. Barber was saying. "It's a wonder some slick female hasn't snapped him up by now."

"He's never been married?"

Mrs. Barber shook his head. "Nope."

"Ouch!" Breena pinched her finger in the teeth of her needle-nosed pliers. *Get your mind on your work, before you permanently maim yourself!* One sharp whack with the rubber mallet, and the piano's rollers snapped back into place. "Have a seat at the keyboard, Mrs. Barber, and rev 'er up; let's see if we've got this baby up and running."

"Here's to happy endings!" Mrs. Barber said as she depressed the foot pedal.

Immediately, a lively tune jangled from the big mahogany box. "Oh, honey, you've done it! You fixed my piano!" Mrs. Barber clapped her hands in time to the music. "Can't you just hear Al Jolson, puttin' words to this melody?" And with neither prompting nor invitation, she belted out the first bars of the ancient song. " 'Swanee, how I love ya, how I love ya, my dear old—' "

Smiling, Breena packed up her tools. Repairing and tuning pianos demanded ingenuity, dexterity, and physical strength. She'd never minded the hard-work aspects of the job, because they guaranteed the end result: seeing and hearing her customers' joy when they'd been reunited with their instruments.

Mrs. Barber stopped singing as suddenly as she'd started. "How much do I owe you?"

Breena filled out a work order, detailing the charges for parts and labor. "You can send a check to that address," she said, handing it to the elderly woman. Customers of Mrs. Barber's age came from a generation with a "do your best" work ethic and pride that demanded all debts be paid, on time and in full. But some lived on fixed incomes and didn't always have the financial wherewithal to pay on the spot for service calls. Asking them to send a check to her workshop, she'd learned, gave them plenty of time to come up with the money, sparing them a boatload of embarrassment. Besides, Breena earned a good living, tending the pianos owned by area churches and schools.

Seventy years old or not, Mrs. Barber was quick. Too quick to let that one slide. "Oh, you're a sly one, honey." In no time, she'd dashed off a check in the full amount of the invoice. "There y'go," she said, tucking it into Breena's shirt pocket. "Now, I'm gonna give you a piece of advice. . .free of charge." And with a snort and a chuckle and an elbow to Breena's ribs, Mrs. Barber instructed, "Don't give anybody a free ride. You do good work; make folks pay for it!"

Nodding and smiling, Breena allowed the feisty lady to usher her to the door.

"You married, honey?"

"No."

"Engaged?"

"No."

"Got yourself a steady beau?"

Breena thought of Keegan. . .and that parting kiss . . . Sighing regretfully, she said, "No."

"What! Pretty and sweet as you are?"

Shrugging, she said, "Guess I just haven't found my Mr. Right yet." But even as she said it, Breena knew she'd found him.

⌘

The scent of roses floated everywhere.

Hiding under the blankets, then the pillow, did nothing but make her short of breath. Even getting up and closing the door didn't block out the sweet, soft fragrance.

Breena tossed and turned for an hour before surrendering. "That's the trouble with a loft apartment," she muttered, firing up the teapot.

Hershey's "since you're up anyway, why not feed me?" expression told her she'd get no sympathy there. Breena fed the cat, then rummaged in the cupboard for a tea bag. *Chamomile is supposed to have natural relaxing properties,* she thought. Breena brewed it extra strong.

Lounging in the overstuffed easy chair near the windows, Breena stared into the vast, velvety sky that blanketed the city below. It was a bright, clear night, complete with a silvery crescent moon and thousands of winking, blinking stars.

Was her mother up there among it all, enjoying an equally beautiful view of earth? Breena's gaze slid toward the bookshelves that flanked the fireplace. On a high shelf, illuminated by the beam of a carefully aimed track light, stood Breena's most treasured possessions: a five-by-seven black and white photograph and a white leather journal.

In the sterling-framed picture, her mother stood alone, one shoulder leaning against the trunk of an ancient weeping willow, smiling serenely, her dark curls cascading down her back like a fur cape. They say the camera doesn't lie. The snapshot, taken on her parents' honeymoon to Niagara Falls, had captured her mother's physical frailty.

And the diary had likely captured Annie Pavan's emotional fragility. As a girl, Breena had watched as her mother, pen in hand, filled in the faint blue lines that striped each page. Her sweet smile, whether she'd been recording chickadee behavior or reacting to a rainbow, told Breena more than the written words could have. . .

But Breena didn't know what Annie had penned in the log, because she'd never been able to bring herself to open it. What if she scanned the precise script and confirmed a link between her wayward behavior and the physical symptoms of Annie's emotional condition?

Better to let sleeping dogs lie, she'd told herself each time she was tempted to pore over her mother's secret thoughts. By now, it had become a habit. . .this business of avoiding unpleasantness. . .so much so that Breena barely realized when she was doing it.

She realized this: she missed her mother!

When had she last said "I love you" to Annie? Sometime before her parents' separation, that much was certain. It had become one of the most agonizing facts of her past. . .that her mother had died, never knowing how much Breena had always loved and appreciated her.

And there was no going back now. No redoing things done wrong. No repairing the damage her own self-centered, immature mindset had caused.

Keegan had been right about that, Breena admitted. Thirty years old or not, she had a long way to go before she could say she'd truly grown up!

Breena forced herself to look away from the keepsakes and focused again on the heavens beyond her window. Surely her mother was up there—*somewhere,* She'd been a good and decent woman—and Breena suspected she'd been close to God, though shy of talking about Him.

"At least she's not in pain anymore," a neighbor had said at the funeral. "She's in a better place now," someone else had responded.

Happy and living eternally without pain. Sixteen-year-old Breena had hoped it was true. She still hoped it was true.

Her eyes filled with tears. "I miss you, Mama," she whispered.

Chapter 7

"Y ou can't get a good night's sleep if you've left dishes in the sink."

It was a proverb coined by his mother, one he'd heard hundreds of times growing up. Raised single-handedly by this loving but no-nonsense, by-the-book woman, Keegan learned to make hospital corners on a bed that would put a Marine Corps drill sergeant to shame. She'd taught him how to cook dozens of mouth-watering gourmet recipes and how to keep house. Anymore, his fastidiously clean house was second nature.

Trying his best to stifle a yawn, he put away the dishes he'd just washed. Living alone all these years, he'd never seen a need for an automatic dishwasher. But the concept—and the contraption itself—was looking better and better.

The clock in the front hall gonged nine times. He rarely hit the hay before ten, but after staring at a computer screen all afternoon, he was completely exhausted. *Give me some perennials and a pile of dirt any day of the week.*

One of the more interesting and exciting jobs he'd held to pay his way through college had been a summer at the "Smith and Wesson" detective agency. His boss, Ernie Sisneros, looked about as much like the stereotypical private eye as the queen of England looks like Mr. Rogers. There had never been a Smith in Ernie's family, and the closest he'd ever got to Wesson was when he fried up a panful of hash browns. But the name gave folks the confidence to call, and Ernie gave them the belief he'd solve their cases.

Keegan had learned a lot that summer. Though the mainstay of his job had been delivering subpoenas and summonses, he'd been assigned to "searches" now and then. He knew how to find things and people and information.

Determined to discover the truth about Breena and her mother, Keegan had parked himself in front of the InfoSeek computer at the library immediately after lunch and hadn't looked up until a quarter to five. By the time he had completed his other errand and was jamming the key into his front door, it was nearly seven.

Just as he'd suspected, Breena had *not* killed her mother. A rare, genetic heart defect had been the cause of death—the kind of disease that would have done her in even if she'd spent her life in a convent.

When he was finished at the library, it hadn't been easy to ring the door-bell of the house where Annie Pavan had died. But Keegan knew he'd get no rest unless he found out why Breena felt responsible for what had happened.

Who better to ask than the only witness to the tragedy?

Breena's father was a nondescript little man with dark hair gone mostly gray, blue eyes that peered suspiciously from a face that was a roadmap of lines and wrinkles, and a mouth that seemed set in a permanent scowl.

He'd been reluctant to let Keegan inside, grumping and groaning about how thoughtless young folks were these days, dropping by unannounced and the like. But by the time he showed Keegan out, anyone watching might have thought Robert Pavan was saying good-bye to a lifelong friend.

Both men learned a lot in the hour they were together. Keegan learned (or rather, relearned) the age-old lesson, "Never judge a book by its cover." And Breena's father figured out that, because of his own behavior, his only child had spent the past fourteen years blaming herself for her mother's death.

Keegan didn't have a clue what to do next, but as he slid between the sheets, he had every confidence the idea would be there in the morning. God had put him and Breena together; there wasn't a doubt in Keegan's mind about that. There also wasn't a doubt that God would show Keegan the way to help free Breena from years of misplaced self-recrimination.

Keegan hoped the path to that end wouldn't be a long and winding one, because Breena deserved to know how much God loved her, as soon as pos-sible. And Keegan was ready to end his search for the right woman, which before had always come up empty-handed.

He knew that a good relationship—a good *marriage*—must be built on a firm foundation. And though he was convinced that Breena had accepted the Lord at that youth rally years ago, she didn't seem to understand how to trust God for her life here and now. Breena might be the woman God intended him to spend the rest of his life with, but she was on mighty shaky ground right now.

But once this mess from Breena's past is cleaned up. . .

Keegan was asleep before he could finish the thought.

❧

Her apartment was beginning to look like a South American jungle. Four times in the six days since she had met Keegan Neil, a delivery truck from That's the Way It Grows had pulled up outside her workshop. Now, in her apartment, there were green and flowering plants on every table, every shelf, every windowsill, and indoor trees in every corner. She had to admit they warmed the place up considerably. "But really," she said to Hershey, "where does he expect me to find the time to water these babies?" Not that it mattered, because in a month, every one of them would be dry and brown and dead.

The cat's bored yawn was interrupted by the doorbell. "That's what you get for being so insensitive," she teased as Hershey disappeared into Breena's bedroom.

She always entered the apartment by way of the workshop downstairs, because the driveway was right beside the entrance. Guests and the occasional Girl Scout cookie pusher used the front entrance, which required a climb up a flight of wide, metal steps. *That's weird,* she thought, positioning herself in front of the peep hole, *I usually hear people long before the bell rings. . . .*

Through the peephole, all Breena could see was a bouquet of mixed cut flowers. *Keegan, are you ever going to quit?* She flung the door open and her heart hammered when she saw her father on the landing, one hand in his pocket, the other holding the flowers.

"Hi," he said in a small, timid voice. "I brought you these."

In a voice that sounded like it came from outside of herself, Breena thanked him for the flowers and waved him inside. "If I'd known you were coming, I would have—"

"Baked a cake?"

Breena couldn't remember the last time she'd seen that playful light in his blue eyes, and she had to fight the impulse to throw her arms around his neck. *Why is he here?* "I was just about to run to the grocery store. There's a sale on chicken; I could get a roaster and fix you a nice—"

"Breena," he said, wending his way into the kitchen, "aren't you going to show your old man around?"

"Well, well, sure," she stammered, "of course. Just. . . just let me put these in water first."

While Breena arranged the bouquet in an empty mayonnaise jar, her father meandered into the living room. "Nice place you've got here. I like it." He stood with his back to her and his hands in his pocket, nodding approvingly. "You have your mother's eye for detail."

She'd lived in this apartment for nearly five years, but despite repeated invitations, he'd never visited before now. Breena set the flowers in the jar on the table and muttered a mousy "Thanks, Dad."

Robert Pavan touched a rose petal. "These from that greenhouse guy?"

Breena nodded and frowned. *That greenhouse guy? How does he know about Keegan? I've never said a word.*

"Must be mighty sweet on you; there are enough roses here to choke a horse!" With a sweep of his arm, he gestured toward the rest of the plants. "Rest of this green stuff from him, too?"

Another nod.

"Looks like he's taken quite a fancy to my little girl."

Had she heard correctly? Was there a tinge of pride . . .and *love*. . .in his voice?

"Got any coffee?"

"I-I brewed a pot just before you—"

"How about pourin' us both a cup then, while I prowl around the rest of the place?"

She watched as he headed for the bedroom, where her unmade bed and a pile of dirty laundry would prove she was still a master at messing things up. "Have you eaten breakfast?" she called after him.

"Well, I dunked a couple Oreos in milk. . . .You know. . . ."

"Why don't I scramble you an egg, make some toast and—"

He met her eyes for the first time since she'd closed the door behind him. . . for the first time in too long. "Maybe later. Right now, I just want to talk."

Talk? About what? Breena's mouth went dry and her palms grew damp. Had he decided to come right out with it, say what he'd been feeling all these years about her part in her mother's death?

Mechanically, she placed cloth napkins, the sugar bowl, a tiny pitcher of milk, and one spoon on the table. Of the two chairs in her kitchen, she liked the one facing the window best. Many a morning, she'd daydream over the morning paper and black coffee as Main Street came to life. She perched on the edge of the other chair, leaving her favorite seat for her father.

"Still taking yours straight, I see," he said, pointing at her mug of black coffee.

A feeble smile was all the answer she could muster. *Funny,* she thought as he stirred milk and sugar into his mug, *I don't feel any relief at all, even though I've been praying for this moment most of my life, it seems.*

"Dad? Why are you here?" She sounded remarkably calm despite the turmoil that now raged inside of her. *Go ahead and get it over with,* she silently fumed. *Tell me you can never forgive me for killing Mom, so at least we can have an honest relationship, if not a loving one!* Now that the moment of truth had arrived, Breena wasn't at all sure it was what she wanted. *At least the other way, I could pretend he loved me, a little. . . .*

"Keegan Neil stopped by to see me the other day."

Keegan? He'd gone to see Dad? Whatever for?

"Said he'd spent the day at the library, researching your past."

What? Breena picked at a nub on the placemat and waited. . . .

"Before you came along, your mother used to tease me, saying living with me was like living alone. . . because I hardly said a word. . . ." He downed a gulp of coffee. "I've never been one for a lot of unnecessary talk."

Especially since the funeral. . .

"I don't know how else to handle this, except to get straight to the point." Robert took her hands in his and forced her, by sheer will, to meet his eyes. "Can you ever forgive me, Breena?"

For a long moment, Breena could only stare in silent disbelief. "Forgive *you?* For what?"

"For letting you think you'd killed your mother." He looked away, but held tight to her hands. "All these years. . .I had no idea. . . ." He swallowed hard, then met her eyes again. "I've been off in a world of my own. Going to work and coming home, watching TV, reading—" A dry chuckle punctuated his words. "Why, I believe I've read every book your mother collected, twice!"

"That would take two lifetimes, Dad," she said, smiling at the memory of her mother's library. The joke was. . .the whole house was the library, and oh, how she loved those books! Every one—even the paperbacks—wore a dust jacket, whether store-bought or fashioned from left-over gift wrap or shelf paper. Alphabetized, and organized by subject matter in the various rooms of the house, Annie could put her finger on a requested title in the blink of an eye.

Robert continued as though Breena hadn't spoken at all. "If I hadn't been such a self-centered—" He shook his head. Then, boring deep into his daughter's eyes, said, "It wasn't your fault, honey. We knew right from the start that she wasn't long for this world."

"Then. . .then why did you two separate? Why all the talk of divorce?"

A deep sigh escaped his lungs. "Because she'd been badgering me for another baby, *for years,* and frankly, I couldn't take a minute more of it. 'You want to leave me, you do it some other way,' I told her."

"And so she went back to Grandma's," Breena whispered, nodding.

"I'd never been able to refuse her anything; guess she figured if I saw how much she wanted more kids, I'd give her that, too. But I wouldn't. *Couldn't.*

"Don't get me wrong, I would have loved a house full of kids like you. But she was dying when we met, and we knew that every morning was its own little miracle. She—"

"You did the right thing, Dad," Breena interrupted. "Another child would surely have—"

"No!" His fist hit the table with such force that the lid to the sugar jar rattled. "Now, you listen to me!" He paused, shook his head again, and in a softer voice continued, "She was lucky to have lived *that* long. Every specialist I took her to after the wedding said she'd have two, three years at best. Having you is what gave her the extra time. Don't you *see*, Breena? You didn't kill your mother. Being a mother is what kept her alive when nothing in the realm of modern medicine could."

"But. . .but all the trouble I caused. All the—"

Chuckling, Robert squeezed her hands. "You're so much like her in so many ways, right down to that stubborn streak of yours. Breena, honey, haven't you heard a word I said? *Wanting* you kept her alive a full year longer than the doctors predicted; *having* you gave her *fifteen years more!*" His lower lip twitched as he struggled not to cry. "You didn't take her from me, honey, you gave me a lifetime with her, when all I'd ever expected was a few years, at best. If you're so all-fired determined to take responsibility for something, take it for *that!*"

He pointed in the direction of the living room. "I saw your mother's journal on the shelf in there. How can you not know how she felt about you? It's all there, in her own handwriting."

Breena could only sit there, shaking her head at the irony of it all. The solution to all her problems had been right at her fingertips for fourteen years.

"I said it before, I'll say it again," he began, "I'm a self-centered, selfish old man. I missed your mother so much, I never took the time to see that you were hurting, too. Plus—" Robert took a deep breath and let it out slowly. "Plus, looking at you, being with you, was a constant reminder of her." He squeezed her hands again. "I know I don't deserve it. . .putting you through all these years of misery. . .but please say you'll forgive me."

"There's nothing to forgive, Dad." It hadn't taken soul-searching, or deep thought, or time; there truly was nothing to forgive. Breena had her father back!

And she had Keegan Neil to thank for it.

Chapter 8

Breena Neil. Mrs. Keegan Neil. Mrs. Neil.

The moment she became aware what her pen had been scribbling, Breena dropped it on the table. Dreaming of becoming his wife was one thing. Putting it in writing was another.

Get hold of yourself, she scolded, gathering up billing statements, stamps, return address labels, *before you—*

The doorbell rang, startling her so badly she nearly dropped the whole stack. *What's wrong with you? That's the second time in a row you didn't hear someone on the steps!* After tucking the materials into a box marked "Bills," Breena hurried to the front door.

I should have gone to bed earlier, instead of staying up all night, reading Mom's diary. . . . Breena rubbed her eyes and looked through the peep hole again.

Keegan stood with one hand in his pocket and the other holding a bouquet of mixed cut flowers. *What is this? Are he and Dad in some sort of cahoots?*

"Hi," he said when she opened the door, "I brought these for you."

Tucking in one corner of her mouth, she accepted the gift. "Thank you. They're beautiful." Then, a nod of her head indicating the rest of the blooming gifts, she added, "You didn't happen to bring something to put them in, did you?"

Laughing, Keegan shook his head. "Sorry. Sometimes I get carried away. . . something you ought to know."

She put the flowers into a tall tumbler and filled it with water. "Something I ought to know?" she repeated. "Why?"

Keegan shrugged. "Well, I just thought that since we'd be seeing more and more of one another, you ought to be aware of my flaws."

"There's a small fortune in greenery in here, and you call that a flaw?" Breena giggled. "You've sure got a lot to learn about making a woman miserable. . . ."

He glanced around the apartment. "Say, I like your place. It's very. . .spac-ey, I mean *spacious.*"

"You were right the first time. Spacey, that's me. Hey, I just made a pitcher of lemonade. Care for a glass?"

"Sure." He grinned mischievously. "A glass would be nice. You gonna put some lemonade in it?"

"Yes, and ice cubes, too." She propped a fist on her hip, pointed a maternal finger at him with the other hand. "Now park it, mister; you and I have some serious talkin' to do."

Both eyebrows rose high on his forehead as his smile dimmed. "Okay. . .but do you mind if I open the door. . .just in case I need to make a quick getaway?"

"I mind very much, as a matter of fact." And in response to his confused frown, Breena added, "I don't want you to get away. Ever."

Beaming, Keegan sat where her father had, just the day before. Laying one hand atop the other, he hooked his pointy-toed boots around the legs of the ladderback and waited.

"Thanks, Keegan," she said, sitting opposite him.

"Wow, you're pretty in the morning light."

"No one has ever done anything so nice for me before."

"Actually, you're pretty in *any* light, but you're especially pretty in—"

"I was up all night, reading my mother's journal. I learned a lot about her, learned a lot about myself, too."

He leaned forward, covered her hands with one of his own, and ran a fingertip over her lashes with the other. "Hard to believe those are real. What are you, part giraffe or something?"

"Giraffe!" she giggled. "What has a gira—"

"I thought for sure you were the type who'd notice details, like the color of a mouse's tail and the fact that calicos are mostly female." He narrowed one eye. "You tellin' me you never noticed before what long eyelashes giraffes have?"

"Well, I've noticed *yours*, Keegan. Are you sure *you're* not part giraffe?" She could feel herself blushing and she took a sip of lemonade in the hopes it would cool her. "Now, back to the subject at hand. . . . You were right, Keegan, about everything. I've—"

"That's the kind of stuff I like to hear. If *that's* the direction this conversation is taking us. . .then I'm sorry for all the interruptions." He rested his chin on a fist. "Go on, continue. What was I so right about?"

Breena rolled her eyes and said, "That I've wasted a lot of time wallowing in self-pity."

"I never said you were wallowing. I said—"

"Keegan, please," she said, laughing despite herself, "this is hard enough!"

"Sorry. . ."

"I understand you did a pretty thorough bit of research on me."

A warm stare was Keegan's only response.

"Well, for your information, I've done a bit of investigating into *your* background."

One brow rose slowly. "Is that a fact?"

"It is. Talking to Agnes is like—"

Keegan groaned, covered his face with one hand. "If you've been talking to Agnes, you probably know more about me than I do."

"I know that your favorite color is red, and that your favorite author is Jack London, and that you hate vanilla ice cream, and. . ."

"What're you smirking about, Breena? C'mon, 'fess up. . . ."

Breena had to be careful here. She didn't know much about men, but she knew this: A man's pride is easily shattered. Even so much as a hint that he might harbor an irrational fear could cause permanent injury to his tender male ego. "Um. . .and you're not terribly fond of thunderstorms."

"I should say not," he spouted. He sat back, crossed both arms over his broad chest. "Let's see how *you'd* react if you got struck by lightning!"

"Oh," she began, chin up and shoulders back, "I know exactly how I'd react."

His chin rose a notch, too. "Well. . . ?"

"I'd shiver under the covers—day or night—until the storm blew over."

Keegan's laughter bounced off every wall in the apartment. "It's not something I'm particularly proud of," he said, suddenly serious, "being afraid of a little rain. I mean, what if you were caught outside in a storm? I don't know if I could trust myself to save—"

"First of all," Breena interrupted, pressing a palm to his whiskered cheek, "Agnes says you're lucky to be alive after that bolt knocked you down. You wouldn't be normal if you didn't get the heebie-jeebies when thunder strikes." Her fingers combed through his hair. "I'm genuinely sorry you've had to live with that for nearly a decade. . .although I must say, it was almost worth it. . . ."

"Worth it? What are you, a sadist?"

She returned his gentle smile. "No," she sighed, "but it did leave you with this sexy streak. . . ."

"Hey," he said, feigning a smoldering, Hollywood-type stare, "I was *born* with a sexy streak. That lightning bolt had nothing to do with it."

Giggling, Breena said, "No, silly. . .I'm talking about the streak in your *hair*."

With no warning whatsoever, Keegan got to his feet, pulling her up with him. "Did you see that Tom Cruise movie. . .the one where he was a secret agent?"

Breena nodded as he wrapped her in a warm embrace.

"Your mission, Breena Pavan," he said, imitating the voice from *Mission Impossible,* "should you choose to accept it, is to meet me at St. John's. Today. One o'clock."

He didn't wait for an answer. Instead, Keegan kissed her as never before. And as she stood, reeling from its dizzying effects, he headed for the door.

"Which St. John's?"

Keegan shrugged. "That's for me to know, and for you to find out," he said, slamming the door behind him.

∞

She found him sitting exactly where he'd been on the day they'd met. . . precisely one week ago. Breena stepped into the pew and sat down beside him. "No Stetson to soften the bench?" she asked, her voice echoing in the empty church.

He looked straight ahead. "Haven't you heard? Stetsons are on the endangered hat list."

"I suppose you're right. Please don't turn me in. I've seen the inside of enough squad cars."

He pretended to take it all very seriously. "I've heard of homicide and suicide, but *haticide?*

Breena bit her lower lip to suppress a giggle. "I need to get you a new one so you don't look like you fell off your horse and landed on your head."

"Hah!" Keegan snorted, then fell silent. For a long moment, neither of them spoke.

"Why did you ask me to meet you here?" Breena finally asked, breaking the silence.

"To ask you to think about the future." He turned on the seat to face her. "And since I never do anything without the Big Guy's approval," he added, a thumb pointing heavenward, "what better place to do it?"

Their silly conversation forgotten, Breena's smile faded. "The future?"

"Well, sure." He said it as though surprised she hadn't been thinking the same thing. "What else?"

Breena licked her lips, which had gone suddenly dry.

"Don't ask me to explain it, 'cause I can't." He held up a hand to stave off any comment she might make. "I've never done anything spur-of-the-moment in my life." He grinned and wiggled his eyebrows. "But then, you already knew that, since you talked to my biographer-slash-accountant.

"I need some spontaneity in my life. I make lists and plans and—" He grew quiet and still for a moment, then grabbed her hands. "I can't explain it," he repeated, "but I think. . .no, I *know* that when you walked in here a week ago and mashed my hat flat, you stole my heart. And darlin', I don't want to live another day without you."

He's. . .he's proposing?

"Keegan," she began slowly, "before you say another word, I think it only fair to warn you. . .I'm not really a Christian. You deserve someone who's as devout as you."

"What do you mean you're not a Christian? Didn't you tell me that you accepted the Lord at that youth rally that your college girlfriend took you to?"

"Well. . .yeah, but I don't go to church."

"So? We can set that right, startin' tomorrow." Keegan put his arm around her shoulder and gave her a reassuring hug.

Breena's mind was swimming with confusion. She had gone forward at the youth rally, with Melissa's encouragement, and she had prayed the prayer. But after all these years of feeling like God had rejected her for what happened to her mother, it was hard to know what she believed. She knew that Jesus was the Lord and Savior. But was He *her* Lord and Savior?

"Breena, listen. If you accepted Jesus back when you were in college, you don't need to do it again. If you've wandered away and made some mistakes, the Bible tells us to repent, or confess our sins, how ever you want to say it, and then get back in the saddle. I'd say God's been waitin' a mighty long time for you to come back."

"Keegan, I understand what you're saying, but that's not the whole story."

"Of course it is."

"No, there's something else. I don't think I'm born again."

"What are you talking about?"

"Well. . .after that revival meeting, Melissa told me I needed to get baptized."

"And. . .?"

"And, it didn't take."

"Didn't take?" Frustrated now, Keegan frowned. "What didn't take."

"My salvation, my. . .my. . .whatever you call it, it didn't take. That same night, after the revival service, I got into the water with the pastor, and re-peated all the right words, and when he went to dunk me. . ."

"What?" Keegan pressed. "When the pastor dunked you, *what?*"

"He dropped me."

The silence was so complete that Breena believed she could have heard one of Hershey's whiskers hit the marble floor, but she could tell by his lurching shoulders that Keegan was laughing at her. "What's so funny?" she demanded, crossing both arms over her chest.

"You think because the pastor slipped up, you're not saved?" Shaking his head, Keegan took a deep breath. "Breena, Breena, Breena. What am I gonna do with you?"

"Well, you can't marry me, that's for sure."

"I can, and I will. . . .if you'll have me, of course."

Breena looked up and was startled by the earnest gleam in Keegan's eyes.

She quickly glanced away and began a serious study of the far wall.

"I know it's crazy, Breena, admitting that I feel this way after such a short time. But I love you! There's nothing I can do about it, so you'll just have to deal with that." He faced forward again and rested both palms on his knees. "But first things first. What you need is to get into a church where you can begin to grow and learn more about God's love for you. Then you'll have confidence about being saved."

"Well, maybe you're right," she agreed half-heartedly.

"Why are you so hard on yourself, Breena? Why not cut yourself a little slack? Give yourself a break once in awhile. The world is a tough enough place without beating up on yourself all the time."

She shrugged. "It *is* silly, I suppose, since you're so good at pointing out my character flaws—"

He faced her again. "Character flaws? Why, there isn't a single solitary thing wrong with you, and I'll whomp anyone who says otherwise."

When he saw the teasing glint in her eyes, he stopped talking and wrapped her in his arms. "Tell me something," Keegan whispered into her hair. "Do you love me?"

"I do."

"And do you want to marry me?"

"I do."

"When?"

She leaned back to get a better look at his wonderful, handsome, loving face. Breena had a pretty good idea what life with Keegan would be like, for he'd already shown his true colors. Without knowing how things might turn out, he'd risked rejection to repair the rift between her and her earthly father; and now he was helping her see that she'd never been abandoned by her Heavenly Father.

She could only hope and pray that, as his wife, she could give him all the things he deserved: She'd cook for him and clean and. . . *Wait a minute! He's the one with the immaculate house and the gourmet kitchen. Maybe he can teach me that stuff, too.* Anyway, whatever Keegan wanted, that's what Breena wanted—no, that's what Breena *needed*—too.

"When?" he asked again.

She leaned over and kissed the tip of his nose. "I don't know what day, but St. John's. One o'clock."

"Um. . .*which* St. John's?"

"That's for me to know and for—"

Her reply was smothered by a hailstorm of kisses.

Stormy Weather
By Tracie Peterson

Chapter 1

Gina looked at the instructions in her hand for the tenth time. "Official Grand Prix Pinewood Derby Kit," one side read. The other side had "Contains Functional Sharp Points" as its title.

"What in the world are functional sharp points?" she asked, looking down into the questioning eyes of her eight-year-old son. "Do you know what this means, Danny?"

The boy shrugged. "Mr. Cameron didn't say. He just said all the Cub Scouts were going to race them some Saturday."

Gina nodded and turned back to the kit. A block of wood, four nails, and four plastic wheels stared back up at her, along with the confusing instructions. "And we're supposed to make this into a car?"

"A race car," Danny corrected.

"Did your scoutmaster say how you were supposed to make this into a race car?" Gina asked, pushing back limp brown hair.

"You have to cut it into the shape of a car and then paint it. He said to have your dad call if he had questions. I told him I didn't have a dad, and he said moms could call him, too."

"I see," Gina said. Three years of widowhood had left a great many holes in her life, including a father to assist Danny in times of crisis. And this was definitely a crisis. The Cub Scout pinewood derby was, according to the date at the top of the page, only a couple of weeks away, and she'd not yet gotten up the courage to carve on the chunk of wood, much less produce a finished race car. Looking from the instructions to the kit to her son, Gina felt an overwhelming desire to lock herself in her bedroom until after the pinewood derby race had passed.

"I guess I'll call him," she muttered and went to the list of phone numbers she kept on the refrigerator. Of course, the refrigerator was also covered with a multitude of other papers and pictures, which made her task even more difficult. By Gina's calculations, the memorabilia and paperwork added a good twenty pounds to the already well-worn fridge door.

"Cub Scouts," she muttered, fanning through the precariously placed information. Cub Scout letters were always on blue paper. Telaine Applebee, the mother of twin boys who always managed to outperform all of the other Scouts, had created their den's newsletter. She thought by putting it on blue paper it would make parents more organized. She could hear Telaine, even now, her high-pitched voice announcing the newsletter like a prize at one of those home-product parties.

"And look," she'd nearly squealed with pride, "it's blue! You'll always know it's Scout information, because it's blue like their uniforms." Only it wasn't blue like their uniforms—more of a sugary shade of sky blue that seemed to match Telaine's perfect eyes.

Gina sighed. It wasn't that she didn't like Telaine. She did. Telaine was a wonderful woman, and Gina would give just about anything to be as organized. But looking at Telaine and seeing her perfect life was like looking into a mirror and finding all your own inadequacies.

"Here it is!" she declared, forgetting about Telaine and the thought that no doubt her twins had already completed turning their wood blocks into race cars.

"They'll probably be featured on the front of *Great Mechanics*," she muttered and picked up the receiver.

Dialing the phone, Gina noted that Danny seemed oblivious to her feelings of inadequacy, but that was the way she wanted it. To share with her eight-year-old the fears and loneliness of being a widow seemed an injustice of grand proportion. Danny just stood there staring at her with such hope—like he expected her to have some magical formula for changing wood into cars. How could she disappoint him when he believed so strongly in her ability to make things right?

The number she'd dialed began ringing and Gina immediately tensed. What would she say? How could she explain that she'd let the project get away from her and now it was nearly time for the race and she hadn't even begun to help Danny put it together?

"Hello?"

The baritone voice at the other end of the phone immediately commanded Gina's attention. "Yes, is this Mr. Cameron, Cub Scout leader for den four?"

"Among other things," the man replied in a tone that betrayed amusement.

Gina smiled to herself and took a deep breath. "Look, we've never met, but my son is one of your Wolf Cubs. No wait, I think he's a Bear Cub or a Bobcat. Oh, I forget." The man laughed, making Gina feel uncertain whether he was laughing at her in a nice way or because she'd just managed to sound like ditz of the year. "I'm sorry," she muttered and tried again. "This is Gina Bowden, Danny's mother."

"Ah, your son is a Bear."

"Especially in the morning," Gina countered.

The man chuckled. "Well, I can't vouch for that, but on Tuesday night, he's definitely a Bear. What can I do for you?"

Gina looked heavenward and rolled her eyes. *Take me away from the monotony. Give me a reason to put on mascara. Teach me what to do when the sidewalk opens up with cracks big enough to swallow small children or when the dryer won't dry but just dings at you like you should know what that means.*

"Hello?"

The masculine voice broke through Gina's thoughts. "Sorry, it's been a bad week," she said softly shaking her head. "This is the problem. I'm looking at this pinebox derby stuff—" Hysterical laughter erupted on the end of the line, causing Gina to pause. "Is something wrong?" More laughter. "You are the Cub Scout leader I'm supposed to call if I need help, aren't you?"

The man collected himself. "Yeah, but it's pinewood derby, not pinebox. We aren't racing coffins out there."

"You might as well be," Gina replied, then laughed at her own mistake. "I'm afraid if I start in on this thing, that's what it'll resemble. Come to think of it, it already resembles that. And just what are functional sharp points?"

"Would you like me to come over and help you and Danny?"

Gina sighed. "Mr. Cameron."

"Gary. Call me Gary."

"Okay, Gary, I would be very grateful if you would come give us a hand. I'm a widow, and although I've tried to be father, mother, taxi driver, Little League coach, and general all-around good sport, I've yet to master woodwork." She paused for a moment, then remembering that strange "check engine" light in the van, she added, "Or car mechanics."

His chuckles warmed her heart. "I have talents in both areas. Do you have time to work on the car right now?" he asked.

Gina smiled, unable to resist. "Which one?"

"Let's start with the wooden one and work our way up," Gary countered.

Gina breathed a sigh of relief. Just thinking about not having to be responsible for the functional sharp points was making it much easier to face the day. "Sure, come on over. The address is 311 Humboldt."

"Be there in ten minutes."

Gina hung up the phone and looked at her forlorn child. "Mr. Cameron is coming right over." Danny's face brightened. Glancing down at her sweat suit, she added, "I'm going to go change my clothes so I don't look like a bag lady. You let him in when he gets here."

Seven minutes later, while Gina was just pulling a brush through her hair,

Gary Cameron was ushered into the house by Danny. She could hear their animated conversation as she came down the stairs.

"Hey, Mr. Cameron, I'm sure glad you could help me make my car."

"No problem, Sport. Where's your mom?" It was that wonderful voice. That wonderful masculine voice. Gina paused at the door just to listen, fearful that if she crossed the threshold too soon, she just might break the spell of the moment. She needn't have worried. Danny broke it for her.

"She's upstairs changing her clothes. She didn't want to look like a rag lady."

"A rag lady?" Gary questioned.

Gina stood six feet away in complete mortification. Gone was the feeling of satisfaction that had come from fixing her hair and putting on makeup. Gone were the plans of appearing in total control and confidence.

"That's *bag* lady, and Danny you really should learn the better part of discretion." The boy shrugged and Gary laughed. Gina felt self-conscious and glanced down at her sweater and jeans.

"You look nothing like a bag lady." He smiled, and Gina noted tiny crow's-feet lined the edges of his eyes. He was obviously a man who liked to laugh. He extended his hand and formally introduced himself. "I'm Gary Cameron."

Holding his gaze a moment longer, Gina felt her pulse quicken. She put her hand in his and felt warm fingers close around hers. "I'm Gina."

For a moment neither one moved, and Gina felt hard-pressed to force herself to be the first to break the companionable silence, but finally she did. "I left the mess on the kitchen table."

"Let's get to it then," Gary said with a smile. "The sky is starting to cloud up and, knowing springtime in Kansas, we could be in for almost anything. Part of our work will need to be done outdoors so as to save you from extra cleanup."

Gina nodded. "It's this way." She walked to the kitchen, Gary following close behind her with Danny at his side. She pointed at the mess. "Nothing like waiting until the last minute," Gina apologized, bending over the pieces, "but I kept thinking sooner or later I would figure out what to do with it." She gazed up mischievously. "I came up with a few ideas, but none of them seemed to benefit Danny or the derby."

Gary held up a small red toolbox. "We'll have you on your way before you know it. We can carve it out today, and if Danny is willing to work hard at sanding it down, I can come back over and we'll work on it some more tomorrow."

"We go to church tomorrow," Danny declared.

"So do I," Gary replied. "But I was thinking maybe the afternoon would work out for us."

"Won't your wife feel neglected?" Gina asked without thinking.

"My wife and son were killed in a car accident four years ago," Gary said matter-of-factly.

"I'm sorry. Danny's father died in an accident three years ago. His car was hit head-on by a drunk driver."

Gary picked up the car kit. "Lot of them out there."

Gina studied the sandy-haired man for a moment, and when he looked up and met her gaze, she suddenly knew that here was a man who understood her pain. Here was a man she could relate to. The look he gave her made Gina tremble at the faded memory of feeling young and loved and happy.

"So would tomorrow work out for you?" Gary asked as though they hadn't just shared a very intimate moment.

"It would be fine with me. What time?"

"How about whenever you're finished with lunch?"

"Why don't you just come for lunch and stay to work on the car?"

Gary smiled. "Sounds great."

"My mom's a good cook," Danny told the man. " 'Cept when she burns something."

Gina tousled his hair. "Which is nearly once a day because some eight-year-old demands that I come see what new creation he's built in the backyard."

"She burned the macaroni and cheese today," Danny announced. "Do you want to see the pan? Mom says it looks like—"

"Danny, I think Mr. Cameron would prefer not to hear about our short-comings. How about you sit down and let him get started with that...that... thing," she interrupted, looking sadly at all the bits and pieces.

Gary laughed. "Your mom's right. We need to get a move on. We'll want to do our cutting outside, and those clouds are getting darker by the minute." Then he turned to her and flashed a quick smile. "Lunch sounds great. Church is out at noon, so, say I come here directly after?"

"Perfect," Gina replied.

Sitting down to the table, she was relieved when Gary picked up the conversation and began to explain the process of carving out the race car. She felt almost exhausted from their first encounter and needed the neutrality of woodwork. It wasn't long until Danny and Gary settled on a plan and were off to the backyard to start sawing away at the block of wood.

Watching from the kitchen window, Gina couldn't remember the last time she'd had this much fun. She and Danny had remained rather isolated after the accident, but now she honestly felt ready to deal with people again. Oh, it wasn't that she didn't have friends. She had several she felt comfortable enough to spend time with. But for the most part, it was go to church on Sunday, homeschool Danny through the week, and go to Scouts on Tuesday nights. Well, Danny went to Scouts. Gina usually sent him with Telaine and her boys and used the quiet evenings to get personal matters done that she couldn't accomplish with Danny in tow.

Telaine had been sympathetic to her needs and, because of her continual ability to be organized even in the face of adversity, Telaine had honestly helped Gina to get through the last three years. But now, Gina felt it was time to throw off her isolation.

It was funny how spending an afternoon with Gary Cameron had helped her to realize that she was ready to get on with her life again. She felt rather like a flower, opening up to the sun. Hadn't God promised He'd turn her mourning into laughter? At this she heard Danny's giggles and saw that Gary was bent over examining something in Danny's hand.

It was the rain that finally drove them into the house. Lightning flashed and thunder shook the windows, but the storm moved through quickly and the trio seemed perfectly content to ignore it as Gary explained how to sand the wood smooth.

The afternoon passed nearly as quickly as the storm, and Gina was almost ashamed when Danny complained of being hungry. She'd completely forgotten to feed the child lunch after the macaroni and cheese fiasco.

"I could use something, myself," Gary said, putting away his coping saw. "How about we go have a hamburger?"

"Can we, Mom?"

Danny's hopeful expression seemed to match the one on Gary's face. Gina grinned. "French fries, too?"

"And onion rings!" Gary declared as though closing an important business deal.

"And maybe a banana split," Danny added.

"Yeah," Gary agreed.

"Let me get my purse," Gina said, but Gary stopped her before she could move.

"My treat," he said in a voice that was nearly a whisper.

Gina could only nod. It'd been so long since anyone had offered to pay their way or treat them to anything. "Let's go."

❧

Later, with half-eaten burgers on the table and Danny off to climb the restaurant's playground equipment, Gina found herself companionably settled with Gary. It was amazing that a chance encounter with Danny's scoutmaster could leave her feeling as though she'd finally found all the answers to a lifetime of questions.

When Gary reached out to cover her hand with his, she bit her bottom lip and looked deep into serious blue eyes. "This seems unreal," she whispered.

"I was thinking the same thing," Gary replied.

Gina swallowed hard. "You can't possibly understand, but I haven't even been out with anyone since Ray died."

"I can understand. I haven't dated since Vicky, and that was high school. I never thought I'd have to do it again, and when she and Jason died, I decided I never would. But there's something about this," he said, looking off to where Danny was happily climbing the wrong way up the slide. "I suppose it sounds cliché, but I don't want it to end. I've been alone for four years and now, all of a sudden, it seems unbearable to go even one more week this way."

"I know," Gina said softly. "I figured I would just handle things on my own; that together, Danny and I could face anything and be just fine. Then Danny started saying things that made me realize how selfish I'd been in hiding away. He misses having a dad around."

"I miss being a dad," Gary said, turning to look at her. His gaze pierced Gina to the heart. "I miss being a husband, too. I don't have any interest in the singles' scene or one-night stands."

Gina swallowed hard. "I can't believe I'm saying all this—it really isn't like me to just open myself up like this. But, sometimes, when Danny's asleep and the house is all quiet, I'm almost afraid the silence will eat me alive." She paused for a moment to collect her thoughts. "Other times, like when the car won't start and I haven't a clue what's wrong or when Danny needs a race car carved out of wood, I feel too inadequate to meet the demands of being a single mom."

"It always hits me when I go out to eat, like this," he said, breaking away from the trancelike stare to look where Danny was happily playing.

Gina glanced at her watch and realized it was getting late. She should be making some comment about going home. But she didn't want to. She thought back on the years of emptiness and knew she didn't want to let this opportunity pass her by. It might seem crazy to have such strong feelings on a first date, and not even a real date at that, but something in her heart told her to take a chance. *Please God*, she prayed silently, *don't let me make a fool of myself.*

Gary spoke again, breaking her thoughts. "There are all these couples and their kids and a single man sticks out like a sore thumb. But I come anyway. And that's why I continue as a scoutmaster. Sometimes it's just nice to hear the laughter."

"We laugh a lot at my house," she said softly.

Gary looked at her with registered understanding. "I'm pretty good at fixing cars, and you've already seen what I can do with wood."

Gina smiled. "And I'm sure the house would be anything but silent with you around."

"So where do we go from here?" Gary asked quite seriously.

Gina felt her pulse quicken. He was interested. He felt the same way she did. She gave a light cough to clear her throat.

"I guess we'll have to let God decide the distant future, but for now we have a date for tomorrow. Dinner at my house."

Gary nodded. "Can I bring something?"

She wanted to laugh and tell him he was already bringing the most important missing ingredient in her frustrating life, but she didn't. "Just yourself," she replied with a smile, then remembered the pinewood derby car. "Oh, and some paint."

"Paint?" he questioned, his mind clearly not following her train of thought.

"For the car," she replied.

"Of course," he said nodding. "Danny said he wanted red, and I just happen to have a can of cherry-red gloss in my garage."

Chapter 2

Sunday dawned overcast and humid. Gina looked from the skies to the half-dressed little boy at her side and sighed. "Looks like another stormy day," she told him, reaching down to button his dress shirt.

"Are we still having s'ketti for lunch?" Danny asked hopefully.

"You bet," Gina replied, helping him tuck the shirt into his pants. "There. Now you look absolutely charming. Every little girl in Sunday school will notice how handsome you are."

"Oh, Mom," the boy replied, his expression very sober, "I can't be worried about that right now. I got lots of time to get a girlfriend and get married. First I want you to get married."

Gina smiled and knelt in front of her son. "I know you want that. And for once in a very long time, I think I want it, too. I think we should both pray about it and trust God for the answer."

"I think Mr. Cameron would make a good husband for you. He's strong and he knows how to fix cars and you don't know how to fix cars," Danny said seriously. "Mr. Cameron also told me that you have a smile that's like sunshine."

Gina felt herself blush. "Oh, he did, did he?" Could it be the heart of a poet beat within that Cub leader facade? "Well, we will just have to see what happens. Now come on or we'll be late for church."

They pulled into the church parking lot just as thunder rumbled low. It continued rumbling off and on throughout Sunday school and church, but always it seemed to hang off in the distance. Gina gave it very little thought, however, as she hurried Danny into the van and headed for home.

She felt as giddy as a schoolgirl going on her first date. A man was actually coming to the house. A handsome man who was interested in her for more than just the pinewood derby.

"Danny, get changed right away and come help me in the kitchen," she called as Danny disappeared into his room. She hurried into her own room and tried to figure out what to wear. She was just reaching for a sleeveless cotton blouse when the weather radio sounded a warning alert. Reaching for the button that would let her hear what the latest weather update revealed, Gina kicked off her shoes and pulled at the zipper in her skirt.

"This is the National Weather Service office in Topeka," the male voice announced. "The Severe Storms Forecast Center in Kansas City, Missouri, has issued Tornado Watch #237 to be in effect from 12:30 p.m. until 6 p.m. This watch is for an area along and sixty miles either side of a line from St. Joseph, Missouri, to Council Grove, Kansas. Some of the counties included in the watch are. . ."

"Great," Gina muttered. "Just what we needed." The man was continuing the routine speech, giving the names of counties to be on the watch for severe weather and telling what a tornado watch entailed. To Gina, who had lived in Kansas all of her life, the information was something she could quote line for line, including the pattern of counties as they were given for a specific area. But even as she mimicked the weatherman's announcement, Gina took the matter in complete seriousness.

"Danny, we're in a tornado watch," she called out. "Make sure you have your bag ready." Danny's bag consisted of treasures he wanted to protect in case they had to make a mad dash for the basement.

"Did you put new batteries in my flashlight?" Danny questioned at the top of his lungs.

"Check it for yourself," Gina replied, slipping on comfortable khaki slacks.

"Wow!" Danny hollered back. "It shines really bright now. Just like when it was new."

"Well, pack it in your bag and take it downstairs," Gina instructed.

Going to the window, Gina glanced out to check the skies. Nothing appeared overly threatening. There were heavy gray clouds off to the west, but otherwise it actually seemed to be clearing in their area. She knew this could be both good and bad. Cloud coverage usually kept the temperature down, and since higher temperatures seemed to feed the elements necessary for stronger storms, she would have just as well preferred the clouds remain.

Deciding not to worry about it, Gina clicked the radio off and grabbed her own bag of precious possessions. Her bag, more like a small suitcase, contained important household papers and photos that were irreplaceable. Usually when the storm season began, she simply took the case downstairs and left it there; but this year the weather had been fairly mild through March, and there hadn't been any real need to worry about it.

Trudging downstairs, Gina found Danny already in the basement. The basement was small and unfinished, but Gina had tried to make it homey for situations just like this. She had put in a small double bed for those times when the storms seemed to rage all night long. It had come in handy last year when the season had been particularly nasty. There were also a table and chairs and several board games she and Danny could play if they wanted to keep their minds off the storms.

There were also more practical things. Under the stairs, Ray had enclosed the area for storage and for protection if a storm was actually bearing down on them. They had heard it was the strongest place for shelter and so it was here that they would take their last line of defense. Gina had placed a supply of batteries, candles, matches, and bottled water on a narrow section of shelving that Ray had built for just such a purpose. There was also a battery-operated television, and Gina stored her extra linens and blankets here as well. The only other thing was an old mattress that had been propped against the wall. Ray had always told her that if a tornado was actually headed for them, they would pull the mattress down on top to help shield their bodies from the possibility of flying debris. They'd never had to use it, but Gina was ready, and it made her feel safe just knowing that it was there.

She knew her friends often laughed about the cautious manner in which she dealt with storms, but she still had nightmares about a time when she had been young and a tornado had devastated the farm she'd lived on. After seeing firsthand what a tornado could do, Gina knew she would never take the matter for granted.

"Mom, are we gonna have a tornado this time?" Danny questioned, securing his bag under the game table.

"I sure hope not. Why don't we say a little prayer just in case." Danny nodded and Gina bowed her head. "Dear God, please keep us safely in Your care, no matter the weather, no matter our fears. Let us remember that You hold us safely in Your hands."

"Amen," Danny said loudly. "Can we eat now?" He looked up at her with a mischievous grin.

"I still have to boil the pasta," she told him. "Let's get upstairs and you can set the table while I see how the sauce is doing."

"Don't forget the bread."

"I won't," she told him, giving his backside a playful swat.

They worked silently, Danny setting the table with the good dishes and Gina trying to imagine what it would be like to have a regular Sunday meal with a man at her table. She tried not to make too much of it. She wasn't one of those women who couldn't cope in life without a man at her side, but she did realize how much nicer it was to have the companionship of another adult. Especially a male adult.

She had just pulled the bread from the oven when the front doorbell sounded. "That's him!" Danny yelled from the living room.

"Well, let him in," Gina replied and hurried to drain the pasta. She arranged spaghetti on each of their plates and had started to ladle the sauce on top when Gary came into the kitchen, a two-liter bottle of cola in his arms along with a bouquet of flowers.

"I brought flowers for the lady of the house and drink for all," he announced, giving her the flowers with a sweeping bow.

Gina laughed. "They're beautiful, but you really shouldn't have."

Gary sobered, his blue eyes seeming to darken as he beheld her. "And why not?"

Gina couldn't think of any reason and simply shrugged. "You're just in time. I only need to slice the bread."

"Let me," Gary said, putting the soda on the counter. He immediately glanced around for a knife.

Gina handed him a slender knife and pointed him in the direction of where she'd placed the bread to cool. Just then, the unmistakable sound of the weather radio shattered their companionable silence.

"Danny, please run up to my room, unplug the radio, and bring it down here," Gina ordered. Danny, knowing the seriousness of the matter, took off in a flash and quickly brought her the radio.

Gina punched the button in time to hear that a tornado warning had been issued for Morris County. "A tornado was spotted on the ground five miles west of the town of Wilsey. People living in and around the areas of Wilsey and Council Grove should take immediate cover."

"And so it begins," Gary said, trying to sound lighthearted about the matter.

Gina nodded and continued listening to the information. "It sounds like the storms are moving our way but not very fast. Maybe we'll have time for lunch before we have to concern ourselves with anything too serious."

"I'm sure we'll be just fine," Gary replied. He held up the bread like a prize. "This is ready."

"Well, let's eat then," Gina declared, bringing the plates of spaghetti to the table.

Gary offered to give the blessing, and when he did, Gina felt tears come to her eyes. Ray used to pray over the meals in a similar manner, and hearing Gary's voice only served to bring back the memory in a bittersweet wave.

Caught up in the memory, Gina didn't even realize Gary had concluded the prayer until Danny asked if he could have some bread. She pulled herself together and looked up with a smile.

"Of course you may," she told her son and watched while Gary handed him a slice.

Gary had just begun to tell them tales of his own days as a Cub Scout when the radio went off once again. This time, it seemed, another storm had popped up in Wabaunsee County just to the west of them. It was only a thunderstorm warning, but both Gary and Gina knew how dangerous these things could be.

Danny ate with great enthusiasm, apparently oblivious to the look that flashed between Gina and Gary. The weather was making it impossible for Gina to eat, but she tried to give the pretense in order to keep Danny calm. Gary smiled reassuringly until another tornado warning, this one issued for towns much closer to their own, sounded on the radio.

"You do have a basement, right?"

She nodded, feeling better knowing that if she had to endure a bad storm, she would at least have Gary's company through the worst of it.

"Danny and I are all prepared."

"Why don't we just move our dinner downstairs?" Gary suggested. "Then we can more or less ignore the radio and just have a good time. We can even work on the car down there, although I wouldn't want to paint it there. The fumes would probably make us all goofy by the end of the day. In fact, with the humidity the way it is, I wouldn't suggest painting it today anyway. We can work on the axles and wheels and add the weights. I even brought a scale to make sure it's regulation weight."

Gina nodded as the radio once again sounded the alarm. "I guess we could move everything downstairs. The basement isn't finished or very nice to look at, but I do have a table and chairs down there. And you do have an after-dinner activity. . . ."

"Then lead the way," Gary said, jumping to his feet. "Danny, you grab up the bread and take your silverware. Gina, you bring your plate and Danny's—oh, and don't forget your silver. I'll bring the rest."

Gina liked the way he took charge and only paused long enough to grab the weather radio as she headed downstairs. They might as well have it with them to know what was going on, even if they didn't have to worry about taking cover. Of course, it was always possible a tornado could plop down nearby and then she would want to get under the staircase, but that wasn't something she wanted to think about just now. She wanted things to be calm and for the storms to go away, and she nearly laughed out loud as she made her way down the basement stairs. How dare stormy weather interfere with her date with Gary!

"This is a real adventure," Danny declared as Gina put his plate on the table. "We're having fun, aren't we, Mom?"

Gina forced a smile. "I think you have the right attitude about it. When life gives you a storm, look for the silver lining."

"Or the basement," Gary called out as he made his way down the stairs. His arms were filled, and Gina hurried to help him. "I'll be right back," he told her as he put his plate on the table. "I'm going to get our drinks and napkins—and my little red toolkit."

Within a few moments he had returned, and as he took his seat at the ancient plastic-top table, the radio announced additional tornado sightings. Gina felt herself tense. She didn't realize how evident it was, however, until Gary reached over and gave her arm a gentle pat.

"You have a nice cozy place here," he said, glancing around the room.

"We had to spend all night down here last year," Danny told him between bites of food. "We even homeschooled down here."

"Oh, so you're homeschooled," Gary replied. And with that he set the conversation in full swing, and soon even Gina was caught up in explanations of how homeschooling worked and what she tried to accomplish. Danny related wonderful field trips they'd taken and how he even joined the soccer team at the local YMCA.

She was so engrossed in the conversation that when the tornado sirens actually went off and the radio weatherman announced that a tornado had been sighted not ten miles from where she lived, Gina was completely surprised.

It was only then that she noticed the rain beating down on the basement window. The window well was already filled with about two inches of water. Lightning flashed and thunder roared right behind it, betraying the fact that the storm was right upon them.

Gina tried to take a deep breath in order to calm herself. She silently prayed for courage and calm in order to keep Danny from being afraid, but already she could read the fear in his eyes. When he left his place at the table and came to her, Gina wordlessly pushed back from the table and took the boy onto her lap. Eight was a difficult age for a child, especially a boy. They needed independence and rough soccer games and all-night campouts with their friends. But sometimes they still needed their mothers' laps and hugs that reassured them that all would be well.

Gina wrapped her arms around Danny's trembling body and kissed his forehead. "We're in God's hands, Danny," she whispered.

Gary reached over and stroked Danny's back. "Don't worry, Sport, it'll be over before you know it." He spoke to Danny, but it was Gina's eyes he looked into.

Gina drew strength from his calm demeanor.

"Why don't we play a game?" Gary suggested.

Danny peaked his head up. "Which one?"

"Hmmm, I don't know, how about—"

Just then a roaring boom of thunder shook the whole house and the lights went out. The room was dark except for the flashes of lightning that seemed to come one right on top of the other and penetrated through the small basement windows.

"How about Blindman's Bluff?" Gary said with a laugh. "We won't even need blindfolds."

Gina laughed, amazed that Gary's presence could give her so much peace. God had known she would need help, and even though the storm raged overhead and the electricity had been knocked out, she realized she wasn't half as afraid as she might have been had she and Danny been alone. Sometimes it was just easier to bear the storms of life when you had someone to stand beside you.

❧

By evening, the storms had calmed and the weather had turned peaceful. The electricity had even been restored, and Gina noted that everything still appeared to be in one piece as they moved back up from the basement. The radio droned softly from the kitchen, announcing the forecast for the evening to be clear.

Gina walked Gary to the front door and laughed. "Well, it wasn't exactly how I figured our first date would go."

Gary stopped in midstep and looked at her seriously. "This wasn't a date."

Gina swallowed hard. Had she misread him? "It wasn't?"

"No," Gary said, shaking his head. "You don't take eight-year-olds on romantic dates. I have something special planned for our first date. You doing anything on Friday night?"

Gina grinned, feeling a sense of elation wash over her. "That depends on what you have in mind. I was going to clean out the refrigerator and wash my hair. Can you top that?"

Gary gave her a look that made her want to melt into a puddle at his feet. "I think I can manage to beat that out. How about I pick you up around seven and we go out for a nice grown-up dinner and then take a walk at the lake?"

Gina tilted her chin up while she considered her options. "Hmmm, that's a tough choice. Dinner with a handsome man and a romantic, moonlit walk or burying myself in condiments and soapsuds." She watched a grin spread across his face. "I guess the fridge can wait."

"Good. Seven o'clock sharp," he said. "Oh, and if you're free on Saturday, we can paint the car. That should give us plenty of time to detail it out for the race."

"Sounds like a winner to me," Gina replied.

She watched him climb into his car and didn't stop watching until he'd backed out of her drive and headed off down Humboldt Street. *This was definitely the start of something exciting,* she thought. *Please God, let it be real.*

Chapter 3

Gary showed up at seven o'clock sharp. He looked down at his navy suit and red-patterned tie and hoped it would meet with Gina's approval. He hadn't felt this nervous since. . .well. . . since the last time he'd showed up for a first date. Taking a deep breath, he punched the doorbell and waited for Gina to answer.

"God, don't let me push too hard or act out of line," Gary prayed aloud. Just then Gina opened the door, and the vision took his breath away. She smiled a smile that went all the way to her blue eyes. . .and to his heart.

"Good evening," Gary said, struggling to control his breathing.

"Good evening," she replied.

He faltered. Should he compliment the way she looked? Should he say that the cream-printed dress looked particularly nice—that he liked the way she'd styled her shoulder-length brown hair? His mouth felt dry.

"Ah. . .um. . .you look really great," he stammered.

She looked down briefly, then returned her gaze to meet his eyes. "Thank you, you do, too."

His mind went blank. What was he supposed to do now?

Gina stepped back from the door. "Would you like to come in for a minute. I just need to check on something upstairs, and I'll be ready to leave."

"Sure," Gary replied, following her into the house. He waited while she went about her business, wishing he felt more at ease. *This shouldn't be such a big deal,* he told himself. But it was a big deal.

It seemed strangely quiet without Danny's rambunctious voice, and Gary figured this would be as good a way to break the ice as any. "Where's your son?" he called out.

"Staying with the Applebee twins," she replied, coming back down the stairs, securing her right earring. "He was very excited to be able to have a sleepover at their house." She lowered her voice to a whisper and added, "They have two horses and some chickens, don't you know."

Gary laughed. "Yes, and a dog who's got a litter of six-week-old puppies as I recall."

Gina nodded. "So are you ready?"

"I thought I was."

This caused Gina to pause and look at him rather sternly. "Is there a problem?"

Gary thought she almost looked alarmed, as if he might back out of their date and ruin the evening. "I'm nervous," he finally admitted.

She grinned. "Me, too. I thought I'd pass out when I opened the door."

This finally broke the tension, and Gary smiled. "That makes two of us. Why are we acting like this? We're grown adults, and we've been through all this before."

"Yes, but not with each other," Gina replied.

"True, but that shouldn't matter."

Gina gave him a look of disbelief. "But of course it matters. You haven't learned my hideous secrets yet. You don't know how I look when I wake up in the morning or how I keep house or cook—with the exception of spaghetti."

"Which was fantastic," Gary interjected. "And exactly what secrets could you have that would make the prospects of spending time with you any less attractive?"

"I don't know, but there are bound to be some. You know how it can be. I remember arguing with Ray over stupid little things."

"Like what?"

"Like not leaving dirty clothes all over the floor but rather in the hamper," Gina began.

"A horrible secret to be sure," Gary teased. "Okay, what else?"

"Well, we used to clash when it came to vacations. I liked to go to quiet places far removed from the tourists. Ray liked to hit all the tourist traps."

"Anything else?"

"I like to read in the evening when Danny goes to bed."

"Hmmm," Gary said, stroking his chin, "Did that habit come about before or after Ray died?"

Gina blushed. "Well, I have to admit, it came about after."

"So. . .if you had something better to do, you might reconsider?" Gary questioned, a mischievous expression on his face.

"I might."

"Well, I just don't see a problem. I'm a very flexible man. I like most foods, love to travel and try new things, but am just as happy to sit still and do nothing. I have given myself a lot of consideration, and I just don't think I have too many flaws that will interfere or create a conflict with our personalities."

Gina smiled. "In all seriousness, we don't know much about each other."

"That's why we're dating," Gary replied. "And I'm starving, so can we continue this conversation at the restaurant?"

Gina nodded. "I was beginning to think I should just warm up some leftovers."

Gary took hold of her arm and maneuvered her toward the door. "Not that I wouldn't enjoy another sampling of your cooking, but I've got special plans for tonight."

He liked the way she looked up at him, her eyes wide with curiosity, her expression betraying her anticipation. She brought back all the excitement of his youth, and suddenly he believed in love at first sight.

Dinner passed in pleasantries and memories of Danny and days gone by. Gary enjoyed listening to Gina talk about her childhood and tried to imagine the brown-haired beauty as a tagalong child in pigtails.

"I've often thought I'd like to move back to the country and live on a farm again," Gina told him.

"Honestly?" Gary questioned. "I've considered such a thing myself."

"You're just saying that to impress me," Gina teased.

"No. I'm serious. I think a farm could be a lot of fun."

Gina laughed lightly. "It's also a lot of work. Things don't just take care of themselves. I'm always trying to explain that to Danny. Especially when he nags me for a puppy."

"I've no doubt that's true," Gary replied. "I didn't mean I wanted to actually run a big farm. Plow the fields and plant and harvest. I doubt I'd be any good at that, and if that's what you had in mind, then maybe we have reached our first clash of personalities."

Gina shook her head. "No, I don't desire to go back to that headache. But I love the way the air smells in the country. The ground freshly plowed, wheat when it nears harvest, the scent of the trees after a summer rain. . ."

Gary smiled and nodded, then his smile faded as he caught sight of someone across the room. He tried to regain control of his emotions, but Gina was too quick for him.

"What's wrong?"

Gary tried to figure out what to say. He didn't want anything to spoil their evening. But, because the man he'd spied was now walking toward their table, Gary knew his wish wasn't going to come true.

Tensing, he took a long drink of his iced tea and waited.

"Hello, Gary."

Gary looked up at the same time Gina did. "Hello, Jess," Gary said rather stiffly.

"I think this is the first time I've seen you out with a woman since Vicky died," the man replied, his voice clearly hostile.

"Gina, this is Jess Masterson. My father-in-law."

Gina reached out her hand, but Jess clearly ignored her. "I suppose you haven't heard yet, but there's going to be a rather sticky issue brought up before the city council."

"And you're no doubt behind it," Gary replied, not even bothering to hide his hostility.

Masterson smiled. "As a matter of fact, I am."

"So why is this sticky issue something you needed to bring up at my dinner?"

The older man shrugged. "Because it has to do with your pet project of Scouting."

"Scouting?" Gary shook his head. "What in the world are you talking about?"

Masterson glanced around the room, noted his party and waved, then turned to Gary and Gina. "I'm strongly pushing to drop all funding for Scouting given by the city."

Gary felt unquestionable anger surfacing. "And what did the Scouts do to offend you?"

"They're an elitist group. They force those who join to participate in religious indoctrination. I'm suggesting," he paused and smiled, "or rather demanding, that the Scouts eliminate any ties to 'God' in their organization or the city will have to discontinue its support. There's that whole separation of church and state thing, you know."

Gary clenched his jaw tightly, and before he could speak, Gina replied, "I'm sorry you feel that way, Mr. Masterson. I'm afraid if they removed the funding from Scouting it would make it more difficult, but I doubt it would do away with the local organization. Even if you could remove a focus on God and country from Scouting, it wouldn't change anything. Scouting is not part of the church or government. We joined voluntarily because we honor the values of Scouting. No one is forcing anyone else to join."

"No, but they are forcing taxpayers to help support the organization. That isn't acceptable when it's such a selective organization."

"And do you speak for the majority, Mr. Masterson, or for a select few?" Gina countered.

Gary wanted to applaud her bold attitude, but he knew that sooner or later Masterson would drag her to the ground over the issue. He started to interject his own thoughts on the matter, but Masterson spoke before he could answer.

"I speak for the law of the land, Miss—"

"Mrs. Bowden," Gina replied.

Masterson scowled as he threw Gary a look of disgust. "Dating married women, Gary?"

Gina slammed down her fork at this. "I am a widow, Mr. Masterson. Not that I think it's any of your concern, but because you are a very rude man I will clear the matter before you continue to prejudge the situation. I am also the mother of a Cub Scout. I fully support the Boy Scouts of America and their desire to put God at the center of their organization. Perhaps if more people put God at the center of their lives, this would never be an issue. However, because you are so intent on bringing up issues of separation of church and state, perhaps you should research the origins of those issues and read for yourself that while our forefathers had no desire to allow government to organize or prohibit religious affairs for the people, Thomas Jefferson wrote quite eloquently of the need for Christian values in government."

"He also wrote of the need to have a revolution every twenty years," Masterson retorted.

"And perhaps we should," Gina replied hotly. "Perhaps if we'd had a revolution the first time someone suggested the elimination of God from the foundations of our society, we wouldn't be in the situation we are today."

"You are naive, Mrs. Bowden."

"And you are out of line, Jess," Gary said, getting to his feet. "I came here for a nice quiet dinner, not for a political-religious debate. I suggest you join your party and allow us our privacy."

Jess Masterson's dark eyes seemed to narrow on Gary as if he were sizing up his opponent. "I simply thought you'd like to know about the situation."

"You could have called me at home. You know the number."

Masterson looked as though he'd like to say more but simply nodded and quickly walked away from the table. Gary watched him rejoin his own group before taking his seat. The evening had been quite successfully ruined as far as he was concerned.

Calling for the check, Gary hoped he might be able to salvage at least part of their date by going on the romantic walk he'd promised. But as they reached the parking lot, a light rain began to fall and his plans were thoroughly thwarted.

But Gina came to the rescue.

"Well, why don't we forget about the walk and go back to my place instead? I have a couple of movies I checked out from the library, and I could fix us some popcorn." She slid into the car and smiled. "Or we could just sit and talk politics."

Gary let his anger fade. "I think the first part sounds good."

Coming around to the driver's side, Gary felt as though he should somehow try to explain Jess Masterson and his anger. When he climbed behind the wheel, he sat silently for several seconds, trying to figure out how best to begin.

"I'm sorry for that," he finally said, not even bothering to start the engine. "Jess has been angry at God ever since Vicky and Jason died."

"He blames God rather than the drunk who hit them?"

"Vicky didn't die right away, and Jess, who was always a bit mixed on his feelings about God and Christianity, began to pray as he'd never prayed in his life. He pleaded with God to save Vicky. She was an only child, you see. And with Jason already dead and Vicky so severely injured, Jess wanted to grab at any lifeline being offered."

"But she died anyway," Gina whispered.

Gary turned to look at her. The compassion and understanding in her expression made him want to take her in his arms. She knew that pain and longing. "Yes, she did. After nearly thirty-six hours of fighting for her life, Vicky died. Jess went ballistic, and Cissy, Vicky's mom, collapsed into my arms in tears. Cissy was a strong believer; so was Vicky. Jason was only four, but he loved to go to Sunday school and church. Cissy and I got through by turning to God, but Jess alienated himself from God and rejected the whole line of comfort. He said if God cared so much, He would never have allowed Vicky and Jason to die in the first place."

"I think that's a pretty normal response," Gina replied. "I remember feeling rather hostile, myself. I knew God was still there for me, but I wasn't sure I wanted His kind of comforting. After all, He could have kept Ray alive and He didn't."

Gary nodded. "I know. I felt that way, too, at least initially. God brought me past that point, however."

"Yes, He did that for me as well, but," Gina said quite seriously, "I wanted to come past that point. I wanted to let go of Ray and the accident and the anger of blaming the man who killed him—blaming anyone. Jess Masterson doesn't appear to be a man who wants to get beyond those things. How does his wife deal with him?"

"She died last year. Cancer," Gary replied flatly.

"Poor man," Gina said, shaking her head. "He must have been devastated."

Gary's heart warmed at Gina's compassion for the man who'd just so angrily berated her. "You're a special lady, Gina Bowden," he said softly, reaching out to touch her cheek.

Gina held his hand in place with her own hand. "I guess this date turned out to be rather revealing, after all. I'm not sorry for what happened. I hope you won't be, either."

Gary took a deep breath and let it back out. She had such a calming effect on him. He smiled. "No, I'm not sorry. I'd pay good money to see you take Jess to task again the way you did in the restaurant. I don't think he expected that out of you."

Gina grinned. "Like I said, it's been a very revealing evening."

"Revealing but not very romantic," Gary said almost apologetically.

"Well," Gina said, removing her hand from his, "the night's still young."

Chapter 4

S aturday dawned in complete pandemonium. Telaine called early to say that Danny had been begging to come home since six that morning. It seemed to have something to do with the fact he was going to work on his pinewood derby car with Mr. Cameron. Then, after assuring Telaine that it was all right to bring Danny home before the agreed upon nine-thirty, Gina had to face the fact that her dryer had given up and was now completely useless.

It had been some time since she'd hung clothes outside, but after wiping down the lines, she went to work and actually found she enjoyed the task. It brought back memories of childhood, when all of their clothes had been line-dried. She remembered how sweet their things had smelled after being outside in the sunshine.

She had just managed to empty her laundry basket when she made out the unmistakable sound of someone pulling into her front driveway. No doubt it was Telaine with Danny. Then a feeling washed over her. *Surely Gary wouldn't be coming at this hour,* she thought, looking down at her watch. It was only just now eight-thirty. She felt her pulse quicken.

She hurried through the house, leaving the empty basket in the laundry room, and had just reached the front door when someone knocked loudly from the other side. Opening it, Gina found herself face-to-face with a delivery man and a huge bouquet of flowers.

"How beautiful!" she exclaimed, taking the flowers in hand.

"Mrs. Bowden, will you sign here?" the man requested.

Gina smiled, smelled the flowers, and nodded. "Who are they from?" she questioned as she took the pen he offered.

"There's a card," the man replied. "That should tell you everything you need to know."

She nodded again and handed the man his pen. "Wait a minute and I'll get your tip."

"No need, ma'am. I've already been tipped sufficiently for this delivery."

With that, he was gone. Gina closed the door slowly and savored the aroma of hothouse flowers. She put the glass vase on the kitchen table and opened the card. After sitting up until midnight talking with Gary, she had little doubt that the flowers were from him.

But they weren't.

My sincerest wish is to be forgiven for my rude behavior. If I offended or otherwise caused you pain, I am sorry.

Jess Masterson.

"Well, I'll be," Gina whispered, looking at the card again to make certain she'd read it correctly.

The bouquet was clearly an expensive one. Gina didn't even recognize some of the flowers included in the arrangement, but the size alone made her well aware that the cost must have been considerable. Leaving them on the kitchen table, Gina threw another load of clothes into the washing machine and then returned to start some baking. She wanted to bake a batch of Danny's favorite cookies. Chocolate chip with nuts.

"Mom! Mom, I'm home!" came a yell as the front door flew open with a resounding bang.

"I'm in the kitchen," she called to her son.

"Mrs. Applebee says to tell you I was good," Danny declared coming into the kitchen. "I got to ride the horse and play with the puppies. Those puppies are sure cute and one of them liked me a whole lot. Do you suppose we could have one? Where's Mr. Cameron?"

All of this came without Danny drawing a single breath or pausing long enough for a comment or answer from his mother. Gina looked at the rambunctious boy and laughed. "He's not here yet. No we can't have a puppy right now. I'm sure they were very cute, however, and I'm glad you got to play with them and ride the horse," she replied in reverse order of his delivery. "I'm also glad you were good for Mrs. Applebee, although I can't imagine it was good that you got her up at the crack of dawn to come home."

Danny's enthusiasm remained high. "They have to get up early to feed the animals," he told her simply. "I didn't wake anybody up. The rooster did that." He came up to Gina to see what she was doing. "Are you making something I like?"

"I sure am. Chocolate chip cookies with pecans."

She had thought it impossible for Danny to look any happier. "All right!" he declared and practically started dancing around the room.

Just then, the doorbell rang. "Mr. Cameron!" Danny exclaimed, heading at a full run for the door.

Gina knew he was probably right. A part of her wanted to run for the door at the same time, but instead she held back and mixed in the final ingredients for the cookies.

"Hello, Danny," she could hear Gary say from the front room. She felt flushed just thinking of the way his voice excited her. Last night had been wonderful, in spite of Jess Masterson. They had talked and shared their hearts on so many things. Gary believed in the power of God to move those pesky mountains of life, and he seemed the perfect counterpart to her own beliefs.

"Mom's making cookies," Danny told Gary as they came into the kitchen. "Can we paint the car today?" he questioned eagerly.

"I don't see why not," Gary replied. "Why don't you go get it?" Danny gave a little cheer and hurried off to his room, while Gary turned his full attention to Gina. "Good morning."

She spoke about the same time he spied the flowers. "Good morning. I see you've noticed my morning surprise."

Gary nodded. "Is it your birthday?"

She laughed. "No. They're from Jess Masterson, complete with apology. Here," she said, picking up the card. "Read for yourself."

Gary took the card and shook his head. "You must have made some impression on the old man. I've never known him to apologize to anyone."

"Well, I have to admit, I was stunned. I thought the flowers were from. . ." She paused, realizing how pretentious it might sound to admit the truth.

"From me?" Gary said, fixing his gaze on her.

Gina licked her lips and felt her face grow hot. "Yes," she finally managed to say.

Gary laughed. "I would have, but I ran by the bookstore this morning and then, well, to be honest—I forgot. The place was in chaos. We're having a sale today, and there were some last-minute changes."

Gary had told her all about his bookstore, Cameron Christian Books and Gifts. Gina was fascinated to know that after many years of patronage to the store, she'd never once met or seen Gary, the owner. "I really didn't expect you to bring flowers. I just figured they were from you because I didn't know who else would have had any interest in sending them."

Gary sobered. "It sure isn't like him."

"Well, if you have his number, I'd like to call him later and thank him for the flowers. And to accept his apology."

Gary reached out and touched one of the blossoms. "I just wonder what he's up to."

Gina frowned. "Does he have to be up to anything?"

Gary shrugged. "Unless he's changed; and after seeing him last night, I don't think that's happened."

"I think we should give the man the benefit of the doubt," Gina replied, wiping her hands on a nearby dish towel. "After all, the Bible says we're to forgive if asked."

Gary seemed to consider her words for a moment. "I just don't like it, that's all. I know Jess Masterson too well, and I'm worried that this is just his way of trying to manipulate you."

"Why would he care what I thought?" Gina asked, her temper starting to get the better of her. That Gary would act so callously and be so skeptical about his father-in-law's apology really bothered her.

"Here's my car!" Danny declared, bounding back into the kitchen.

He was totally unaware of the tension, and Gina intended to keep it that way. "I'm sure you and Mr. Cameron want to get to work right away. You can either work in here or out on the patio; the choice is yours."

"Outside!" Danny declared.

"Yes, I think that would be best since we'll be spray painting," Gary agreed. He looked at Gina for a moment, his expression apologetic, then turned to Danny. "Do you have some newspapers?"

"I've been saving them just like you told me to do," Danny replied with great pride.

"Good, then go spread them on the patio table and we'll get right to work."

Danny nodded and took off through the laundry room and out the back door.

"Look, I'm sorry," Gary said to Gina.

"Are you really, or should I doubt your apology as well?"

"Touché," Gary said, stuffing his hands into his pockets. "I guess I acted out of line."

Gina grinned. "It's all a part of that 'getting to know you' stuff. I just didn't want to think that when my apologies were necessary, you'd believe them less than sincere."

Gary nodded. "Point well taken."

❧

Later that evening, with Danny happily preoccupied with a naval battle in the bathtub, Gina picked up the telephone in her bedroom and dialed the number Gary had left for Jess Masterson.

"Hello?" a gravelly voice sounded.

"Mr. Masterson?"

"Yes."

"This is Gina Bowden. I wanted to thank you for the flowers and the apology."

There was silence for several seconds before Jess Masterson replied. "Well, I did feel bad for acting so rudely. I appreciate your willingness to look the other way."

Gina wasn't sure she agreed with his wording, but she didn't want to create yet another scene by challenging his statement, especially when she wanted to ask him more about his stand against the Boy Scouts. "May I ask you a question?"

"Certainly," Masterson replied.

"I wondered why you were so set on fighting this thing out with the Boy Scouts. I mean, I know firsthand there is a lot of local support for Scouting. I suppose I'm just curious as to why you would ruin a good thing for everyone else just because you're angry at God."

"Who said I'm doing it because I'm angry at God?" Masterson retorted, his voice betraying his anger. "I suppose that was Gary's analysis."

"Well, isn't it true? I mean, what does it matter to you if the Boy Scouts make it an issue to honor God and country?"

"It matters that they are treating others unfairly by demanding an allegiance to God."

"I fail to see how it is unfair. No one is forced to join the Boy Scouts. It isn't a requirement in order to be educated in the public school system. It isn't necessary in order to be able to vote or serve in government or other forms of public service. It is an elective club, rather like your country club, Mr. Masterson."

"But my country club doesn't interfere in my religious beliefs. I may still join the country club so long as I adhere to the rules of the club and pay my dues."

"It's no different for the Scouts," Gina countered. "We adhere to the rules. Rules about being honorable to God and country. Promises to do our best, to help other people. Oh, and we pay dues that are a whole lot less exclusive than the dues you pay to your country club."

Masterson was silent for several moments. When he spoke, it so surprised Gina that she could do little more than agree to his idea.

"I'd like to come over and talk about this in more detail. Perhaps you could arrange for Gary to be present as well."

"When?"

"How about tomorrow?"

"We have church in the morning, but the afternoon would be fine. Say around three?"

"Thank you, that would be fine," Jess replied. "I'll see you then."

"Oh, do you have the address?" Gina questioned, forgetting about the flower delivery.

"Yes, it was in the telephone book. That's how I arranged for the flowers."

"Of course," Gina said, feeling rather silly. "Until tomorrow then."

As she hung up the phone, she heard the unmistakable sound of water being drained from the bathtub. Danny had apparently finished with his bath. She stared at the telephone for a moment, wondering why Jess Masterson would make it a point to come all the way over to her house to talk about his fight against funding for the Boy Scouts.

"I'm ready for bed," Danny announced from the doorway. Once again he'd failed to dry off before putting on his pajamas, and Gina wanted to laugh out loud at the way the material clung and bunched.

"Come here," she said with a grin. "Let me get you untwisted." She turned him around and found the entire back of the pajama top was caught up around his shoulders, leaving most of his back bare.

She adjusted his shirt, then prayed with him, and finally kissed him soundly before tucking him into his bed down the hall.

"Mommy," Danny said sleepily, "do you think if you and Mr. Cameron get married, I could call him Dad? I mean, do you think Daddy would mind?"

Gina felt her throat grow tight. "Honey, Mr. Cameron and I are just friends right now. I don't know if God would have me marry him or not, but I'm sure that's a question we don't need to worry about right now."

"I want to call him Dad when you get married," Danny said, not seeming overly concerned with Gina's words. "I'm going to pray and ask God to 'splain it to Daddy in heaven. I don't want to hurt his feelings."

Gina kissed him on the forehead. "I think Daddy will understand perfectly," she told her son. "Now get some sleep. I love you very much."

"I love you, too," Danny said yawning loudly. "And Mommy?"

"Yes?"

"I had a lot of fun today."

She smiled and tousled his hair. "I'm glad. I did, too."

There was a comfort in knowing he was safe and happy and healthy. A comfort that Gina wouldn't trade for anything in the world. Not companionship with Gary or any other man. She wanted to remarry and give Danny a father, but it had to be right. It had to be the right man and the right time. He had to be someone she could love and respect and someone who would love her and Danny as if they had belonged to him from the start. Gary had made a special place in both their hearts, but Gina knew it was important to be careful.

Back in her own room, Gina stretched out on her bed and picked up her book, a wordy intellectual piece on New Age religions. Telaine had suggested it, but Gina found it rather dry and boring. Putting it aside, her mind turned to Gary's comments on whether she read because of a lack of anything else to do. She smiled. Of course, he was partly right. She loved to read, however, and would find time for it whether she was married or single. But this time of night had always belonged to just her and Ray.

She allowed her mind to run back over the memories of her marriage. She was happy as a wife and mother. She couldn't imagine wanting anything more out of life. She didn't mind that other women wanted it all—careers, travel, children, husbands—even politics. But she was happy with things being simple and noninvasive. Even now her modest home was paid for, and she had Ray's life insurance money in the bank, which paid their living expenses. No boss called her to come in when she had something else planned with her family. No political scandal brewed outside her door while the world waited for her to make a wrong step. No one knew or cared who Gina Bowden was. It had become a comfortable anonymity.

Would a relationship with Gary change that? She thought of his involvement with the community. His bookstore. His Scouting leadership. She had learned only that morning that he was heavily active in his church and couldn't help but wonder how that might change things for her and Danny should their relationship grow more serious.

Chapter 5

Gary didn't like the idea of Jess Masterson arranging to speak to Gina. He couldn't imagine what possible good it would do. Did the old man think he could persuade her to join his cause? Furthermore, he still found it of concern that after nearly four years of absolutely no communication, Jess Masterson had also requested that Gary be present.

Pulling into Gina's driveway, Gary was just about to switch off the car when the radio announced that the area was once again under a tornado watch. *Good old Kansas weather,* Gary thought as he shut off the engine and made his way to the house.

"You're early," Gina said, greeting him before he could even ring the doorbell.

"I know," Gary said. "I guess I wanted to make sure I got here first."

"Didn't want to leave me at the mercy of the angry councilman?" Gina teased.

"Something like that."

"Well, come on in. I was just cleaning up in the kitchen."

"They've just put us in another tornado watch."

Gina nodded and picked up a dish towel. "Yes, the weather alert radio just went off. Danny's putting his things downstairs."

"You're acting a bit prematurely, aren't you?" Gary was more than a little aware of Gina's preoccupation with storms.

"As a Scout I would think you'd approve. 'Be prepared!' Isn't that the motto?" She picked up a glass and began drying it. "We don't just sit in the basement the whole time we're in a watch. We just make ready so we can go about our business until the time comes that we need to go to the basement. The last thing I want is to have Danny running around here like some sort of frantic ninny, trying to gather up things important to him and make his way to the basement."

"But the things aren't important," Gary pressed. "Are you sure you aren't teaching him to value possessions more than life?"

Gina continued drying the glass even though Gary could see it was already dry. He'd pushed her too hard, and now she was no doubt angry at

243

him. But to his surprise, Gina put the glass in the cupboard and picked up another.

"I suppose," she finally said, "that it might look that way to you, but it's not. Danny knows the things are unimportant. Property can be replaced and memories will live forever in your heart and mind. Being responsible for his bag of treasures is one way he feels he has some control over the situation. My mother used to do this with me and it helped a lot.

"My parents' farmhouse was built at the turn of the century, so we had to go out into the weather to get to the storm cave, and it always scared me. So, my mother decided to do what her mother had done when she was a child and give each of us kids an old pillowcase to put a few of our favorite things in. When the weather looked threatening, she'd have us take our stuff down into the storm cave. That way, we had a vested interest in the cave, and it was more than just some place to get to when the storms came." Gina put the glass in the cupboard and leaned back against the counter. "I like to believe that I'm helping Danny have some control over his environment. He focuses on what he can do to be ready rather than stewing about the upcoming storm."

Gary nodded. "That makes sense. I'm sorry if I sounded out of line."

Gina smiled and continued drying dishes. "A lot of folks go around doing nothing about the weather. They feel that God will protect them, and of course, He protects us all. But I feel it's important to take precautions. After all, people have been killed in these storms."

The way she looked as she said that final sentence made Gary wonder if she'd lost someone she loved in a storm. "You sound like you know better than some."

Gina nodded. "A good friend of mine died when I was thirteen. She used to laugh at my fear of storms. She and her mother teased me and said it wasn't Christian the way I fretted about things. They lived about a mile north of us and one spring a bad storm system went through and a tornado hit ground about a quarter mile southwest of our farm. I'd just come from helping Dad turn the cows out into the pasture in case things got bad. We could see it bearing down on us, and Mom and the others were already making a mad dash for the cave. I was so scared I could hardly move. The roar was bad enough, but the sight of that thing. . ." Gina shuddered and grew silent for several moments.

Gary got up and went to her. He felt bad for having made her relive such a nightmare. Gently, he pulled her into his arms and hugged her close. "You don't have to tell me any more."

Gina seemed not to hear him. "It destroyed our farm and it kept going north, where it destroyed my friend's farm, too. Only they hadn't bothered to take shelter. They weren't paying attention to the weather, and we were too far away to hear any warning siren blown in the city. The house collapsed on top of them." She began trembling.

"Shhh," Gary hushed her and stroked her hair. "It's all right."

Gina looked up at him and tried to smile. "I'm sorry. Sometimes it's still so hard to remember."

Gary cupped her chin with his hand. He looked for several seconds into her eyes. Without a doubt he had fallen in love with this woman. And now, seeing her so vulnerable and weak, he loved her even more. He wanted to protect her—to keep her safe from anything that might harm her.

She watched him with an expression that implied concern and curiosity. He hesitated only a moment, then lowered his lips to hers. Just then, the weather radio sounded, startling both of them nearly out of their wits. Gary laughed and Gina pushed away to punch the radio on. As she did, the tornado sirens started up.

"Guess we don't have to ask what the radio has to say," Gary declared, grabbing the radio and pushing Gina toward the basement stairs.

"Where's Danny?" she questioned, seeing that the basement light was off.

"I'll find him," Gary assured her. "You get downstairs." He handed her the radio, then went off in the direction of the living room.

"Danny!" he called, looking around the room. Seeing no sign of the boy, he bounded up the stairs, the constant blaring of tornado sirens in his ears. "Danny!"

The boy came streaking down the hall. "Dad!" He threw himself into Gary's arms. Neither one said anything about Danny's usage of the word *Dad*.

"Come on, Sport. Your mom's already in the basement," Gary said, lifting the boy and carrying him downstairs.

As Gary reached the bottom step, he made out the sound of knocking on the front door. Opening it, Gary came face-to-face with a stunned Jess Masterson. "Come on, Jess," Gary commanded. "Basement's this way."

The older man nodded and followed Gary. Gary felt the rapid beating of Danny's heart as the boy clung to him tightly. He longed to comfort the child, but the most important thing was to get them both out of harm's way. Gary hadn't needed to look for long at the greenish-black clouds that he saw overhead when he'd opened the door for Jess. He knew the signs were all there. The color of the clouds. The puffy fullness—indicating wind. They might well be in for it this time.

They made their way down the stairs with Gina grabbing Danny out of

Gary's arms before he even reached the bottom step.

"Oh, Danny," she said, holding him tight. "I was so worried about you. Where were you?"

"I went to your room," Danny said, his lower lip quivering. "I thought you were there."

Gina hugged him close. "We're all right now, Danny. We don't have to worry. Did you say a prayer?" she questioned, taking a seat at the table.

"I think we were both saying prayers," Gary interjected, trying to lighten the mood. Outside the rain had picked up, and the unmistakable sound of hail pounded down.

Gina nodded and Danny popped his head up. "I prayed." He paused only a moment and added, "Look, Mom. We found this guy at the door."

Gina looked up and smiled. "Ah, Mr. Masterson. So glad you could join us."

Gary looked over to meet Jess's expression. "You timed that just right."

"I was rather concerned," Masterson replied. "I could see that storm coming up fast and wondered if I'd even get here before the rain started."

The lights flickered and Gary looked at Gina. "Flashlights?"

She nodded. "Danny, go get your bag and get your flashlight ready." The boy seemed to calm at this and nodded. He slipped off her lap and Gina smiled at Gary. He knew what she was thinking. Giving Danny an action, something to occupy his mind, had given the boy a sense of renewed strength.

Gina got up and went to the stairway enclosure. Opening the door, she handed out a battery-operated lantern. "I picked this up the other day. They were having a sale and I figured it would be—"

B – O – O – M!

Thunder shook the house so hard that for the briefest moment before the lights went out, Gary could see Gina's expression of sheer panic. He switched on the lantern, and Danny turned on his flashlight. By the time they could see each other again, Gina had pulled her facade of calm into place. Gary admired that she wanted to appear strong for her child, but he worried about her.

"We may be here for a spell," Gary said, motioning to the table and chairs. "Might as well have a seat, Jess."

The older man nodded and took a seat. Gina did likewise. Gary noted that Danny was already busy rummaging through his bag, apparently oblivious to the drone of the weather updates and the raging storm outside. He was safe and he knew it. He knew it because routine told him it was true, and his mother's calm assured him that all was well in spite of the storm. Gary could easily see that even Gina was calming.

"So, Mr. Masterson," Gina said with a smile, "you wanted to talk with Gary and me?"

Jess chuckled. "Yes, well, I wanted to better explain my position regarding the Boy Scouts."

Danny perked up at this. "Are you a Boy Scout?" he questioned, pulling something out of his bag and coming to the table. "I'm a Cub Scout. Do you want to see my pinewood derby car?" His hopeful expression seemed to penetrate Jess Masterson's resolve.

"Sure, son," Masterson said, exchanging a quick glance with Gary before turning to the boy. "Let's see what you've done there."

"We've been working for about two weeks on it," Danny told him. "See how fast the wheels go?" The little boy ran his hand against the wheels and watched them spin.

"They do indeed go fast," Masterson agreed.

Gary listened in silence as the boy explained how they were going to have a race on the following Saturday. Danny's enthusiasm was so contagious, in fact, that when he invited Jess Masterson to be his special guest at the derby, the old man surprised them all by accepting.

Gary shook his head and walked to the window well in order to see if he could make out anything. It was usually on the back side of a thunderstorm that tornadoes made their deadly path. He glanced to where Jess Masterson was nodding to something Danny had said. Compared to his father-in-law, tornadoes were predictable.

Chapter 6

W ell," Gina said as she met Gary at the door to the church community center, "it looks like clear skies for the derby."

"After last Sunday's storm," he replied, "I'm ready for clear skies from here on out."

Gina laughed. "Me, too. Thanks for helping me clean up." She could still see the mess of downed tree branches in her mind.

"No problem. Pity you don't have a fireplace."

"I'm just grateful we didn't have any more damage. I heard that the tornado touched down near a housing development on the west side of town. Destroyed about six houses."

"I heard that, too. We were fortunate no one was killed," Gary said softly.

"Yes," Gina said nodding. The thought made her shudder, and she turned quickly to watch Danny rush by her, his Cub Scout hat sitting rather cockeyed and his necktie twisted in the back. She compared his haphazard appearance with that of Gary Cameron, who stood before her wearing the adult uniform as if he were born in it. She realized all at once that he was watching her study him. Feeling her face grow hot, Gina looked away to where the boys were playing around the derby's inclined track.

"Is Jess here yet?"

"Nope, not yet. I still can't believe he agreed to come today."

"I know," Gina replied. "He hardly said two words to me after Danny latched onto him during the storm."

"Me either. I tried to call him once during the week, but I only got the answering machine. You do realize the council meets next Thursday night?"

Gina nodded. She knew Gary was worried about Masterson's plans for the Scout funding, but she also knew he was troubled by more than just that. Reaching out, she touched his arm. "What are you afraid of?"

His eyes widened for just a moment before he regained control. Then, as if deciding she deserved his honesty, Gary's expression softened. "I just don't want to see anyone hurt. Especially that little boy." He nodded to where Danny was proudly showing off his car. "I've come to care a great deal about him."

Gina smiled. "I have, too."

"Do you know he called me Dad?"

"When?" Gina questioned, remembering Danny's request to call Gary Dad if and when they married.

"During the storm. It was when I found him upstairs. He was terrified and he called me Dad."

Gina nodded. "I don't doubt it for a minute. He cares a lot about you, and. . ." She hesitated to continue.

"And?" Gary questioned, taking hold of her hand as if they were the only people in the room.

Gina licked her lips. "And he asked me if he could call you Dad after we got married."

Gary's expression revealed surprise, almost shock. Gina tried to pull her hand away, fearing that she should never have mentioned the "M" word.

Gary held her hand fast and asked, "What did you tell him?"

"That he needed to give it time and let God show us the direction to take."

"And has He?"

"Has who—what?" she asked, feeling her senses overcome by the way he was looking at her. He seemed to reach into her soul with his eyes. Her mouth felt cottony and her hands began to tremble.

"Mr. Cameron! Mr. Cameron!" one of the Bear Cubs was shouting from across the room.

Gary grinned as if sensing his power over her. "We can discuss it later. But," he said, pausing to lean closer to her, "I think God's already shown me plenty. The path seems very clear, and if I have my way about it, we'll be making derby cars for years to come."

"Danny won't be a Cub Scout forever," Gina teased.

Gary winked. "No, but it'll take a while to get all his brothers through Cubs." With that he walked away, leaving Gina to stare after him. *His brothers! Gary was implying—*

"Hello, Gina."

Gina turned to find a very casually dressed Jess Masterson. "Hello, Mr. Masterson." She felt both regret and relief that Masterson had chosen that moment to show up.

"Now I thought we agreed that you were going to call me Jess."

Gina gave him a slight smile and eyed him as one might when considering a rattlesnake. *Caution!* Her mind seemed to warn. "I'm glad you could come, Jess," she offered.

He smiled. "I know you are making an effort where I'm concerned, but really I'm not such a bad guy."

"Why don't we take a seat. It will take awhile for the leaders to get everything ready. We might as well make ourselves comfortable."

Jess nodded and followed her to a gathering of empty chairs. "I don't want you to hate me, Gina."

Gina realized how very reserved her actions must have seemed to the older man. Asking God for guidance, she took a seat and turned to Jess. "I don't hate you," she began. "I don't understand you, but I don't hate you."

Jess looked at her in a rather puzzled manner. "What don't you understand?"

Gina folded her hands and looked at them as though they were the most interesting things in the world. "Why would a grown man set out to ruin the pleasure of children? Why do grown-up politics have to creep into everything in life?" She forced herself to look at Jess. "I believe in my heart that you are doing this for two reasons."

Jess looked rather surprised. "Do continue."

Gina swallowed the lump in her throat. "I think first of all you're angry at God for not saving Vicky. I can understand that. God knows I was angry at Him after Ray died. See, my husband died in a car accident like your daughter. A drunk driver hit him broadside and killed him instantly."

"I'm sorry," Jess said, stiffening in his chair. "I didn't know."

"I think you want to get back at God, but we both know that won't work," Gina continued. "Secondly, I think you want very much to hurt Gary because he lived and Vicky and Jason died." Jess paled and looked rather shocked. But Gina didn't give him time to answer. "You and Gary could have gained strength from each other, but instead you somehow hold him responsible."

"I don't suppose Gary bothered to tell you, but Vicky and Jason were only in that car because they were on their way to pick him up from a late night of inventory work at the bookstore," Jess said rather haughtily.

"Yes, I know," Gina replied. "And my husband was on his way home to me after a business trip. Should I blame myself? Was it my fault he was killed? Better yet, maybe I should blame Danny; after all, Ray was in a hurry to get back to us because Danny's birthday was the next day." She paused and looked him square in the eye. "Or was it the fault of the drunk behind the wheel? And beyond that, do I blame God because He took away someone I loved, when it was God who gave him to me in the first place?"

"Ah, the old, 'The Lord giveth and the Lord taketh away,' " Masterson replied. This time anger was clear in his voice.

"Blessed be the name of the Lord," Gina finished.

"Meaning what?" Jess's eyes flashed in rage.

Gina reacted without thinking and placed her hand on Jess's arm. "Meaning, God is still God whether we blame Him or praise Him. Meaning God is still in charge even when we think He has somehow forgotten our zip code. Meaning God was with our loved ones when those drunks crossed their paths, and He was there when they breathed their last breath on earth and took their first steps into heaven."

Jess's expression remained fixed and rigid. "You can believe that way if it brings you comfort."

Gina smiled and squeezed his arm. "It does, Jess. It honestly does. Just knowing I don't have to bear the weight alone is more comforting than any kind of retaliation I can think of. You can go ahead with your plans against the Boy Scouts, but it won't change the fact that Vicky and Jason loved God." She paused and looked him in the eye, hoping she wasn't about to go too far. "It won't change that your wife loved Him either."

"What do you know of my wife?"

"I know what Gary told me. How she stood fast in her faith in spite of Vicky and Jason's death."

"She turned to God, but not to me," Jess said, and this time his voice sounded tired—resigned.

"She always had God, but maybe when she lost you, God became even more precious."

Jess's eyes widened in surprise. "How dare you say something like that! You didn't know her. You don't know me."

Gina released her hold on him and smiled. "Maybe I know you better than you think. I've been hurt just like you. I've lost people I loved, and I pushed away the love of others because I feared ever feeling that emptiness again. Jess, you go ahead and do what you think you need to do, but it won't change how you feel inside right now. I just want you to remember that."

"Mr. Masterson!" Danny exclaimed. "You came!"

The man eyed Gina for a moment, then turned to greet Danny. "I told you I'd be here, and I'm a man of my word."

"Come see my car," Danny said, reaching out to take Masterson by the arm.

Gina forced a smile, Masterson's words echoing in her head. *I'm a man of my word,* he'd said, making it both a threat and an affirmation.

❧

The afternoon passed in noisy exultation. Gina laughed to watch the boys line the pinewood derby track. It was hard to imagine that something so simple could give such pleasure. From time to time, she also caught sight of Danny with Jess Masterson. The man seemed completely caught up in the moment, and Gina actually found herself glad he'd come.

The awards were handed out, and Danny enthusiastically received the award for "Best Design." She smiled, knowing that if Gary hadn't bothered to take the time to help the child, Danny would have been racing a block of wood. She smiled, wondering if they had an award for the "Most Boring Design." No doubt she could have helped Danny win that one.

When the celebration was over, they gathered their things, and while Gina helped Gary, Danny was busily talking to Jess Masterson. She headed over to rescue the man, but as she drew close enough to hear their conversation, she halted in surprise.

"I had a very nice time, Danny. Thank you for inviting me. I'd almost forgotten what it was like to be young."

"I'm glad you came," Danny replied, entwining his fingers with Masterson's. "I need a grandpa and you need a boy so you won't forget about being young. Maybe you could ask my mom about coming over all the time. You could even come to church with us."

Jess Masterson looked up to meet Gina's fixed stare. She thought she saw the glistening of tears in the old man's eyes. She knew for certain there were tears in her own eyes. When Masterson appeared to be at a loss for words, Gina rescued him.

"Danny, come give me a hand with the chairs." She smiled at Jess. "You're always welcome at our house," she said, as if to answer the unspoken question in regard to Danny's statement. "And at our church."

"Thank you," Jess replied. "I need to go. Will you tell Gary good-bye for me?"

"Of course," Gina replied. She watched the man leave, wondering what the future would hold and whether or not he would accomplish his goal of removing funding from the Boy Scouts. Either way, she knew he was struggling to find his way out of sorrow and loneliness, and depriving the Scouts of city money wasn't going to change a thing.

Chapter 7

Gina and Gary nervously took their seats at the city council meeting. Neither had spoken to Jess after the derby, and neither knew what kind of scene they would have to endure tonight. But they had prayed about the situation and had agreed to trust God for the outcome. It would be hard on the Scouts to lose the help of the city, but it wouldn't put an end to the organization.

The meeting was brought to order, and after the rhetoric of various reports, the issue of Jess Masterson's proposal was brought to the attention of the council. Jess, who'd arrived late and had barely taken a seat before the meeting started, cleared his voice and shuffled some papers in his hands.

"If it pleases the council," he began, "I'd like to withdraw my proposal. I would also like to propose the council disregard anything I've said over the last few months." He grinned rather sheepishly and added, "I'm not sure exactly what all that might entail, but I'm certain it was probably less than well thought out."

Silence held the room as Jess continued. "I'm afraid my judgment has been altered by the recent events of my life. Some of you know I lost a daughter and grandson in a car accident. Then last year I lost my wife of forty years. Those aren't the kinds of things a man easily deals with. I'm afraid I didn't deal well with them at all."

Gina felt tears come to her eyes and did nothing to try to hide them. She smiled at Jess when he looked her way—hoping—praying that her expression offered reassurance.

"Instead of my original proposal," Jess said, nodding slightly at Gina, "I'm offering something else." He picked up a stack of papers and handed them down the table to the council. "My resignation."

There were gasps of surprise in the audience, but no one was as surprised as Gary and Gina.

"It's time I retired and did some of the things fellows my age have earned the right to do. There's a little boy out there who told me the other day he needed a grandpa. He also said that I needed a boy to remind me about being young." Jess grinned. "I think he was exactly right."

Gina tightly gripped Gary's hand. "This is unbelievable," she whispered. "I thought it was impossible for us to change his mind."

"I don't think *we* did," Gary countered. "I think Danny did."

Gina nodded. "He sure took to Jess. I guess I just never realized all the missing aspects in Danny's life. It's like he has holes in his life I never even suspected were there."

"Well, we need to get to the business of filling in those empty places, don't we?" Gary said softly.

Gina felt her breath quicken. She knew what Gary was implying. It was time to make a commitment. "Maybe we could leave the meeting?"

The council was already going through the motions of dismissing Jess's earlier proposal and accepting his resignation. As soon as the vote was complete, Gary grabbed Gina's hand and pulled her up with him. They made their way to the back door, and Gary had already opened it when Gina stopped. Turning, she caught sight of Jess watching them. Smiling, she did the only thing she knew would clearly explain her gratitude. She blew him a kiss. Jess Masterson couldn't have looked more shocked had she shaken her fist at him, but then a tiny smile crept across his face.

Gary pulled Gina into the hall, his own expression rather stunned.

"What's the matter?" Gina questioned. "You look as though you've seen a ghost."

"Vicky used to always blow Jess a kiss good-bye whenever we got ready to leave. I guess seeing you do that just now. . .well. . .it just surprised me."

"I'd say it surprised you both," Gina replied, fearful that she'd caused more harm than good. "I hope I didn't upset him."

"From the expression on his face, I think he was touched," Gary said, raising her hand to his lips. "I know I was."

Gina felt overwhelmed by the emotions coursing through her heart and mind and soul. *God always had a way of breaking down doors,* she thought as Gary led her to the car.

They picked up Danny at the Applebees' farm, then made their way to Gina's house. Danny chattered at full speed, telling about the puppies and how much he wanted one. Gina quickly realized that any private discussion she and Gary had hoped for was now out of the question.

Gary must have realized it, too, because after they arrived home, he told Gina he needed to run some errands and couldn't stay. Disappointed but understanding, Gina bid him good-bye and watched as Danny gave Gary a big hug. Perhaps it was better this way. She needed to talk to Danny about the future and help him through any questions he might have.

As soon as Gary was gone, she turned to her son. "We need to talk," she said quite seriously.

"Did I do something wrong?" Danny asked, his face contorting as he appeared to consider the possibilities.

"No, silly," Gina said, tousling his hair. "Come sit with me on the couch. I want to talk about us. . .and about Gary."

Danny nodded. "Are you going to get married now?"

Gina laughed. "Nothing like jumping right in, eh? Well, we might as well talk it through. Would you like for me to marry Gary?"

"Yes!" Danny replied enthusiastically. "I want him to be my dad."

Gina nodded. "I know you've said that before. But I want you to realize how things might change for us."

Danny sobered. "Okay."

"Having a dad around will be a lot of fun for you. You will be able to do things with him while I do other things, and then there will be times when we have fun all together. But if I marry Gary, you will also have to mind him. Do you understand that?"

"Sure," Danny replied as if what she'd said was a given fact. "I mind him at Scouts already. Mom," he said reaching out to hug her, "I want a dad. I promise I can mind."

Gina felt her heartstrings plucked in a most evident way. "I know you can. I want you to have a dad, and I think Gary would make a great dad and a good husband. I think God has finally shown me that we would make a good family."

Danny let out a yip of excitement. "I'm gonna have a dad and a grandpa!" He got up from the couch and danced around the room.

Gina laughed at his enthusiasm. "Danny, come back here. Nothing is settled yet. Gary and I haven't even talked about getting married. I mean, not really. We need to talk about it first, and then we need to give ourselves plenty of time to make plans and get to know each other better. I need for you to know him better, too."

Danny threw himself into her arms and looked up at her. His baby face was fading more and more each day, and in its place had grown a boy's hopeful expression. "How long will it take?"

Gina laughed again and tickled Danny lightly under his arms. "Not long. Not near as long as it's taken to find the right person for the job."

⧳

Gina had fully expected Gary to call her later that night, and when he didn't, she felt an emptiness inside that her newest fiction novel couldn't fill. Then when Gary didn't call on Friday or Saturday, Gina thought perhaps she'd done something to offend him. She thought back to her actions reminding everyone of Vicky and worried that she'd created a major mess of things.

Sunday found her and Danny just going through the paces. How empty it seemed without Gary. It was as if a vital part of their lives had been suddenly taken from them. It reminded her too much of how she'd felt after losing Ray. Finally, on Sunday night she broke down and gave Gary a call.

But he wasn't there. His answering machine clicked on and asked her to leave a message, but that was the only sound of his voice that Gina had. Going to bed that night, she tossed and turned fitfully. What was happening? Had Gary given up on the idea of making a commitment to her and Danny?

Monday morning, Gina awoke more tired than when she'd gone to bed. Going through the familiar routine of homeschool studies and daily chores did nothing to help calm her fears. Gina had just managed to finish cleaning the bathroom, while Danny worked on multiplication facts, when the telephone rang.

"Mrs. Bowden?" a decidedly aged voice questioned from the other end of the line.

"Yes?"

"This is Nora down at Cameron Christian Books and Gifts."

Gina felt her body tense. Why should this woman be calling her? Had something happened to Gary? She could still hear the voice of the police officer who'd come to tell her about Ray's accident.

"Is something wrong?" Gina questioned, praying silently for strength.

"No," the woman assured. "Well. . .that is. . .I hope you'll forgive me, but I've neglected my duties, and now I fear I've been the cause of making you worry."

"I don't understand," Gina replied softly.

"Gary asked me to give you a message last Friday and I totally forgot."

Gina felt relief wash over her. "A message?"

"Yes. Gary wanted me to tell you that he needed a few days of prayer for a special situation. He thought you'd understand. He took off for a three-day weekend. I expect him back any time, but I was supposed to let you know last Friday. I hope you'll forgive me."

Gina was so happy to hear that nothing horrible had happened to Gary that she would have overlooked any mistake the woman might have laid claim to. "That's all right, Nora. I understand how these things go." Gina listened as the woman apologized once again, then thanked her and hung up with renewed enthusiasm for the day.

Danny brought his paper to her. "I'm finished. Can I have a recess break?"

Gina smiled. "Sure thing. Oh, and that was a woman who works at Gary's bookstore. She said she forgot to call us last Friday and tell us that Gary was taking a short trip away from town."

Danny's face brightened. "So he's coming back?"

Gina nodded. "Yes, I'm sure he will. Now you go play and I'll call you in about fifteen minutes. We still have social studies, but then we'll be done."

Danny hurried out the back door, while Gina followed in order to check on the clothes hanging on the line in the backyard. Silently she thanked God for Nora's call. She looked heavenward, noting the building clouds. It looked like the weather might once again grow threatening. Glancing at her watch, Gina saw that it was nearly three o'clock. Their worst storms took place in late afternoon and early evening. If she was fortunate, the clothes would have time to dry before the rain set in.

By five o'clock, Gina was hurrying to pull the clothes from the line. The area had been put into a severe thunderstorm watch, and from the look of the weather radar on television, storms were popping up all around them. The unmistakable darkness of the clouds to the south gave Gina little doubt the storms would soon be upon them as well.

She fixed them a light supper while Danny played quietly upstairs. The first sound of thunder rumbled in the distance, and Gina silently prayed for safety from the storm. "Danny!" she called, putting two plates on the table. "Supper!"

Danny came bounding downstairs, his storm bag in hand. He put it by the basement door and looked up at his mother. "I brought this down just in case. I don't want to be stuck upstairs again if the sirens go off."

Gina frowned. She didn't want her son so paranoid that he couldn't go about his business when storms came. Sitting down to the table, she took hold of his hand. "Danny, we don't have to be afraid of the stormy weather. God is watching over us. He will take care us, no matter what happens. You believe that, don't you?"

Danny's eyes were wide as he nodded. "I think so," he said doubtfully. "But sometimes people die in storms. You told me about your friend."

Gina gently stroked his hand. "I know. Sometimes bad things do happen. Sometimes storms destroy homes and lives. Sometimes people are hurt by other storms in life, as well. But Danny, I promise you—God has it all under control. He won't leave us to go through it alone. The Bible says He will be with us always."

"But sometimes you get afraid," Danny said quite seriously.

"Yes," Gina nodded. "Yes, I do. But that's when I forget to give it to God. The times I get afraid are those times when I try to take care of everything myself. When I try to be in charge—instead of letting God be in charge. Understand?"

Danny nodded. "But you said that we should be prepared."

"And we should. We should use the knowledge God has given us to help take proper care of each other and of our things. But we don't sit in the basement all day, every day for fear that a little rain cloud might send us a tornado. It's the same way with other things in life. When the threat of bad things comes, we have to do what we know is right in order to get through those times. Sometimes we get hurt—"

"Like when Daddy died?" Danny interjected.

"Yes," Gina whispered, her voice heavy with emotion. "Like when Daddy died. But God brought us through that. He showed us that we were still loved by Him and that we would always be loved by Him. He's taken good care of us, hasn't He?"

"Yup, and God sent us Mr. Cameron."

Gina smiled. "That's right, He did."

The weather alert radio blared out its warning tone, interrupting Gina's conversation. Giving Danny a reassuring smile, she went to the radio and pressed the button. The thunderstorm watch had been changed to a tornado watch after two separate storms had produced small tornadoes in the surrounding area. She was still trying to listen to the details when someone rang the front doorbell.

"Danny, go answer the door, please," she told her son.

She finished listening to the report as Danny ran for the door and came back beaming from ear to ear, Gary Cameron following right behind.

"Looks like we're in for it again," Gary announced. "I don't like the looks of those clouds."

"Mom said God will take care of us," Danny offered.

"I agree totally," Gary replied as lightning flashed.

There was little doubt that a storm of great intensity was nearly upon them. Gina tried to maintain her composure. "Danny, go ahead and take your bag downstairs and then we'll have lunch."

"Can we eat in the basement again?"

Gina laughed and cast a quick glance at Gary. "I don't think we have to go that far. At least not yet. Remember what I said about not being afraid of the storms?"

"But I thought it was fun eating down there," Danny countered, picking up his bag. "It was like an adventure."

"Well, I suppose if you really want to. . . ," Gina said, her voice trailing off.

"Come on, Sport," Gary said, picking up his plate. "I'll get you settled downstairs, then come back up and convince your mother that it will be a lot of fun. We'll even play a board game or two."

Danny cheered and headed down the stairs.

"I thought we didn't want him to be paranoid about storms," Gina said in a barely audible voice.

"We don't, but like I said, those clouds didn't look good. Besides, when I come back upstairs, I have some important questions to ask you, and I'd like to do it without an audience." He winked at her, then bounded down the steps before she could reply.

Gina felt her heartbeat quicken and her hands go clammy. Did he want to ask her what she hoped he would ask? Had he thought through all the complications in their lives and sorted through his feelings to know that marriage to Gina was the right move to make?

By the time he returned, Gina was leaning casually against the kitchen counter. She tried her best to look disinterested and nonchalant but knew she was doing a miserable job of it. "So what did you want to ask me?"

Gary smiled and leaned against the jamb of the basement door. "How do you feel about having more kids?"

"I've always wanted more children," she said quite seriously. "How many did you have in mind?"

"Three, maybe four?"

Gina bit at her lower lip as if considering the matter. "I think that's workable. What else?"

"Houses and living arrangements," he said flatly. "I prefer to think of us both starting over. A new house in the country is what I have in mind."

Gina tried to keep from smiling, but she couldn't help it. "I know a good real estate lady. Anything else you want to ask me?"

"That just about does it," Gary said. Then without a single word, he crossed the room and swept her into his arms. "I've missed you more than I ever imagined possible." His mouth came down on hers and Gina melted against him in absolute rapture. "I love you, Gina Bowden," he whispered, pulling back only long enough to speak.

Gina tightened her hold on him and let her kiss be her agreeing comment on his declaration. Without warning, he pulled back and grinned. "Marry me?"

She laughed, and as she opened her mouth to speak, the weather alert radio sounded. Both of them broke into laughter as the weatherman announced the need to take cover from the strengthening storm.

"Ah, Kansas stormy weather," Gina mused, allowing Gary to hurry her to the basement door. "Grab the radio, will you?" She turned on the top step to await him.

"Sure thing," he replied, reaching back to the counter.

He quickly retrieved the radio and gave her a gentle push to start her down the steps. "There's never a dull moment around here," he declared.

"I warned you, our house is anything but quiet," Gina replied.

Gary smiled at Danny, who started to babble about the sirens and his good idea to eat lunch in the basement. "We're having another adventure, aren't we, Mom?"

"That we are. Say, how would you like it if I made this an even better adventure?" Gina questioned.

Both Gary and Danny looked at her, but it was Danny who questioned. "How?"

"By letting you in on a great surprise," she replied, enjoying her son's curiosity and Gary's puzzled stare. "Gary just asked me to marry him, and I'm just about to say yes."

Danny cheered and jumped up from the table to hug his arms around Gary's waist. "I knew you would be my new dad. I just knew it!"

Gary looked down at Danny for a moment before returning his gaze to Gina. "She hasn't said yes, yet, Sport."

Danny pulled back. "Say it, Mom. Say it so Dad knows you mean it."

Gina laughed in spite of the weather outside. "Yes," she said simply. "Yes, I will marry you, Gary Cameron."

Danny cheered again, but this time Gary joined him and lifted him high in the air to toss him up in joyful celebration. "She said yes, Sport! That makes it official." He caught Danny and held him against his shoulder and held open his other arm to Gina.

"Now we can be a real family." The pleasure in Danny's voice was clear.

Gina laughed and came quite happily into Gary's embrace. "A real family," Gina murmured and silently thanked God for the miracle He'd given her. Even stormy weather couldn't spoil the moment.

Epilogue

A year later, on a clear April evening, Gina and Gary were married in the church where Gary had grown up. Gina loved the people and the wonderful way she'd been welcomed into their family, but most of all, she loved Gary and the way he loved her and Danny.

"You look rather pleased with yourself, Mrs. Cameron," Gary whispered in her ear as their guests gathered around to see them cut the wedding cake.

"I am rather pleased, Mr. Cameron," she replied, giving him what she hoped was a rather sultry look.

Gary raised a single brow and Gina thought she saw sweat form on his forehead. Grinning, she leaned against him ever so slightly. "You're looking a bit stressed, my dear." She held up the knife. "But we mustn't disappoint our guests."

"Just remember," he whispered against her ear, "I wanted to elope."

Gina felt a shiver run from her head to her toes. His warm breath against her neck was nearly enough to make her drop her facade of composure. "We're supposed to. . .ah. . . cut the cake together," she stammered.

Gary took hold of her hand and closed it around the knife's handle. "The quicker we get to it, the sooner we can leave on our honeymoon," he teased and laughed out loud as Gina quickly plunged the knife into the cake.

The reception was a tremendous success, and Gina's heart was warmed by the sight of her son and Jess Masterson sharing company and having a wonderful time. Jess had acted as Gary's best man, while Danny stood up as Gina's only attendant.

"I'm surprised you held the reception in the church basement," Telaine Applebee said, coming to give her best wishes to Gina and Gary. "They have a perfectly wonderful reception hall upstairs. I don't think anyone's used this area in years, at least not for a wedding."

Gina exchanged a quick smile with Gary before answering. "Scout motto."

Telaine looked at her oddly. "Scout motto?"

"Be prepared," Gary countered.

"Yes, I know what the motto is, but what does that have to do with the reception being in the basement?" Telaine asked.

"Gina figured we'd outwit any chances of stormy weather," Gary replied with a grin.

"That's right," Gina replied. "It took me long enough to find this man, I wasn't going to risk losing him in a mad dash for the basement."

Everyone around them laughed at this, while Gina felt Gary's arms close around her from behind. "There wasn't a chance of you losing me," he whispered only loud enough for Gina to hear. "Storms or calm, you're stuck with me for life, Mrs. Cameron."

Gina leaned against him and grinned. "Good thing. See, there's this pinewood derby coming up in two weeks and. . ."

The Bouquet

Prologue

by Gail Sattler

Abby's hand shook as she reached for the bouquet.

Her bridal bouquet.

After months of preparation, she was no longer Abby Edmonds—at least not on paper. She was now Mrs. Stanleigh Chenkowski.

For the first time today, Abby was able to stand by herself and not listen to relatives recount highlights of their own wedding days thirty years ago or pose for pictures. For a few minutes, she had some time to see what was happening around her.

Currently, a large group of guests had their attention fixed on the beautiful groom's cake, made to look just like Stan's dog. Since the cake resembled Bowser so much, no one, including Stan, had the heart to cut it. Even Rose, who made the cake, couldn't be the first one to insert the knife.

Guests sat at the tables around the room, nibbling goodies, eating wedding cake, and sipping coffee and tea. Other people stood in small groups, just talking.

Away from the action, Abby surveyed the banquet room of the Country Meadows Inn one last time. The red and white streamers, hearts, and bells were exquisite, the decorating perfect.

Her wedding day was almost over. Everything had progressed without a hitch.

The ceremony had been beautiful, and there hadn't been a dry eye in the house, except, strangely, for her own. Because she'd caught Stan sniffling when she hadn't been, Abby promised Stan she would remind him on every anniversary. Abby snickered to herself. She always kept her promises.

Following the ceremony, because the weather was a typical March day for Vermont, they'd taken the portrait pictures inside a studio, then come back to the inn for the reception.

The meal had been delicious. The speeches were performed without incident or too much embarrassment, although she couldn't say the same about the video her brother and his friends had made and shown their guests. Abby wasn't very pleased her courtship with Stan had been turned into a comedic documentary, but the video had provided a nice break from the rush and festivities.

For now, the wedding cake had been cut, and it was time to get ready to throw the bouquet to her still-single guests.

Abby picked up the small bouquet and ran her fingers over the soft petals of the fragrant roses in varying hues of red, pink, peach, and even a few in yellow. Felicity had outdone herself with the beautiful arrangement. Abby almost didn't want to give it away, but of course she had to. Besides, her brother David was a semi-professional photographer, and he had taken enough pictures that she would never forget its beauty.

"Abby?" a little voice piped up beside her.

Abby looked down. "Hi, Jenni. Are you enjoying yourself? I want to thank you for spreading the rose petals so nicely at the church today. You did a good job as flower girl." She smiled, thinking of how cute Jenni and Cody, the ring bearer, were together.

Jenni beamed from ear to ear. "Thanks!" she squealed. "Mrs. Edmonds told me to tell you that it's time to throw the bouquet."

Abby bit back her grin. "Tell her that I'm going to do it right now."

As Jenni giggled and skipped back to Abby's mother, Abby sighed. This was her last official function of the day, and then her wedding would be over.

She craned her neck to see Stan, all decked out in his white tuxedo, through the crowd. At the same moment, he turned around and looked back at her, smiling.

Abby's heart pounded. She loved Stan more than she did yesterday, and even more than this morning. Today they had been joined as husband and wife in a ceremony witnessed by their friends, their families, and God. And now it was time to leave their guests and begin their lives together as a married couple.

Abby raised one arm and waved at the room full of people. "Attention! Everybody! I'm going to throw the bouquet! Everyone who wants to see if they're going to be next to get married, come now!"

Most of her single guests hurried into a circle behind her. She could see Kathy, Brenda, Nanci, all her cousins, and a bunch of Stan's cousins, whose names she couldn't remember, shuffling into a circle. Even little Jenni, who was only six years old, was in the middle. All faces were expectant and hopeful as they waited.

However, some faces were missing. But before Abby had a chance to tell them to join in the fun, the women already gathered began calling out to her to hurry up.

Abby turned around and tightened her grip on the bouquet. "Okay, Lord," she mumbled, "I've had my day. You gave me Stan, and You made me the happiest woman on earth. But now it's someone else's turn. You know who needs this the most."

Abby sucked in a deep breath, closed her eyes, and flung the bouquet over her head.

The weight of the flowers had barely left her hands when she spun around to see who would catch it.

Before she stopped moving, a collective gasp echoed through the room.

All heads were turned up, way up, toward the ceiling. Abby also tilted her head to watch.

The bouquet was not arcing gracefully through the air; she'd accidentally thrown it too hard. Instead of floating into the circle of anxious single women, the bouquet zipped through the air, straight for the whirring ceiling fan in the middle of the room.

Abby covered her mouth with her hands. "No!" she shouted, but her voice came out muffled between her fingers.

With a dull thud, followed by a series of crisp snaps, her beautiful bouquet shattered.

Only shredded leaves floated to the women below. The larger pieces of the bouquet, their speed increased by the force and velocity of the spinning fan blades, shot past the ladies huddled in the middle of the room and hurled along on paths of their own.

Flowers by Felicity
By Janet Lee Barton

Dedication

To my Lord and Savior for showing me the way.
To my family for your love and encouragement always.
To my granddaughters, Mariah, Paige, and Sarah:
when it's time—remember to look to the Lord
for the mate of His choosing.
I love you all!

Chapter 1

Felicity Carmichael's heart slammed against the inside of her chest as she witnessed pieces of the bridal bouquet she'd worked so hard on fly out over the room in all directions. She caught her breath as one of the clumps shot straight toward her. Instinctively, she closed her eyes and reached up to catch it just before it smashed her in the face.

Opening first one eye and then the other, she looked down at the small tuft of flowers she held and fleetingly wondered if catching only a portion of a bouquet meant anything. She shook her head and sighed. *It was nothing but a near miss. . .just like her two previous engagements.* No. She wasn't going to think about that now.

Clasping the flowers to her heart, she took a deep breath and willed her racing pulse to slow down. She looked down at the mangled little cluster of flowers, and her heart sank. All her work had been torn to bits in a matter of seconds. She closed her eyes once more to fight against the threat of tears. When she opened them, it was only to immediately blink against the bright light of a camera flash going off somewhere very close.

David, the bride's brother, had been taking pictures of his sister Abby's wedding reception all afternoon. From what Abby had told her about him, Felicity was pretty sure he'd be teasing his sister forever about her pitching style. . .especially after witnessing the aftermath of that pitch.

She watched him turn to catch his sister doubled over laughing at the expressions on the faces of the women who'd hoped to catch her bouquet. Felicity couldn't help but chuckle herself. If Abby wasn't upset, she certainly shouldn't be. After all, it wasn't her wedding day.

Looking around, Felicity shook her head but couldn't keep from chuckling as she watched David continue to take pictures of the wedding reception and the havoc the flying bouquet had caused. He moved around the room snapping pictures right and left. How he could hold the camera still with his shoulders shaking with laughter was beyond her. No telling what those photos were going to look like. But she found it hard to take her eyes off him. A handsome man with thick dark hair and blue-green eyes, he was even better looking when he smiled or laughed—his eyes crinkling at the corners and a dimple suddenly appearing out of nowhere.

Felicity was surprised at the way her pulse sped up when he turned and caught her staring. He began to walk toward her. She didn't realize she'd been holding her breath until his parents stopped him and she released the pent-up air in her lungs with a *whoosh*.

Feeling the heat rising on her cheeks, Felicity didn't know whether to be relieved or disappointed when he turned and started in a different direction, but the way her pulse began to race, she decided it might be for the best if she found something to do besides watch David Edmonds. It didn't take long. . . there were bits and pieces of the bride's bouquet everywhere. Felicity gently put the tiny portion of bouquet she'd caught into her skirt pocket and began to pick up some of the scattered blooms off the floor.

❧

David hadn't had time to think since he'd dodged the flying flower bundle that flew past his ear. For a scant second he'd wondered if he was seeing things and then realized what it was he *had* seen. The look of shock on his sister's face as she'd thrown her bouquet had him aiming his camera first at her and then at her attendants, who'd been waiting to catch the bouquet. Their expressions were priceless. As Abby dissolved into laughter, he turned to the room.

He took a picture of Felicity Carmichael, Abby's friend and the florist who'd made the bouquet, holding one of the errant flower bundles close to her chest. There was a vulnerable look in her eyes that made him want to stop and talk to her, but laughter from across the room had him aiming his camera in a different direction just in time to catch his best friend, Geoff Manfrey, reaching for the clump of flowers stuck on top of his head.

David felt the mirth building in his chest. . .his chuckles inching toward huge guffaws. . .but he didn't dare let them out as he watched the responses of the people who'd caught or been hit by parts of the shredded bouquet. Somehow he didn't think most of them would appreciate it. It wasn't easy holding the camera steady while he tried not to laugh, but he didn't want to miss one good shot. Thankfully, Abby didn't seem too upset. . .at first. But when her expression changed to one of concern and she darted across the room, he followed.

It took him longer as he framed first one and then another shot. By the time he got there, a crowd had gathered around the cake table—or what was left of it—and the caterer, Rose something, and Stan's best man, Lucas Montgomery. David couldn't get close enough to really see what was happening, and he wondered if the bouquet had anything to do with it. He then dismissed that idea. They were flowers after all. How much damage could they do?

He turned and saw Felicity across the room and suddenly remembered that Abby had suggested that he interview her for the newspaper—that it would be a way of helping Felicity's business out since she had given Abby such a great price on the flowers. It was the least he could do for someone who'd helped make his sister's wedding so beautiful, and he started toward her to try to set up an interview. But he was stopped by his parents telling him that Abby and Stan would be leaving soon, and when he looked back, he didn't see Felicity. He made a mental note to try to talk to her later. He took a couple more pictures and decided he'd better head toward the door so that he could take the going-away pictures of his sister and her new husband.

He looked at his watch. If the newlyweds hurried, he'd be able to get these pictures developed and into the Sunday paper. He turned quickly, stumbled, and almost tripped over Felicity, who was bent down picking floral bits up off the floor.

"Oh! I'm so sorry," he said, extending a hand to help her up. "Are you all right?"

Her laughter was light and lilting, and as he looked into her eyes, he was surprised by the way his heart began to beat faster. He'd seen Felicity many times over the last few months—at church, although they didn't attend the same Sunday school class, and at times on the street as they passed each other coming or going from his sister's house just next door to hers. But he'd never been really up close like this. Her eyes were the most unusual shade of brown. . .almost gold. They sort of shimmered as she looked up at him, and something in his chest seemed to flip into his stomach. He was pretty sure it was his heart.

"I'm fine," she said, sounding a little out of breath.

"Good. I think we've already had one casualty today." Funny. He sounded the same way—as if he'd been out running.

"Oh?" Felicity looked around. "Who?"

"The wedding cake."

"The cake?" She looked confused.

"Yes. It seems to have crashed to the floor." David looked back toward the cake table, but the crowd had dispersed and Rose and Lucas were nowhere to be seen. He shrugged. "I'm not sure what happened."

"That's a shame," she said, shaking her head. "I was looking forward to a piece of that cake. Oh well."

David chuckled. "You can have a piece of the groom's cake."

"Of Bowser? Oh. . .I'm not sure I can do that."

The groom's cake was adorable. . .shaped and decorated to look just like Stan's basset hound.

"From what's left of it by now, you probably wouldn't recognize him." David wasn't sure what to say next, but he wanted to keep talking to her. "I noticed that you caught one of the pieces of the bouquet. I guess this means there will be more than one bride coming out of this wedding."

Felicity shook her head. "I don't think it works that way."

"No?"

"No."

Her smile seemed a little wistful, and David wondered why he hadn't noticed how really pretty she was before. "I've been—"

"David!" Abby called. She and Stan were hovering by the front door of the inn. "Are you going to get pictures of us leaving?"

He looked down at Felicity. "I'm sorry. Duty calls."

"Abby wants those pictures." She grinned and motioned back to the newlyweds. "And it looks like Stan wants to leave. You'd better go."

David turned to look at his sister and her new husband. Stan was motioning for him to hurry. He chuckled and grinned at Felicity. "Looks like you're right. I guess I'd better go. . .if you're sure you're not hurt?"

"I'm fine."

"Okay, then. I'll talk to you later." He hurried away, a little put off by his sister's timing, now that he realized he'd like to get to know her neighbor a whole lot better.

⤳⤳

A light snow had begun to fall when Felicity left the reception. The temperature had been steadily dropping all evening, and by the time she'd changed clothes and fixed herself a light supper, the snow was beginning to accumulate on the sidewalk outside. She cleaned up the kitchen and then went to take a warm bath.

Dressed in her warmest robe, she made herself a cup of hot chocolate and carried it into the living room. Felicity looked out the window and shivered before settling into her recliner. She took a sip of the warm liquid in her cup and picked up the remains of Abby's bouquet that were lying on the table beside her. She still couldn't believe that it'd been sliced into pieces.

Had her work been inferior? Felicity shook her head. She'd spent hours on that bouquet. The fragile blooms just couldn't stand up to the force of the fan. She twirled the small clump around in her fingers and thought about what David had said. Could he be right. . .that catching a portion of a bouquet would have the same results as catching a whole one? She shrugged and shook her head. Did it really matter? No. . .not for her.

David certainly was an attractive man. Especially up close. She'd seen him many times, but she'd never really talked to him. She wondered why that was when she and Abby were such good friends. Of course they'd gone to college together, and David was already out of college by then. Felicity had only been living in Loudon for about a year, having moved here when her parents decided to retire in Florida. Besides, Abby knew how relationship-shy she was after her two broken engagements and probably hadn't wanted her to think she was trying to set her up with her brother.

Abby knew Felicity well enough to know she'd run the other way, because her heart had been broken too many times. Months ago Felicity had come to the conclusion that the Lord intended for her to stay single, and that was the reason she'd put everything she had into opening her own flower shop. Flowers by Felicity was all she had time for now, and she needed to put all of her energies into making a go of it.

She'd only been open a few months, and while she had enough business to hire one other person to help, she was barely getting by. It seemed her hired help was clearing more take-home money than she was. Of course, right now she was putting everything she made back into the business. She was just lucky the shop had a small house attached to it so that she wasn't paying for both a business and a place to live.

Abby's wedding was the first one she'd supplied flowers for, and she hoped word of mouth would garner her more business. Everything had looked lovely. Abby's attendants' skirts were multicolored, and she'd wanted the flowers to be made up of roses of those very same colors. Finding just the right shades of red, yellow, pink, deep rose, and peach had been quite a challenge. But Felicity had contacted all her suppliers and managed to order in enough for Abby's bouquet, the attendants' smaller ones, and the table arrangements at the inn.

Abby had been thrilled with the final result. . .and the price Felicity had given her. She wasn't making much of anything on this project, but she hoped it would pay off in more business.

She sighed, thinking back over the day. It had been a beautiful wedding. Abby and Stan seemed to have found that elusive true love that Felicity had given up on. She really was happy for them. . .if a little sad for herself. She still longed for a love of her own, but it wasn't to be, and she certainly didn't need to sit around moping about it. She flipped on the television and tried to find something to take her mind off weddings and happy endings. It didn't take long.

It was the news hour, and none of the stories were uplifting. The weather was going to get worse during the night, with record snow accumulations for this time of year predicted. Felicity shivered and hit the OFF button on the remote. She took a sip of hot chocolate and picked up the book on the table beside her chair.

It held all the answers she needed and the assurance that she was indeed loved. She flipped open her precious and well-worn Bible. She loved seeing what the Lord had in store for her when she turned to His Word and sought His guidance.

Chapter 2

David looked over the Living section of the paper and chuckled. Abby would probably throttle him when she got home and saw this spread, but one day she would hug his neck for getting these pictures. He'd worked hard to get them ready to go into tomorrow's edition.

He especially loved the one of Abby as she realized she'd thrown her bouquet into the fan. He did feel a little funny about the one he'd taken of Felicity clasping that little bunch of flowers to her heart when she was looking so vulnerable, but it was too late to take it out now. At least she wasn't wearing it on top of her head! David laughed just thinking about what Geoff's reaction would be when he saw his picture. His friend would have plenty to say, of that there was no doubt.

David had looked for Felicity after he took the pictures of Abby and Stan leaving the reception but couldn't find her anywhere. He'd call and try to set up an interview tomorrow. There was no need to write a note to remind himself—he wanted to see her again. His sister's suggestion of an article for the paper just gave him a convenient excuse to be able to do that. He folded the paper under his arm and turned off his computer before heading home for the night.

⌘

The next morning, Felicity looked out her window to a snow-covered world. It was beautiful, even though she dreaded having to drive on slick roads the few miles to church. Hurrying downstairs and through her shop, she shivered and pulled her robe close as she opened the front door and quickly retrieved her paper. The sun was up—hopefully most of the snow would be melted by the time she got ready to leave. It didn't tend to stay around too long this time of year.

She stomped the snow off her shoes before going back inside and hurrying into the kitchen to pour herself a cup of hot coffee. Sitting down at the breakfast nook, she held the warm cup in both hands and sniffed the aromatic liquid before taking her first sip. She scanned the headlines and saw a note in the upper right-hand corner of the paper: "Edmonds-Perry Wedding: Article and pictures in Living section."

She quickly flipped through the newspaper sections until she found the one she was looking for and pulled it out. There on the front page was a beautiful picture of Abby and Stan leaving the church for the reception at the inn, and another one as they left the inn while everyone blew bubbles on them. They did make a beautiful couple. And David really was a great photographer. It was nice he could occasionally still use his talent for the newspaper he ran.

Felicity turned to the inside middle of the section and almost choked on the coffee she'd just swallowed. There in full, living color was a picture of her bouquet flying in all different directions. The caption under the photograph read, "Flowers by Felicity."

The fan that shredded her creation was nowhere in sight. Nowhere in the small accompanying article was there an explanation of *why* the bouquet had broken apart. But all over the two-page spread were pictures of the aftermath. One showed her holding her little clump close, looking. . .confused? Sad? She wasn't sure, but she wasn't thrilled that David had caught her with that expression on her face. In another photo, a man she recognized from church wore one of the bundles on top of his head while observers laughed. It *was* kind of funny. Felicity found herself chuckling in spite of herself—but only for a moment. As she looked back over the picture layout and saw absolutely no mention of the fan, she wondered just how many people were going to think she did shoddy work. Worry about the effect on her business fueled a building anger.

David could have managed to show the fan along with the flowers, couldn't he? Or at the very least, the article could have explained it all. Didn't he realize how much damage he might be doing to her business with these pictures?

Well, before the day was out, he'd know. She couldn't wait to give him a piece of her mind. Felicity was pretty sure he was in the other adult Sunday school class—she knew he wasn't in hers—but she always saw him at church. While she usually sat with Abby, he sat across the way with friends from his class. One thing she was certain about: she would make sure to find him. Oh, yes, she would.

Felicity hurried to get ready, wanting to allow herself plenty of time to get to church. She dressed warmly in a long brown suede skirt, soft butter-yellow sweater, and her favorite boots. The calendar might say spring was just around the corner, but it sure didn't seem that way as she pulled on her coat, opened the front door, and headed for her car.

She was glad she'd allowed a little extra time as she followed a snowplow down the road. By the time she'd parked her car and made her way up the front steps and into the building, there wasn't any time to look for David. She slipped into class and was a little relieved that no one had time to ask about the pictures in the paper.

As soon as class was over, however, several people came up to ask how the bouquet had fallen apart. Her fears that those who weren't at the wedding to see what had happened would get the wrong idea were realized. Thankfully, several people had been there, and they jumped in with the explanation of the fan before Felicity had a chance to. She was too busy trying to tamp down her anger at David. It was probably a very good thing they weren't in the same class.

Felicity sent up a silent prayer that the Lord would help her get past her frustration with the situation and her irritation with David. By the time she'd taken a seat for the worship service, Felicity was having second thoughts about talking to David at church. Once she sat down for the worship service and saw him across the room talking to old Mrs. Donaldson, she decided she'd be better off just going to the paper the next morning and confronting him there. This wasn't the place to make a scene. . .and maybe by tomorrow she could laugh about it all.

❧

David saw Felicity across the room and smiled at her, but she didn't smile back. In fact, she looked almost angry from the way she was frowning, but then she looked away with the same expression on her face, and he wondered if she might be nearsighted.

Once the worship service started, though, the frown left her face, and David found himself glancing her way off and on during the rest of the service. There was something about her. . .she seemed kind of reserved, and he admitted to himself that he wanted to get to know her better. He hoped he'd be able to talk to her after the service.

It quickly became apparent that wasn't going to happen as he was stopped by first one and then another church member laughing and commenting on the pictures in the paper of Abby and Stan's wedding. By the time he got free, Felicity Carmichael was nowhere to be found.

He thought about asking his best friend, Geoff Manfrey, to have lunch with him, but he seemed in deep conversation with Clarissa Evans and her little sister, Jenni. Hmm. When they all walked off together, he wondered what the conversation was about. It looked like lunch with Geoff was out.

Normally content with his own company, David couldn't understand why he suddenly felt so alone. . .but he did. He could go grab a quick bite somewhere and then play a little golf. *Right. In the snow.* Maybe he'd pick up some fast food and go home and watch a little golf on television. That was something he did a lot in the winter, but it didn't sound so great to him now. He headed down the aisle and into the foyer.

"David! Son, where are you going in such a rush?"

David turned to see his mother hurrying up to him.

"Want to come over for Sunday dinner? Your dad and I feel a little at loose ends with all of Abby's wedding preparations over with."

"Oh, so now you have time for me?" he teased.

"David, you know we always have time for you. You stay so busy, it's usually the other way around," his mother admonished him gently.

"Well, I would certainly love to have dinner with you, Mom. I'm feeling a little at loose ends today myself."

His mother raised an eyebrow and chuckled. "Oh, so now *you* have time for us?"

His dark mood immediately lifted, and he laughed as he put an arm around his mother's shoulders and gave her a hug. "It appears I do."

Laughing together, they headed toward his dad, who was waiting by the door. Family. What would he do without them?

⌘

Felicity was glad to see Monday morning come. Usually she loved weekends—especially Sundays. But not this one. She'd spent most of the afternoon trying not to think of David and the pictures he'd put in the paper, but she hadn't been very successful. The day was too quiet and gave her too much time to think about the handsome newspaperman.

For weeks now, she'd spent most Sundays with Abby, helping her plan the wedding. Staying busy. But yesterday there was nothing going on—no wedding showers to go to, no last-minute plans to attend to—and the day had stretched out before her. . .long and a little lonely.

She'd straightened up her house and emptied the trash, adding the offending newspaper to it. She never wanted to see those pictures again. Nor did she want to see David, she told herself. She'd worried and wrestled with whether to go see him most of the night, but she felt the need to tell him he should be more careful about what he put in his newspaper—before he hurt someone else's business.

This morning, she was trying to talk herself out of it until her helper, Nellie Barclay, came in at ten.

"Oh, Felicity—I saw those pictures in the paper! How in the world did that bouquet break up like that? I watched you tape those stems and put it all together. There's no way it should have come apart like that."

Felicity felt a little better just knowing that at least one person knew how carefully she'd put that bouquet together. But if Nellie, who worked with her on a daily business, was wondering about it, half the town would be, too. As the morning wore on, she knew she'd never rest until she made her way to the *Loudon Daily News* office.

Leaving Nellie in charge, Felicity pulled on a jacket and headed outside. The sun was peeking out behind the clouds, and she hoped that by mid-afternoon most of the snow would be gone.

Her shop was in an older section of town, just off the main street, and it was only a few blocks from David's office. Nervous butterflies fluttered in her stomach as she made her way into the newspaper building. She took the elevator up to the executive offices and walked up to the receptionist.

"Is Mr. Edmonds in? I'd like to see him if possible."

The receptionist looked her up and down. "I'm sorry, but he's in a meeting right now. His schedule is pretty tight today. Would you like to schedule a meeting for tomorrow or the next day?"

Felicity could feel her courage sinking. If she left now, she probably wouldn't come back. "No, I'd really like to see him today if that's possible."

"Then you can take a seat. When his meeting is over, I'll see if he has time to see you. What is your name?"

"Felicity Carmichael."

"Oh. The *flower* girl." She shook her head. "Too bad that bouquet didn't hold together."

Felicity clenched her teeth and watched as the receptionist wrote down her name and glanced at her watch.

"He should be through anytime now. I'll check with him then to see if he has time to see you." In a condescending tone, she added, "But I don't think he will."

The receptionist bared her teeth in the phoniest and most insincere smile Felicity had ever seen and motioned across the room. "You can sit down and wait over there."

Praying for the Lord to forgive her for wanting to call the woman at the desk *guard dog*, and to keep those very words from passing her lips, Felicity somehow managed to find the nameplate on the desk. "Thank you, Myra."

And thank You, Lord.

She turned, let out a deep breath of relief that she hadn't made a scene, and took a seat in one of the chairs facing the door to David's office. She wanted to make sure that she could see when his meeting was over. If nothing else, she'd just wait until he took a lunch break and catch him then.

One way or another, the *flower girl* was meeting up with the *picture boy*. Today.

Chapter 3

When the office door opened fifteen minutes later, Felicity had only a moment to wonder if she could leave before David saw her waiting. Her bravado was quickly disappearing. Besides, what was the point? The damage had been done. She'd just have to depend on word of mouth from those at the wedding to let people know pictures didn't always tell the truth.

But before she could leave, David spotted her. "Felicity! What a nice surprise. I was just going to have Myra look up your number for me." He walked toward her with a smile. "Are you here to see me?"

Felicity nodded. "If you have time."

"Of course I do. Myra should have buzzed me to let me know you were here. I hope you haven't been waiting long."

"You were in a meeting, Mr. Edmonds," Myra said. "I didn't think you'd want to be disturbed. I'm sorry."

"It's all right, Myra. Just be sure to buzz me the next time Ms. Carmichael comes to see me, please. Felicity, come on into my office and tell me what I can do for you."

The look his receptionist shot Felicity wasn't pleasant, but at least it was apparent that Myra's guard status was self-imposed. Felicity held her head a little higher as she followed David into his office.

❧

David couldn't believe Felicity was actually there to see him. She'd been on his mind ever since the wedding, and he had planned to contact her later in the day. He waited for her to take the chair in front of his desk before he sat down. "It's great to see you. What brings you here today?"

He watched as Felicity sighed and looked over at him with those big golden eyes. She was lovely, but she seemed a little nervous. "What is it, Felicity? Is something wrong?"

She let out a huge sigh. "Do you realize the harm you've done?"

David's heart skittered in his chest. "What harm? What are you talking about?"

"You honestly don't know?"

David shook his head. He didn't. But whatever it was, it was obvious that Felicity wasn't happy about it. She sat there, chewing her bottom lip and wringing her hands. He couldn't for the life of him figure out what he might have done that could cause her such distress. Whatever it was, it must have been bad. He stood and came around his desk and took the extra seat beside her. Propping his forearms on his knees, he looked into her eyes. "Felicity, I'm sorry. I don't know what I did. Please tell me."

"Those pictures you put in the paper of the wedding. . . the bouquet flying apart and no mention of the fan?" She flipped her hand in the air as if to remind him of the flying flowers. "It looks as though my work on the bouquet was inferior. . .that it didn't hold together."

David sank back into the chair, letting the breath he'd been holding swoosh out of his lungs. "You're right. I didn't mention the fan. I guess I assumed everyone there knew what caused the bouquet to fall apart."

"Everyone there *did* know. It's all the other people in town who read the *Loudon Daily News* who I'm concerned about—unless the only people who read your paper are the ones who attended the wedding? You'd have what? About two hundred subscribers?"

"Ahh, no. We wouldn't be in business if that were the case."

Felicity smiled at him, but it never reached her eyes. "I didn't think so. And that's my point. Are those subscribers who weren't at the wedding going to want to order flowers from a florist who they think does shoddy work? No, of course they aren't."

She shook her head and rubbed her fingers across her forehead as if to ease a headache. David was feeling worse by the minute.

"I'm just starting out, David. This wasn't the kind of publicity I was hoping would come from doing Abby's flowers."

"I am so sorry, Felicity. I truly am." And he was. He gave himself a mental kick in the seat of the pants. "Obviously. . . I wasn't thinking. How can I make it up to you? I can put an explanation in tomorrow's morning paper. . .a correction of sorts."

"No. That will only look like I complained and forced you to. It won't help." Felicity stood up and pulled her purse strap over her shoulder.

David felt like a rat, knowing he'd hurt her. She turned to go, but he stood and beat her to the door. "Felicity, I truly am sorry. I never meant to hurt you or your business. Let me take you to lunch so we can talk about how I can make it up to you?"

For a moment he thought she was going to say yes. Then she shook her head and smiled at him. "No, thank you. I've got to get back to work. Besides, you've apologized. There's really nothing else you can do."

There has to be something I can do! I can't just let her walk out of my life, hating me. But before he could come up with any answer, that's exactly what she did.

❧

Felicity swept past Myra and hurried to the elevator before she changed her mind and told David she would go to lunch with him. He'd really been very sweet, and he'd seemed sincerely sorry. She'd been tempted to accept his invitation to lunch. . .but she just couldn't. She had a feeling she could be way too attracted to David Edmonds, and that was the last thing she needed. She couldn't take the chance of being hurt again.

Besides, she'd said what she'd come to say. He'd apologized. That was it. That was all there ever could be. She had a business to run, and she'd best get back to it. It was lunchtime, and Nellie was probably starving. Felicity hurried down the street, trying to put David out of her thoughts.

She found Nellie on the phone, taking an order for an arrangement for a baby shower scheduled for that weekend. Felicity smiled. She loved doing those.

She waited on a man who came in from the street and ordered a dozen red roses. Maybe she wouldn't starve. And surely, one day people would forget the bouquet that flung its flowers from one end of County Meadow Inn to the other.

❧

David spent most of the next few hours trying to figure out how to make things up to Felicity. . .and how to get her to go to dinner with him. He was interested in her. . .more than a little. Why hadn't he realized that he might be hurting her business by putting that picture of the bouquet breaking into pieces in the paper? David sighed and shook his head. He'd been too intent on putting together a layout that he knew would get a rise out of his sister.

They did that, the two of them. If he wasn't getting the best of Abby, she was playing a trick on him. That's what siblings did, wasn't it? Only this time, it looked as though someone else was being hurt by his prank, and for that he truly was sorry.

What could he do? Maybe he'd send Felicity flowers. Yeah. Right. From her competitor. That was bound to make her want to have dinner with him.

Myra buzzed him to remind him of a meeting with his advertising manager scheduled for later that afternoon. He had half a mind to cancel the meeting. Sales were up. Ed did a good job and didn't need any supervision in his area. They didn't have to meet today. David needed to spend his time trying to come up with something that would help Felicity, and. . .*advertising.*

David tapped his fingers on his desk. Maybe he had the answer. Would Felicity go for it? He grinned. How could she not?

⁓

At first he thought Felicity was gone for the day, but he knew Ms. Barclay from church, and when he told her he was there to see Felicity, Nellie just led him back to a workroom where Felicity was working on a huge arrangement.

She didn't see them standing in the doorway at first, and David watched as she wrapped the stem of a purple flower with florist tape and place it just so in a vase among other flowers of the same kind and some yellow ones he thought were daffodils. It was a beautiful arrangement. Felicity was very good at what she did. It was too bad anyone might have other ideas from his own thoughtlessness.

"Felicity, Mr. Edmonds is here to see you," Nellie announced before turning to go back to the front of the shop.

Felicity seemed surprised to see him. . .and not very happy about it, either. She raised an eyebrow as if to ask what he was doing there. "David? What can I do for you?"

"Well, I came to make amends—I hope."

"You've already apologized. You don't need to do anything more."

"Oh, but I do. I have an idea. Please. . .have dinner with me and let me tell you about it."

Felicity shook her head. "I can't. I have to finish—"

"Don't say no. We can go after you get through. You choose the time."

She hesitated for a moment and shook her head again. "David, this really isn't necessary."

How was he going to convince her to have dinner with him? "Felicity, Abby is going to be mad enough at me as it is. Please let me at least be able to tell her I tried to make it up to you."

It worked. Felicity smiled at him and chuckled. "All right. I've seen Abby when she's angry. I'll take pity on you, 'cause she *is* going to be mad at you. Pick me up at about seven."

David nodded. "I'll be here." *With bells on, if I thought it would help.*

⁓

Felicity looked at herself in the mirror and wondered one more time if she'd lost her mind. She had absolutely no business going to dinner with David. None. But the simple fact was she wanted to. And she was curious to find out his idea for making things up to her.

She had no idea where he was taking her for dinner, but she dressed in what she hoped would work for just about any place he chose. After much deliberation, she'd chosen an aqua sweater and matching pants. It was cold again and looked like more snow might be on the way. She was beginning to wonder if spring was ever going to arrive in Vermont.

When the doorbell rang, she hurried to answer it, trying to ignore the rapid beat of her heart. This was not a date. David was here to make amends. That was all. And she'd do well to remember that fact.

But the smile on his face and the way he looked at her when she opened the door did nothing to slow her pulse rate. He looked wonderful in brown slacks, a cream-colored sweater, and a leather jacket.

"Hi. I hope you're hungry. I made reservations at Salvagio's. Do you like Italian? If not, we can go somewhere else."

"No, I love Italian food. And Salvagio's is one of my favorite places to eat."

"Good. It's one of mine, too." He helped her on with her coat and waited for her to grab her purse before guiding her down the walk to his car.

Felicity felt special as he opened the door and helped her inside. She kept telling herself it was only a business dinner. . . at most, simply dinner with her best friend's brother. But when he looked over at her and smiled before starting the car and putting it in gear, she knew she was in trouble. Because suddenly, it felt like a date with a handsome man.

Chapter 4

D avid kept telling himself this wasn't a date. No matter how attracted he was to Felicity Carmichael. She was only with him because he had a plan to make things up to her for hurting her business—and to keep Abby from being furious with him when she got home—and because she was nice.

When they got to the restaurant and found a line already in progress, even on a Monday night, he was glad he'd called ahead and made reservations. Salvagio's was one of the most popular restaurants in Loudon, and he considered Nick Salvagio a good friend. But when Nick kissed Felicity on the cheek, it didn't settle well with David.

"Felicity, you look lovely tonight. And, David. . .it's great to see you, my friend. What a good night—two of my favorite people, here together." He grinned at David. "Are you celebrating anything special?"

David had a feeling Nick was trying to find out if the two of them were seriously seeing each other, and he wasn't of a mind to let him know for sure. "More like I'm here to make amends to Felicity for something."

That stirred Nick's curiosity; David could tell from the way he raised an eyebrow in his direction and grinned. "I see."

David only wished what Nick thought was going on between him and Felicity was right. . .that they were dating. As it was, if she didn't like the idea he'd come up with, David wondered if it might be the first and last time he took her to dinner. Looking down at her as they followed Nick through the dimly lit dining room, he knew that he wanted it to be the first of many evenings they would share. Enough that he sent up a silent prayer. *Lord, please let me convince Felicity that I'm sorry and that I truly want to see her business succeed.*

Once seated at the candlelit table, they gave their attention to the menu. David knew what he wanted, but he was curious to see what Felicity would order. When the waiter appeared, he asked her if she'd decided.

Felicity nodded. "I'd like the Fettuccine Salvagio, a house salad, and iced tea, please."

David grinned and nodded. "I'll have the same." Nick's specialty of sliced Italian sausages on top of a bed of fettuccine with a spiced-up Alfredo sauce had become his favorite dish.

He handed the menus to the waiter and looked over at Felicity. "Thank you for coming with me tonight. You know, I looked for you after I finished taking pictures of Abby and Stan leaving the reception. Abby had suggested that I interview you for the paper. I'd still like to do that, if you are willing."

She leaned her head to the side and smiled at him. "David. It's all right. You don't need to do that."

"No. Really, I'd like to. And maybe we can slide in an explanation about the flowers and the fan?"

"This is your plan to help my business and make things up to me?"

David shook his head and took a sip of water before answering. "Not entirely. I think it could help your business if done right. But I was planning on doing that anyway, so it wouldn't really be making anything up to you. It would be a way to get your name out there, though. Some free publicity."

"I guess it would. . . ."

"I promise you can look over the copy before it goes to print." David grinned at her.

"Well, then. How can I refuse?"

The waiter brought their drinks and salads just then, and once the man left their table, Felicity put her napkin in her lap and asked David if he'd say a blessing. He bowed his head and gave thanks for the food they were about to eat, wondering when the last time was that he'd dated a woman who expected a prayer to be said before they ate. It felt good to be around Felicity. It made him feel like a better man somehow.

They took several bites of salad before David continued with their conversation. "The making things up to you part would be to offer you free advertising for the next year."

"Oh, David." Felicity looked startled. "That's quite an offer. And it's much too generous. I can't let you do it. Hopefully in a year no one will remember those pictures in the paper."

"Please. I want to do it. It's my paper, so it's not like I'll be out any actual money."

"But you'll be losing money—I've checked the prices of running an ad in your paper."

David looked into her eyes and knew it would be money he could live without. "Felicity, you're a businesswoman. Can you really afford to turn down my offer?"

She looked up at him and then back at her salad. She took a sip of her tea. Her gaze met his once more. She chuckled and shook her head. "No. I can't."

"Good. It's settled then. We'll discuss layout ideas later this week." David extended his hand across the table and waited for Felicity to take it. When she did, he was struck by how small and warm her hand was as his fingers tightened around hers for a moment.

Felicity pulled her hand away when the waiter brought their meal to the table. "A small ad will be fine. . .more than enough, David."

"We'll see." Afraid she'd change her mind about the ad, he quickly changed the subject, "Now, how about getting to that interview? Tell me. . . when did you decide you wanted to become a florist?"

"Oh, I think when I was a child, I fell in love with flowers. . .my grand-mother and mother always had flower gardens, and fresh arrangements were part of our daily life. I've always loved the different textures, colors, and fragrances of flowers. Loved working them into arrangements. I think they are one of the most beautiful parts of God's creation."

"And how did you get started in the business? Did you need any kind of formal training?"

David thought he could listen to the sound of her laughter forever. "I started in the business when I was about sixteen. I went to the florist in my hometown and asked if they needed help. I've been working in florist shops ever since. But I majored in business in college and got an associate degree in Floral Design and Marketing. When I decided I wanted to open my own shop, I applied for a small business loan, and here I am."

Sitting across from me. As David spent the next hour learning all he could about her, he could think of nowhere else he'd rather be.

❧

Sitting across the table from David and finishing up the cheesecake they'd ordered for dessert, Felicity couldn't remember when she'd talked so much about herself or her life.

"And why did you decide to open your own shop?" David asked.

"I couldn't think of anything else I'd rather do for a living." She wasn't about to tell him that when it became obvious after two broken engagements that she would be her sole provider, she realized she needed to decide what she was going to do with the rest of her life. And that if she was never going to be a wife and mother as she longed to be, she might as well make a living doing something she loved.

He smiled across the table at her. "Not everyone can lay claim to that."

"No, they can't." Felicity did feel blessed in her career choice. . .especially if she could just manage to make a living at it.

"And you've been open for business for how long?"

"Just since the first of the year."

"Oh, you are just starting out, aren't you?"

Felicity leaned back in her chair. "I am. I'm just thankful that the shop has a house attached to it. Otherwise, I'm not sure I could make it. But I'm hoping that by the end of the year, I can see a profit."

David pushed his dessert plate to the side and rested his forearms on the table, leaning in and looking at her intently. "I can see why you were so upset with me. I truly am sorry, Felicity. Please forgive my thoughtlessness."

How could she possibly refuse to forgive him? He was sincere; she had no doubt of that. Besides, she already had forgiven him. "David, of course I do. I know you meant no harm."

"Thank you. I promise to do all I can to help you make that profit by the end of the year."

"That isn't your responsibility, David."

"Maybe not, but I do feel that I might have hurt your chances some. I intend to change that, though. I'll come by tomorrow afternoon. What time do you close up shop?"

"Usually around five o'clock. Sometimes I work longer, but the shop closes to business then."

"So I'll be there about quitting time. I'll have a copy of the article for you to approve, and hopefully we can talk about advertising."

"I'll be there."

David asked a few more questions about her business, but they finished their meal making small talk. . .finding out about the people they both knew, trying to figure out how they'd never really met with his sister living right next door to Felicity.

By the time David pulled his car up to her house, Felicity found herself wishing the evening didn't have to come to an end. She couldn't remember when she'd had such a good time. The meal was wonderful, which was no surprise; the food at Salvagio's was always superb. It was David's company that made the evening stand out. He seemed genuinely interested in her work. . .in her. Of course, he was trying to make her feel better. . .and he didn't want his sister to chew him out when she got home. Besides, he was a newspaperman. He knew how to interview.

Aware that she'd enjoyed herself way too much, she opened her car door almost before he came to a stop. "Thank you, again, David. It was a wonderful meal. No need to see me inside."

"But I—"

"No—really," Felicity was already out of the car. "I left a light on. Thanks again." She hurried up the walk, but in her haste, she got the heel of her boot caught in a crack in the cement. She turned and swayed, dropped her purse, and struggled to right herself before she fell on the hard walk.

David must have gotten out of the car anyway, because he seemed to appear out of nowhere and was by her side, steadying her. "Are you all right?"

Well, so much for the graceful exit. "I'm fine. Thank you."

He handed her the purse he'd picked up and held on to her elbow as he guided her to her front door. "I'm glad," David said, waiting as she rummaged through her purse, looking for her keys

"My keys aren't here."

"Did you drop them when you tripped?"

She dug some more. "I might have."

David was already back out on the walk looking for them. "Ahh! Here they are," he said, bending to pick them up from the lawn. He turned, sprinted back to the porch, and held the keys out to her.

Felicity took them from him and unlocked the door, trying not to let him see the embarrassed tears that were trying to form. What a klutz she must have looked like! He really was sweet. "Thank you."

"You're welcome." As if he knew how she was feeling, he turned to go. "Thank you for a great evening!"

She waved at him before shutting her front door. *A memorable one, anyway.* One she certainly wasn't going to forget anytime soon.

⁂

The next day, David found himself looking forward to stopping by Felicity's shop that afternoon. She'd been on his mind all day. He couldn't remember when he'd enjoyed an evening more. Felicity was wonderful company. He'd had to keep reminding himself that he wasn't on a date— he was there to interview her and to help undo some of the harm he might have done with the Sunday photo spread. But it didn't ring true. He wished it had been a date, and if he had his way, there would be another and another. But it wasn't going to be easy. While Felicity had been warm and open at the restaurant, by the time they got back to her house, she seemed to turn cool.

He did know he wasn't going to put all of his apples in one basket. He'd take the copy of the interview to her for her approval, but he was going to draw out a decision on the advertising for her shop. If everything were settled today, he wouldn't have a good reason to stop by her shop again. And he wanted every excuse he could get to see Felicity Carmichael.

Abby might not be happy with him about the wedding pictures he'd picked for the paper, but he wasn't too thrilled with her, either. His little sister had a lot of explaining to do when she got home. After all the times she'd tried to get him together with one or the other of her friends, he wanted to know just why she hadn't tried to set him up with Felicity—the one and only woman who'd captured his interest in months!

Chapter 5

Felicity looked at the clock for the fourth time in the last ten minutes. She'd had Nellie leave early so she could stop by the hospital to deliver a bouquet made up of tiny baby-pink roses to the mother of a brand-new little girl. Felicity had been looking for David to show up ever since. She sighed and shook her head. She had no business looking forward to his visit. Hadn't she asked the Lord to show her what His will for her life was after her last broken engagement? And hadn't the opportunity to open her own shop come up just days later?

Besides, she couldn't afford to have her heart broken again. She just couldn't. First Ned and then Marcus. She'd thought she'd found the man of her dreams both times. And *both* times she'd been mistaken. Ned had decided marriage wasn't for him. Marcus had decided that one of her best friends was for him. Felicity had decided that men—none of them—could be trusted. . .with the exception of her dad and granddad. Evidently, the mold had been thrown away after them.

So why was she watching the clock and listening for the bell over her shop door to ring? Because she couldn't quit thinking about David Edmonds. He'd been so nice last night. . .showing real concern when she'd nearly fallen and going back to look for her keys.

At the restaurant, it'd almost felt like a date with the two of them getting to know each other a little better. She'd found out that he and Abby had been pulling pranks on each other all their lives. . .but he was a little nervous about this last one. He'd included a few less-than-flattering shots of his sister in the Living section layout, and he had a feeling Abby wouldn't rest until she found a way to pay him back. Felicity chuckled. Knowing Abby, David was probably right.

She finished the birthday bouquet she was making for a young woman turning eighteen. It was made up of a mix of cream and pink roses, and Felicity was pleased with the results as she put it in the cooler to be delivered the next morning. Next, she checked the order pad for the last few orders Nellie had taken to see what needed to be done before she called it a day.

There was an anniversary bouquet to be made for a man to pick up around four in the afternoon. He wanted it to be special for the forty years they'd been married. Then there were several orders to be sent to a funeral home. Felicity didn't recognize the name of the deceased, but it wouldn't matter. She always gave a lot of time and care to funeral arrangements, knowing how much they meant to those who were grieving the loss of a loved one.

She checked her stock and made a list of the flowers and greenery that she needed to order from her suppliers early the next morning. As she was making a list, the bell over the door rang out, and a young man entered the shop.

Felicity put a hand to her chest and shook her head. "Oh, I'm sorry. We're closed. I just hadn't turned the sign around."

"Oh, please, ma'am, I really need some flowers tonight." He looked about nineteen and was very worried. "I forgot my girlfriend's birthday, and I really need to make it up to her. I'll pay double."

Felicity smiled at him, thinking how lucky his girlfriend was. Would that either of her fiancés had cared that much about her birthday. "Let me see what I have."

She had her head in the flower cooler when the bell over the door jingled once more, and she wondered if maybe she should consider lengthening her hours of operation if she could have this kind of business later in the day. Her heart did a funny little somersault when she turned to see David standing there.

He looked at his watch. "I thought you closed at five?"

"Normally, I do," she answered, ducking back into the cooler. She hoped the coolness from inside it would excuse the give-away color she felt flood her cheeks.

She took a breath and brought out a half-dozen red roses and several sprigs of baby's breath. She held them out for the young man to inspect. "Think these will do?"

"They'll be just fine, ma'am. Thank you."

"Do you want them in a vase or boxed?"

"Boxed will be fine." He reached for his wallet. "How much do I owe you?"

Felicity wrapped the flowers in green tissue paper and carefully laid them in a long box. She quoted him a price, and he grinned. "Are you sure? At this late notice?"

She nodded and took the cash he handed her. "I'm sure. Just let your friends know how reasonable my prices are, okay?"

"I'll do that; I certainly will. You have a good evening, and thank you."

"You're welcome," Felicity said, following him to the door. She flipped the closed sign to the outside before turning to face David.

He smiled at her. "That was nice of you. You could have asked twice as much for those roses."

"I know. But he seemed so worried when he came in, I kind of felt sorry for him. It's his girlfriend's birthday, and he'd forgotten."

"Oh. I see. Still, you gave him a great price."

She shrugged and grinned. "My prices *are* good. I try to make sure they are better than most of my competitors."

He handed her a piece of paper. "Maybe I should add that to this copy. I plan on putting it in the Living section of the Sunday paper. . .along with some great pictures of the flowers that you did. I did get some really good shots before the fan incident."

Felicity took the paper from him. "You don't have to do the Sunday paper, David."

"But I'm going to." He looked around the shop. "Are you ready to close? Want to go pick up a bite to eat? You can inspect the copy and give me the go ahead. . .or not?"

She knew she shouldn't. She should just look over the article and tell him yes or no and send him on his way. That's what she should do. Her heart skipped a beat as he inclined his head and smiled a slow smile.

"Come on. You have to eat sometime."

Oh, yes, she knew what she *should* do, and she knew what she wanted to do. The latter won out. "Okay. Only, it's my treat tonight. I put a pot of soup on earlier. We can eat at my place."

Thank You, Lord. Never in his wildest dreams had David expected to be having supper with Felicity, but here he was. . . sitting in her cheery kitchen, smelling fresh cornbread cooking, and drinking in the sight of her across the table from him.

She looked up from reading the article he'd written and smiled at him. "Thank you, David. It's very flattering and a wonderful plug for my shop."

"That's what we're aiming for—lots of business for you. Which reminds me, I've got several ideas for ads. Have you had time to think about what you'd like?"

"David, this article is enough. You don't need to. . ."

Oh, yes, he did. In just a few short days, he'd realized he wanted to get to know this woman much better. She was like a breath of fresh spring air. . . even with small patches of snow still on the ground. Besides, he truly wanted to help her business get on its feet. She'd been so nice to that young man. And she had given Abby a really great deal on the flowers for her wedding.

"Felicity, that's already been settled. I'll get some ideas to you later in the week."

"All right, thank you, then. But there's no hurry. I know you have a business to run, too."

David sighed with relief when she gave in.

Felicity got up to check on the cornbread. It was golden brown when she took it out of the oven. She ladled up two large bowls of beef vegetable soup and set one in front of him. He couldn't remember the last time he'd had homemade soup. The very smell of it had his mouth watering in anticipation.

Felicity brought her own bowl and a basket of cornbread to the table. She refilled their tea glasses and sat down. "Would you say the blessing, please?"

David bowed his head. "Dear Father, we thank You for this day, for this food. And thank You for prompting Felicity to ask me to share this meal she prepared. Please forgive us our sins and help us live each day to Your glory. In Jesus' name, amen."

They began to eat, and David felt a contentment he didn't quite understand, sitting at Felicity's table, eating her delicious soup and the cornbread that, spread with butter, melted in his mouth. But the meal seemed to satisfy more than just his stomach, and he knew it had more to do with whom he was sharing the meal with than what he was eating.

"This is wonderful, Felicity. You are a great cook."

"Thank you. I like cooking almost as much as I like flower arranging."

"Well, if the flower shop bombs, you can always open a—oh, I'm sorry." David clamped his mouth shut and shook his head. Would he never learn to keep his foot *out* of his mouth? He shrugged and said, "Abby says I have no tact at all. I think I just proved her right."

"It's all right, David." Felicity laughed. "That isn't a bad idea, actually. I think I like florists' hours better, though. Speaking of Abby. . .she and Stan are due home at the end of the week, aren't they?"

"Yes. Stan couldn't take any more time off from work, and they wanted to have a little time to settle in before Monday. I still can't believe my baby sister is a married woman now."

"It will seem a little strange to find Stan answering the phone or the door. Abby and I have been used to running back and forth through the hedge. Maybe I'll start calling first."

"I'm sure you'll be welcome there anytime. Stan's a pretty easygoing guy. I think they are going to be very happy together."

"So do I. He's really nice, and I'm very happy for Abby."

Felicity refilled his bowl, and the next half hour passed much faster than David wanted it to as they talked about Abby and Stan, their families, and anything else that came to mind. He would have liked to stay longer, but he had a feeling he might wear out his welcome, and that was the last thing he wanted to do.

"Let me help you with the dishes," he said as Felicity took their empty bowls to the sink.

"Oh, no. That's not necessary. Besides, the house may be old, but the kitchen is modern. I have a dishwasher."

David glanced down at the gleaming, stainless steel appliance built in beside the sink. "So you do. I'll be glad to help, though."

"Thanks, David. I can handle it." Felicity smiled at him as she came back to the table and gathered their glasses and the empty basket that had held the cornbread.

Obviously, it was time for him to go. . .whether he wanted to or not. He stood up. "I guess I'll be on my way, then. Thank you for the wonderful meal."

Felicity walked him to the door. "You're welcome. I'm glad you enjoyed it. And thank you for that nice article."

David gazed down at her as they stood in the doorway. He wanted to ask her out, but he had a feeling now wasn't the time. Patience was something the Lord was continually trying to teach him, and he acknowledged that this might be one of those moments when he should try to exercise that quality. He smiled down at her.

"It was easy to write. I'll try to get some ad ideas to you soon. If you come up with anything you'd like to do, just give me a call."

"All right. . ." Felicity paused.

David decided not to linger. He didn't want her to refuse the advertising space. . .not when it was the only good reason she might agree to see him again. He started down the steps. "I'll be in contact. Good night, Felicity."

Chapter 6

Felicity watched until David got in his car and pulled away from the curb before going back to the kitchen. She'd enjoyed the company immensely, but she told herself it was just because she felt a little at loose ends. All the preparations leading up to Abby's wedding had kept them both busy, and now she wasn't quite sure how to fill her time.

With Abby married and on her honeymoon, Felicity admitted to herself that she still wished for a love of her own, and she was trying very hard not to be envious. She was happy for Abby and Stan. . .truly she was.

She just wasn't totally happy for herself. And she didn't know why she was dwelling on it now. Her life plan had been decided with the last broken engagement. She had a living to make, a new business to see to, and that's *all* she had time for.

She certainly didn't have time to mope around wishing for what couldn't be. . .or thinking about how empty her kitchen felt since David left. Sensing the need to keep busy, instead of loading her dishwasher, she filled the sink with dishes, hot water, and dish soap.

But washing them by hand did nothing to help her mood. It only made her wonder what it would have been like to share the task with David. He was much too nice for her heart's sake. It beat faster just thinking of him, and she was certain that wasn't a good thing. Besides, he was her best friend's brother. She didn't need to be thinking about him romantically. She didn't need to be thinking of him at all!

Dear Lord, I'm sure David Edmonds isn't in Your plan for my future. We've already mapped it out, haven't we? So, please help me put him out of my mind. I don't need the distraction right now. And I certainly don't need another heartache. In Jesus' name, amen.

She finished cleaning the kitchen and went back into the shop to finish making up her list for what to order the next day and to see if there were any messages on the answering machine. The light was blinking, and she was pleased to hear someone from the Loudon First National Bank asking her to call the next day with a quote for doing a weekly arrangement for the bank's lobby.

Maybe the pictures David had put in the paper hadn't done too much harm after all. Felicity put a note on her "to-do" list to call them first thing the next morning and replaced thoughts of her handsome supper companion with ideas of the different kinds of arrangements she could offer the bank.

The next day, Felicity was pleased with the order the bank gave her, but a little disappointed in business in general. She wasn't sure if it had fallen off or if she'd just hit a slow spell, but she tried not to worry about it. She hoped that the newspaper article in the coming Sunday paper would help.

David called several times that week, but each time she was in the middle of a project and asked Nellie to take a message. He always said he'd just call back later. Much as she wanted to see him or talk to him again, she was fully aware that she was trying to avoid doing just that. The way her pulse raced each time Nellie told her he was on the phone, Felicity decided that it would just be easier on her if she could keep from seeing him any more than absolutely necessary.

⧉

Abby and Stan had returned on Saturday afternoon, and when Abby called with an invitation to come over for brunch after church on Sunday, Felicity was happy to accept.

The interview in Sunday's paper went over very well. Several people at church were complimentary about it, and Felicity knew she needed to thank David for the publicity. She looked around for him, but he was talking to several people across the room and she didn't want to disturb him, so she went on home to freshen up. She brushed her hair and applied fresh lipstick before going outside and hurrying through the hedge to her friend's back door.

She was glad Abby and Stan were back and looked forward to catching up and hearing all about their trip. But it was only when David came to the back door, accompanied by Bowser, that she acknowledged deep down she was hoping he would be here, too.

"Hi, Felicity. Abby didn't tell me you were coming over."

"Hi." *She didn't tell me about you, either.* Felicity hoped the color she felt stealing up her cheeks didn't give away how flustered she was at seeing him again. She bent to pat Bowser on the head and let him lick her hand, trying to give herself time to regain some of her composure.

Abby came up behind David and shoved him out of the way. Hugging Felicity, she asked, "Did he apologize for that awful spread in the paper last week? I've been on his case ever since I looked at it. I can't believe he put so many unflattering shots of me in there!"

Felicity couldn't help but chuckle at the way David rolled his eyes behind his sister's back. She shook her head at him and answered Abby, "Yes, he did. And he's trying to make up for it. Did you see the interview he did with me in today's paper?"

"No, I haven't had time to read it, but it's a good thing he's trying to make amends. Otherwise, he'd be—"

"Disowned," David said, grinning, with his hand over his heart. "But I've asked forgiveness, sister mine. If Felicity can forgive me, surely you can, too."

"I know you better than Felicity does," Abby answered.

David looked over at his new brother-in-law. "You can step in and take up for me anytime now, Stan."

Stan laughed and shook his head. "Not on your life, Buddy. We're still newlyweds."

"Aw, please forgive me, Abby. I really am sorry," David implored his sister.

She winked at Felicity. "Well, if you promise to make it up to Felicity and if you behave yourself from now on—hard as I know that will be for you. . ."

David gave her a bear hug. "Thanks, Sis. I really didn't mean to cause problems for Felicity. And you looked beautiful—even with your mouth wide open and your eyes closed. But I promise not to ever put that kind of picture of you in the paper again."

Abby punched him on the shoulder. "You'd better not."

He kissed his sister on the cheek, gave an exaggerated sigh of relief, and grinned at Felicity.

The doorbell rang, and Abby hurried to answer it. Felicity was relieved to see more of Abby's family and friends joining them, thinking that there should be a certain amount of safety in numbers. . .because she needed to keep her heart safe from David.

But by the time the afternoon came to an end, she knew she was in real danger. She liked the interaction between David and his sister, between him and his parents. Liked more about him each time she saw him. She wanted to see more of him. But when she looked over and found him studying her from across the kitchen and giving her that slow, sweet smile of his, Felicity knew that was exactly what she couldn't do. Not if she wanted to save herself from more heartbreak.

⚜

By the end of the next week, and after calling in favors from everyone he could think of—asking them to put any flower orders they might need, or even a few they might not need, into Flowers by Felicity—David began to wonder if he'd hurt his own cause.

Felicity was up to her ears with work. He stopped by on Friday evening, hoping to get her to go to dinner so that they could discuss some of the ad copy his advertising department had come up with, only to find her and Nellie knee-deep in buckets of cut flowers. ·

"What's all this?"

"Peach amaryllis, white amaryllis, purple anemones, red anemones, yellow tulips, roses, broom, artichoke leaves, and—"

"No. I mean, what's up?"

She shrugged at him and grinned. "I don't know. Suddenly, I have more business than I've ever had. I think I have you to thank for that."

"That's the point of it all, right?" He smiled at her and looked around. Her worktable was covered with vases and bowls of different shapes and sizes, some kind of green foam stuff, and greenery. Buckets of flowers were all over the place.

"The Wildwood Country Club called late this afternoon. Some kind of reception is being held there tomorrow evening, and they wanted thirty table arrangements by four o'clock tomorrow afternoon. I needed to get started tonight because I've never had an order from them before, and I want to be sure and have everything ready on time."

Remind me to kick myself later, Lord. I want to help her business, but I certainly don't want her so busy she doesn't have time for me. David almost snorted at his vain assumption that she might want to spend *any* time with him—the goal was to get her to that point. But he had to have time to do that. . .and if she was working nonstop, what chance did he have?

"I was going to see if you wanted to grab a bite to eat and go over some ideas for your ads." He could easily see that wasn't going to happen. . .at least not tonight.

"As it stands now, the only way I'm going to eat for a while is if I have something sent in, but thank you anyway."

"Well, how about I go pick something up and bring it back here?"

"Oh, there's no need. I can call and order a pizza."

How was he going to get around that, David wondered, thinking as fast as he could. "I can go pick one up. It'd be a lot quicker."

"I—"

"Let me do this for you, Felicity. Please."

She hesitated for a moment, then she smiled at him. "Yes, all right. Thank you, David. Maybe by the time you get back, we'll have everything set up so that Nellie and I can finish up first thing in the morning. She wiped her hands on her work smock and grabbed the phone. "I'll call in an order to Mario's Pizza. Any kind you are partial to?"

David shook his head, knowing he'd eat any kind she ordered. He headed toward the door. "You pick. Just put it in my name and surprise me."

Chapter 7

Felicity gave the order for the pizza and hung up the phone, staring at the door David had just gone out of. How had he done that? She'd been determined *not* to see more of him, and now it appeared she'd be sharing a meal with him once more. Did she have no backbone at all?

"Are you all right, Felicity?" Nellie asked, bringing her out of her reverie.

"I'm fine. I'm just trying to gather my thoughts." *And protect my heart.* But Felicity had a feeling it was already too late for that. She was afraid she was quickly losing her heart to David Edmonds. She shook her head. She was just going to have to be more on guard.

Trying to get her mind off of him and back on business, she experimented with several different arrangements to find the one she liked best. She made one up of white roses, ornamental cabbage leaves, and rose leaves, and another of anemones of different colors.

She was just putting the finishing touches on one made up of the peach and white amaryllis, broom, and sprigs of cineraria, all the while telling herself that she was going to make sure she didn't fall in love with David. And that was all well and good. . .until he walked back in the door with the pizza and a huge smile on his face. Her heartbeat went into overdrive.

"How did you know I liked a lot of meat on my pizza? And thick crust?"

"Just a wild guess?" Felicity arched an eyebrow at him and grinned. "I think Abby mentioned it one time. And besides, that's the kind Nellie and I like, too."

"Can you take a break and eat while it's warm?"

"I think we're at a good stopping place."

"If you don't need me, I think I'll take off and go home," Nellie said. "But I can come in early, if you want me to."

"That'd be great. Can you come in about seven o'clock?"

"I'll see you then," Nellie said, gathering her purse and a sweater before heading out the door.

"Are you finished for tonight?" David asked.

"I've just got to decide which arrangement I think will work. They left it up to me, and I'm a little nervous about it." She brushed off her hands, took the pizza box from him, and headed toward the door leading into the kitchen. "I'll set the table. Come on back, David. But first, look at those arrangements, will you? And let me know which one you like best?"

David followed only minutes later. "Can I help?"

"No, thanks." She'd already put out the plates and was bringing glasses filled with iced tea to the table.

She liked the way David waited until she sat down across from her before taking his seat, and she was pleased that he bowed his head and said a prayer before she had a chance to ask him to. He opened the box and motioned for her to help herself first.

She slid a slice filled with cheese, pepperoni, and sausage onto her plate. "Mmm, this smells delicious."

"Not nearly as good as your soup does," David said, taking a couple of pieces out of the box.

Felicity knew she shouldn't be so pleased at his compliment, but she was. Very. She changed the subject. "Which arrangement do you think I should go with?"

"I'm not sure you should take my advice, but I really liked the peach and white one."

"Oh, I am so glad. That's the one I like, too—and it will actually take me less time to put together!"

"Do you need any help tonight? I'm sure we could get Abby and Stan over here for a while."

"Oh, I'd hate to ask them. . ."

David grinned and headed for the phone hanging on the wall. "I don't mind at all."

In only a few minutes, the newlyweds were knocking at Abby's back door. Felicity couldn't remember work ever being quite so much fun as they spent the next few hours putting together the flower arrangements. David, Abby, and Stan proved to be quick studies, and it only took a time or two of showing them how to fill the white bowls about three-quarters full of water, trim the flower stems to the right size, and place them just so in the bowls, before they got it right.

But the laughter and companionship were wonderful and well worth the few mangled flowers on the floor. After they'd put the finished products in the cooler, ready to be delivered the next day, Felicity turned to the trio of friends. "I can't thank you all enough. It would have taken me hours tonight or working up until delivery time tomorrow to get them ready without your help."

"It was fun," Abby said with a yawn.

"It really was," Stan added as he put an arm around his wife's shoulder and turned her toward the door. "Call us anytime."

Felicity saw them out and turned to David. "Thank you again, David—for helping and for calling in Abby and Stan."

"No problem. But we never got around to discussing the ad for the paper."

"Oh, don't worry about that."

"Felicity, there's going to be an ad. I'd like your input."

She yawned and chuckled. "I'm sorry. I'm too tired to think anymore tonight."

David nodded and headed for the door. "I can see you are. I'll get back with you about it tomorrow or the next day. Thanks for letting me help out."

He stood in the doorway a moment, then reached out and gently touched her cheek. "You look exhausted. Try to get some rest, okay?"

She nodded and missed his touch when he dropped his hand and backed out the door. Felicity shut the door behind him and suddenly felt like crying. This man was so sweet. She was afraid she was really falling for him. . .and she couldn't let that happen. Couldn't open herself up to more hurt.

She pushed herself away from the door and went to call Nellie to tell her there was no need to come in early. But it didn't keep her from thinking about David. Oh, why couldn't she have met him before she'd put up a wall around her heart and promised herself never to take it down?

❧

Felicity was avoiding him again. David knew she was. Oh, he'd seen her for a minute at church on Sunday. But each time he'd called the last few days, he either got Nellie or listened to Felicity's voice on her answering machine. He didn't bother to leave a message with either. He was afraid it would become way too obvious that she didn't want to talk to him if she didn't return his calls. So he kept hope alive by telling Nellie he'd call back or hanging up before the tone sounded on the answering machine.

He was afraid he was falling in love with Felicity Carmichael in spite of the fact that she seemed determined not to see him. But he wasn't a quitter, and he wasn't about to give up now. There was something about the way soft color stole up her cheeks when he looked at her a moment too long. And the way the pulse at the base of her throat beat when he touched her cheek the other night. He had a feeling she cared about him, too, but how in the world was he going to find out when she wouldn't even talk to him on the phone?

By quitting time on Thursday, David did the only thing he could think of that would work. He picked up the phone and dialed. "Sis? I need your help."

"What with?" Abby asked.

"Felicity." That's all he needed to say. Abby immediately asked him over for supper, and David silently sent up a prayer, thanking the Lord above for family.

On his way over to his sister's, and thinking he had the perfect excuse for being in the neighborhood because he really needed an okay on the advertising copy he'd made up, he stopped by Felicity's shop. While he finally got her to look at the ad, she still tried to talk him out of it.

"David, I know I keep repeating myself, but you *really* don't need to do this. Business is picking up. . .most likely because of the article you did. In a few months, I could probably afford to put an ad in myself."

"Felicity, please quit trying to talk me out of it. I owe you this. Do you like it or not?" His tone was sharper than he meant it to be; he was just so frustrated at feeling like his relationship with her was going backward instead of forward.

Her tone turned cool. "It's fine."

"Aww, Felicity. I'm sorry. I didn't mean to—"

"No, I'm sorry. You are the one doing me a favor. I'm being ungracious." She handed the ad copy back to him. "It's wonderful, and I do thank you."

Her phone rang just then, and she hurriedly answered it. David couldn't help but think it was odd how she never answered when he called. He'd planned to ask her to dinner the next night, but he had a feeling she'd turn him down flat, and he wanted to avoid an open rejection for as long as possible.

So he took his leave by just waving at her and heading over to his sister's. He sure hoped Abby had some ideas that would help, because with the ad approved, he was fast running out of reasons to stop by Felicity's shop. He needed his sister's advice more than ever.

❧

When Abby came over the next afternoon, Felicity was glad to take a break. They went to her kitchen, and she made some iced tea for the two of them.

"So? How's married life?"

Abby blushed and smiled. "It's wonderful. Stan is so good to me."

"I'm glad. It's wonderful to see you so happy, Abby."

"Thanks. I wish. . ."

"What?"

Abby shook her head. "Nothing. Catch me up on you. How's business?"

"It's great. I really do have your brother to thank for that. Between his article and the ad he plans to put in the paper, I think I may have to hire another person."

"That's wonderful, Felicity. And it's only what you deserve. He owed you after that spread he put in of my wedding!"

Felicity's heart sank. Abby only confirmed what she'd been thinking. That David was just trying to make things up to her. She was sure that was the only reason he'd been showing her any attention at all.

"Well, he's more than made up for that. I've tried to tell him so. . .but maybe you need to tell him."

"You sound a little put out, Felicity. Has David done something else to upset you?"

"No! He's been wonderful, and I—"

"He thinks he's being a pest and getting on your nerves."

"He told you that?"

Abby was quiet for a moment. "I think he's interested in you. He's a little aggravated at me. . .that I never introduced you to him."

Could what Abby was telling her be true? And what did it matter if it was? He wouldn't be interested for long. . .no one ever was. And she couldn't afford to find out because she already cared too much.

"You knew I'd run in the opposite direction—"

"So, you're still relationship shy?" Abby took a sip of her tea and waited.

"I think I always will be." She couldn't afford to be anything else.

Abby shrugged. "No reason you and David can't just be friends. I'd sure like you to be."

Felicity felt a sudden relief she wasn't sure she understood. But she liked the idea of being friends with David. . .a lot better than thinking their business was over with and she'd never see him again. "A person can't have too many of those."

⌘

For the next several weeks, Abby and her new husband did their best to get David and Felicity together. Abby had told him about Felicity's broken engagements and warned him that he'd have to go slow if he wanted to get past her determination not to get involved with anyone again. But she thought they'd make a great couple, and she agreed to help his cause.

It was growing warmer, and they had cookouts and cook-ins, sometimes with other friends, sometimes just the four of them. It took a few weeks, but finally, Felicity seemed to be warming up to him again. David was beginning to feel he was making progress. . .little by little.

Felicity had even sat with them in church for several Sundays. Well, more to the point, she hadn't objected when he sat beside her. Neither did she seem totally comfortable with it. But he was beginning to think she did care about him. He hoped so. Because he was ready to let her know how he felt about her.

One night, Stan and Abby invited them over for supper and then to a movie. The plan was for Stan and Abby to back out at the last minute, leaving David and Felicity to go alone. David just hoped she didn't refuse to go with him.

He was standing beside Stan at the grill outside, pretending not to be watching for her, when Felicity cut through the hedge, bringing a chocolate cake. It was still cool out, especially of an evening, and she had on a lightweight moss-green sweater and matching pants. She looked lovely.

"You guys be sure and don't burn those burgers tonight, okay?" she teased them, reaching down to scratch Bowser behind the ears, who was lying right next to the grill. "Bowser likes them medium-well, don't you, Boy?"

David and Stan chuckled. Last time they grilled out, they'd been talking about the upcoming baseball season and their inattention had resulted in charred steaks.

"I'll watch real close to make sure Stan pays attention this time," David said as she headed inside to help Abby.

Felicity giggled, and when she smiled at him, David knew he was a goner. He loved her. Loved her sweetness and her spunkiness. Loved the way she was a loyal friend to his sister and the way she conducted her business. He loved that she loved the Lord with all her heart. He just plain loved her. And he wanted to tell her. It was time.

He worried all through the meal that Felicity would refuse to go to the movies when she found out Abby and Stan weren't going. He held his breath, waiting for her response, when Abby said, "You know, I'm really tired tonight. I hope I'm not coming down with anything. Would you two mind if Stan and I don't go to the movies tonight?"

"That's no problem. We can all go another night," Felicity said.

David's heart sank.

"No, this is the last weekend it's showing, and we'll feel bad if you miss it, too. You two go and let us know how it is," Abby insisted. "If it's good, we'll buy it when it comes out."

"It's okay with me, if it's okay with Felicity," David said. *Dear Lord, please let it be all right with her.* He waited for Felicity's response.

She shrugged. "Sure. Let me help you with dishes, and we'll be off."

Thank You, Lord. Tonight, please guide and direct me on how to let her know I care.

The movie was a romantic comedy with a happy ending that left them both in a good mood. When David suggested that they go to a nearby coffee shop for a cappuccino, he was pleasantly surprised when she agreed. At long last, he felt like they were on a *real* date.

Chapter 8

Felicity couldn't remember enjoying herself more. David was just fun to be around. Over the past few weeks, spending time with him and Abby and Stan, they'd had some really good times. She'd gotten to know him so well. He enjoyed the same movies, the same kind of foods, games, and humor that she did. They both had a soft spot for old people, and sitting beside him in church, she'd found out their favorite hymns were the same. She had more in common with him than with anyone else she'd ever known. It was no wonder she found it impossible to say no to going to a movie with him tonight.

But as she sat across from him, sipping a hot cappuccino, she knew tonight was different. This truly felt like a date, and she'd convinced herself that they were just great friends. But her heartbeat didn't lie, and it told her she was only kidding herself. She cared about this man. . .more than a little. She was falling in love with him.

She hated seeing the evening end because she knew it couldn't happen again. It was one thing to spend an evening in the company of others. . . another thing entirely to spend it with only David. She might begin to think a relationship was possible, and she couldn't afford to do that. She couldn't. Truth was, she'd been fooling herself for the last few months, and the only way to handle things now was to put an end to the time they spent together.

Still, when David drove her home, she didn't want the evening to come to a close. . .she wanted it to go on forever. When he walked her to her door, took her keys from her, and unlocked the door, she turned to thank him, and the look in his eyes was almost her undoing. If she didn't get a grip, she'd convince herself that he really cared.

David smiled down at her. "Thank you for going with me. It was. . .nice. . . just the two of us."

Felicity's heart beat against her ribs as his hand came up to cup the side of her face. "I. . .it was a good movie."

David's head dipped close, and his lips quickly touched the corner of her mouth. He raised his head. "Felicity, I'd like us to do this again. . .go out. . . just the two of us."

"I'm not sure that would be a good idea." Her voice sounded breathless even to her own ears.

"Why not?" His head dipped once more, and his lips touched hers gently, tenderly.

"Hmm. . ." She couldn't remember why not as she responded to his kiss.

When she pulled back, David leaned his forehead against hers. "Felicity, I'm falling in love with you."

That did it. Snapped her right back into her senses. She'd heard those words before. . .from two other men. She shouldn't have believed them then, and she couldn't believe David now.

She backed up toward the door. "No, David. You don't mean that. . .and I. . . No. You can't mean that. You only think you love me. I've been here before."

"I'm not like those other men. I never want to hurt you, Felicity."

She shook her head. "I can't do this again. I just can't. Good night, David." She opened the door, slipped into the safety of her home, and shut the door, leaving David outside. She wanted nothing more than to open the door and rush right back into his arms. But she couldn't do that. She had to stop spending time with him. She had to.

The thought of not seeing him again sent a piercing pain shooting through her heart, but she knew she had no choice. She had to put a stop to the time they spent together. It wasn't meant to be. She and the Lord had a plan for her life, and it didn't include having her heart broken once again.

❧

David thought his heart truly would break in the timeless moments he stood there just looking at the door. What had he done wrong? He forced himself to turn and step off Felicity's porch and start down the walk. He looked over at Abby and Stan's. There were lights on downstairs. He needed advice, needed to talk to someone. Now. He headed toward his sister's, but watched as the light went out first in the kitchen, then in the living room. Stan and Abby were calling it an evening. Evidently, he wasn't going to get any advice tonight. His sigh sounded almost like a moan to his ears.

He bowed his head. *Lord, please help me here. I think Felicity cares for me as much as I care for her. I don't think that kiss lied. But if I'm wrong, please make it plainer to me than a door closed in my face.*

He shook his head, sighed deeply, and headed for his car. How could it possibly be any plainer?

Felicity was glad when Abby asked her to come over for lunch the next day. She needed to confide in her. . .even though she was David's sister. Abby knew her past, and she would understand why Felicity couldn't continue to join her and Stan and David. Why she couldn't see him anymore. She left Nellie in charge of the shop and hurried through the hedge that separated the two properties.

Abby had everything ready when Felicity arrived, and they sat down at the kitchen table. She'd made a salad with crusty rolls on the side. After saying a blessing, Abby poured tea into their glasses and asked about the movie.

"It was great. You and Stan will like it."

"Did you do anything afterward?"

"We had cappuccino at that new coffee house near the theater."

"And?"

"He brought me home." *And kissed me.*

"And what?"

I lost my heart once more. "He told me he was falling in love with me."

"Oh?" Abby took a sip of tea and paused for a moment. "And what did you say?"

"I told him he only thinks he is. . .and I ran inside. I shut the door right in his face." Felicity laid her head on the table and began to cry.

"Oh, Felicity, honey, don't cry. He'll be all right." Abby patted her shoulder. "How do *you* feel about him?"

"I. . .he's. . .I. . . It doesn't matter." Felicity sniffed and raised her head. "It's not meant to be. Oh, Abby. . .I certainly don't want to hurt him, if what he said is true. . .but you know I can't go down that road again. I just. . .it's not God's plan for me, and I have to accept that."

Abby got up to get her a tissue and handed it to her. "Felicity, I don't think David is lying to you. He does care very much."

"I thought Ned and Marcus cared, too, Abby. But they changed their minds at the last minute. I just can't take that chance again. You *know* that."

"I know you think the path for your life has been decided and that marriage and a family are out because of those two jerks. But what if you are wrong this time, Felicity?"

"But I asked the Lord for guidance, and He opened up the way for me to start my own business, Abby."

Abby propped her elbow on the table and cradled her chin in her hand. "And you've always assumed that meant you weren't supposed to fall in love again?"

Felicity nodded and wiped her eyes. "That's what I think, yes."

"What if the business was the way to get you together with your true love?"

"Oh, Abby. That would be wishful thinking."

"Would it? You do care about him then."

Felicity nodded and wiped at fresh tears.

"Maybe you've been assuming too much. . .been wrong about what God has been trying to do for you," Abby said, handing her another tissue.

Felicity's heart skipped a beat and then another. Could that be possible? She shook her head. "Oh, Abby. If that was the case, I think the Lord would make it very plain to me."

Abby chuckled and patted her hand. "As plain as the nose on your face, huh?"

"It sure would help."

"Well, I think you may have misread God's will for you, Abby. Sometimes we get ahead of His will for us. We don't always wait for Him. Pray about it and see what happens. You know that verse in Proverbs three, verse five. . .to lean not on your own understanding?"

"Yes."

"Well, maybe you need to tell the Lord that you don't understand and ask Him to make it clear."

Hope stirred in Felicity's chest. She tamped it down. The Lord had made it clear to her already. . .hadn't He?

⊱⊰

David told himself to get over it. Obviously, Felicity didn't care about him the way he cared about her. But he kept reliving the evening before—the kiss they'd shared—and he just couldn't believe she didn't have some feelings for him. They'd shared so much the past few weeks, grown more and more comfortable with each other, laughed with one another, and there was just something about the way she looked at him, smiled at him. He honestly felt she had feelings for him, too. But she didn't want to care, and he didn't know how to get past the hurts of her past.

He couldn't concentrate on anything, and by Sunday he was truly miserable. Felicity was late for church, and she took a seat at the back of the sanctuary instead of sitting in her usual spot on the pew beside Abby, Stan, and him. When the service was over, she didn't linger. Instead, she hurried out the door.

Abby touched him on the shoulder. "Want to join us? We're going out for lunch."

He didn't have anything else to do. . .and felt like he never would. "Sure."

David followed the couple to a favorite Mexican restaurant, and once they'd given their orders, he started quizzing his sister. "Is Felicity all right?"

"Oh, I'd say she's as well as you are." Abby grinned at him.

"What do you mean by that? I'm fine." David dipped a chip into salsa and stuck it in his mouth.

Abby looked at her husband and grinned. "Does he look all right to you, Hon?"

Stan chuckled. "Seems a little lovesick to me."

David sighed. "You know about the other night? Did she tell you she shut the door in my face?"

"You probably moved too fast. You are too impatient, David. I told you it would take time." Abby dunked her tortilla chip into some guacamole dip.

"I know. You're right. I am. I should have—"

"She's scared, David. That's all it is. She's afraid to believe she could have a future with you. And she has this idea that it's not in God's plans for her to marry and have a family. I think she's as impatient as you in her own way. She may not have waited on the Lord to show her His plan for her life before she decided what it was."

"Well, how do I convince her that I'm sincere, that I do love her, and that I won't hurt her? I want to do God's will, too."

"I know you do. So you need to pray about it. And I don't know how you are going to convince her. It's not going to be easy. You're going to have to do something big. . .something that will persuade her you truly love her."

"Got any ideas?"

"No, but I know it has to be big enough to prove to her that what you feel is real and lasting. And most of all that it's in God's plan for *both* your lives. In the meantime, don't give up."

David had no intention of giving up. And he prayed. But it took several weeks before he finally came up with a plan. During that time he questioned if he should keep trying. Felicity continued to avoid him. If he showed up at Abby and Stan's while she was there, she quickly found an excuse to leave. Once he even saw her start out her door and head toward his sister's until she saw his car in the drive. Then she turned and retraced her steps back home.

Yet each time he did see her, there was something in her eyes that kept him on target. . .trying to come up with something big enough to prove to her that he was serious about her. Abby seemed convinced that Felicity really cared about him and that if he went about it right, he had a chance to win her over. He prayed she was right.

Now as he thought about the plan he'd come up with—the one he was sure the Lord had given him because he didn't think he would have come up with it on his own—he prayed he was doing the right thing. And it was something big like Abby said it would need to be. Very big.

After tomorrow, there was no way Felicity could doubt that he truly cared about her. The only question left was whether she felt the same about him. David bowed his head, knowing that he was either going to be the happiest man in the world the next day. . .or become the laughingstock of the whole town. *Dear Lord, I pray that I am part of Your plan for Felicity's life. That there is a place for me there. I love her. I won't hurt her. Please let this work. In Jesus' name, amen.*

Chapter 9

The last few weeks seemed to have dragged by to Felicity. She missed the fun evenings with Abby and Stan. . .and David. She really missed him more each day. Oh, she saw him when she was at Abby's and he suddenly showed up, or at church—even though she made sure she was late coming into the sanctuary from class so that most seats were taken, making it necessary for her to sit in the back. But nothing was the same, and she was sure it never would be again.

Thoughts of closing her business and moving away had crossed her mind. She wasn't sure she could handle seeing him come and go from next door for the rest of her life. There would come a day when he'd find someone else, marry, and have a family. Then she'd have to contend with watching children who could have been hers grow up right before her eyes. The thought almost made her physically sick. She didn't want David marrying anyone else. Didn't want to watch him have a life that didn't include her.

But if she sold her business and moved, how would she be living in God's will for her. . .or at least what she thought was His will? *Could Abby be right? Could I have gotten it all wrong? Oh, dear Lord, if I'm wrong, please show me. If I decided what Your will for my life was on my own, please forgive me. Please give me understanding.*

Business was good and getting better, and it kept her busy during the day, but her nights were lonesome. She'd almost quit running over to Abby's for fear of running into David—although that's exactly what she wanted to do. She hadn't realized just how much a part of her life he'd become until now—and the emptiness she felt with him gone seemed to be growing daily. It hurt that she hadn't heard from him, that he hadn't come by or called, that he'd given up so easily.

Okay, maybe not so easily. He told me he loved me—put his heart on the line—and I slammed the door in his face. Felicity's heart twisted over the pain she was afraid she'd inflicted on him. Tears formed as she thought how that must have made him feel. She would have been crushed had he done that to her, yet she expected him to ask for more awful behavior? Felicity shook her head. Not likely.

She threw herself into her work, but it didn't take her mind off of David. . . or the kiss they'd shared. . .or the love she could no longer deny feeling for him. It was getting so hard to face seeing David yet not really being with him that Felicity was seriously contemplating changing churches. Yet she knew she wouldn't. She loved her church family, and she was due to start teaching the preschool class for the summer quarter.

As she woke on Sunday morning, both wanting and dreading to see David, afraid she'd see him sitting beside another woman one day, she prayed for strength to get out of bed, get dressed, and focus her mind on the Lord rather than on the man she loved. She prayed that seeing David would get easier to bear and that she would get over the love that seemed to be growing by the minute. *Dear Lord, please help me to accept Your will in my life, and most especially, to know what it is. If it's only to run this business You've made possible for me to have, please help me get past this, get over David. But if I've been wrong all this time in thinking You intend for me to stay single, please make it clear to me, Lord. In Jesus' name, amen.*

She went through to the kitchen to put the coffee on and then outside to pick up her Sunday paper. Placing it on the table to be read with breakfast, she left it there and went to get dressed for Sunday school.

She found a sleeveless green dress with matching jacket. It was light and summery, and she hoped wearing it would lighten her mood. Hard to believe that it was only late spring. Abby's wedding seemed so long ago. In truth she knew that it was only the past few weeks that had dragged. The time after Abby's wedding—with David—had sped by until the night he told her he loved her. Oh, how she'd wanted to believe him. But she'd believed two other men and had been wrong. How could she trust her judgment anymore?

She couldn't. That's why she needed the Lord to show her if she was wrong. . .or if David was sincere.

She warmed a frozen waffle in the toaster oven and poured herself a cup of coffee. Sitting down at the breakfast table, she took a bite of waffle, pulled the newspaper out of its protective plastic bag, and opened it to the front page. Her heart seemed to jump and stop all at the same time as she read the headline:

NEWSPAPER EDITOR PROPOSES TO LOCAL FLORIST
SEE LIVING SECTION FOR DETAILS

Felicity's heart began beating again and hammered in her chest as she tore through the paper, trying to locate the article. It was short and sweet:

Felicity Carmichael, I think I fell in love with you from the moment I nearly tripped over you at my sister's wedding. I know I was in love with you the night I told you so. And I love you more each day. I can only hope you feel the same way. It's with that hope that I ask you now—Felicity, will you marry me?

Tears rushed to her eyes. David. Silly, adorable, precious David. She turned the paper all around. It looked like an ordinary Sunday paper with ad inserts and all. But he must have had these few pages made up just for her. . .for this proposal to her. *Oh, dear Lord, can I believe him? I want to so badly. Please help me to know.*

Her phone rang. She hurried to answer. "Hello?"

"Well? Are you going to tell him yes?" Abby asked.

"What?" How could Abby know?

"You have seen the paper, haven't you?"

Felicity's heartbeat pounded in her ears. "You saw it, too?"

Abby laughed. "By now, half the town has seen it. I told him he had to find some big way to let you know how he felt. That brother of mine! I think he succeeded."

Felicity tried to chuckle around a joyful sob. "I think he did, too."

She'd no more than hung up with Abby when the phone rang once more. This time it was Nellie. "Felicity, if you don't tell that wonderful man yes, I will!"

Nellie didn't even wait for an answer before hanging up. The phone rang at the same time her doorbell did. Felicity took the cordless phone with her to the door.

It was in all the papers. All over town. He did love her. He had to. Only a man deeply in love would lay his heart out for acceptance or rejection in full view of the entire town. *Thank You, Lord, for letting me know how he truly feels. Thank You.*

David was at the door. . .and his mother was on the phone. Felicity could only stand there grinning at him as his mother said, "My dear Felicity. I just had to tell you that my son must love you very much. This is just not like him. If you had any doubts before, I can tell you he is sincere. I hope you'll tell him yes."

At a loss for words, Felicity could only nod into the telephone.

"Who's on the phone?" David asked.

She held it out to him and finally found her voice. "Your mother."

David took the receiver from her. "Mom? Yes. I'd like to get her answer now. You'll be the second to know, I promise." With that, he punched the end button and pitched the phone to the couch. He turned back to Felicity and took her hands in his, pulling her close.

"Felicity, have you seen the paper?"

Her heart felt as if it might burst with the love she felt for this man. She nodded.

Still clasping her hands, David knelt on one knee. "I meant it. I love you. . . with all my heart. I know you've been hurt in the past, but I only want to make you happy for as long as I live. Will you please marry me and let me spend the rest of our lives proving it to you?"

Tears streaming down her face at the way the Lord had answered her prayers, Felicity tugged David's hands, and he got to his feet. He pulled her into his embrace, and she looked deep into his eyes. "Oh, David. I love you, too. And yes, oh, yes, I will marry you."

He lowered his head. Their lips met in a lingering kiss meant to mend the hurts of the past and seal the promise of their love for each other. . .for all time.

Epilogue

They said their vows two weeks later on a balmy summer evening in Abby's backyard garden. Felicity was dressed in a white satin A-line gown with beaded Venice lace and delicate cap sleeves gracing the top of the shoulders. Her only attendant was Abby, dressed in a peach Georgette flutter sleeve A-line with a chiffon ruched empire waist.

David had pressed for the date, saying he didn't want Felicity to have a chance to back out, but she knew there was no chance of that happening. She was more than happy to comply. She didn't want him to change his mind, either. Deep down, she felt they both knew that wasn't going to happen. The Lord had brought them together. . .in spite of their blundering along the way.

As David took her in his arms and they shared their first kiss as husband and wife, Felicity thanked the Lord above for leaving her no doubt about how this man felt about her. And she was pretty sure the Lord approved of their impatience this time. . .after all, it'd taken them long enough to figure out His plans.

When the time came to throw her bouquet, she was thankful there was no fan to tear it apart. It sailed through the air the way it was meant to. . .a beautiful bouquet of white roses, gardenias, and lily of the valley made by. . . Felicity, of course.

Petals of Promise
By Diann Hunt

Dedication

To my mother-in-law and father-in-law,
Alice and Byron Hunt.
Thank you for the blessing of your son,
my husband, Jim.
I love you.

Special thanks to my coauthors,
Janet Barton, Sandra Petit, and Gail Sattler.
It was great to work with you!

Chapter 1

Konni Strong reached toward the smiling baby girl perched in her mother's arms. "Hi, Zoe. Want to come to—"

"Watch it!" a deep voice called out beside her.

Before Konni could turn, a bundle of shredded roses plunked into her open palms.

She blinked. Her mouth went dry; her throat constricted. She stared at the flowers that mocked her like a bad dream. Her mind whirled. *Weddings. . . bouquets. . .vows. . .*

"I–I have to go outside," she said to Zoe's mother between shallow breaths. "I'm sorry." Petals dropped from her shaking fingers to the floor. Without so much as looking up, she bolted.

Straight into the arms of the man with the deep voice.

Konni thought she heard him grunt when her body slammed into his chest like an amateur skier against a sturdy tree. His arms grabbed her, holding her perfectly still. Mortified, she reluctantly looked up into his dark, compassionate eyes. As if a slight breeze had swept across the back of her neck, she shivered. "I–I. . ."

A grin spread across his face. Firm arms continued to hold her. She glanced from his hands to his face.

Amusement fanned the corners of his eyes with fine lines. "Oh, sorry," he said, but the smirk on his face indicated he wasn't sorry in the least. He released her.

Oh, how she wished she could crawl into a hole.

Her eighteen-year-old daughter, Emily, stood nearby and leaned over to whisper in Konni's ear, "Hmm, beautiful widow reaches for baby, catches a piece of the bridal bouquet, and runs into the arms of a handsome stranger. It definitely has potential." Emily curled Konni's fingers around the dropped bouquet pieces.

The stranger held Konni's gaze, and she almost gulped out loud. She ignored her daughter's comments completely.

"I nearly got hit in the face with those flowers," he said, nodding toward the petals still in her hands.

"What happened, anyway?" she asked.

He laughed and pointed toward the commotion in the back of the room. "I think the bride threw her bouquet a little too hard. It hit the ceiling fan and broke into pieces." He turned back to Konni. "By the way, I'm Rick Hamilton, the new superintendent of schools for Hartley South School District."

Emily let out a soft whistle in her mother's ear.

Konni turned to her. "Emily, dear," she said through clenched teeth, "would you please get me some more punch?" She batted her eyes sweetly but felt sure she got her meaning across.

Emily frowned. "All right, but I'll be back." Though said in a singsong fashion, Konni thought the words held an unveiled threat.

Konni turned back to Rick. "Excuse me." She sounded positively nasal. With a quick cough, she attempted to pull up a rich contralto. "I'm Konni Strong, aunt of the bride. That was my daughter, Emily," she said, pointing to the young woman as she made her way toward the punch line. "We attend this church."

He nodded. "Your niece told me." His eyes twinkled with secrets.

"Really?" she asked, wondering what else Abby had told him. "Since Stan is a principal, I assume you are here on his behalf?"

"Yep. Couldn't miss the groom's wedding." Lifting his punch cup, he took a drink. "I moved here this school year from the Midwest."

"So is your family with you?" She tried to sound nonchalant.

"No family. My mom and dad are both gone. I'm an only child." His eyes pinned hers before he added, with emphasis, "Never married."

"Oh, I'm sorry."

"Over my parents or the never married part?" he teased.

Suddenly her tongue felt like a beached whale. Before she could make it move, he continued. "Dad's been gone ten years, Mom four. The never married part was a choice I made long ago."

She scratched away the nerves tingling her neck.

He took a drink of punch. "I do have a dog, though, if that counts. Read's a black lab. He doesn't like weddings." His mouth split into a wide grin.

"Read?"

"The basis of all learning."

"Good name."

"Abby tells me you're not married?" He lifted his punch to his lips, but his eyes held hers as if he didn't want to miss her response.

"Well, no, actually, I'm not married. Now." She paused a moment and scratched the top of her hand that held the bouquet pieces. "Eric died five years ago."

"Oh, I'm sorry," he said as though he meant it.

"Thank you." When Konni looked down, she could see a rash developing on her right hand. Her body's response to stress. She sighed and glanced up at Rick. He was looking across the room. Quickly, she shoved her hand behind her. Oh, she hated these rashes. There wasn't a thing she could do about them except scratch and try to relax. She felt like a walking scratch 'n' sniff sticker.

She took another deep breath. *Calm down. Everything is fine.*

A few people beyond Rick smiled and looked their way. Well-meaning friends nodded and gave her the thumbs-up. She felt her face grow hot. Goodness, couldn't she even talk to a man without friends trying to hook her up? She sighed, knowing she'd soon be on their project list. Again. She rolled her eyes.

"Something wrong?"

"Oh, no, I was just. . .oh, well, uh. . ."

"Here you go, Mom." Emily offered the cup filled with punch.

Funny how things change, Konni thought. Suddenly, she was glad to see her daughter. Konni breathed an inward sigh of relief. "Mr. Hamilton, this is my daughter, Emily."

"Nice to meet you."

"Yeah, you, too."

"Mr. Hamilton is the superintendent—"

"Please, call me Rick."

Konni looked at him with surprise. She glanced at Emily, whose eyes positively sparkled. Oh, just wait till she got that girl home. "Emily, Rick is the new superintendent of schools."

"Great!" Emily said with definite approval in her voice and far too much enthusiasm.

Konni made a face at her.

"Would you like to sit down?" Rick asked. "Seems a little crowded right here." Before she could answer, he was already maneuvering her through the crowd. "Oh," he stooped down and lifted something from the floor, "I think you dropped this." He handed her another cluster of the petals she had dropped.

"Oh, uh, thanks." Suddenly, the last five minutes became a tangle of confusion. If only she could run, get away from the stares, the handsome stranger, the warmth of his hand against her back. But no matter how she felt, good manners prevailed. Pushing panic aside, she took a deep breath and continued toward the table.

She wished the people would leave her be. Oh, she knew they meant well, but couldn't she talk to a man without them charting her social calendar for the next six months? She shrugged mentally. Key word here, *man*. They thought she'd been far too long without one. What did they know anyway? She had done just fine for the past five years since Eric's death, and she would continue to do so.

Rick, Konni, and Emily slipped into chairs at the corner of a table, away from other people—though not away from the glances. What must Rick be thinking? He surely noticed how people studied them like biology students over a microscope.

Emily grinned as if she knew something the others did not. Konni threw her a go-somewhere-else-to-sit look. A friend came up to Emily and they chatted quietly.

"Do I have a punch mustache?"

Konni looked at Rick in surprise. "I'm sorry?"

"My mouth. Is there a red punch mustache above my mouth?"

She felt almost too embarrassed to look. "No, why?"

"Everyone seems to be staring at us, so I thought I must look funny." He studied her with a smile in his eyes. "It certainly can't be you. I mean, forgive me if I'm out of line, but, well, you look, um, all in place." He stammered for the words like an awkward boy with his first crush.

Konni thought he said the words in a most charming way. "Oh," she finally answered, "people with nothing better to do, I suppose."

He drank more punch, his eyes looking at her, never blinking.

She squirmed a little in her seat.

Putting the cup down, Rick settled back in his chair, his lean torso stretched into a relaxed position. "Since I started in the middle of the school year, I'm fairly new to the community. I don't really know many people outside the school setting."

Konni nodded. She looked at her hands. Why did she bite her nails? For once, she wished she had taken Emily's advice and polished them. She sighed. "So, do you go to church anywhere?"

"I've been attending the big community church on Main Street, but it's really too large for my taste. I prefer a small, intimate fellowship."

"That's how this church is, and I love it."

"Maybe I'll give it a try."

She almost choked. As if she didn't have enough to do to quiet the tongues from today's little chat. If he started going to her church, the endless get-togethers pairing the two of them would never cease. Her friends would not be happy till they got her to the marriage altar. She groaned inwardly.

"So, how long have you lived here?" he asked.

"Forever. All my life, actually."

Emily's friend walked away, and Emily turned to join the conversation.

"Do you have any kids, Mr. Hamilton?" Though Emily tried to mask the question with an air of nonchalance, she was obviously on a searching expedition. She looked at her mother and smiled sweetly before biting into a sandwich. Konni squinted and tried to imagine Emily with duct tape over her mouth.

"No kids. Never married." His knowing eyes sparkled with good humor.

Several people stood and pushed their chairs back up to the tables, then headed outside. Konni turned toward the noise of people shuffling out the door.

"Well, looks like the crowd is thinning out. The happy couple must be preparing to leave." Konni motioned toward the crush of people. She stood, grabbing her coat and purse. She couldn't leave soon enough. Emily and Rick followed suit.

A cold breeze whipped past them, causing Konni's hair to blow all over her face. Though cropped to neck length, she had lots of it. She pushed the black strands from her eyes.

Rick smiled.

That made her feel good inside. She rebuked herself. After all, she'd kept her vow to Eric for five years and didn't want to break it now.

"Here they come," rippled through the crowd. Everyone lined the sidewalk as the happy couple came through the doors and headed for the limo. Well-wishes, farewells, and bubbles filled the air.

Once the car pulled away, the guests scattered like falling leaves on a windy afternoon.

"Where did you park?"

She pointed toward her car.

He nodded and continued to walk with her. "Did you say you work outside the home?"

"No, I didn't say, but I do. I own an antique shop. Forgotten Treasures."

He nodded. "I've heard of that."

"It's a great little shop," Emily piped up. Konni had forgotten her daughter was still there.

"I'm sure it is. I like antiques myself. I might come in and check it out."

"Good." Why did she say "good"? She didn't want to encourage him. Not that he cared one way or the other. She stopped at her car door and turned to him. "Well, Mr. Hamilton—Rick—it's been a pleasure." She shifted the bouquet pieces into her left hand so she could extend her right hand.

"Konni, the pleasure has been all mine." He dwarfed her hand in his. "Hopefully, I'll see you again."

Before she could respond, he turned and walked toward his car. Her heart swirled with emotions she didn't want to deal with just now. She didn't like the effect this man had on her, and the farther away she stayed from him, the better.

She turned to get in the car, but not before glancing at her daughter, who stood on the passenger's side waiting to get in. Emily looked at her. "At least give him a chance, Mom."

"Get in the car, Emily."

Emily climbed in, and Konni turned her head once more toward Rick, who was driving by just then. He caught her staring and raised his hand to wave. She waved in return, mad at herself for glancing back.

After all, she didn't want to give him the wrong impression.

Chapter 2

Rick stared at the paperwork spread across his oak desk. Seemed no end to his responsibilities. He didn't especially enjoy working on a Saturday, but he'd been swamped with paperwork since the wedding a couple weeks ago. He didn't mind too much. Work energized him. In fact, he looked forward to it each day. His chair squeaked as he scrunched into the soft leather and leaned back.

Yet things seemed different somehow. He couldn't understand it. He liked his job; it was going well. Why did he feel unsettled?

Konni Strong's image intruded his thoughts, surprising him. More and more, her face seemed to pop up like an energetic kindergartner. The short dark hair, delicate features, thick lashes that fringed eyes the color of rich, brown leather. Eyes that held a hint of sadness. A look that made him want to shelter her, hold her tight, and tell her everything would be right with her world. He shook himself. How could he make a promise like that? With his upbringing, what did he know about taking care of a woman? He didn't trust himself.

That's why all these years he had dabbled only in surface relationships. No tangles. No worries. Still, he couldn't deny his loneliness. He blew out a sigh. He decided he needed some good companionship. As they say, "All work, no play. . ." He thought a little longer. Konni didn't seem interested in a serious relationship. Maybe he'd attend her church in the morning and invite her out to dinner. No harm in that. He stretched long and hard in his seat. That's what he'd do.

With his decision made, he bent back over the papers and set to work.

The next morning, Konni got a call from Rick, asking about church service times. She gave him the information, hung up the phone, and stared at it a full moment. Since she hadn't talked to him in two weeks, she'd figured he had decided against coming to Hope Village. Well, she didn't have time to think about it now. She needed to get ready. Rummaging through her dresser drawer, she pulled out a packet of black panty hose.

With her fingers wrapped around the ends of the package, she yanked off the tape. When she shook the nylons free, her jaw dropped. "I'd have to be Malibu Barbie to wear these things!" she said out loud. She blew out a gust of air and made a gesture of rolling up her sleeves.

With the tip of her tongue poking slightly through the right side of her mouth, she worked the feet between her fingers until she could gracefully slip her toes in. Gradually, she inched the material up her legs. Once she reached her knees, the delicate fabric fought back. "Come on, work with me here," she said between grunts and labored breathing.

She paused a moment to catch her breath. Like a rubber band, the hosiery snapped tight against her thighs, cutting off circulation. Her pulse throbbed through her leg veins with the steady rhythm of marching soldiers. She figured that couldn't be good, so she fell onto the bed and declared war.

Yanking, twisting, and basically squirming her way across the scattered bed covers, Konni worked with determination to pour her legs into the panty hose, come what may. Perspiration beaded her forehead, but still she persisted. Harder and harder, she tugged like a woman on a mission. With victory just in sight, she gave a final thrust that catapulted her body across the family cat. Trixie's meow would have won an Oscar for special effects in a horror movie. Konni screamed. Her thumbnail ripped through the material as her legs tangled with the cat, the covers, and the control tops.

Things were not pretty.

Emily's footsteps pattered from the hallway to the bedroom door. "You okay?"

Konni gasped for air and stared in disbelief at the white pad of her thumb that poked through the ragged hole in the hose. She didn't know whether to cry or create a finger puppet. She made a face at her daughter. Emily covered her mouth to stifle a chuckle.

"I'm fine," Konni said in a huff, trying to stand, "but I'm not so sure about Trixie."

This time they both laughed.

When had she put on the extra pounds? Had she really let herself go after Eric's death? She hadn't thought so, but now, her eyes opened to the truth.

Though it took some doing, Konni pulled herself free from the covers and the nylons. With renewed determination, she decided she would start a diet and exercise program.

After her morning doughnut.

"Do you think he'll come today?" Emily asked while examining her fingernails, as if only partially interested in Konni's response.

Konni played along. "Who, dear?"

Emily looked up at her with a start. "Rick Hamilton, that's who."

Konni feigned surprise. "I'm sure I don't know what his plans are."

Emily stared at her.

"Okay, he just called. He'll be there this morning."

Emily was more excited than she let on. "That's nice," she finally commented before heading back to her room.

Though Emily had loved her father, she made it clear time and again she wanted Konni to move on with her life. No doubt before going off to college, Emily wanted her mother's happiness intact.

What Emily didn't understand was that Konni didn't need a man to be happy.

Konni sighed. She was a bit curious as to why Rick hadn't called or come to church before now. At the wedding, he had seemed anxious to get to know her. Maybe he had met someone else. Not that it mattered. She meant it on the day of Eric's funeral when she vowed to never remarry. Though others had told her she needed to get on with her life, she didn't care. Eric Strong was the only man for her.

Past, present, and future.

❧

Tired from the long week, and restless for reasons she couldn't explain, Konni punched her pillow into position for the umpteenth time. Rick's presence at church the previous Sunday had done little to calm her inner turmoil. Once she finally got comfortable, the phone rang. Grating her frazzled nerves, she almost fell off the bed. "Okay, so I'm a little edgy," she said to Trixie, as the feline walked by, appearing as though she couldn't care less about Konni's problems. "Hello?"

Rick Hamilton's deep voice greeted her on the other end of the line. "Hi, Konni. Hope I didn't wake you."

She shot straight up in bed. Her heart leapt to her throat. "Uh, no." From where she sat, she could see herself in the dresser mirror. She worked her fingers through her hair to straighten it.

"Good. I'm not trying to stalk you or anything, but Emily gave me your number and said I should call you." He paused a second, then added, "We didn't really have a chance to talk last week at church."

"I know. I'm sorry about that. What with the Sunday school promotion and all, there was a lot going on."

"Not a problem. Those things happen." He cleared his throat. "I was wondering. . .well, I didn't know if you might want to go to dinner on Friday night. Nothing real fancy. Steak and potatoes restaurant. Are you game?"

Her mind screamed *no*, but her voice said, "Yeah, why not?" before her good sense could stop her. After all, shouldn't she offer Christian kindness and friendship? Though the feeling there was more to it than that gnawed at her.

"Great. I've been so bored around here. I mean, I have coworkers but no real friendships, you know?"

She smiled. "Yes, I understand."

"Thanks, Konni. I'll look forward to it."

"Me, too."

She gave him her address; they chatted a little longer and finally said their good-byes. Konni could hardly get through the conversation as she tried to think of a way to move and leave no forwarding address for her daughter. . . .

❧

The next evening, Konni clicked off the TV and dabbed at her eyes.

"Why do you watch *Little House on the Prairie*? You know it always makes you cry," Emily said from her recliner before biting into an apple.

"I know." Konni grabbed a tissue and blew her nose.

"So, what's going on?"

Konni sat on the couch with her feet propped on the coffee table. An empty popcorn bowl perched in her lap, she shoved the last kernel in her mouth and looked up. "Nothing. Why?" She brushed the crumbs from her pajama top.

"Well, it's just that you only eat like that when you're nervous."

"Eat like what?"

"Well, you know, kind of fast and furious. Last meal kind of thing." Emily's words held no disrespect, just bald truth.

Konni resisted the urge to whack Emily up the side of the head with the bowl. Visions of fighting with her panty hose surfaced. She gave an inner wince. "I'm fine."

"Come on, Mom. Something is going on. I know you. Can't you tell me what it is?"

Konni scratched her neck. Uh-oh, the rash was back. She felt like a dog with fleas. Emily saw her scratching and threw her an I-caught-you look. Why did Konni feel like the kid here instead of the mom? She hated this role reversal thing. Wasn't it too early for that? She took a deep breath. "All right, I don't want you to make a big deal out of this—"

"Are you sick?" Emily's worried eyes searched her mother's.

"Oh, no, honey, nothing like that."

Emily visibly relaxed. Poor kid. Last thing she needed was to deal with another blow like that in her young life.

Konni licked her lips. "It's really nothing. I'm just, well. . ." If only Emily would quit looking like she was hanging on her every word. Konni swallowed.

"Well, I don't know why I'm stammering like a child. I'm just going to dinner with Rick Hamilton on Friday night, that's all."

"What?" Emily let out a scream and jumped off her chair. She ran to the couch. "Mom, that's fantastic!" Emily hugged her fiercely.

"Now, you see. That's why I didn't want to tell you."

"Why?" Emily pulled back, surprised.

"Because it's not a big deal, and I don't want you to make it into something it's not."

"Mom, it's a huge deal! You are going on a date! I'm so proud of you." Another hug.

"No, it's not a date. We're friends, period."

Emily nodded, giving her mother a patronizing smile.

"You stop that this minute, Emily Marie."

"Okay, okay, so it's not a date." Emily parroted what Konni wanted to hear. "Where you going?"

"Roy's Steakhouse."

Emily nodded. "Nice. Nice."

Konni stuffed a pillow in Emily's lap. "Glad you approve."

"What are you wearing?"

Konni thought a moment. She started to chew on her thumbnail. "I don't know."

"Mom, stop chewing your nails." Emily was off and running. "Oh, Mom, you could put your sign up at the store that you're closing early and get your nails done."

Konni raised her chin. "Absolutely not." She felt downright offended at the suggestion. After all, she wasn't changing her routine for anyone, certainly not a man with whom she had no intention whatsoever of getting involved.

Emily raised her hand. "Okay, okay, just a suggestion." She tapped the eraser end of a pencil against her forehead. After a moment, her eyes lit up. "I know! You look great in that red pantsuit."

"Oh, Em, you know how I hate that thing."

"You hate it because men stop and take notice. Aunt Cheryl knew what she was doing when she bought it for your birthday. You look awesome in that suit, Mom."

"You and my sister are conspiring against me."

"Your red shoes with the gold buttons look great with it."

Konni chewed off her next nail. "I don't know. Might be too fancy."

Emily brushed the comment aside. "No, no, it's casual-classy. Perfect to wear there. I've got some polish that will look good on your nails." Before Konni could comment, Emily ran to her room and came back with a bottle of cherry nail polish.

"I'll look like a tomato in all that red."

"You'll look gorgeous. I'll just put this on and you can see if you like it." Emily placed a board on her lap and pulled her mom's hand to her. Quickly, before Konni could chew off any more nails, Emily opened the polish and began to apply it to Konni's fingernails.

"Oh, Emily." Konni hated all the primping, but she knew her daughter enjoyed every minute of it.

Once Emily finished the job, Konni had to admit her nails did look nice. Besides, they matched the rash on her hands.

"Now, if they chip at all, just touch them up with this," Emily said as she replaced the cap and screwed it tightly closed.

Konni blew out a long sigh.

"Mom, everything will be fine. You'll see."

Konni nodded. "He's just a friend. You remember that." She waggled a red fingernail under Emily's nose.

"I'll remember," Emily said, doing the Scout's honor sign.

"You still going to Alexis's house Friday night?"

Emily smiled. "Yeah. Why, are you trying to get rid of me?"

Konni gasped. "Absolutely not!"

"Okay, okay, I'm just teasing." Emily turned a serious expression to her mom. "I'm really glad you're doing this, Mom."

Upon seeing her daughter's hopeful face, Konni didn't know how to respond. Emily reached over, dropped a kiss on Konni's forehead, and headed for the door. "See you in the morning."

"Okay, honey."

Emily walked into the hall.

"Em?"

She turned. "Yeah?"

"Thanks."

A huge grin spread across Emily's face. "No problem." With that, she went to bed.

Konni watched her daughter and smiled in spite of herself. She knew Emily felt proud to help her in this way. Still, Konni wanted everyone to know right from the start, she and Rick were friends. Only friends. Period.

She walked over to the closet and pulled out her red pantsuit. Maybe she would wear it Friday night.

Chapter 3

Rick clicked on the wide-screen TV and raked his fingers through his hair. What had he gotten himself into? He wanted a friendly date. That's all. Yet after talking with Konni, he sensed this was a big step for her. Maybe a bigger step than he wanted her to take.

He turned on a reality show and walked into the kitchen. Plopping some ice cubes in a glass, he poured himself a soda. The fizz rose up over the rim of the glass and spilled onto the counter. Rick grabbed a dishcloth.

"I mean, it's not like we're getting married or anything," he said to Read. The lab's ears perked, his eyes fixed on his owner. Rick sipped the remaining suds from the top of his glass, cleaned the overflow from the counter, and looked back at his dog. "I haven't stayed single this long for nothing. I'm not about to get into that trap. Those people live in misery. That's not for me."

Read cocked his head as though listening with a compassionate ear. The action seemed to shake Rick to his senses. He laughed, bent down, and scratched behind Read's ear. "Thanks for listening, ol' buddy. There will never be anyone but you for me." Rick stood, grabbed his glass again, and headed back into the living room. Read jumped up, wagged his tail, and trotted alongside.

Rick placed his glass on the coffee table. He leaned back and sank into the plump leather cushions of his sofa. With a glance at the reality show, he picked up the remote and clicked his way through the channels, pausing here and there along the way. His eyes glazed as images flickered across the screen.

Thoughts of his childhood surfaced again. He was nine. His mom clutched him close to her side, trying to leave the house while his alcoholic father blocked their way. No matter how hard he tried, Rick could not erase the memory of his dad's face at that moment, twisted in anger, breath reeking of whiskey. A twinge of fear from that scene haunted him still.

He blew out a sigh and clicked off the TV. Looking down, he stared into his open palms. Never did he want to break a woman's heart the way his dad had broken his mother's heart. Better to stay single and not risk it.

Read pushed his head under Rick's hands for attention. Rick smiled and rubbed the dog's neck. "You know, Read, it's not unusual for me to work late. Maybe I'll just let Konni know I need to stay at the office Friday night." Read's eyes met Rick's. "Well, there's truth in that." Rick felt defensive. "My desk is piled with papers needing my attention. I'll just stop by her antique shop tomorrow. That will be best for both of us," he said, ignoring the doubt that pricked his heart.

⸎

Konni flipped through the musty magazines a customer had dropped off. The periodicals appeared in pretty good shape despite their years. Recognizing some of the products and famous people of her youth, Konni sighed at the passing of time. Why couldn't things stay the same forever? She hated change, and she hated growing old. Why, just that morning she had plucked a gray hair. Okay, maybe two or three. . .hundred. Time to color. The thought made her mood dive south.

Stacking the magazines in a neat pile, Konni pulled out her inventory book, slipped on her reading glasses, and added the items to her growing list.

The bell on the front door jangled.

Konni took off her glasses and looked up. A slightly bent, frail wisp of a woman entered the store. Wrapped in a green tweed coat, neatly pressed and buttoned to the top, the old woman walked rather sprightly toward the counter. A sheer green scarf covered the white hair that fell in soft curls and dusted the nape of her neck. She carried a shiny black handbag with a small handle and gold clasp. Rubber-soled black shoes covered her feet, while sensible hosiery supported her aged legs. Once she reached the counter, a kind smile touched her mouth and a twinkle lit her eyes.

"Hi," she said in a shaky voice. "I'm Irene Kenner." She extended a gnarled hand.

"Konni Strong. How may I help you?" Konni's heart went soft at the sight of the woman.

Irene Kenner looked about the store. "You got a place to sit around here?"

Konni liked the woman's no-nonsense approach. "Oh, yes." Konni grabbed a chair and brought it to the mysterious stranger.

Mrs. Kenner eased herself into a seat plumped with padding, laid her purse across her lap, and looked up at Konni with a smile. "My mind tells me I'm twenty-five, but my body tells me the truth." A slight smirk tinged the corners of her mouth. "I do okay for an eighty-five-year-old, I reckon."

Konni nodded and waited for the woman to state her business.

Mrs. Kenner's eyes grew serious. "Married to a wonderful man for thirty-five years," she began. "Orville." She looked away from Konni, as if she'd stepped into the past.

Uh-oh. Something told Konni this could take awhile. Oh well, the work would have to wait.

"I've wasted too many years. Too many," Mrs. Kenner said with a touch of sorrow. She seemed to linger in remembrance, then turned to Konni. "But no more." Bright enthusiasm flickered in pale, clouded eyes. She smacked the purse on her lap for emphasis.

"I want to sell a desk."

Konni smiled.

"Do you know I wrote love letters to my husband on that desk more than sixty-five years ago?" She waved her hand. "Of course you don't. We've only just met." She laughed at herself. "The desk was a good hundred years old then. My parents loved antiques." She shrugged again. "Got a neighbor girl who needs to go to college. She works two jobs, has all the financial aid she can get, and it's still not enough. Parents barely make ends meet." She shook her head. "I mean to help her. I'm going to sell my desk." Her lips pursed into a thin line as though the matter was settled.

Amazed that someone could part with such a prize, Konni studied her. "The desk has been in your family for a long time. Are you sure that you want to sell it?"

The woman nodded emphatically. "What good does it do collecting dust at my house? Can't see a thing to write. For crying out loud, half the time, I can't even see the desk. I keep bumpin' into it." She groaned and rubbed her knee as if there was a fresh bruise underneath her dress. "Might as well do some good."

Konni stepped cautiously onto personal ground. "Might your family want it?"

"I have no family," she said matter-of-factly. Her hand steadied her purse.

Realizing the woman's mind was made up, Konni interrupted the brief silence. "Where might I see it?"

"I thought you'd never ask." With great care, Mrs. Kenner reached shaky fingers into her purse and pulled out a slip of paper. "Here's my address. I live just down the road. Within walking distance."

Konni looked at her in surprise. "You walked?"

"Course. How do you think I keep my figure?" An ornery grin escaped her.

Konni chuckled. "Would Saturday evening, say around seven o'clock, be all right?"

Mrs. Kenner nodded.

The doorbell jangled, causing them both to look up. Rick Hamilton entered the store. Konni's heart flipped.

"Hi, Rick. Nice to see you," she said as he approached. Her eyes took in the heavy beige sweater that swept across his thick chest and broad shoulders.

She ventured a glance at the well-scrubbed jeans that stretched down long legs and stopped short of brown leather shoes.

"Hi, Konni." He turned to Mrs. Kenner and tipped his head. "Ma'am."

"Rick, this is Irene Kenner. Mrs. Kenner, Rick Hamilton. Rick is superintendent of schools for Hartley South School District."

"Is that a fact?" She looked him over. "You'll do just fine. We need good men in such important positions." She studied him. "I can tell you're a good one," she said finally and snapped her head once with approval.

Rick looked at Konni, and they laughed. He turned to the old woman. "You can tell already?"

She attempted to rise. Rick reached over and assisted her to her feet. She poked a crooked finger under his nose. "Oh, don't let this body fool you. I may look like an old hound dog, but my mind is sharp. I can read people pretty well."

"Uh-oh, I'd better watch myself," he said with a laugh.

Mrs. Kenner smiled. Her slow, steady gaze drifted from Rick to Konni and back to Rick. "Well, I'll leave you young folks to your business. I'll see you Saturday, Konni Strong."

Konni nodded and smiled. She and Rick escorted Mrs. Kenner through the door into the crisp air. They watched her walk steadily into the quiet street lined with towering maples and quaint lampposts. High above, the whir of an airplane caught Konni's attention as it soared against the backdrop of a spring sky full of sailing clouds. Just once she would like to experience such freedom. To fly among the clouds, to allow her spirit to give way in complete abandon to protocols, convention, and. . .vows. She gasped almost audibly. Whatever made her think that?

"Nice woman," Rick said, jarring Konni to attention.

She nodded, though still stinging from the betrayal of her private thoughts. She mentally shook herself. "Do you know she's eighty-five?" Konni asked, her eyes once again on Mrs. Kenner.

"She gets around pretty well."

Konni turned to Rick. "So what brings you here?"

He swallowed hard and stared at her.

"Is something wrong?"

"Uh, no. I just wanted to look around your shop and, uh, remind you about dinner tomorrow night."

She laughed and opened the door into her shop. "You afraid I'll back out?"

Rick laughed, but something about his mannerisms made Konni wonder if there was more to his visit than he let on.

On Friday night, Konni's bedroom smelled of perfume and hair spray. Weary from the effort and stress of getting ready for a date, she finally allowed herself to edge in front of her full-length mirror. Her red neck matched her pantsuit. Emily came in and stood behind her mother.

"You look great, Mom."

"I look like Bob the Tomato. Round and red." She could hear the panic in her voice. All she wanted to do was curl under a soft blanket and watch an old movie.

Emily laughed and shook her head. She walked over to her mother's dresser and picked through the jewelry. She held up a dainty golden necklace and turned to Konni. "Here, this will look great with your outfit."

Konni reluctantly walked over to Emily and looked at the necklace Eric had bought her on their fifth anniversary. "Not that one," she said in a whisper.

With knowing eyes, Emily looked at Konni. "I'm sorry." She squeezed her hand. "You don't really need one."

Just then the doorbell rang. They both jumped. Emily squealed and placed a kiss on her mother's cheek. Konni groaned and scratched her neck once more.

"Come on, Mom, you're going to have a great time. I promise." Emily grabbed Konni's hand.

Alarm shot through Konni. Her feet thudded to a halt. "I can't go like this. If people see me rush through the parking lot, they'll think I'm a flashing traffic signal. I'll cause a wreck. I'm much too conspicuous!" Konni turned to rush back to her bedroom; Emily grabbed her.

Holding her by both arms, Emily looked straight into Konni's eyes. "Mom, calm down. You look wonderful."

Konni thought she might lose her lunch, which, of course, would do nothing for her red pantsuit. She took a deep breath. She stood there a moment or two to calm herself. Goodness, what had gotten into her? *Dinner. Two friends going to dinner.*

The doorbell rang again. Emily and Konni both glanced toward the front door. "You gonna be okay, Mom?"

Konni closed her eyes, took another breath, and nodded.

"Okay, let's go." Emily helped Konni down the stairs to the front door; then Emily stepped aside and went into the living room.

Konni glanced once more at her daughter and received a thumbs-up. She opened the door.

Rick's approving eyes met hers. A large grin stretched across his face. "Hi."

He stood tall before her, dressed in khakis with a sharp crease, a button-down shirt, and a brown leather jacket. Konni stood mute like a figurine in a wax museum.

Rick's eyebrows raised; amusement danced in his eyes. "May I come in?"

Konni gulped. "Oh, yes." She let out a nervous laugh and stepped aside. She turned toward Emily and rolled her eyes. Emily covered a giggle.

"Just let me grab my bag and coat," Konni said.

Rick exchanged some chitchat with Emily while Konni stepped in the bathroom to check her rash once more. A glance in the mirror told her what she needed to know. Once at the restaurant, someone might possibly toss her into a salad bowl. Okay, a very large salad bowl. She sighed and walked back into the living room.

"You ready?" Rick asked

Konni nodded and looked toward Emily. "You and Alexis behave yourselves," she said in the expected parental tone.

Emily smiled. "We'll be good as gold. I promise."

Konni eyed her with suspicion. "Why does that make me nervous?"

Emily laughed. "I'll be back around ten o'clock tomorrow morning. Is that okay?"

Konni kissed her daughter on the forehead. "That's fine, honey. You girls have a good time."

"You, too." Emily gave her a motherly look.

Konni felt like a sixteen-year-old going on her first date. She half expected Emily to dole out a curfew. Rick smiled and cast a wink at Emily, then ushered Konni out the door. She felt his hand on the small of her back. A gentle and protective touch. She liked it. Too much. She told herself to jerk away but argued it would be a rude thing to do.

It's okay. You're friends. You're only friends.

Rick opened the door and helped her in. While he walked back to the driver's side, she looked at her hands and admired her nail polish. Reluctantly, she admitted to herself she did feel quite feminine.

"Want some music?" he asked as he closed the door and started the engine.

"Sure."

He clicked on the knob and turned to an easy-listening station. A saxophone crooned a romantic melody that melted the stress from Konni's shoulders and soothed her down to her toes. It was just what she needed after her tension-filled day. She felt sure if she were a cat, she'd start to purr.

"You hungry?" Rick asked, breaking through her momentary trance.

She turned to him and smiled. "Yes."

"Good. I am, too."

Chapter 4

After dinner at Roy's Steakhouse, Rick and Konni went to the Chatting Grounds Coffeehouse. The clock inched toward closing time, but Rick didn't want the night to end. Seeing Konni at Forgotten Treasures had made him want to keep the date. He was glad he hadn't canceled it. He and Konni were having a good time.

Konni laughed at something someone had commented in passing; then she took the last sip of her latte. She placed the cup back on the table and glanced around. "Must be near closing," she said in a voice that hinted at disappointment.

"I know a diner, a fifties kind of place that stays open until one o'clock. That would give us a little more time. Are you game?" As soon as he spoke the words, he was afraid he had pushed her too far. One look in her eyes removed his fear.

"Why not?" A carefree grin lit her face—an expression that told him she truly was enjoying herself.

"Great."

They rose from the wooden chairs, threw their cups in the trash, and left the coffee shop. In practically no time at all, they arrived at Della's Diner.

Rick shut off the engine and walked to the passenger's side of his navy SUV. He opened the door and let Konni out, noticing she had touched up her lipstick.

Once inside, she eased into the booth, and he slid across from her.

"Hey, Rick," a plump, gray-haired lady called from behind the counter of the near-empty room.

"Hi, Della. What's the owner doing working so late?"

She shrugged, edging her way over with menus. "The waitress called in sick. My backup left for vacation. That leaves me." She tossed a weak smile and pulled a pencil from behind her ear. Reaching into her pocket, she lifted a customer order pad. "What will it be?"

Rick held up his hand. "Sorry, Della, no food tonight. Just coffee will be fine." He looked at Konni to make sure that's all she wanted.

"Please. Decaf," she said.

"Better do the same for me, or I'll never get to sleep tonight," Rick added.

Della laughed. "You'll have trouble sleeping all right, but it won't be from the coffee," she murmured as she walked away.

Rick heard her and turned to Konni. She rummaged through her purse and didn't seem to notice the comment. He had to smile in spite of himself. Della, always the matchmaker.

Konni looked up at him. "What is it?"

"Hmm?"

"You're smiling."

"Oh, that." He ran his fingers absently across his chin and shrugged. "Just having a good time, I guess." He kept his eyes fixed on her.

Konni smiled back. "Rick, this has been a wonderful evening."

Uh-oh, here it comes. "It's been great, but..." He studied his fingers and gritted his teeth, waiting on what would follow. Silence. Surprised, he glanced up. She looked at him.

"Did I say something wrong?" she asked, concern on her face.

"Not at all. I just thought—"

Her dark eyes searched his face, causing his tongue to stick to the roof of his mouth like a glob of peanut butter.

"Well?" A smile played in her teasing eyes.

"Okay, I thought you were going to say something like, "It's been great, but, blah, blah, blah," you know, like maybe you didn't want to see me again." Oh, now he'd done it. A shadow flickered across her face. He had to slow down or he'd blow it. He reached his hands out and cupped hers in his own. "Look, I'm sorry. I don't mean to..."

She looked as though she wanted to rescue him from digging a deeper hole. "It's okay, Rick. I understand."

He blew out a sigh of relief and leaned back in his seat. Their eyes engaged, neither breathing a word.

Della approached with a pot of coffee, shaking them from their thoughts. She poured the steaming liquid into china cups she placed in front of them.

"Wow, fine china. I've not seen those before, Della. Are we getting the red carpet treatment?"

The owner winked at Rick. "Just for you and your friend, Kiddo. Just for you." She patted his arm, then looked at Konni and smiled before walking away.

Konni chuckled. "I'd say you must come here quite often," she said, easing the hot liquid to her lips.

"Guilty as charged." He lifted his cup and took a drink. Putting it back in the saucer, he glanced at Konni. "What's a bachelor like me gonna do for dinner? Della keeps me from starving." He patted his midsection. "She does a great job, I might add."

"What, you don't cook?" Konni feigned shock.

"Can't even boil water," he said, trying his best to put on the sad look of a stray puppy.

Konni laughed. "Okay, that settles it. You'll have to let me fix dinner for you next Friday."

Rick's hand jerked and tipped his coffee. With his other hand, he stopped the spill. "Really?" he asked, cleaning coffee droplets from his cup and saucer.

She shrugged. "It's the least I can do for a starving friend."

He nodded his head with pleasure. "It's done then. Seven o'clock all right?"

She took another drink. He could detect a smile behind her cup. "Seven o'clock will be fine."

"To next Friday then," he said, lifting his cup to hers till they clinked.

⁂

The next morning, Konni put away the clean dishes from the dishwasher, clanging pots and pans in the process.

"You okay, Mom?" Emily asked when she walked in the door.

Konni turned with a start. "Oh, hi, Em. I didn't hear you come in."

"You look a mess," Emily said, her eyes intent on Konni's face.

"Thanks a lot."

Emily grabbed her mother's hand and led her to the chair by the table. "What's wrong, Mom? Was the date a total bust? You look like you haven't slept all night."

"I haven't slept. Why, I didn't even get home until two o'clock this morning!" She could hear her voice rise; a panic attack threatened to strike. Her fingers scratched the rash on her neck.

Emily's eyes grew wide as grapes. "Mom, that's terrific!"

Konni's hands clamped the sides of her face. "It is not!" She rose from her chair and began to pace as Emily looked on. "It's not supposed to be like this. I'm not some silly teenager—" She stopped abruptly and glanced at Emily. "Sorry." She continued to pace, her arms raising and lowering for emphasis. "Look, I don't want to do this. I don't have the energy, nor the. . .the. . .well, I just can't do it, that's all."

Emily stood and faced her. "Why not? He's a great guy, and you obviously had a wonderful time. What are you worried about, Mom? What's stopping you?" She looked straight into Konni's eyes.

Konni stared at her, speechless.

"Mom. . ." Emily swallowed for a moment as if allowing herself time to consider the words. "Dad is gone. Nothing we do will ever change that. We both need to face it and get on with our lives." Emily placed her hands on Konni's shoulders. "You know that's what Dad would want."

Whether from fatigue or the emotional turmoil of the last twenty-four hours, Konni didn't know, but try as she might, she couldn't stop the tears from falling.

"Oh, Mom." Emily pulled her into an enormous embrace. "It's gonna be okay."

There she went again, acting like the mom. It was just what Konni needed to bring her to her senses. She pulled away and wiped her face with a nearby paper towel. "You're right. We'll be fine." She raised her chin and shoulders. Her jaw tensed. They would be fine, but she didn't feel like talking to Emily about it just yet.

Emily seemed to sense it. "Anytime you want to talk, Mom, I'm here for you."

Now, Konni really felt like a failure. Her daughter had to take care of her instead of the other way around. Konni needed time to think, a place where she could not be bothered.

She knew just where to go.

⟡

Konni took measured steps under an overcast sky. The April winds blew a chill her way. She pulled her coat closer and glanced up. Gray clouds shadowed her footsteps like unexpected feelings shadowed her heart.

Frost kept the ground cold and hard. Winter. The season of her life since Eric's death. Gone were the soft, moldable ways of yesteryear. A hardened heart burdened her chest, making it difficult some days just to breathe. At least the ground would thaw soon, but Konni feared winter would never leave her.

Yet last night with Rick, a thin shred of warmth had seeped through her veins, frightening her. Not that she wanted to stay in a winter fog, but the vow reminded her that she had no choice.

A nervous squirrel darted across the path and scurried up a tree. If only she could do that. Run and hide, not have to deal with anything.

Her footsteps finally stopped in front of the familiar marker. ERIC STRONG. BELOVED HUSBAND AND FATHER. WE WILL ALWAYS LOVE YOU.

As she read the words once again, they pricked her conscience. "Some love, huh, Eric?" Konni dropped to her knees beside the grave. Her knees throbbed from the impact, but she didn't care. Right now, nothing mattered. She pulled a tissue from her pocket as big plops of tears fell from her eyes and splashed onto her legs. "I shouldn't have gone out with him." She wiped her face, trying to keep up with the tears. "You took such good care of me, in life and in death. How could I possibly see someone else?"

She bit her lip. "Everyone tells me it's time to move on, Eric." Her eyes bore into the grave marker. "What do they know? Have they lost their best friend and lover? Do memories haunt them until their head hurts? Do they struggle to get out of bed in the morning? To put one foot in front of the other? To breathe?"

Blame shifted with the passing winds. "Why did you leave me, Eric? Why? I needed you! I need you still!" She hit the ground hard with her fists until her hands started to bleed. She cried with abandon, like the wail of someone betrayed. Angry, swollen eyes glared at the heavens. "Why did you take him from me? It's not fair! I need him!" Things she knew she shouldn't say shot into the air like illegal fireworks.

Konni had rarely allowed herself to cry over Eric's death. Yet now, among the whispers of the wind, she held nothing back. Tears gushed like blood from an open wound. She cried until her strength was gone.

The wind seemed to echo her vow, taunting and mocking, as she made her way back to the car. Yet Eric's face brushed across her mind. A face that told her it was time to move on.

Without him.

By the time she settled behind the steering wheel, her breathing came easier, but she was no closer to answers for the future.

Out of nowhere, Isaiah 41:10, a verse she had memorized in her younger days, came to her: "Fear thou not; for I am with thee: be not dismayed; for I am thy God: I will strengthen thee; yea, I will help thee; yea, I will uphold thee with the right hand of my righteousness."

The words comforted her heart like good news from an old friend. Yet how could God be there for her when she had blamed Him for her pain? Konni put her key in the ignition and started the car. If only she could trust Him with her future.

"Fear thou not; for I am with thee. . ."

"But what if I lose someone else?"

"Be not dismayed; for I am thy God."

"I can't bear any more pain—"

"I will strengthen thee; yea, I will help thee—"

Tears flowed down her cheeks once again as she pulled onto the country road. "But. . ." Her words paused in her throat. "I haven't cared about anything for so long—even You."

"I will uphold thee with the right hand of my righteousness."

Peace spread over her cold heart like sunshine over snow. In the quiet of the country roads, inside her vehicle, Konni sensed her life was changing.

Was she ready for it?

Chapter 5

The morning quickly melted into early evening before Konni traveled the road toward Mrs. Kenner's house. Glancing in her rearview mirror, she could see the sun setting in a blaze of pink. Her car slowed in front of Forgotten Treasures, the soft glow from the security light spilling through the window onto the sidewalk. Everything appeared in order.

From her car radio, the oldies station beat out a song popular in Konni's teen years, and she ventured a few blocks farther. The familiar tune made her feel young and carefree, a feeling she had long forgotten—until last night. *Not now. I don't want to think about Rick now.* She clicked off the radio.

Once she arrived at Mrs. Kenner's house, she pulled next to the curb, causing tires to scrunch on the pebbly gravel. She reached for her purse, opened the groaning door, and climbed out. Cold, damp air chilled her face the moment she stepped into it, reminding her of the night before.

A brick path lined her way toward the porch. Konni glanced up to see Mrs. Kenner wrapped in her coat, rocking gently on a weather-beaten swing. Konni warmed with the sight of the old woman's wind-ruffled hair and the smile on her face.

Mrs. Kenner's hand clutched Konni's in a hearty greeting. The kind woman looked most eager for company. "You got a minute?"

"Sure."

Mrs. Kenner patted the seat beside her. Konni sat down.

The woman studied Konni for a moment. "You doing all right, Child?"

The woman has the heart of a grandmother. What a shame she has no children. "I'm fine."

"I'm not so sure," she said, pointing to Konni's eyes.

Konni dropped her gaze.

Mrs. Kenner paused a long moment. "Well. They say tea is good for the soul." She thumped her hands on her lap. "Let's have some." Without further ado, she stood and walked into the house.

Konni followed Mrs. Kenner like a child following her teacher. A small but tidy room lined the way toward the kitchen. Konni took a deep breath, pulling in a calming fragrance. On the table, she saw an antique crock over-stuffed with a fresh bouquet. In the corner sat a ragged box littered with silk flowers.

Mrs. Kenner followed her gaze. "Oh, that." She filled the teakettle with water, placed it on the stove, then turned to Konni. "I used to set out silk flowers." She pulled some cups from her shelf. "They collected dust. Just like me," she said with a laugh. "Honestly, it occurred to me my life was like that. Stale as an old biscuit." She shrugged, placing the cups in saucers. "I might be eighty-five, but I'm still kickin'. I figure as long as I'm kickin', there's life to be lived. I keep fresh flowers to remind me every day is new and exciting. Meant to be savored like a good bowl of grits. So on Saturday mornings, I go to the florist and gather my bouquets for the week."

Konni smiled and thought about the wisdom of her words.

"Guess you can tell I'm from the South, huh?" A grin tipped the corners of her mouth.

Konni laughed. "I admit I had my suspicions."

"Me and Orville came here back in 1965. Our kinfolk were all from Tennessee." She turned abruptly to Konni. "Course, they're all dead now," she said matter-of-factly.

The woman hesitated, her eyes fixed on Konni. "You must be anxious to see the desk." Konni nodded and followed Mrs. Kenner into a side room that appeared to be a study. Bookshelves lined one wall; a rocking chair and desk were the only other pieces of furniture.

Konni gasped when she saw the antique desk, recognizing at once its value. Her fingers ran along the fine wood, well maintained over the years.

"You like it," Mrs. Kenner said more as a statement than a question.

Konni nodded. "How ever can you part with it?"

The old woman shrugged. "To give a girl a future."

They discussed its value and made arrangements to get it to the store. With business settled, they grabbed their tea and sat on the soft cushions of a well-kept antique sofa.

Konni shared bits of her life with Eric while Mrs. Kenner listened with interest. "I've talked far too long," Konni said, with a glance toward her watch. Lifting her cup and saucer, she stood, reached over, and took Mrs. Kenner's empty cup and saucer, then headed for the kitchen. Placing the dishes in the dishwasher, she turned to go. The bright flowers caught her attention. Mrs. Kenner's words played over in her mind. "I keep fresh flowers to remind me life is meant to be savored." Something stirred inside Konni. Was her life stale? One glance at her outdated pants and top answered her. She knew when she had stopped caring.

"Oh, dear, you didn't need to do that."

Konni turned to Mrs. Kenner with a start. "No problem. Thank you for the tea. I'll be back next week for the desk." Without thinking, Konni reached over and gave the woman a hug. The action surprised her. She didn't normally hug people she hardly knew, but there was something about this woman. . . .

Rick pulled into the church parking area. A rush of adrenaline pulsed through him once he spotted Konni's car. Grabbing his Bible, he stuffed his keys in his pocket and headed out the door. A few people greeted him upon his entrance into the church, and someone passed him a bulletin. He made small talk as he looked around for Konni.

"Good morning, Rick," Konni's voice called from behind.

He turned to her. "Hello." The sight of her caused his heart to jump off track like a runaway locomotive. For a moment, neither of them said anything as they stood close together. Rick fingered the cuff of his shirt, feeling the jitters of a kid on the first day of school. He cleared his throat. "You want to sit together?"

"Well. . ." She considered his question for a long moment.

Rick wondered at her hesitation. Hadn't she enjoyed herself on Friday night? He thought things had changed a little between them.

Her eyes flickered downward.

"Konni?"

She seemed to have pushed away her fear for the moment and looked back to him with apology. "Sure." A guarded smile lit her face.

Rick led the way into the sanctuary. He pondered the complexities of the woman walking beside him. Complex, yes, but somehow he felt she was worth the challenge.

The service couldn't be over soon enough to suit Konni. She still didn't know how she felt about things. Her vow to Eric hung over her heart like a heavy cloud.

She and Rick made their way from the sanctuary, amid greetings and friendly chatter. Rick turned to her. "Want to go to lunch?"

His question surprised her. She stumbled over her tongue, trying to find an appropriate response. "I. . .uh. . . well, I—"

"I'll take that as a yes." He laughed and touched her elbow, leading her away from curious friends. They stepped through the church doors into the sunshine. A concerned expression shadowed his face. "I'm sorry. I shouldn't have asked you within the hearing of others. I didn't mean to put you on the spot." He lifted her chin, causing her eyes to meet his.

The tenderness in his voice made her feel as though a breeze had caressed her. Her resolve melted away like the morning dew. "Thank you, Rick," she said with all sincerity. "I'd love to go to lunch with you." She stubbornly pushed aside all guilt and confusion and allowed herself the luxury of a friend.

The surprise on his face was so abrupt that Konni struggled to hide a smirk.

He laughed. The sound of his laughter made her feel content, like enjoying coffee with an old friend.

⁂

Tuesday night, Rick stopped by Konni's house unexpectedly after dinner. Konni had just popped in a DVD, so she invited him to join her. She put some kettle corn in the microwave and poured soda into glasses filled with cubed ice.

Once the movie started, Konni sat on the couch, munching on their snack, and stole a glance at Rick. Her emotions tossed about like a bag of popping corn. Attraction sparked between them, she couldn't deny that. The more time they spent together, the more she liked him. Why, in the short time of their relationship, he had managed to make her rashes disappear.

Their relationship. Was this a relationship? She gulped and almost swallowed a corn kernel whole. A rather unladylike cough escaped her, causing Rick to jerk around.

"You okay?"

She nodded, grabbing her drink from the coffee table. His attention still on her, Konni felt herself flush. She swallowed the cold liquid, trying desperately to bring herself under control.

Once she put her drink down, Rick scooted closer to her and gently hit her back a couple of times. The coughing finally subsided.

"Thanks," she said when she found her voice. She turned to him. His hand still rested behind her. Their eyes locked, neither daring to blink.

A gentle nudge from his hand on her back pulled her closer to him. Konni's pulse rushed in her ears in thunderous throbs. As they inched forward, Rick's gaze fell upon her lips. She trembled in his arms, her lips eager to receive his touch. When he was but a whisper away, the sudden *swoosh* of the front door jarred them apart like two school kids getting caught in a smooch behind the bleachers.

Emily stepped inside the door and froze in place. Konni could almost visualize the image of their guilt-ridden faces. Rick broke through the awkward silence.

"Well," he said, with a hand slap on his knees, "I'd best get home."

"Don't you want to finish the movie?"

He shook his head, already making his way to the door. "Got a big day tomorrow."

Konni practically had to run to keep up with him. Emily stepped out of the way, still gaping at the scene but saying nothing. Konni threw her a make-yourself-scarce look. Emily quickly retreated to the kitchen.

Konni turned toward Rick, who was halfway into his car by now. When she arrived at his car door, he had already started the engine. He held up his hand to stop her from saying anything. "I don't know what got into me. I apologize."

Before she could utter a word, he rushed out of her driveway with a squeal of tires.

Chapter 6

When Rick finally settled into his bed, he folded his hands behind his head and stared at the spackled ceiling. He couldn't imagine what had come over him when he almost kissed Konni. That wasn't his style. He'd spent enough time talking to her to know she struggled with the idea of dating again. He exhaled. "She'll never want to see me again, that's for sure."

No matter how he worked it, he didn't know how to fix things. He'd blown it, pure and simple.

With a jerk, he yanked off the covers. He stood and pulled a lightweight robe over his bare chest and long boxers and made his way to the kitchen. Lifting the cold water jug from the fridge, he poured himself a glass and drank it down without stopping for a breath. He swiped his hand across his mouth, placed the glass in the sink, and looked down at Read.

Crouching until he was eye level with the lab, Rick scratched Read behind the ears. "I really messed up tonight," Rick said, staring blankly into the black fur. The dog threw him a tell-me-all-about-it-but-don't-stop-scratching look. In spite of himself, Rick laughed and calmed down a bit. He continued to scratch; then with a final pat on Read's sleek coat, Rick stood and walked back to the bedroom. Once inside the room, he knelt down at his bedside and did what he realized he should have done the moment he met Konni Strong.

He prayed.

⬥

As always, Saturday found Konni working at Forgotten Treasures. She walked through the store and checked to make sure the inventory looked nice for browsing customers. Satisfied with the turn of a rocker here, the scoot of a trunk there, she made a few phone calls to follow up on possible purchases. Once finished with the calls, she settled into her chair with a glass of iced tea in front of her. She cleared various papers away like unwanted thoughts.

Flashes of Tuesday night with Rick confused her. First, she had determined to stay away from him; then just as she found herself wanting more of his company, he seemed to distance himself. Why?

He had called on Thursday night, saying he couldn't come for dinner on Friday. "Too much work." Still, she wondered if something else lurked behind his excuse.

Her hands reached for the logbook to glance over the length of stay for some of her antiques. The front door jangled.

When she glanced up, she saw Mrs. Kenner walking through the store. The old woman waved and inched her way toward the counter. Konni could see that her friend held a couple of books in her arms.

"I'm sorry, Mrs. Kenner, I didn't realize you were carrying something." Konni rushed to the woman's side and took the books from her hands.

"Posh! I'm not an invalid, for crying out loud. You treat me like I'm an old woman!"

Konni looked at her in surprise. She held a giggle in her throat.

The woman tossed an ornery grin. "Okay, I may be past my prime, but like I said, I'm still kickin'." She winked. "And my name is Irene." She brushed the air with a wave of her hand. "You make me feel like my mother when you say 'Mrs.'"

Konni laughed and laid the books on the counter. When she looked at them, she realized they were journals. She wondered how Irene could part with something so personal.

"They're not for sale. They're for you to read."

Surprised, Konni looked up at her.

Taking a few more steps, Irene slipped into the chair Konni had brought out on Irene's last visit. "I thought you might like to know some of my story. Of course, it's not the entire story, but it is the most interesting part," she said with a wiggle of her eyebrows. "It shows some of my thirty-five year marriage to Orville." She searched Konni's face. "But of course, if you're too busy—"

"Oh my, no," Konni said with her hand up. "I would love to read your journals—if you don't feel it's too personal."

Irene shrugged. "For others to read, perhaps, but somehow I feel like the Lord wants me to share them with you."

Konni stared at her, not knowing what to say. How could she argue with what the Lord wanted? Reading someone's journals was like taking a glimpse into their soul. Konni could never reveal herself to someone like that.

"I also have some china I'd like you to look at."

"Whom are you selling it for?" Konni teased.

"A single woman from our church who works two jobs just to put food on the table."

"I don't know that china will bring you much in the way of money."

"Oh, but I believe this china will," Irene said with a mischievous grin. "It belonged to my great-great-grandparents. Now *that's* old."

They both laughed. Konni shook her head. "You're full of surprises."

Irene took a few moments to rise to her feet. "I'd better get home before I tucker out. By the way. . ." She stopped and with intense eyes stared at Konni. "How is Mr. Hamilton?"

Konni blinked. "Uh, he's fine," she stammered.

"He's a good one, I'm telling ya." With an expression that said she knew more than she let on, Irene Kenner turned toward the door. "Come by the house after work, and I'll show you the china," she called over her shoulder before she stepped into the spring air.

⤜⤛

"So how does that make you feel—reading those journals, I mean?" Konni's sister asked while they followed the hostess who led them to a table.

They eased into their booth. "I don't know, Cheryl. As I read the love story between Irene and Orville, it's like reading of my own life with Eric. Wonderful marriage, both strong in the Lord, he died fairly young. Fifties, I think."

Cheryl sipped from the glass of water the waitress had placed before her. "That's too weird."

"Yeah. I suppose she wanted me to read them since I lost my husband."

Cheryl shrugged, then after a moment leaned into the table. "You know, Konni, God could be in this."

"Fear thou not; for I am with thee. . . ."

Konni nodded but said nothing.

"So, tell me about this Rick guy. Emily says he's really cute." Cheryl's voice was lighthearted and encouraging, but Konni wasn't sure she wanted to talk about it.

"I admit I like him a lot, but things are still, well, a little strained between us. Besides, I'm not sure I want another relationship." She shrugged. "It's really a non-issue. He hasn't called for a while."

Before Cheryl could comment, the waitress showed up and took their orders. They handed her their menus and went back to their conversation. "Maybe he feels your apprehension," Cheryl offered.

"I don't know." Konni sighed. "Life was easier before he came along."

Cheryl reached out and grabbed Konni's hand. "It's time to live again, Konni. Eric would want that."

Konni thought of her time at Eric's grave, the sense of him releasing her from the vow. Still not sure she could talk about it, she looked away. Her eyes fell upon a scene that made her stomach plunge. Across the room in a cozy corner table sat Rick Hamilton and a woman with hair the color of corn silk. She wore a shapely dress that complimented all the right places and accentuated her endless legs. No wonder Rick was acting strange. He had other interests. *How could I have been so stupid?*

"Hey, you okay?"

Konni barely heard the words over the roar of her confusion. She couldn't blame him really. She glanced down at her own frumpy clothes. Maybe it was time to make some changes. Reluctantly, she turned toward her sister. "I'm fine." A trickle of determination stirred, then charged through her like a rushing river.

"Ma'am?" Konni called to her waitress.

The woman hurried to the table. "Yes?"

"I'm not as hungry as I thought. Could I cancel my previous order and just get a house salad, fat-free dressing, no croutons or cheese, please?"

The waitress made a quick note, then scurried off.

"What was that all about?" Cheryl asked with a slight smile.

Yes, she'd make some changes. Starting right now. Konni lifted her chin. "You know, I think I'm going to get my nails done."

Cheryl's eyes widened. "Now I know you're not okay. What's up?"

Konni forced herself to laugh. "Nothing's up. I just want to take care of myself. Is there anything wrong with that?"

Cheryl eyed her suspiciously. "Why, no. Nothing wrong at all."

❧

Konni worked out all the frustrations of recent days exercising to her workout video. Maybe her vow was made in haste. Jump, two, three, kick! Maybe the others were right. Eric would want her to branch out. Twist, two, three, pant, four, five, six, gasp!

Why didn't Rick tell her he was dating someone else? Arm thrust, punch, two, three. Not that he owed her an explanation. After all, they didn't have "an understanding." Punch, four, five, six. Her pulse thumped harder than her feet on the aerobic stepper. Nobody owed her anything. She pushed her body harder. It's time she started a new life. From now on—jump, push, kick, wheeze—others would see the new Konni Strong.

She only hoped the determination wouldn't ebb with her fading energy.

❧

Rick finished his five-mile run and pushed through the front door. As usual, Read stood ready to greet him. Bending over, Rick patted the hound on the head a few times and staggered to the kitchen, pulling the water jug from the fridge. He'd hoped to settle some things in his mind during his run, but instead he found himself more confused than ever.

He missed Konni, no doubt about it. But should he risk a relationship? His father had failed. What if Rick failed, too?

Then, as if he didn't have enough to think about, assistant superintendent Haley Green showed up with "business matters." Though hidden behind a barrage of paperwork, her true agenda was all too obvious.

Admittedly, she was a beautiful woman. Still, he had no interest in her. How could he when Konni Strong bombarded his thoughts day and night?

He wanted to forget the whole thing. Shove Konni from his life, from his heart.

From his heart?

Where did that come from? He couldn't possibly be in love. He didn't know her well enough. His mind argued that he knew her well enough to know something was different about her.

Okay, he could live with that. Now what? He still didn't want to get into a serious relationship. Couldn't she stop haunting his every thought? His head hurt from thinking.

Lifting his glass, he guzzled the cold water as fast as he could, hoping the chilled liquid would refresh him and maybe clear his mind at the same time. It cooled his body, but his thoughts still burned with Konni's image.

There was nothing he could do. Their relationship shifted the night he had tried to kiss her. End of story.

End of relationship.

He stopped drinking for a brief moment. He was forgetting one thing. Rick Hamilton was not a quitter. He had apologized about the near-kiss attempt. Maybe she wouldn't write him off completely.

What about church? He liked Hope Village. Why stop going there? And if he happened to bump into Konni in such a small church, well. . .

Excitement surged through him. He finished his ice water. By the time he lowered his glass, his mind was made up. He would win Konni Strong back.

He just didn't know how.

⟡

When Konni spotted Rick inside the church foyer, her heart skipped a beat. She struggled to pull her gaze away from him, but he caught her attention and waved. Anticipation sparked through her with every step that brought him closer.

"Good morning," he said, sounding a bit hesitant.

"Hi."

"You look great." The look in his eyes told her he meant it.

Konni could feel herself flush. "Thanks." Maybe the diet and exercise were helping. She curled a wisp of hair behind her ear, hoping he'd notice her manicured nails.

He looked at her and smiled. "Want to sit together?"

His voice smoothed her heart like cool water over pebbles. Without hesitation, she nodded.

Rick led the way, and Konni followed, wondering just where her life was headed.

Chapter 7

The smell of steak and baked breads filled the air as Konni and Rick waited for their meals. "I'm glad you agreed to lunch," Rick said.

Konni shrugged. "You saved me from a cold sandwich. When Emily goes to her friend's house, I never feel like cooking just for me."

Rick eyed her carefully, hesitating a moment. "I wasn't sure you'd want to see me again."

"Why is that?" She studied him.

Feeling a bit restless, he fidgeted with an edge of the cloth napkin. "Um, well, I know you're still a little uncomfortable with dating."

"What makes you think that?"

He stopped fingering the cloth and looked at her with surprise. "Well, aren't you?"

She paused a moment. "Well, okay, maybe a little."

They both laughed.

"But it's getting easier," she added.

Her words gave him hope. "Good!" He wanted to probe further into her heart. To ask her about her feelings for Eric. After all, he didn't want to play second fiddle to anyone. Not even her late husband. Yet the time didn't seem right.

"How are things with the school corporation?"

"Going well. Very busy, winding things down for the year."

She nodded and spread her napkin on her lap as the waitress placed their food before them. When the waitress left, Rick reached for Konni's hand. He noticed the surprise on her face but bowed his head before she could comment. He offered the Lord thanks for their meal, then pulled his hand away.

Konni reached for her fork and looked to him. "That was nice. Thank you."

Her comment surprised him. Why would she thank him for praying?

"I appreciate your walk with the Lord, Rick. It's made me examine my own heart. I mean, I used to have that close communion with the Lord, but that was before. . ." Her voice broke off.

He understood. "You still miss him, don't you?"

They sat in the quiet of the moment while Konni searched for the right words. "I miss the life we shared." She blankly stirred the corn on her plate. "What about you? Why have you never married?"

He noticed how she quickly changed the subject, apparently uncomfortable with talk about herself. "I suppose it scares me," he answered. "I never had a good example of what a husband should be. Dad was an alcoholic. When he drank, he abused my mother and me. I don't want to be like that."

Konni searched his face a moment. "You think because your dad wasn't a good husband that you won't be?"

He laid his fork down. "Seems logical, don't you think?"

A warm smile lit her face. "You're not your father, you know."

"So you think there's hope?" He cocked an eyebrow.

"There's always hope."

"Really?" He winced inwardly as he realized he'd spoken almost too eagerly.

"Really," she said with conviction.

Oh, he liked the sound of that. Made him feel anything was possible.

If only he could believe it.

⚉

Konni rolled her head from side to side as she waited for her e-mail to pop up. She didn't normally receive much mail—an occasional letter from out-of-town friends and sometimes work-related notes since she didn't have a computer at the store. She had to admit, since Rick started e-mailing her, she could hardly wait to check for messages in the evening. It had almost become the highlight of her day. Seemed they could talk easier via computer than on the telephone.

The e-mail displayed across her screen, but she saw nothing from Rick. Before disappointment set in, an instant message popped up, asking if she'd accept a message from "Readerleader." Konni laughed. She could only imagine who that must be. Though not an expert with instant messaging, she had IM'd with her sister a couple of times before. Her fingers tingled with excitement.

"Excuse me, dear lady, do you always accept messages from strangers?"

Konni felt as giddy as when she discovered a rare antique. "Only ones with obvious names like 'Readerleader.'" She clicked the message back with a laugh.

"Okay, so I'm predictable. I thought you might be online about now. This instant message thing is a bit mysterious and all, don't you think? I feel somewhat like Romeo sneaking a secret message to Juliet."

Konni let out a giggle. "I admit it's a little easier to talk this way than face-to-face. Takes the pressure off, don't you agree?"

"Definitely. Now, since rejection might be a little less painful this way, what do you say we go to dinner Friday night?"

Uh-oh, am I ready for this? After all, he had never explained his relationship to the other woman Konni had seen him with in the restaurant. Konni wondered if she should confront him. She bit her thumbnail. They had no claims on one another. Maybe she should just let it go and see how it all turned out. Her hands hovered over the keyboard. She noticed a growing rash.

Another message from Rick popped up on the screen. "Okay, you're hesitating. Am I pushing too fast? Please tell me, Konni. I don't want to make you uncomfortable."

Even though his words played on the screen, she could almost hear his voice. For an instant, she wondered what it would feel like to be held in his arms. She gasped. What was going on with her? "I have to work."

"Oh, okay."

She could read his disappointment between the lines. "How about meeting for coffee Saturday afternoon?" There. They wouldn't have to be out late. A quick cup of coffee, then home.

"Great! I'll pick you up around, say, three-thirty?"

"How about we meet there?"

"Oh, right. So family members don't catch us. Have it your way, dear Juliet. See you then. R (Romeo or Rick, whichever you prefer)."

Dare she trust her heart to him? The answer came as a surprise to her. Rick Hamilton had already stolen her heart.

"Don't hurt me, Romeo," she whispered into the softness of her room. Then she looked toward heaven and prayed, "Please, God, I can't go through losing someone I love again."

❧

"Hey, Gal," Irene said as she slipped into the shop.

"Irene! So good to see you. I was afraid you wouldn't come," Konni said, grabbing a chair for her friend.

"Ah, but it's Saturday. I have to come see you on Saturday."

Konni laughed. "I'll make us some tea and be right back."

Irene nodded, settling into her familiar spot.

Konni returned with the tea and handed a cup to Irene. She sat in her chair across from Irene.

"Thank you for selling the desk and china," Irene offered.

"I was so pleased to get such a price for them both," Konni said and sipped from her cup.

"I suspect you didn't take your cut." Irene looked at Konni as a mother questioning her child.

Konni wasn't offended but rather smiled. "Why should you get all the blessing of helping a girl go to school and a mother feed her children?"

Irene laughed, deepening the wrinkles in her soft but aged face. She took another drink. "You've read my journals then?"

"Yes." They grew quiet. Konni looked into her cup. "You knew they would help me." She glanced up.

Kindness glowed from Irene's face. "I hoped they would."

"I've been a fool. You see, I made a vow—"

Irene quieted Konni with a wave of her hand. "You needn't tell me, dear. God knows your heart. What's important is that you move on from here."

Konni swallowed hard. "I loved Eric so much, Irene."

The old woman leaned over and placed her hand on Konni's. "I know. But our memories of Orville and Eric will always be with us. They shared a part of our lives that belonged to them alone. No one can take that from us. But now is the time for new memories."

A tear slid down Konni's cheek and plopped on Irene's hand. "Oh, I'm sorry."

The older woman reached up and brushed Konni's face with her fingers. "God has a plan for you. Trust Him."

Konni grabbed the gnarled fingers that rubbed against her face. She squeezed Irene's hand lightly. "What would I do without you?"

"No need to worry. I'm like an ol' wart—hard to get rid of."

Konni wiped her face and laughed.

"The world is uncertain, Konni, but God's love for us never changes. Oh, I almost forgot! I brought something else." Irene reached into a large bag beside her chair and pulled out a worn leather Bible. The old woman's eyes twinkled like a kid with a secret as she handed the sacred pages to Konni.

"Irene, you always surprise me." Konni flipped through the pages and saw that the Bible had been in the family for six generations.

"Oh my, Irene, I can't let you part with this."

She shook her head. "Our church has a missionary family in Papua New Guinea. They need financial support. They're sharing the Good News. I'll sell this Bible and give them the money."

Konni stared at her. "I want to be just like you when I grow up."

Irene looked at her aghast. "What? I haven't grown up myself yet!"

❧

Rick walked Konni out to her car. A sliver of moon sailed overhead, granting a shaft of light below. Konni stood beside her car door, facing him.

"Thanks for meeting me tonight," Rick said.

"I'm sorry I had to reschedule it for this late. Trying to get Emily ready for college is quite a job," she said with a laugh.

"No problem. I'm just glad you could still make it. I really enjoy our times together, Konni." Emotion touched his eyes, causing something inside her to stir. He looked at her, never blinking, as if waiting on her to say something. Finally, he released a sigh. "Well, I'll see you tomorrow at church."

A look of defeat shadowed his eyes before he turned to go. "Rick?" She grabbed his hand. "Thank you. For everything."

The words seemed just the encouragement he needed. Rick stepped closer. She felt her pulse race to her throat. He glanced around the deserted parking lot, then looked down into her eyes. With a gentle touch, his fingers traced the outline of her face. His hand reached tenderly behind her neck, working, sifting through strands of hair, causing her skin to tingle with life. His eyes held a question to which hers answered yes. He moved to her waiting lips and eagerly caressed hers with his own.

A tender moment that she never wanted to end fell upon them. It seemed as if the whole world grew silent while under moonlit shadows, Rick Hamilton took Konni's breath away.

Chapter 8

Hi, Rick!" Konni's voice called from behind him in the church sanctuary. He turned to her. "Good morning." Her face looked as happy as he felt. No doubt about it, their relationship had taken a turn for the better.

"Want to sit over there?" she asked, pointing to a pew halfway toward the front.

"Sure." He escorted her through the room, passing out greetings along the way. The praise band played quiet songs of worship as Konni and Rick settled into their seats.

Rick warred with himself over whether or not he should grab Konni's hand. They were, after all, in public, and he wasn't sure how she would respond. His heart pounded hard against his chest like a schoolboy in love. He told himself he was being silly. After all, he was forty-eight-years old. Just as he lifted his hand to reach for hers, she abruptly turned to him. Fortunately, she didn't see him almost jump out of his skin.

"Oh dear, I forgot to tell Rhonda where I placed her new quarterly. Will you excuse me a moment, Rick?"

He swallowed hard. His Adam's apple seemed to wedge itself between his collarbones like an elevator stuck on the basement floor. "Oh, sure."

Konni smiled and walked away. Rick figured it was just as well. They'd had a great time last night. In honest moments over coffee, they shared their fears and dreams of the future. They talked of a relationship and the risks involved. Still, they had agreed to take baby steps together and see where it led them.

One thing Rick knew for sure, he didn't want to do anything to blow his chances with her this time. As fragile as her heart was, he may not get another chance.

"Well, good morning, Rick. I was hoping you'd be here. May I sit down?"

Rick turned to the voice and looked up into the smiling face of Haley Green.

❦

"Hey, Mom, you doing okay?" Emily's expression suggested a problem.

Konni almost laughed, then thought better of it when she saw the seriousness on her daughter's face. "I'm fine. Why? Do I look all flushed or something?" She winked, remembering she had told Emily about Rick's kiss last night.

"Mom, let's go sit down somewhere." Emily tugged on Konni's arm.

"Emily, what is the matter with you? The service is about to begin. I need to get back in and sit down with Rick. He'll wonder where I am."

"Wow!" interjected Emily's friend Nate. "Who is that gorgeous blond with your friend, Mrs. Strong? Is that his sister or something? I'd sure like to meet the likes of her." Emily turned to Nate and gouged him in the side. "Ouch! What did I do?"

Konni stared at both of them, then went to the sanctuary door and peered in. There beside Rick sat the woman she had seen him with in the restaurant. Konni swallowed hard. She turned back to Emily.

"Mom, you want to go?"

Konni took a deep breath and shook her head. "I can't run from my problems, Em."

Emily reached up and gave her mom a hug. "I'll be praying for you."

"I'll be fine, honey. You go on to service."

Emily nodded. Konni watched as Emily walked up to a group of her friends and they made their way into the sanctuary. Emily tossed one more glance toward her mom. Konni waved just before the kids stepped out of sight.

How humiliating. The whole church would notice Rick sitting with that woman. "Poor Konni," they would say, offering her sorrowful glances and hugs. She inhaled long and deeply. Her chin lifted, shoulders straightened. She could do this. Stepping into the sanctuary, Konni slipped into an empty spot in the back row.

The service seemed to take forever. Konni didn't hear a word of the message. It took all her efforts to contain her racing emotions. She wanted to teach Emily to face her problems, so Konni forced herself to stay. But as soon as the benediction was over, Konni rushed through the crowd to get to her car.

"Konni!"

She could hear Rick's voice but kept moving.

"Konni!" He was closer now. She had no choice. She turned to him. "Yes?"

"Where were you? You never came back."

She couldn't let him think for a moment she was jealous. "Oh, I got caught up with some business."

He looked at her as though he didn't believe her. "Want to go to lunch?"

She shook her head. "Not today, Rick." Adrenaline made her bold. "You know, I've really been thinking about last night, and I just don't think I'm ready for a relationship, Rick." Her breath was short and choppy, like she'd been running a marathon. "I'm sorry." With that, she turned on her heels, all but ran to her car, and climbed in.

Starting the engine, she pulled her car into gear and never once looked back.

❦

Rick's jaw dropped. With honest confusion, he watched Konni's car leave the lot. "What was that all about?"

"Hmm? Did you say something, Rick?" Haley stepped up behind him, placing her hand possessively on his arm. Concern filled her eyes.

His glance went from her hand, to her face, to Konni's fleeing car.

The answer became all too clear.

❦

Thankful that Emily wouldn't be home for a while, Konni went into her bedroom and threw herself on the bed. She couldn't believe she had fallen so hard for Rick and was now dealing with yet another loss.

She leaned back against her pillows. What had happened today? One minute, she sat happily with Rick; the next minute, someone had taken her place. Just that fast. Did she know him so little? Was he playing two women at the same time? He did, after all, call himself "Romeo." Maybe there was more to it than she realized.

She shook her head. It made no sense. Rick didn't seem that type of guy. Oh, she didn't know what to think anymore. Her heart uttered a prayer for guidance and strength. Only this time, a new verse came to mind, 2 Corinthians 5:17: "Therefore if any man be in Christ, he is a new creature: old things are passed away; behold, all things are become new."

It seemed an odd verse to come to her mind at that moment. "What are you trying to tell me, Lord?" The words played over and over.

Hadn't she allowed the Lord to touch her life afresh? Hadn't she put her past behind her—or at least attempted to? Okay, she was still working on that one.

She had taken a huge leap, allowing Rick passage into her heart. Now pain exploded in her chest with one blow. In the midst of her turmoil, a thought struck her. She hadn't given Rick a chance to explain. But he didn't owe her an explanation, did he? She stared at the ceiling. Still, if he had wanted to offer one, she hadn't given him the chance.

Whether she wanted to admit it or not, she had run away. Just like she'd been running for the past five years. Running from anything that remotely resembled conflict, rejection, or loss.

Misery sank to the pit of her stomach. Just then, the phone on her night-stand rang, startling her.

She let it ring. The caller could leave a message. If it was Emily, Konni would know and could answer.

"Yeah, Konni, this is Rick. Hey, I just wanted to say, well, I'm not sure what happened this morning, but if it has to do with the woman you saw me with at church, I can explain. Will you give me the chance?"

Oh, she wanted to reach over and grab the phone and tell him how she truly felt, but the image of the woman beside him at church kept Konni per-fectly still, like a mummy in grave clothes. She waited, then decided to give him a chance. She reached for the phone, but instead of Rick's voice, the dial tone buzzed in her ear.

She rolled over on her bed. She'd allow herself a little time to sulk, then she'd pull up her boot straps and get back into the game of life. Rick's excuses could not lessen the pain of her embarrassment at being replaced on Sunday. She balled herself into the pillow. Somehow, she'd get through this.

She had to.

⚘

"Are you okay?" Haley asked when Rick returned to their booth.

"I'm fine. I just needed to make a phone call." He sat down in his seat, and Haley made an obvious shift to his side. Though uncomfortable, he was glad he brought her to lunch to deal with this matter before it got out of control.

"I'm just glad you're back." Her hand reached over to stroke his arm.

He shrank away. "Look, Haley, you're a beautiful woman—"

"Don't. Please don't." She stopped him. After a moment's hesitation, she started gathering her things from the booth. "I knew you cared for her; I just thought I could turn your head my way," she said, edging toward the other end of the seat. "Guess I hadn't figured on you being in love."

Rick stared at her, not knowing what to say. He didn't want to hurt her.

"I know we still have to work together, but once I know where I stand, it's not a problem. So we'll keep things strictly professional from here on out, okay?"

"Look, Haley, I'm sorry."

"Yeah, that's what all the good ones say." She threw him a meager smile and left him to eat lunch alone.

Rick sat in his recliner and stared at the phone in his hand, the dial tone blaring at him like a sassy teenager. How many messages had he left on Konni's answering machine over the past two weeks? Couldn't she at least return one phone call? What about the e-mails? She made it obvious she wanted nothing more to do with him.

He hadn't returned to Hope Village. Though it had become his own church home, he didn't want Konni to quit going because of him. He prayed for guidance. The situation seemed hopeless. He told himself he should let her go. Yet she was the one who had told him there was always hope. There had to be something else he could do.

The coffee shop. Saturday was the day she usually showed up there. At least he could make one last effort. If she still brushed him off, well, then he knew what to do.

His heart would say good-bye to Konni Strong.

Chapter 9

Rick rushed over to Chatting Grounds Coffeehouse, all the while praying for God's direction, whether that meant a future with or without Konni. He had to know where this was going.

He stepped out of his car and pushed through the entrance of the shop. Looking around, he didn't see Konni. Disappointed but not yet defeated, he went to the counter and ordered a latte.

Once he received his drink, he sat down behind a wooden table and tried to relax. Sipping the hot beverage, he mulled the situation over in his mind like a child's hands worked through Play-Doh. Before he could come up with an answer, the door swished open and in walked Konni. His stomach churned.

He gave her a moment to order her drink, and while she waited for it, he walked up behind her.

"Konni, please don't run."

She turned to him with a start. "Rick! Hi." Her face flushed.

"Konni, please, can we talk? Just this one time, and I'll never bother you again." He kept his voice soft and low, for her ears only.

She bit her lip and looked toward the lady who fixed her drink. "Where are you sitting?"

He finally took a breath and pointed toward his table. She nodded. He went back to the table, and once her drink was ready, she joined him.

"Look, I'm not sure what happened between us, but if it has anything to do with Haley, it's all a misunderstanding."

"Haley?"

He nodded. "She's the woman you saw me with at church. She's works with me as an assistant superintendent. We're coworkers. Nothing more."

"You don't owe me an explanation, Rick."

He grabbed her hand. She looked up at him. "Yes, I do. I want to pursue this thing between us, find out where it takes us."

She pulled her hand away. "I've found out something about myself in the past few weeks, Rick. I care a lot about you. I really do. But I don't want a serious relationship. With anyone. Ever."

"You can't mean that, Konni. You have your whole life ahead of you."

"Why does everyone keep saying that? Life is full of pain. I don't like pain, Rick." She paused. "I guess I just want to play it safe."

"Occasional dinner and coffee dates, that's it?"

She looked at him with defeat. "I'm afraid so. I'm sure you don't want that, so we'll leave it here."

His eyes pinned hers. "Actually, I'll take that. For now."

Konni shifted in her seat and took a drink.

"I'm not ready to give up on us, Konni Strong. Not yet." Rick threw her a look that said he meant every word.

The summer sun warmed Konni's back as she carried the last load of Emily's belongings into the college dorm.

"You sure you have to start now? Why can't you wait till the fall like most kids?" Konni asked.

"Mom, I told you, they only offer these classes in the summer. Might as well get them over with."

Konni nodded reluctantly.

"You sure you'll be all right?" Emily eyed her carefully.

"Here we go again, you playing the mom role."

They both laughed. Konni's eyes scanned the messy room. "The question is, will *you* be all right?"

Emily laughed. "I'll be fine."

Konni pulled her daughter into a long embrace and kissed her on the cheek. "Call anytime, okay? Study hard; come home when you can. Go easy on the guys."

"Yeah, right. You know guys are off-limits for me. I can't risk losing my scholarship."

"Just don't forget to enjoy yourself once in a while, Em."

"You're a good one to talk," Emily said with a laugh. "Give Rick a chance, will ya, Mom? He's a nice guy, and I think he really cares about you."

"I'm doing okay, really. You don't have to have a man to be happy, you know." Konni poked her finger in Emily's side.

Emily giggled, then stared her mother square in the face. "Are you happy?"

The light bantering stopped. Konni shrugged. "Let's just say I'm working on it." Konni smiled. "Keep in touch, okay? I love you."

"Love you, too, Mom."

Konni walked out the door, feeling lonelier than she'd ever felt in her life.

Rick and Konni had met for coffee and dinner a couple of times, but staying true to her word, Konni kept her distance. They were definitely back at the "friend" level.

He knew she grieved over Emily's absence. Konni lived her days locked in a world of memories, and he had no clue how to break her free. Things had been going so well until the interruption with Haley. Konni had been too vulnerable at the time. Too fragile. Now he didn't know if she would ever trust him—or anyone else—again.

The TV murmured in the distance while he wondered where this left him. After all, he couldn't wait forever. Could he? The phone rang, jarring him to his senses. "Hello?"

"Yes, I'm looking for a Dr. Rick Hamilton, superintendent of Hartley South School District in Loudon, Vermont," the male voice said.

"This is Rick Hamilton."

"Yes, Dr. Hamilton, this is Dr. Wedgewood calling from Macon County, Florida. We are currently in search of a superintendent for our school corporation here in Macon County. Your name has been referred to us, and we wanted to talk to you about a possible job change. Would you be interested?"

Rick's mind raced with what to do. He didn't normally switch positions so frequently. After all, he hadn't been in Loudon for a full year yet. He wouldn't leave Konni for the world if he thought there was any hope, yet if she wanted nothing more than friendship, he didn't know if he could stick around.

"Dr. Hamilton?"

"Yes, I'm still here."

"Well, I can tell we have taken you by surprise. How about we give you a week to think about it? If you decide you're interested, call us. We'll talk. Would that work for you?"

"That would be fine. I appreciate your consideration," Rick said. He spent the next few minutes getting the necessary contact information. When he finally hung the phone up, his hands were trembling. After spending time in prayer, Rick finally decided what he would do.

Without telling Konni of his job offer, he would declare his love to her. If she accepted it, he would stay. If she refused him, he would leave. His future was in her hands.

He prayed Konni Strong would make the right decision.

❧

"So, you doing okay?" Rick asked Konni over coffee.

She cradled the cup in her hands and looked up. "Yeah."

"Look, Konni, I called you here because it's a private place where we can talk. I can't put this off any longer."

She looked at him, apprehension in her eyes.

He held up his hand. "Just hear me out. Then you can come to whatever conclusion you want."

Konni nodded and kept silent.

"When I came here, I didn't know anyone. Attending Stan and Abby's wedding changed all that. They brought you into my life. We became great friends and then something more—or at least I thought it was more.

"I never thought I'd get serious about anyone. People thought of me as a confirmed bachelor, and, well, that's what I was—and I liked it that way. I told you the reasons why. Fear of failure, I guess.

"But you—you changed all that. I was willing to risk failure rather than risk losing you. Still, misunderstandings happened and brought us to where we are today.

"We can't change the past, Konni, but we can change the future."

Rick took a deep breath. "I know you probably don't want to hear this, but I have to say it anyway. I love you. I've loved you from the moment you plowed into my chest at the wedding; it just took me awhile to realize it."

Konni's head felt hot. Rick spoke the words she had longed to hear, and now she didn't know if she could accept them. Love held too much pain. If she didn't get involved, if she just lived her life in a safe haven, she wouldn't get hurt. Ever. Though she loved him in a whole new way from Eric, she didn't think she could give her heart away again.

Rick grabbed her hand. "Being a confirmed bachelor, I never thought I'd say this. I'm ready to take a risk, Konni. I want to share my life with you. I'm asking you to be my wife."

Konni sat speechless in a hazy fog of confusion.

"I'm not asking for your answer right now. I know you said you didn't want a serious relationship, but please, think about it. Pray about it. I'll call you in a couple of days. We can talk it over then."

The kindness in his voice, the loving words felt like a gentle touch to her parched senses. Outwardly, she merely nodded. How could she lose him? But then how could she open her heart to yet another wound?

Rick threw their empty cups into the canister. He grabbed her hand and walked her to her car. Once they got there, he pulled her hand up to his lips. A look of desperation shadowed his face. He closed his eyes and for one long moment pressed his lips hard against the back of her hand. He looked at her. "No matter what our future holds, I will always love you, Konni."

Without a word, she turned and slipped into her car. All the while, her heart cried out in the darkness, *Father, please, show me what to do.*

❧

"Oh, Irene, I just don't know which way to turn," Konni said, after explaining and discussing her problem with her friend.

Irene quietly walked over to a carved wooden jewelry box. She opened the lid and slipped out a beautiful gold chain with a small watch encircled with diamonds. She walked back and placed it in the palm of Konni's hand.

"Oh, my, Irene, this is beautiful."

"My wedding gift. Orville gave that to me more than sixty-five years ago." She shook her head. "Hard to believe it's been so long." She looked at the watch with remembrance. " 'Irene,' he said, 'we need to enjoy every moment together. Life don't hold no guarantees.' " Irene laughed. "His English wasn't the best." She turned serious once again. "Bless his heart, he was right."

Tears formed in Konni's eyes.

"I want you to have this."

"What?" Konni asked incredulously.

Irene folded Konni's fingers over the necklace. "It's my reminder to you. Enjoy your moments, Konni. True love doesn't always come when we're ready for it. Life doesn't hold any guarantees. You could marry Rick, and yes, he could die."

Her voice fell to a whisper; she looked Konni full in the face, still holding her hand. "Or you could let him go and *you* will die."

Konni understood. She nodded and pulled Irene into a strong hug. "I love you."

"And I love you, dear." Irene pulled away.

They talked a little longer; then Konni excused herself, knowing she had much to think about. From her car, she waved to Irene and pulled onto the road. Her thoughts raced. Could she trust her heart again? What of the pain? She couldn't bear any more. Yet if she lost Rick now, she'd have pain just the same. Working the matter over in her mind, she drove into the country—how far, she didn't know. All the while, her cluttered thoughts tossed about like ragged books cleared from an attic.

By the time her car had turned back toward town and reached Rick's house, she'd decided Irene was right. Peace had settled over her, and her mind was made up.

❧

Rick heard a car door in his driveway and couldn't imagine who would visit him at such a late hour. He brushed the chips from his T-shirt and denim shorts, making his way to the door. He twisted the knob and pulled the door open.

Konni stood in the entrance. "Do you have a minute, Rick?" Red, puffy eyes greeted him, but something in them said she had come to a decision.

Rick let out a shaky grin and stepped aside. "You want something to drink?" he asked, closing the door behind him.

"No, thanks." Konni sat on the couch. She smiled and patted the seat beside her.

That encouraged him. Surely she wouldn't be that chipper if she had bad news. Somewhat guarded, he sat down and looked at her.

She grabbed his hands, shooting sparks up his arms. "Rick, I've been wrong. I've been so afraid of getting hurt, it's like I put my heart in a box and tucked it in a secret hideaway that no one could reach. I won't tell you this is easy. I'm frightened. Very frightened. But I love you, and to quote the man I love, 'I'm willing to take this risk, because I can't take the risk of losing you.'"

Rick pulled Konni into his arms, his chest tight against her so that he could feel the beating of her heart. Never had he loved anyone so deeply. Feverishly, he kissed her hair, her eyes, her forehead, and finally her lips, as if the moment might slip away. Their laughs mingled with tears.

"I want to marry you, Konni Strong."

"And I want to be your wife, Rick Hamilton." She kissed him this time. Long and hard.

When they pulled away, Rick told Konni of his job offer and how he had let her make his decision for him.

"When I think of how I could have lost you forever. . ." Konni stopped. "Thankfully, the Lord used Irene to guide me and bring me to my senses." She showed Rick the watch and explained the story.

He wiggled his eyebrows. "Hmm, she did say I was a good one."

Konni laughed. "And she was right."

"So, when are we getting married?"

"Well, it takes awhile to get everything ready, but just a small wedding should do it—you've never done this before, so I want it to be nice for you."

"It will be great for me because you'll be there." He kissed her again. She snuggled into him on the sofa, her head against his shoulder.

"I know one thing for sure," she said.

"Hmm, what's that?" he asked, his fingers gently stroking her hair.

"I know just the petals I want to tuck into my bouquet."

"You still have those bouquet pieces?"

"Uh-huh. For some reason I couldn't part with them. But I never dreamed those petals would open a whole new world for me. For us."

"I like the sound of that," he whispered into her ear. "Petals of promise. I promise to love you forever, Konni."

She turned her smiling face up to him once again. "Could you seal that promise with a kiss?"

Rick's eyes held hers. He lowered his lips, brushing them tenderly against her own, thus sealing his promise on her lips, and on her heart, to love her forever. . . .

Rose in Bloom
By Sandra Petit

Dedication

God's timing is always perfect. And He wastes nothing.
Through every event, every activity, every person
who has touched my life, He has brought me to this point,
and I am truly grateful. Many have traveled along with me
through the journey, but a special few I'd like to acknowledge.
A big hug of appreciation to my husband, Todd,
and my children, Kate and Ben, for their love and support.
My parents, Leoncia and Austin Stevens, have encouraged
me wholeheartedly in whatever endeavor I have attempted.
Their faith in me has helped me to press on.
Lastly, a special thanks to my wonderful friend,
Gail Sattler, who was so generous in sharing
her most valuable asset—herself.

Chapter 1

The words Rose Bentley was about to speak froze in her throat as she caught sight of a movement out of the corner of her eye.

A small bundle of flowers, transformed into a missile when the bridal bouquet hit the ceiling fan, hurtled toward the prize wedding cake she'd made as her gift for Abby and Stan's nuptials.

Ignoring propriety, Rose sucked in a deep breath and leaped toward the flowers, praying she'd retained enough skill and agility from her softball days to save her culinary creation.

She stretched her arm to its limit, plucked the flowers from the air, and dropped neatly back to the ground in one smooth motion. She grinned as she stared at the blossoms in her hand. *Easy as snagging a pop fly.*

Her triumphant smile suddenly faded. The pink roses were beautiful, even though the fan had clipped some of the delicate petals, but these weren't ordinary flowers. Since they were part of the bride's bouquet, catching them traditionally meant she would be the next to marry.

That couldn't happen. Rose was still building her catering business, and at twenty-nine years old, she was finally starting to achieve some degree of success. Putting her business aside to marry wasn't on her agenda.

Rose wound her arm back to hurl the offending arrangement to the waiting single women gathered in the center of the large banquet hall at Country Meadows Inn—and hit a rock hard jaw.

Just as she began to turn, the jaw's owner grabbed her outstretched arm in an attempt to steady himself. Unsuccessful, he fell backward. Rose couldn't do anything except scream as he pulled her along with him.

Air whooshed out of her lungs, and the two of them crashed into the table, which collapsed beneath them. Plates, napkins, cake, and little bottles of Vermont maple syrup flew through the air. Then everything seemed to hit the ground at the same time with a resounding crash. Rose landed on her arm with a thud and felt a searing pain in her right shoulder as she lay still, holding the small piece of Abby's bouquet in her hand.

Best man Lucas Montgomery groaned, bringing her attention to his face.

His wide blue eyes bored into hers. White frosting covered his strong, chiseled chin, and the tiny plastic bridegroom was lodged in his charcoal-black hair, glued in place by a blob of the sticky white icing.

Abby's beautiful cake—the one Rose had spent days making—lay in ruins on the floor around them.

By the heat on her face, Rose knew her cheeks were flaming. She tried to raise herself off Lucas, but sank back in pain.

"Ow!"

"What's wrong?" Lucas asked, his voice filled with concern. "Is it your arm?"

"Yes. No, the shoulder I think." She blinked back tears and gritted her teeth with the pain. She inhaled sharply as he turned her gently so her back was to his chest.

"I'll help you up."

He wrapped his arms around her to help her keep the injured arm immobile, then sat up, bringing her with him. She closed her eyes and fought the pain and nausea that rolled over her. She recognized the sensations, having dislocated her shoulder years ago playing softball. Her doctor had warned her it could happen again. The memories were not pleasant.

Lord, help me get through this.

Lucas helped her to her feet. Before she could say anything, footsteps echoed behind her. "Rosie! Are you okay?" Her bridal gown flowing around her, Abby came to an abrupt halt a few inches from Rose.

Laughter sounded from other parts of the room, but there were muffled conversations in the area surrounding the cake as some guests realized she'd been hurt. People began to gather around to see if they could help.

Rose opened her mouth to answer Abby, but the lump in her throat prevented her from speaking. She ached for someone to take care of her. It was at times like this that being independent wasn't such fun. The thought had no sooner left her than her widowed sister, Alexandra, raced up.

"Rosie. Are you all right?"

Lucas saved her the trouble of answering. "It looks like her shoulder is dislocated. I grabbed her as I was going down." He turned to face Rose. "This is my fault. I'm so sorry."

"It was an accident," Rose said quietly, though even she could hear the strain in her voice. She moved to step away from him, but his arm tightened around her.

"You need to see a doctor right away. I'll drive you."

"I can take her," Alexandra said.

"I–I can't just leave. . . ." Rose's voice trailed off. She closed her eyes against another wave of nausea as she leaned into Lucas.

"Yes, you can. Abby?" Lucas looked at Abby.

"You can't take the baby to the hospital," Rose said to Alexandra, before Abby could reply. "It's no place for Mia."

Stan appeared beside Abby. "Lucas, if you can take care of Rose, we'll take care of everything here. We already have a crew for cleanup, and I'm sure arrangements can be made to get Rose's van to her later."

Lucas nodded. "I'll take care of her."

Someone handed Abby a stack of napkins, and she began to wipe frosting from Rose's arm. "I'm so sorry. I feel like this was my fault. If I hadn't thrown the bouquet. . ." Her voice trailed off as tears filled her eyes.

Rose laid her hand on Abby's and moved it away. Abby couldn't know that even that slight jarring was painful. "It wasn't your fault. It wasn't anyone's fault."

Stan moved up beside Abby and put his arm around her. "It was an accident, Sweetheart."

Lucas looked at Rose. "We'd better get going."

Rose hesitated. "There are still some people who didn't get cake."

The three of them looked at her, and Rose felt her face heat once again. "I guess that's not really a problem since there isn't any more cake. I'm so sorry, Abby. I'll make you another cake."

"That might not be for a while," Lucas said.

Rose's eyes widened even as she grimaced. "I have to make a cake just like this for Wednesday night. It takes three days to make. I don't have any choice. It's too late for them to get someone else. And Abby needs wedding cake for her first anniversary. It's tradition. She has to freeze it."

Rose noticed Stan watching Abby. His brow was drawn with concern, his entire attention on his bride. Soon Abby would leave Country Meadows Inn as Mrs. Stanleigh Chenkowski. The thought caused moisture to pool in Rose's eyes, but it wasn't because of her physical pain.

Lord, what about me? I know I asked You to help me get my business started. And You did that. Thank You. But I admit I'm coveting the love I see in Stan's eyes, the way he looks at Abby as though she's the only one in the room. Help me find someone who will look at me that way, Lord. Someone who will understand how important my business is to me. I feel so alone right now. I know that's foolish. You're with me, Lord. Please give me peace.

"We'll work out your baking schedule later. Right now, you need to get to a hospital." Lucas's voice pulled Rose back to her current situation.

"Don't worry about the guests," Stan put in, his gaze shifting to Rose. "They can eat the Bowser cake."

Rose gave him a weak smile. She was proud of the groom's cake, which she had shaped to look like Stan's basset hound. The chocolate cake and frosting had turned out just right. Rose worried that no one would want to "eat" Bowser, but she guessed if it were the only cake left, they'd enjoy the tasty treat.

Rose glanced at Lucas. He had taken the worst of the fall, shielding her with his broad shoulders from being immersed in the creamy white icing. She cringed.

"It was my fault you fell in the first place."

"You do pack a wallop." He rubbed his jaw where her fist had connected, then winked. "Come on. Let's get this shoulder taken care of."

"All right." Rose turned to her sister. "I'll call you later."

Lucas placed Rose's coat over her shoulders since she couldn't move her arm to put it on. He gently wrapped his arm around her and guided her toward the door as they left the reception, the errant bouquet still in Rose's hand.

∞

Lucas looked at Rose, asleep on the seat beside him, as he drove to her apartment. Rose's sister was going to meet them at the apartment and stay the night with her.

The trip to the hospital had been difficult. Rose was in a lot of pain, and more than once he detected a tear slipping down her face, each one a stab at his heart. The attending physician couldn't give her anything for the pain until X-rays were taken, which he'd ordered immediately. When the diagnosis was confirmed, Rose was finally given medication, and the doctor popped her shoulder back in, giving her some relief. He'd given instructions that she was to rest the arm for several weeks.

Rose said she'd dislocated her shoulder twice before in high school, and the doctor told them that was probably why it had been so easy to dislocate again. Still, Lucas felt responsible.

He drove into the parking lot, turned off the engine, and walked around to the other side of the car to open Rose's door. He touched her good shoulder lightly.

"Rose?" She glanced up at him, groggy from the pain pills.

He picked up the piece of the bouquet she'd caught at the reception. He assumed it meant a lot to her, so he wanted to make sure she didn't lose it. It was the least he could do. He crooked his arm around her waist and helped her up the stairs, surprised at how small she was. How could such a little thing pack such a punch? He chuckled at the memory of her fist hitting his face.

When he got to the door, he knocked softly. Rose's sister opened the door, holding her baby. A large cat was wrapped around her legs.

"How is she?"

"I'm fine," Rose grumbled. "And I'm right here."

"Like you'd tell me the truth. Lucas?"

"She's a little loopy from the medication," Lucas replied, "but otherwise, okay. She's to take it easy and not use that arm for a while." He guided Rose to the sofa, removed her coat, and eased her down. The cat crept up and plopped itself down beside Rose, who murmured to it. "She'll probably sleep through the night."

"Thanks for taking her to the hospital."

"If you need anything—anything—call me." Lucas pulled out a business card and placed it on the table next to the sofa. "My home and cell phone numbers are on there. I don't have a business number yet since those plans aren't finalized."

"I'm sure we'll be fine." She pulled a brightly colored afghan over Rose.

"I guess I'll get going. Rose, I'm really sorry about this."

Rose rolled her eyes. "I know. But you wouldn't have fallen if I hadn't hit you in the jaw."

He laughed. "Point taken. Your right hook almost knocked me out. Nevertheless, I feel responsible. If there's anything I can do, all you have to do is ask."

"Have you ever baked a wedding cake?"

His mouth dropped open. "No, but I am in the restaurant business. My brother is the cook. I can read, though, and I'm sure I could follow instructions."

"Like I told you, I have to bake an anniversary cake for the Warners for Wednesday night. It takes three days, so I don't have time to look for another worker. If you're really serious, I could use your help on Monday. I can probably find someone else for the rest of the week."

"You don't need to find anyone else. I'll be glad to help. Besides, I owe Abby that top layer. I need to replace it."

Her deep sigh tore at his heart. "I guess I don't really have any choice."

"Then I'll see you on Monday."

"Thanks." She reached into her purse and pulled out a business card. "Here's the address."

Lucas tucked the card into his pocket.

Rose gave him a small smile. "Don't feel so bad. It could have been worse."

He didn't know how, but he accepted her words to ease his conscience.

❦

Lucas steered the car toward home. He loved living in the suburbs of Loudon, Vermont. Though the two-story house reflected his prosperity, it was too large for a single man living alone. Now that his business success was all but assured, his greatest desire was to have a family to fill the big house. He prayed daily for God to grant his wish.

Sighing, he entered the house, threw his keys on the small table by the door, and hung his jacket on the nearby coatrack.

Since it was getting late, he headed upstairs to shower and prepare for bed. Pulling his loose change out of his pocket, he felt the card Rose had given him fall into his hand and glanced down at it.

> *Rosie's Catering*
> *311 Arby Avenue*

His eyes widened and a lump formed in his throat. He and his brother, Nick, had just purchased 311 Arby Avenue for their new restaurant. It was apparently also the building Rose rented for her catering shop.

Lucas ran a hand over his face. This was not good. He knew his brother had scoured the city for the perfect building to use for the new venture that would bring them back home, close to their parents. Nick said the Arby property had all the facilities they needed in a perfect location. They had agreed to make the purchase when the owner assured them the present renter was not interested in buying. A suspicion crept into his mind, however, that if Rose was the tenant in question, she knew nothing about the sale.

A catering business brought the food to the customer, so location wasn't as big an issue as it was with a restaurant. He needed the location; she didn't.

If she didn't know the building had been sold out from under her, she would soon. He'd faxed the signed agreement to Jerrold Inkman that morning. He was now legally bound. Not only that, but he really wanted this building. It was perfect for his needs. However, he didn't want to hurt Rose. He'd already caused her enough problems. Besides that, she was a nice woman, and he wanted to get to know her better.

As trite as it seemed, the moment he'd seen her, he'd felt an attraction. He'd even gone so far as to ask Stan about her.

"Nice, but focused on her career," Stan had said.

His shoulders slumped. He'd finally met a woman who interested him, and very soon she was going to hate the sight of him. He didn't want that to happen. The image of Rose's deep brown eyes looking down at him as he lay among the cake would haunt his dreams tonight.

And he realized Stan was correct. Rose's business was her life 24-7. That being the case, he'd make it his life, too, at least until her shoulder healed—and she got to know him better. Of course, she might run him over with her van once she found out he was shoving Rosie's Catering into the street.

Lucas sighed. Maybe she wouldn't have to find out. Not right away. Not that he'd lie to her. He wouldn't do that. He simply wouldn't tell her everything, making him guilty only of omission. He could let her landlord be the bearer of the bad news. *After* she realized she couldn't live without Lucas Montgomery.

He headed for the shower, deep in thought. Before he went to sleep tonight, he concluded it would be a good idea to spend some time in prayer. A lot of time.

Chapter 2

Lucas stared at the recipe in his hands. It listed amounts and ingredients but didn't tell him when everything needed to be done or how. He glanced at Rose. She said she wasn't in pain, just uncomfortable. She refused to take any pills because they made her sleepy. There was nothing he could do about it. She was an adult. He couldn't force her to take medication she didn't want to take, so he gave up and moved on.

"What do I do first?" he asked.

Rose yawned. "Make some coffee, and let's have breakfast. It always takes me awhile to get going on a Monday morning."

Coffee. That was something he could do. He was glad he'd picked up breakfast on his way in. A few minutes later, he joined her at the table and said a brief blessing over the food. He watched closely to be sure Rose didn't have any trouble and refilled her cup when it was empty.

"What made you decide to become a caterer?" he asked, taking a bite of his bacon, egg, and cheese biscuit.

"Not what. Who. Abby. I was always interested in baking, but I didn't have the money for the course. She encouraged me to share my feelings with Mom and Dad. They financed my education at the Culinary Arts Institute. It took all their savings and then some."

"They must be very proud of you."

She bit her lip, and her voice caught as she spoke. "They were killed in a car accident the night I catered my first party—but yes, I think they were proud."

"I'm sorry. That must have been rough." He reached over and squeezed her hand.

"It was. I still miss them." She paused. "I don't usually talk about it except with Alex."

Lucas winced. Who was Alex? "I'm glad you can talk to me. I'd like for us to be friends." He gave her an encouraging smile, squeezed her hand again, and released it. She returned the smile with a sad one of her own. He couldn't pull his eyes away. Those deep brown eyes showed every emotion.

Lucas's heart beat faster, but he resisted the urge to lift his hand and touch the light brown hair that framed her face. Instead, he stood. It was time to start baking.

❧

Rose watched Lucas struggling to get the top off the tub of flour, frustrated that she couldn't help. "It should just come off," she grumbled. "I never have any trouble with it."

"I think it's glued on," Lucas muttered as he pulled hard.

Rose backed up, shielding her arm. Lucas jerked the top off; the tub hit the edge of the counter, then slid out of his hand. He reached to catch the tub and slipped. Both tub and Lucas hit the floor. A cloud of white flour flew into the air and settled on top of Lucas. Rose giggled, and Lucas shifted his gaze to glare at her.

"You should have put your apron on," Rose quipped.

His scowl deepened. "Men don't wear aprons."

"Right."

Rose bit her lip and struggled to contain her laughter.

Lucas stood and dusted himself off. "Where's your broom and dustpan?"

Rose pointed to the closet in the corner. "I'd help if I could."

"Not a problem."

A wedding cake was not a beginner project. Doing it herself would take less time than explaining it to him, but she didn't have any choice. She had an obligation to make this cake for Wednesday. It took three days. There wasn't room for error.

Since Lucas was willing, she was going to have to accept his help, even if she wasn't sure she wanted to spend several days in his company.

The Warners had contracted her to bake an anniversary cake months ago. They would repeat their wedding vows and then host a reception where everyone could share in their joy. Fifty years together. It was remarkable. Rose wondered if she would ever find a man who would love her that much. When she married, she wanted it to be forever.

Her gaze moved to Lucas. He had dressed casually, in jeans and a yellow T-shirt. His face was clean-shaven, and when he'd helped her inside, the woodsy scent of his aftershave had tickled her nose.

His blue eyes had dark circles under them as though he hadn't slept well, and his black hair—now heavily dusted with flour—had that mussed look one might get from driving with the top down, though she knew he certainly wasn't doing that in Vermont in March. He looked like a man who desperately needed caffeine, which was why she'd suggested coffee.

She knew he felt guilty about her injury even though she'd told him several times it wasn't his fault.

Lucas interrupted her thoughts. "All cleaned up. What do I need to do now?"

"Put on an apron," Rose said, laughing. "Then the ingredients need to be measured out. The measuring cups are in that cabinet to your right. Then you can get the pans ready."

Grumbling, Lucas reluctantly grabbed an apron, then gathered ingredients and sat at the table with Rose.

"Maybe I could help," Rose said.

Lucas looked up. "Your job is supervisor. Doc said you have to take it easy for a few days."

Rose sighed. "All right, but we can't mix it all at one time, so we'll make the four small cakes first. That's eight cups of batter."

Lucas finished measuring and set the ingredients aside. "Now you want me to get the pans ready?" At her nod, he looked at the pans and grinned wryly. "How does one make a pan ready? Do you want me to have a talk with it? Explain what's going to happen?"

Rose stared at him. Then her mouth turned up, and she started to laugh until tears streamed down her face. Lucas was smiling. Finally, she pursed her lips together and got herself under control. She suddenly realized she'd been so intent on making a success of her business, she hadn't laughed much lately. It felt good.

She took a deep breath. "Um. The pans. You need to spread a thin layer of cake release on the bottom and sides of each pan with a pastry brush. It helps the cake to slide out of the pan more easily. It's the yellow container there on the counter. I'll turn the oven on to preheat." She stood, half expecting Lucas to object, but he simply began to work.

While Lucas prepared the pans, Rose carefully carried the measured ingredients, one at a time, to the counter where her large mixing bowl sat.

"I didn't realize how much batter it would take."

Rose turned. Lucas was standing right behind her. Having him so close made her breath catch. She moved slightly to put some distance between them. "We're making six double-layer cakes, and one of those is sixteen-inches square. That's a lot of batter."

"Hmm. You can sit down now. I'll do this. Do I just put it all in there and turn it on?"

Rose blinked. "Well, yes, but slowly and carefully. You don't want batter to go flying all over the place. And you need to use the spatula along the sides." She sighed, frustrated. How could she explain it to him?

Lucas placed his finger under her chin and lifted it so her eyes met his.

"Hey. I know this is hard for you, but there's no choice here. We'll do the best we can. I'm really trying. Okay?"

Rose bit her lip and nodded. He was trying. She could see that. It wasn't his fault he didn't know what he was doing. "You're doing a good job. I appreciate it." She watched him mix the batter.

"How much of this goes in each pan?" Lucas asked.

"Fill them halfway."

He nodded and proceeded to do just that. The first cakes were placed in the oven and the timer set.

"So that's that," Lucas said, a big smile on his face.

Rose laughed. "Not exactly. Now we need to prepare the cardboard pieces the cakes will sit on. The two large cakes are stacked."

"Cardboard pieces?"

"Uh-huh. We'll need waxed paper, scissors, and my cutter to make the center hole in the cardboard."

Lucas gathered the pieces, and Rose explained what to do.

"That doesn't sound complicated," Lucas said. "Why don't you rest while I do that? Want some more coffee? A danish? A pain pill?"

Rose hesitated. "No pain pills, but I'll have some coffee."

Lucas brought her a cup of coffee, then began to work. As he worked, he talked, inserting humorous anecdotes about things that had happened at his restaurants. Rose found herself enjoying the time and laughing more than she had in a long time.

Lucas insisted on ordering lunch from the Chinese restaurant down the street. As they sat down to eat, Lucas reached across the table for her hand and bowed his head. Rose hoped he didn't notice the way her pulse had increased at his touch. As soon as he said "Amen," she pulled her hand away and began to eat. But she almost choked at the first words out of Lucas's mouth.

"So, Rose, who's Alex?" he asked.

Rose's brows drew together. Lucas sat staring at her, his elbow on the table, his chin propped up with his hand.

"Alex—Alexandra—is my sister. I thought you knew that. Didn't I tell you she was staying with me the night I dislocated my shoulder?"

"Your sister was there, yes, but you didn't say that Alex was your sister, and you were in no shape to introduce us."

"Sorry. Alex is my sister. She's twenty-five, four years younger than I am. She's a widow and owns her own carpentry business. You met her baby daughter, Mia." Rose grinned mischievously. "Is that what you wanted to know?"

Chapter 3

Lucas's eyes lost their focus for a second, and he smiled. Perhaps he would get the chance to know Rose better. If she could forgive him for not telling her about his latest purchase.

"I know you said your parents are gone, and now I know you have a sister. Are there any other Bentley siblings?"

"No. What about you?"

"Just Nick and me. We get together for lunch at my parents' house often, usually on Sundays after church when we can make it."

"That's nice. Sounds like you're all close."

"We are. My folks aren't pushy, but they do keep reminding us what's important. It's not all work all the time." He paused and pointed his fork at her. "Who reminds Rose when it's time to put down the mixer and have some fun?"

Rose choked on her drink, then raised her head to stare at him. "I have fun."

He lifted one brow. "What do you do for fun?" Lucas fought a smile as he watched her struggle to come up with something.

"I–I–I go to church."

He couldn't stop his grin. "That's a good thing, of course, but I'd hardly consider it entertainment. What church do you attend?"

"Lakeview Bible."

"I've been there a couple of times. Large congregation." He didn't tell her that he'd tried Lakeview when he first returned to town and that he'd felt lost in the crowd there. While there wasn't anything wrong with attending a large church, Lucas felt more comfortable in a smaller congregation. When he'd found Hope Village, it had felt like coming home.

"Where do you go?"

He smiled. "Hope Village at the edge of town. It's like a family. Everyone knows everyone. Why don't you come to church with me on Sunday and see for yourself?"

"I don't know. Maybe."

Lucas nodded. He didn't want to push her, but he didn't know how much time he had. Surely it wouldn't be long before her landlord let her know her building had been sold, although hopefully it would be awhile before she found out to whom. When he'd entered the building that morning, he'd been surprised to find Rose only used the kitchen and office area. He hoped Inkman, the current owner, wasn't charging her for the entire building. He and Nick were going to open up the large front room for the restaurant and put in a refrigerated storage area in the attached warehouse. If business was good enough, the warehouse could be converted into additional seating later.

Rose stood and began to clear the table, but Lucas gently moved her aside and took care of the cleanup.

He listened carefully as Rose showed him how to check the cakes and remove them from the oven. After a few minutes, he removed them from the pans and set them on cardboard to finish cooling.

Lucas noticed the garbage can was full and decided to empty it. He lifted the bag from the large container and stepped to the door. He was turning the knob to open the back door when Rose whirled around.

"What. . .oh, no! Don't open the—"

Lucas turned his head as he pushed the door open. "What did you say? I didn't hear—"

A massive weight bumped against him. Unable to regain his balance, he felt himself falling to the floor as two huge dogs raced over him. Too stunned to move, Lucas remained on the floor, flat on his back, still grasping the garbage bag in his right hand. Cold air entered the room from the alley.

Rose screamed, and a huge crash echoed in the room. Lucas released the bag, jumped to his feet, and rushed to her side. Assured that she was all right, he surveyed the room.

The cakes they'd just spent the morning baking were in pieces on the floor—at least the pieces that weren't inside the dogs were on the floor. Rose was trying to grab one of the dogs. Lucas had a vision of her falling and spraining an ankle to go with her dislocated shoulder—again because of him.

"Rose, wait!" He grabbed hold of the two dogs and dragged them back outside, shutting the door firmly behind them. Then he picked up the garbage bag that had started the mess and very carefully exited the door and set the bag in the bin behind the shop, making sure the cover was tightly closed.

Returning to the kitchen, he stood next to Rose as they appraised the damage.

"I'm sorry. I had no idea."

"It's not your fault," she muttered. "I should have told you about the dogs. I've never seen anything like it, but these dogs love cake. Whenever I'm baking, they sit and wait by the door."

Lucas studied the disaster. "Does this happen every time you take out the garbage? Have you spoken to their owners? Or the animal control office?"

She sighed. "No. They're really nice dogs. They just love cake. If I have to open the door, I'm really careful. If I time it right, they're distracted when Wang puts his garbage out and they're down the street."

Lucas ran a hand down his face. "I'll sweep it up. And I'll pay for what was wasted. Then I guess we have to start over."

"I guess so." Her voice was tight, but she didn't yell at him.

He didn't quite know what to say to get himself out of this, but before he could come up with anything, the *Mission Impossible* theme song sounded in the room. Grinning at Rose, he lifted the cell phone attached to his waistband and pulled it open, leaning on the broom. "Montgomery."

"Lucas. Where are you?"

Lucas ignored the question. "What's the problem, Nick?"

"The Arby building owner, Mr. Inkman, hasn't informed his tenant of the sale or prepared the building, but his wife's had an automobile accident. He needs more time to take care of her, so he'd like us to wait to take possession. What do you think?"

It only took Lucas a moment to see that this would give him more time with Rose before she discovered the sale. "That sounds okay, but I'll talk to him." Lucas opened his mouth to say more, but suddenly realized Rose could hear every word he was saying. "I'll get back to you soon."

He ended the call and closed the phone.

"Do you need to go?" Rose asked.

He shrugged. "There are always problems. It can wait."

"If you need to take care of something, I understand. Maybe Alex can come and help me. The cakes will have to cool overnight anyway."

"I'm not going to desert you."

She scowled at him. "It's not your problem. I usually bake alone. It's only because—"

"You work too hard."

"I work as hard as I need to. My reputation is important to me. Failing is not an option, even if I have to stay up all night. I'll figure it out."

Lucas heard the defensive tone in her voice and knew he'd stepped over the line. He had no right to tell her what to do. He remembered the late nights when he'd opened his first restaurant. Starting a business was hard work. Yet he couldn't help worrying about Rose and wanting to make sure she didn't drive herself too hard. He also realized this was her business, and she wanted it to succeed as much as he wanted his own to do so. "All right.

Look, I'll mix up another batch of cakes, and while they're in the oven, I can take care of my problem and pick up some dinner for us. Does that sound okay to you?"

She sighed. "I suppose so. I'm sorry I snapped at you. Maybe it will go faster since we've done it once already. But we'd only done one batch, and there are six cakes to make, plus the replacement wedding layer."

"Abby's cake is no rush. She's not using it until her anniversary, right? I'll make it. I promise. We'll just take care of the rush job first."

He gathered all the supplies once again and set about making new cakes. As Rose had said, the second time went faster because he knew more about what he was doing. Once the cakes were in the oven, Rose went to lie down in the office, and Lucas hurried out the door to get their dinner and take care of Inkman, without Rose overhearing the conversation.

When he returned, Rose was sitting at the table. She looked up when he entered, relief evident in her face.

"Everything okay here?"

She nodded. "The cakes are almost done. I was worried you wouldn't get back in time."

"I said I would, and I keep my promises." It hadn't taken long to work things out with Inkman. The man was distraught and worried about his wife. Since Lucas was in no hurry to take possession, he'd okayed the delay and even agreed to give Inkman his money so his wife could receive the best treatment. Inkman promised to talk to his tenant as soon as things settled down for him. Since Lucas and Nick had agreed to give Rose time to find a new place to operate, he hoped that would ease the way to a relationship other than business with the woman who appeared to be capturing his heart.

Lucas removed the new cakes from the oven and mixed the next batch. It was very late when they finally finished all the baking, but Rose insisted all the cakes had to be finished before they could leave. They needed the next two days for other things. While he didn't understand how it could take three days to bake one cake, he had already caused Rose enough distress. If she wanted the cakes baked today, they'd be baked today. Her eyes were drooping, and he could see how tired she was.

When he'd taken the last cake out of the oven and cleaned up, he drove her home, promising to pick her up the following morning.

He left quickly because he was afraid after the dog disaster that she might decide she'd rather have another helper.

He didn't want her to say something like, "Don't come back."

Chapter 4

Lucas hesitantly knocked on Rose's door at six o'clock the next morning. He knew how tired he was, and he was sure Rose was in no better shape. After yesterday's disaster, he couldn't imagine what his welcome would be. Rose had been upset with him, he knew, though she hadn't reacted as he'd expected.

Before he'd fallen asleep, he'd prayed for Rose and for God's will regarding their blossoming relationship.

"Morning." Rose stood with the door open, wearing a button-down blouse and long denim skirt. Dark circles lined her eyes, and she yawned. "You're right on time."

"You look exhausted."

She frowned. "I'm fine. We can go now."

She stepped out, and Lucas moved his hand to the small of her back to guide her. Rose, however, didn't seem to want any assistance. She stiffened and moved ahead of him. He knew it distressed her to accept his help in making the cake. He wondered if she even allowed God to help her. That would be something they'd need to discuss before he allowed their relationship to go further. He knew she attended church, but he also knew that not everyone warming a church pew was a true believer, and it was important to him that any woman he was seriously involved with put God first.

When they arrived at the shop, he made coffee and set out the doughnuts he'd picked up for breakfast. He bowed his head and said a blessing before biting into a powdered doughnut, being careful not to get the fine powder all over everything. He'd seen enough flour yesterday to last him quite a long time.

"Do you always come in so early?"

Rose smiled. "Sometimes earlier. Depends on what I need to do."

"I'm not trying to criticize. It just seems you work so hard, even with an injury."

"I work hard because I want my business to be a success. I'm sure you work just as hard at your business. Why aren't you working, by the way?"

He shrugged. "My other restaurants are out of town. I have a manager at each restaurant, and I keep in touch through phone and fax. My brother left for Boston this morning to handle some problems."

"Oh. I thought your brother was the chef."

"He is, but we share the responsibilities. It's Nick's turn." Lucas watched as Rose took a sip of her coffee. "I was thinking about the wedding," he tried again.

"The wedding where we decided to wear the cake instead of eat it?" Her lips curved upward into a soft smile, and Lucas felt his heart kick into gear. *Slow down. She's just a friend. A beautiful friend. At least right now.*

He grinned. "That's the one."

"I remember." This time she chuckled.

"You caught those flowers like a pro."

"Alex and I were on the school softball team for years. I wasn't really that much of an athlete, but Alex loved it. That's where I hurt my shoulder before."

"We could use you on our church softball team. Your sister, too."

"Isn't it too cold for softball?"

"Actually, we start practicing in a few weeks, though it's a little cool, and our games begin locally in late April or May, depending on what other teams are available. Of course, your arm has to heal before you can play."

Rose grinned. "I've seen guys play football the next week after dislocating a shoulder."

Lucas gave her a scowl. "The doctor said weeks."

She laughed. "I know. I'll think about it and talk to Alex, too. Don't team members have to belong to your church?"

"We often invite friends to help us out since the church is so small. We play other churches in the area. Both sides have booths for donated foods, which we sell during the games. Each game's profit goes to a different charity or ministry effort. People come out to have some fun and support their favorite charities."

"Sounds like fun and a worthwhile project, too."

"It is. It's family entertainment, and it helps people who need it. My offer's still good to come to church with me on Sunday. You could meet some of the other members of the team even if you can't practice yet."

Rose looked down. "I don't know that I want to change churches."

"I didn't ask you to change. I just asked you to visit. Pastor Charles is a terrific speaker. I think you'll enjoy hearing him." Lucas angled his head slightly in the direction of the radio, tuned to a Christian station. "I also notice you like contemporary Christian music. We have a praise band and sing a lot of the contemporary songs."

"Sounds nice. I'll think about it."

"Great! I'll pick you up at nine for Sunday school."

"I didn't say I'd go."

He gave her a wide grin. "You didn't say you wouldn't."

⌘

Rose handed the cake leveler to Lucas. "You're going to level the cake so the layers will fit well together. Keep the legs of the leveler flat on the counter and cut into the cake at the same height, using an easy sliding motion." She demonstrated with her free hand. "Each cake needs to be leveled, so you'll have to adjust the height of the leveler with the different cakes. If you'll open the cans of apricots, I'll make the glaze while you're doing that."

"What's the glaze for?" Lucas opened the cans, then picked up the leveler and eyed the cake as he adjusted the height of the equipment.

"To keep the crumbs from messing up the icing."

"Will we have to let that cool overnight?"

"No. It will harden in fifteen minutes." She hesitated. "Then we start the fondant."

Lucas tilted his head to stare at her. The leveler wobbled, but he returned his attention before any damage was done. "The what?"

"Fondant. I used European fondant on the first cake." Rose bit her lip as she wondered if perhaps she should use an easier rolled fondant or simple icing. European fondant was difficult to make correctly. It took timing and skills she'd developed in her years as a pastry chef.

Besides that, her head was starting to ache. She lifted her hand to massage her temple.

"Problem?" Lucas raised an eyebrow as he looked at her.

"No." If she told him she had a headache, Lucas would insist she rest, and there wasn't time for that. She had to deliver this cake on time. Lucas was right. She did work hard, but it was necessary. For Alex and Mia. She owed them this.

Lucas finished leveling the cakes as Rose boiled the apricot preserves for the glaze. She approved his work, and then they each took a pastry brush and coated the cakes with the glaze. Though it was more difficult with her left hand, she could still handle the brush, and it made her feel useful.

Cakes set aside to dry, Rose considered her next words carefully.

"This is when I would normally make the fondant."

Lucas nodded.

"It's very precise. And it takes a long time."

Lucas grinned. "Are you trying to politely tell me you don't think I can do it?"

The heat of a blush crept up Rose's neck as she swallowed and nodded. "You don't understand."

Lucas stepped closer, and Rose sucked in a breath. He was invading her space, and though she wasn't afraid of him, she was uncomfortable. When he lifted her hand, however, she couldn't seem to pull away.

"I do understand, Rose. You've been doing this for a long time. I don't have a clue what I'm doing. But you do. And you can get me through it. You're going to be right here beside me." The way he said the words made her blink. It sounded intimate, though she knew he was just talking about her help in making the fondant. "It's going to work out. Have faith. Okay?" He gave her hand a squeeze, then let it drop. "Now what do we do first?"

Rose released the breath she'd been holding and stared at him. He was right. She needed to have more faith. God knew what this meant to her, and He would help them through it. Hadn't He gotten them through the disaster yesterday? Though they'd had to do everything twice, it was done.

With focused determination, she gathered the glucose, sugar, and water. European fondant had to be heated to exactly 240 degrees Fahrenheit and then allowed to cool to 110 degrees or it would become coarse and tough rather than smooth and pliable as it was supposed to be.

Lucas didn't attempt conversation or interrupt her. He just did what she told him to do. He concentrated totally on the job at hand. Since he was busy, Rose was able to watch him work. No man should look so good—his black hair, strong chin, and gorgeous blue eyes made her feel like a teenager with a hormone overload. She refused to give in to it. She was more than the sum of her hormones. And Lucas was more than the sum of his good looks. He was gentle and kind. He'd taken time from his own schedule to help her with this job, something he didn't have to do. It touched her heart.

After he poured the mixture onto the marble slab and sprinkled it with water, he started to work it with a steel scraper, folding it onto itself over and over again. Though the work was physical, it was brainless, and Lucas talked to her as he worked, bringing a smile to her face with his stories of his brother, Nick, and vacations they'd taken as children. He even coerced her into sharing memories of her parents, bringing both happy and sad tears.

When the fondant was finished, Lucas insisted she lie down to rest while he cleaned the kitchen. She was so tired that she agreed. He walked her to the office, and when she lay down, he touched her cheek gently before he left.

Rose closed her eyes. The warmth from Lucas's touch stayed with her long after he left the room. She dozed, and when she awoke, the lamp was on low and muted sounds were coming from the other room. She slid off the sofa and walked back to the kitchen.

Lucas had cleaned all the dishes and sat at the table, radio playing softly, hands folded on his stomach, chin on his chest, sound asleep. A smile tugged at her lips, knowing he was still there because he hadn't wanted to wake her. It had been a long time since anyone had taken such care of her.

Rose tiptoed to the chair and laid her hand lightly on his shoulder. "Lucas?"

His eyes opened and he smiled, reaching up to hold her hand that rested on his shoulder. "Hey. How are you feeling?"

"Rested. I think we should go home now, though. Thanks for cleaning up."

"Not a problem. I'll drive you home."

She nodded and followed him out, locking the door behind them.

Chapter 5

Lucas felt great relief when Rose pronounced the fondant usable. He'd already made the filling for the cakes, and Rose had explained how to apply a border around the edges and then fill in the center. When the second layer was placed on top, the filling spread perfectly.

He understood how much it frustrated her not to be able to help. He would have hated standing by and watching someone else do his work. Regardless of that, he was impressed with the way she had handled things. She'd accepted his help graciously, not even yelling when things went wrong.

Working side by side with Rose, Lucas found himself enjoying the camaraderie as they bantered back and forth. He loved listening to her easy laughter and watching her eyes crinkle when he said something that amused her. He found himself working harder to keep that smile in place. And he found himself wanting to talk to her about things he didn't normally discuss with others. It was becoming harder not to tell her about the building purchase. The guilt weighed him down.

When the filling was done, Rose carefully coached him in the application of the creamy fondant.

Lucas then prepared to make icing from the recipe Rose gave him. His brow furrowed as he concentrated on the instructions. Making icing couldn't be that hard, could it?

"Don't worry. You can't ruin it." The musical lilt of Rose's voice caressed him from across the room. "I've laid out all the ingredients so you can't use the wrong ones. We can adjust the amounts when you're done if it's not the right consistency."

Lucas turned to quirk an eyebrow at her. "Do I hear a note of sarcasm? You think I'm going to mess it up, don't you?"

Rose lowered her head, and he knew she was giggling as her shoulders shook in a quick rhythm. He loved being the cause of her merriment.

He understood that Rose had no intention of starting a relationship. Her business was still in its infancy. Independent as she was, he was sure she wanted to make it on her own. And he was sure she'd succeed, if having to change locations didn't discourage her from continuing to try. He sighed softly.

Lucas worked carefully, wanting to show that he respected her work and could share in it if necessary. She seemed pleased with the effort when they stopped for the day to let the whole thing dry overnight.

They stood together at the sink. Lucas washed his hands and then took Rose's hand in his to wash it for her. Her skin was soft, and he lifted his head to tell her so, but the words stuck in his throat. The look in her eyes was almost too much for him. His gaze lowered, and he had to fight against an urge to brush his lips over hers.

"We'd better go if we're going to do this again tomorrow," Rose said softly.

Lucas swallowed and nodded. He patted her hand dry, then locked up the building and drove her home.

~❧~

"Where's your apron?" Rose asked.

Lucas frowned. "We're not doing any baking today. No need for the aprons."

"Lucas." She stared at him, her eyes narrowing.

Lucas shook his head but acquiesced, tying an apron around his waist. He didn't want to think about why he gave in so easily, but he couldn't help smiling as he helped Rose wrap her huge apron around her thin frame.

"Let's get to that icing," he said with a laugh.

Rose showed him how to place the templates on the sides and mark them and then trace the designs with royal icing. He put together the church and steeple, then added icing to his creation. Rose had miniature flower arrangements to put on the four small square cakes.

When they sat down to eat a quick lunch of spaghetti with garlic bread, Rose complimented him on his efforts.

"I have to admit you've surprised me. I appreciate your help more than I can say."

"It's certainly been different from my regular workweek. I've enjoyed it." He wanted to say that he'd enjoyed being with her, but he didn't think Rose was ready to hear that.

At the end of the day, Lucas retrieved a camera from his car and took pictures of the finished cake. He stepped back to survey their work.

"Job well done, Miss Bentley."

"I wasn't sure we could do it."

"I admit to having some doubts myself. Especially when those dogs bowled me over."

"The look on your face was priceless." Her eyes sparkled with glee.

Lucas chuckled. "I'm sure it was." He lifted a hand to push a strand of wayward brown hair behind her ear. "You deserve a reward for doing this twice in as many weeks."

"Reward?" Her eyes widened as he took a step closer.

"Uh-huh." He lifted a hand and cupped the back of her head, then leaned over and touched his lips gently to hers, careful of her shoulder. It was a sweet kiss, not meant to frighten or pressure her. He was relieved when she didn't pull back but accepted the kiss and even seemed to enjoy it. He released her and smiled. "It's been fun."

"Your fun is my work." She met his eyes briefly and then looked away.

His smile faded. "That's right. I don't have to do it 24-7." At her look, he changed the subject. "When do you need to deliver this?"

She hesitated. "We could take it over to the church now and set it up."

Lucas nodded. He noticed she'd automatically included him in her plans and was inexplicably pleased. "Then that's what we'll do."

It wasn't as easy as it sounded, but finally they were able to load, transport, and deliver the cake to the church.

"Who's going to cut and serve?" Lucas asked.

Rose frowned. "I had planned to since I usually attend Bible study on Wednesdays anyway." She paused. "I think I could still do that. It only takes one hand to slice."

"Then it has to be put on plates. You'll need help, and you've already had a long day. I'll stay and help you."

"You've had a long day, too, and this is not your responsibility. You've done enough. Besides, don't you attend Bible study at your church?"

Lucas shook his head. "Not tonight. I'll take you home so you can rest awhile, and I'll pick you up in time for the ceremony. No arguments."

❧

"I can't believe you helped Rose make this cake." Mrs. Warner gave Lucas a bright smile. "When I heard about her accident on Saturday, I was really worried, but everything looks wonderful—and tastes wonderful, too." She turned to Rose. "What a blessing Mr. Montgomery was available to help."

Rose smiled. "Yes, ma'am, it was."

Lucas held his hands out in front of him in protest. "I only followed Rose's instructions."

He thought back to the ceremony they'd enjoyed just an hour earlier. The older couple had stood and professed their vows to one another, to keep God at the center of their lives and love one another forever. Their love was a wonder to see. Fifty years. Would he ever find a love like that?

His gaze moved to Rose, who stood chatting with other church members as she ate a piece of cake at Mrs. Warner's insistence. He cared for Rose. Perhaps more than cared. He had to admit he was hoping for a deeper relationship, but love? It was too soon to entertain those kinds of thoughts. He wanted her success as much as she did. He just wished it didn't have to be in his building.

He suddenly realized Rose was watching him, her brows bunched together, the skin between them wrinkled. He moved to her side. "Hey." He had a strange urge to lean down and kiss her cheek, but he reined it in. "No bouquets today, huh?"

She laughed. "No. This cake is safe."

"Good. I'd hate to have to spend the next three days making another one of these. As it is, we still have to remake Abby's cake."

Rose tapped her chin, a habit he'd noticed she had when she was concentrating—or pretending to. "You mean you didn't enjoy working at the catering shop this week?"

Lucas rubbed the back of his neck. "Yes, I did, but I don't think I'm cut out to do it full-time."

"Don't you do any cooking at the restaurant?

"That's Nick's job, and he loves it."

He paused, looking over the mingling crowd. This certainly was a much larger church than his. "Have you thought more about visiting Hope Village?"

Rose looked up at him. He almost lifted his hand to touch her face. Tiny freckles lined her nose, and she wore little makeup. *Lord, if this isn't the woman You want for me, please slam the door shut now.*

"Yes, I have. I guess I wouldn't mind going one Sunday."

A little voice inside him yelled, "Hallelujah!" but Lucas schooled his face into a neutral expression. "How about this Sunday? I can pick you up at nine for Sunday school."

"This Sunday?"

"Sure. Unless you've already got plans."

"I planned on going to church, so I guess that's fine."

"Great. So what's on the agenda for tomorrow's baking—besides Abby's cake?"

"I don't have a wedding this Saturday, but I do have a birthday party. The little boy doesn't like cake, though, so I'm making a chocolate chip cookie cake and several other kinds of cookies. It's nothing really difficult."

"Can I sample the wares?"

She laughed. "I suppose a taste test would be wise."

"It's a tough job, but I'm willing to accept the challenge." Lucas winked at her and linked his hand with hers. "Maybe the job wouldn't be so bad if I got to taste all the baking."

He stayed close to her the rest of the evening. Because of her injury, several ladies in the church insisted on taking care of cleanup and the leftover cake. He and Rose left early.

As Lucas made his way home, he rejoiced that Rose had agreed to attend church with him on Sunday. He'd see that she met the softball team members, but more than that, he would make sure she felt right at home at Hope Village Church. He wanted her worshiping next to him for a long time to come.

Chapter 6

Sunday morning Rose dressed carefully in a dark blue skirt and white silk blouse. A little nervous about going to a new church, she wasn't sure how Lucas had convinced her. Lakeview had been her home church since her parents died. Even so, she doubted anyone would even notice she missed today's service. She was just one person out of many. She took a last brief look in the mirror, knowing Lucas would arrive at any moment to pick her up.

The doorbell chimed, and she walked sedately to open it.

"Good mor—" Lucas stopped, his brow wrinkled.

"What's wrong?"

"You're. . .um. . ." He fidgeted.

"What?"

"Um, well, you're. . .too dressed up."

Rose looked down at her outfit. "This is what I always wear to church." Then she noticed what he was wearing. Jeans and a sport shirt with a casual heavy jacket. "You wear jeans to church?"

"Yes. I told you it was casual." He hesitated. "Look, if you're comfortable, it's fine. Let's go." He picked up the coat she'd thrown over the back of the sofa and held it out to her, but Rose hesitated.

"I'll change."

"You don't have to. I shouldn't have said anything. It doesn't matter what you wear."

Rose bit her lip. "I don't want to stand out. I have jeans." She hurried to her room and pulled out a pair of jeans. The skirt came off easily, but unbuttoning the silk blouse with one hand and replacing it with a cotton one took time. She worried that they would be late. Finally, she finished wiggling into her jeans. She grabbed socks and a pair of boots and headed back out to the living room.

"Would you help me with these?" she asked nervously.

"Sure. Sit on the couch, and I'll do it."

She sat and Lucas knelt, working her feet into the socks. She giggled when his fingers brushed the bottom of her foot, tickling her. He held each boot out, she worked her foot into it, then Lucas zipped it up.

Lucas's lips curved in a bright smile of approval. Rose returned his look with relief, though she wasn't sure why what he thought mattered to her.

When they drove up to the small church, Lucas pulled into a parking spot and walked around the car to open her door.

"Want me to carry that for you?" He pointed to her purse and Bible.

"You want to carry my purse?"

Lucas grinned. "I'm a man of the twenty-first century. If you need me to, I'm willing."

Rose laughed. "Thanks, but I think I can handle the purse. You can carry my Bible if you want to." He accepted the Bible, and Rose slipped out of the car.

Lucas placed his hand at the small of her back as he led her to the front door. A couple stood just inside, distributing bulletins. Lucas accepted one and slipped it inside his Bible.

"Hi, Don. This is my friend Rose Bentley. She's going to visit with us today." Lucas turned to Rose. "This is Don Barnes, the catcher on our softball team, and his wife, Marcia."

Rose nodded. "Nice to meet you." At her church, no one really talked to her. She just entered and sat down. If she continued to attend here, she'd have to get used to being noticed.

Lucas greeted friends as he led her upstairs to his Sunday school classroom. Rose noticed that he kept his hand at her back and made every attempt to shield her injured arm from jostling by the crowd.

The Sunday school lesson was on following God's will for your life. She was impressed with the questions that were asked and by how generous the group was in sharing incidents from their own lives, making them very vulnerable as their faults were displayed for all to see.

When the class was over, they entered the sanctuary and found a seat close to the front. After a few minutes, the praise band started playing, and soon the congregation was singing a rousing chorus of "I Want to Know You" as people slowly made their way to their seats. The music eased into a worshipful "Amazing Love."

Rose joined in, glad she was familiar with the songs. As the service continued, she was surprised to find she recognized almost every song as one she had on CD at her apartment.

Rose was glad she had changed her clothes. Everyone was dressed casually as Lucas had told her. The pastor even wore casual clothes, though not jeans. His message, however, was anything but casual. Behind the entertaining humor was a suggestion that perhaps too many people let someone else carry the church load.

Church attendance, while good, was not enough. There were needs that could only be met if the people were willing to make sacrifices. Had she made any sacrifices lately that weren't for her own good or the sake of her business? Rose was ashamed to admit to herself she'd been focused solely on her own goals. She'd let God occupy the outer reaches of her life instead of keeping Him in front of her where He should be. She determined to do better in that regard.

"Want to go get something to eat?" Lucas asked as the closing chords of the last song faded away.

"I don't know, Lucas. I appreciate you taking me to church this morning, but I don't want to give you the wrong idea."

Lucas reached over and took her hand. It was a habit she was getting used to, and she was tempted to withdraw it for that very reason.

"And what idea would that be, Rose?"

She lowered her lashes and spoke softly so passersby wouldn't overhear her. "You know what idea. I don't have the time to invest in a relationship right now. I do want that in my life, but the timing isn't right. We've already spent the week together—"

"That was work."

"Yes, but—"

"I know what you're saying, Rose. I won't try to push you into anything. We can be friends. But remember, work isn't everything. I work hard, but I take time out for other things as well. Besides, God's timing and yours might not coincide."

Since she'd been thinking the same thing recently, Rose didn't respond.

"We'll just grab a burger. Okay?"

"All right," she finally agreed. "Just lunch."

Suddenly, someone called Lucas's name, and they turned as one to see an older couple walking toward them.

"Mom, Dad!" Lucas turned to Rose. "Mom and Dad don't attend here, but they do come occasionally because they're friends with Pastor Charles's family. They prefer 'Amazing Grace' to 'Bring It On.'" He grinned.

A woman with graying brown hair walked up to them, hand in hand with an older version of Lucas. "Lucas, we wanted to invite you and your friend to lunch. It won't be anything fancy. I have baked beans in the Crock-Pot, but there's fresh apple pie for dessert."

Lucas smiled. "Mom, Dad, this is Rose Bentley. Rose, my mom, Evelyn, and my dad, Lucien. Mom's a great cook. What do you say?"

Rose stared at Lucas. They seemed like a nice couple, but she'd just told Lucas she didn't want to get involved, and here he wanted to take her home to have a meal with his parents. It seemed a little too cozy for her, but she couldn't see a way to politely refuse.

"That would be nice. Can Lucas and I bring anything?"

"I think we have everything we need, but thanks for the offer. We'll look forward to seeing you soon." Evelyn smiled and put her hand on her husband's arm as the two walked off together.

⟋⟍

Lucas sensed Rose was annoyed with him. He knew she didn't want a relationship. At least she said she didn't. While he knew he was ready to settle down, he wasn't sure if Rose was the one God intended for him. It was still early in their relationship to determine that, but it didn't seem as though God had slammed the door on the relationship, either.

There were so many things he liked about her. All he had to do was convince Rose to give them a chance. He was determined to be available to help her as long as she couldn't work. After all, it was his fault she was injured.

The meal with his parents went without incident, and he knew Rose enjoyed the food from her comments as they ate. His mother entertained them with embarrassing tales of his youth. He laughed along with the others. When the last bite of pie had been eaten, Lucas thanked his parents for the meal and escorted Rose to the car.

"Would you mind if I stopped at home for a few minutes? I need to pick up some papers I promised to take to Nick. You're welcome to come along." Bringing Rose to meet Nick was risky. While he really preferred they never meet face-to-face, he knew that was unrealistic. He tried not to dwell on what her reaction would be when she saw the two of them side by side. Worst of all, Lucas didn't want to find she had more in common with Nick.

"I suppose that would be all right."

A short time later, he left her in his living room while he went to his office for the papers. When he returned, Rose was seated at the card table in front of a partially completed jigsaw puzzle of the Starship Enterprise.

"You build puzzles," Rose said. He could hear the smile in her voice as she took in the completed puzzles he'd mounted and framed and used to adorn his walls.

Lucas smiled. "Yes. I admit it. I'm a jigsaw puzzle fanatic." He crossed to the large picture window in the room, gazing out at his front yard. Without turning around, he continued. "I started doing them to relax during a difficult time in my life. I guess in a way the puzzles are representative of that time. Every day seemed like one big puzzle to me. I figured if I couldn't solve the puzzle that was my life, at least I could solve these." He took a breath and went on, wanting Rose to understand. "I was fighting God, angry with Him for some of the things that had happened to me. I ran with a bad crowd. I walked away from the church." He shoved his hands in his pockets. "I got an education, though. Some part of me knew that was important. God was trying to get my attention, but my eyes and ears were closed."

He lowered his voice. "Then Nick gave me some advice I've never forgotten. It certainly wasn't the first time I'd heard it, but I guess it was God's timing. This time it made sense. He told me to give God control of everything in my life, not just select portions."

"Easy to say, though not so easy to do." Her voice came from close behind him, but he didn't turn around.

"Exactly. Thing was, I thought I was following God's plan. I thought I trusted Him to handle things. Turns out I was just trying to turn God my way. I finally admitted I hadn't a clue what to do. I opened my heart to God and let Him work in my life." He faced her then. "Nick always loved to cook, and he's very gregarious. We decided to open a restaurant together. Neither of us ever believed it would be a national project. Boston, Napa, Denver, New Orleans."

"Is there a Mrs. Nick?" Rose asked lightly.

"No. Not yet, anyway."

"So you let God lead you, and now you've got all these restaurants. Successful?"

"Yep."

"And a new one soon?"

Lucas hesitated. "Yes. Nick and I plan to be based here, close to our parents. So what about you? How did you get to where you are?"

"I told you my parents sent me to culinary arts school."

"Yes, but anyone can go to school. Not everyone will make a success of it. You seem to have done that."

She nodded. "I'm doing okay." Her deep sigh tore at his heart. "I guess I'm not very good at letting God lead me, either. The catering shop is my obsession. I want to pay back the money my parents used for my education. Alex and Mia can use that money. It's not fair that she has no inheritance because my folks used it on me."

"That's admirable, Rose, but I'm sure Alex doesn't expect you to do that."

"Of course she doesn't, but I do." She stood. "Are you ready to go?"

He nodded and followed her to the car. Soon they were on the road to Nick's place, where Rose would learn another secret in his life. He hoped it wouldn't turn her away from him.

Chapter 7

This is where your brother lives?"

Lucas glanced at Rose, who was staring at the red wooden building that resembled a barn. He smiled. "Yes." He walked around the car and opened the door to help Rose out. "Nick's house in California looked just like it. Wait until you see the inside."

Rose gave a noncommittal nod as she followed him to the front door. Lucas felt his heart speed up.

The door opened wide, and Nick greeted them, his gaze landing on Rose. "Lucas! And you brought an angel."

Lucas heard Rose's gasp and cringed.

"Nick, this is Rose. I told you about her catering business. Rose, this is my brother, Nick. You may notice we look a bit alike."

"A bit?" Rose's brow disappeared beneath her bangs.

Lucas glanced at Nick, who stood in the doorway, an amused smirk on his face. "Okay, more than a bit. Why don't we go inside?"

Nick stepped back and motioned for them to enter. "A fellow chef. We should have lots to talk about."

Lucas clenched his fists as Nick gave Rose the smile that kept women at his side. He didn't want Rose at Nick's side.

The aroma of simmering food grew stronger as Nick continued on into the ultramodern kitchen.

Lucas turned to Rose and tried to read her expression. It wasn't very difficult. She was miffed.

"You should have told me you had a twin," she muttered.

"Don't you like surprises?" Lucas forced himself to smile, even though it was almost painful.

"No, actually, I don't. I never have," Rose said between gritted teeth.

"We'll have to change that. Maybe a more gradual introduction would have been better." Lucas gave her another weak smile. "Guess I should have told you sooner. I'm sorry. Yes, Nick and I are twins, but we're quite different. When we were kids, it wasn't cool for guys to cook. I spent a lot of time with a bloody nose, fighting boys who made fun of Nick's hobby." He glanced briefly at Nick.

Nick grinned. "Yeah. Lucas had the 'older brother' thing down pat. He *is* a few minutes older than I am. I liked to cook, and I didn't care who knew it. But in self-defense, and to keep Lucas from those bloody noses, I joined the football team. Kept me in shape. I had lots of friends, despite the cooking—most of them female."

Lucas grimaced when Rose giggled. Already she was succumbing to Nick's charm, and Lucas felt himself fade into the background as he always did when Nick was around and there was a woman in the room. "As we got older, things turned around. Nobody cares now that Nick cooks. Women flock to him like bees to honey." *Including you.*

Nick spoke up. "I think that's enough of a trip down memory lane, Lucas. I made lamb stew. Stay and have some." He spoke to both of them but looked at Rose, pulling out a chair and motioning for her to sit. Before either of them could answer, Nick winked at Rose. "I hope my brother is treating you right." He grinned widely.

"Yes, he is." A fine blush crept over her face, giving her a sweet innocence.

"Haven't fallen into any more cakes?"

Rose laughed, and Lucas felt the heat creep up his own neck. Then Rose replied. "That was an accident—my fault, really."

Nick snorted. "Right. You're a sweetheart. So, how about a bowl of stew?"

Lucas, still standing, pulled the papers out of his pocket and laid them on the table. "We've already eaten. We just stopped by to bring you these."

Nick picked up the papers and tossed them on the countertop. He glanced at Lucas. "Thanks." He angled his head toward Rose. "Lucas is efficient, a good business manager. I'm a good cook." He leaned in a little closer, invading Rose's space.

Lucas wanted to throw him against a wall, but Rose didn't seem to mind.

"Do you like to eat out?" Nick asked her, lowering his voice and waggling his brows.

"Yes, I do."

Lucas watched his brother flirt with Rose.

Nick waved toward the stove. "Come on. Just a small bowl?" He covered his heart with his hands. "You'll break my heart if you don't let me feed you."

Rose laughed. "Okay. A small bowl."

Nick rose and fixed two steaming bowls of stew, which he set in front of them.

Lucas sniffed appreciatively, hoping to take Nick's attention away from Rose. "I love your lamb stew, Nick."

Nick mumbled, "Thanks," but didn't move his gaze from Rose.

Lucas also looked at Rose. "We can't stay long. I have to get Rose home."

"What's the rush?" Nick asked, leaning over to stir Rose's stew. "It's hot. Be careful."

Rose lowered her eyes. "Lucas is right. I really have to get back." Nick dipped the spoon in the bowl and lifted a bite to her lips. Rose opened her mouth, and he slid the spoon inside. Her eyes widened. "This is fabulous."

Lucas clenched his hands at his side, watching Rose respond to Nick's attentions.

Nick dropped the spoon, which Rose picked up as she continued to eat.

"That means a lot coming from another cook. I think the new restaurant should do well. It's in a prime location. Has Lucas shown you—"

"Nick, why don't you put those papers in your office?" Suddenly, the room became too hot for Lucas. He hadn't considered that Nick might bring up the restaurant. This wasn't the way he wanted Rose to learn about the building purchase.

❧

Rose was quiet on the drive home. Though Nick was a mirror image of Lucas, he was very different in personality, much more outgoing and flirtatious, while Lucas was quieter—not shy certainly, but not as comfortable in a party crowd as Nick would be.

"What did you think of Nick?" Lucas asked.

She turned slightly to face him. "I think he's very nice and a very talented cook, but you should have told me you had a look-alike in town."

Lucas had the grace to blush. "You're right. I just didn't know how to approach it. I wanted to get to know you first."

"Why would that matter?" He was quiet for so long, Rose thought he wasn't going to answer.

"Nick can be, um, overwhelming. Once he decides to pursue a woman, he doesn't really allow time for anyone else."

She lifted her brows in surprise. "I don't think Nick intends to pursue me, but even if he did, I have no intention of starting a relationship with anyone, particularly not a restaurant owner."

Lucas turned his head slightly. "Does that include me?"

"It includes every male in the city. I'm too busy building my business to expend time and energy maintaining a relationship. I thought I'd made that clear."

He frowned, then apparently decided to change the subject. "So are you going to join our softball team?"

"Is Nick on the team?" she teased.

"Yeah. He's a great hitter." She saw his sidelong glance but ignored it.

"He wasn't at church this morning."

"No, he attends with Mom and Dad. It's hard when we're both in the same place. People get confused. We've learned to handle it for the most part."

"Was Nick part of the puzzle you were trying to put together before you came back to the Lord?"

Lucas pulled into Rose's driveway. He shifted into park and turned off the ignition, then faced her. "As you could see, we're mirror images. Since we look alike, some assume we have the same personality as well. We don't. I didn't always appreciate Nick's unique qualities."

"Like his love of cooking. But you came to accept it?"

"Accept? Yes, and more. I value him. We get along well most times."

Lucas escorted Rose to her apartment. When she opened the door, a soft meow greeted them. Rose reached down to pick up the tortoiseshell Maine Coon that wrapped himself around her leg.

"I don't think you've been formally introduced," she said, lifting her head to meet Lucas's eyes. "Meet Bleu, named after Le Cordon Bleu Institute."

Lucas laughed and reached out to pet the cat, which purred softly. She lifted Bleu, kissed the top of his head, and then set him down.

"Would you like something to drink? Soda? Coffee?"

Lucas shook his head. "I really should go. The church youth meet in the late afternoon for a Bible study, and I usually try to be there. You're welcome to come with me if you'd like."

"Maybe another time. I'll think about the softball team." When his brow lifted, she added, "Of course it would have to be after I get the okay from the doctor. When do you need to know?"

"Whenever you're ready. Changes are accepted without question unless you're a really bad player."

"Then they'd kick me out?"

"Nah, but they'd grumble at me."

She laughed. "When do you practice?"

"Saturday afternoons, two o'clock."

"At the church?"

"Yes. There's a big field behind the building."

She opened the door for him. "If I decide to participate, I'll let you know."

"Great. The team will love me if that throwing arm is any indication of your talents."

Rose laughed and shut the door behind Lucas. She leaned against it, feeling more alive than she'd felt in a long time.

Chapter 8

"Batter up!"

Rose leaped from the bench and ran to stand at home plate. She hefted the bat and took a few practice swings. This was only her second time playing with the team, and it was an important game. It had taken more than four weeks for her shoulder to heal, and she was still supposed to be careful. She doubted her doctor would consider softball a recommended sport, but she decided she couldn't live her life worrying about being injured. She enjoyed playing with the group and wanted to do a good job.

She knew that Lucas, on the other hand, constantly worried about her playing so soon after her injury.

Nick yelled his encouragement over the roar of the crowd, and Rose knew, without looking, that Lucas was sitting quietly praying for her safety. It gave her a nice feeling, but it also concerned her that they'd become so close in such a short time.

Once Nick had seen she was only interested in his friendship, he'd backed off. He still liked to shower attention on her to tease Lucas. After that first visit to Nick's place, she and Lucas had not discussed relationships. She'd made it clear she didn't want one, but she had a feeling Lucas had conveniently forgotten that fact. Sometimes her conscience pricked her as they spent so much time together.

She closed her eyes briefly. *Lord, I know this is only a game, but it's an important one. I know the other team is praying just as hard, so I'll ask that no one gets hurt and we all go home friends. If You could see Your way clear to give us a reason to celebrate when it's over, however, I'd be grateful.*

The first swing was a strike. Rose put her head down and closed her eyes again. *And if I could not look too stupid up here, I'd really appreciate that, too, Lord.*

The second swing was a strike. Rose took a breath. The pitcher, a man, smiled at her and winked. Rose smiled back.

When the ball came at her, she knew she had to swing. She barely hit it and the ball rolled out of bounds.

"Foul!"

She could hear a combination of voices behind her.

"You can do it, Rosie!" That was Alex.

"Hit it high!" Nick yelled.

Rose took a second to glance over her shoulder. Lucas was standing, his fingers linked in the fence. He gave her a smile and a thumbs-up, and she turned back to face the pitcher, determined to win this game. If she struck out, it was over. If she got a base hit, at least someone else would be the one to win or lose. She'd have done her part.

Concentrating, she watched the pitcher. The man turned around and faced his teammates. She knew he was giving them hand signals, but of course, she didn't know which ones. Their team had similar signals depending on what kind of ball the pitcher had decided to throw.

When he turned around, his face was serious. He wound his arm and threw.

Rose watched the ball come at her, ready to swing. Her bat struck the ball with a satisfying crack. It flew high. She dropped the bat and ran, knowing the crowd in the stands was screaming. She prayed it wouldn't be a fly ball so she wouldn't have to walk back to the plate in disgrace. She kept her eyes on the base, trying not to think of where the ball was. As she got close to first base, Don signaled her to go on. She took his word and headed out. At second, Marcia yelled, "Go, girl!"

Her side ached, and she was gasping for air. This was not the sort of exercise a caterer got on a daily basis. She continued to run, but when she rounded third, she had to look. The ball was in the air, heading home. She put on a burst of speed and dropped to slide into home plate, just as she heard the ball slap into the catcher's mitt and saw the player stumble while trying to tag her.

As Rose lay on the ground waiting for the call, she saw Lucas running toward her. It seemed forever before she heard the umpire yell. "Safe!"

The crowd went wild. The game was over, and her team had won.

Lucas reached her side as she started to get up. He dropped to the ground and laid his hand on her shoulder to stop her from rising too quickly.

"Slow and easy, Rose." Someone handed him a cup of water, and he encouraged her to drink. His hand unconsciously rubbed her back, and she felt his gaze on her as he tried to decide if she was all right.

Then others were crowding around, inquiring about her. She struggled to get up, but Lucas held her still. "Take it easy, honey."

"I'm okay," she murmured in his ear. "Just a little winded. Don't make a fuss."

Alex dropped down beside her, holding Mia. "Big Sis, I'm proud of you." She leaned down and gave her a hug. Rose glanced over her sister's shoulder and saw Nick coming in for his hug. Lucas backed off, watching.

"I'll fix you a celebration dinner," Nick told her. "Everybody come to my house."

"We'll meet you there, Nick. I have to change my clothes." Rose looked down at her jeans, covered with dirt.

Lucas spoke up. "That sounds like a good idea."

Alex settled Mia on her hip, gave a little wave, and left the field, followed closely by Nick.

∞

Lucas turned to Rose and helped her up. "You okay? You didn't hurt your arm again, did you?"

"I'm fine. My arm's fine. It's been a long time since I hit a home run."

Lucas grinned at her. "Felt good, huh?"

She beamed. "It felt terrific!"

He led her to his car and drove to her apartment where Rose stopped downstairs to pick up her mail. Bleu greeted them at the front door.

"Hey, Bleu. Miss me?" He watched her pick up the cat but quickly moved to take Bleu from her. Fortunately, the cat didn't object.

"You need to change quickly. Everyone's waiting for us."

"Okay."

Lucas sprawled on the sofa in the living room while Rose changed into clean jeans. When she returned, she stood in front of him. He smiled and held his hands out.

She took them, but before she could pull him up, Lucas pulled her down to the sofa.

"I've thought about it, and I think they can wait a bit. That was a tiring game," Lucas said, grinning.

Rose laughed and shook her head. "Nick is fixing food. I'm going. You can stay here if you want to."

Lucas groaned. "Oh, all right. I'm coming." He stood, lifting her up as well, and suddenly realized they were standing toe to toe. Rose looked up into his face, and his eyes met hers. "I was proud of you today. You did good," he whispered.

She ducked her head shyly, and he lifted her chin with his finger. Without thinking about it, he lowered his head and touched his lips to hers in a gentle kiss. Her arms went around his neck, and he pulled her to him.

He felt her smile as he captured her lips once again. Then he backed up. "Guess we'd better go," he said, his voice husky.

She nodded and led the way to the front door where Bleu had knocked the mail to the floor. Rose picked up the letters, scanning them quickly.

"Oh, look, here's one from my landlord." Rose picked out one letter from the group.

Lucas plucked the letter from her hand, hoping she'd forgive his rudeness. "You can read it later, can't you? Nick's cooking, remember?" Though Rose's brows came together as she looked at him, she said nothing and followed him to the car.

Time's up. I have to tell her today.

Cars filled Nick's driveway and spilled out onto the street. Apparently he had invited the entire team to join them.

Lucas walked with Rose to the den, where she was soon surrounded. She was everybody's hero, and though she'd never admit it, he thought she was enjoying the attention. He headed to the kitchen and found Nick busily preparing tacos. When he returned to the den, Rose was no longer there.

"Where's Rose?" he asked Alex.

Alex looked up. "She went that way." She pointed her thumb in the direction of the hall.

Lucas waited awhile, but when Rose didn't return, he began to wonder if something was wrong. He decided he'd better check and see. He walked down the hall and was passing Nick's office when he saw her.

She was kneeling on the floor near Nick's desk, scattered papers around her, one particular paper in her hand. Lucas recognized the purchase agreement for the Arby Avenue building.

"Rose?" Her head lifted, and the agony in her face made his breath catch. "What are you doing in here?"

She stared at him. "Nick said I could use the phone." Her face contorted, and he cringed to see her anger directed at him. "You bought my building. For your restaurant." She looked down at the paper. "It's dated over a month ago. How could you do this? And how could you not tell me?"

He extended his hands, palms outward. "I can explain."

She stood and backed away from him. "There is no explanation."

Lucas watched the emotions crossing her face—rage, disillusionment, and betrayal. It was the last that tore his heart in two.

"It's not the way you think. There were reasons I—"

"I thought I knew you. I guess I was wrong. Please tell Nick I'm sorry. I'll get Alex to take me home."

"Please let me explain. Don't go like this."

She shook her head. "I can't stay here." She shoved her way past him and grabbed Alex's arm. "I need to leave. Will you drive me?"

Alex looked from her to Lucas and stood slowly, juggling Mia on her hip. "Sure. You okay?"

"Yes. I just need to leave. Now."

She turned and walked away without another word, head held high, not looking back once.

Lucas squeezed his eyes shut.

What now, Lord? I've messed up royally. I should have told her long ago. Is this it? Is it over?

Chapter 9

Rose stared at the letter in her hand:

Dear Miss Bentley,

Please be advised that I have sold the building at 311 Arby Avenue, which you presently rent. The new owners will honor your lease, which expires at the end of next month. That should give you sufficient time to find a new location.

My apologies for any inconvenience the change in ownership causes. I wish you success in your business.

Sincerely,
Jerrold Inkman

He had sold the building. *Her* building. And Lucas had bought it. The entire time he'd worked with her in the shop, he had known. The past weeks he'd taken her out to eat after practice, attended service and Sunday school with her, coaxed her to attend midweek Bible study with him—all that time, he'd known he was going to be evicting her. She clenched her hand in anger, crumpling the paper.

God never promised everything would go smoothly in life, but He did promise to be there with her whatever happened. *Sure need You now, Lord.*

She sank onto the sofa as tears began to fall. Bleu slipped onto her lap, and she petted the chubby cat. God's timing was always perfect. He had brought her closer to Him knowing she would need His comfort. The irony that God had used Lucas, her betrayer, to do that was not lost on her. She'd grown under Lucas's ministry, and now she had to move forward—without him.

She closed her eyes. Lucas had kissed her, right here in her living room, all the while knowing what he'd done. If he could do that, he didn't care for her as she'd hoped he did. It was best that he was out of her life. Her heart would be a lot steadier with Lucas gone. She could concentrate on her business, which was what she should have been doing anyway. Wherever it was located.

She regretted she'd have to give up the friends she'd made at Hope Village. She'd also have to leave the softball team. That was all right. She would find a way to minister in her own church. God would still come first in her life, even if she didn't understand why He'd allowed this to happen.

On Sunday, Rose returned to Lakeview Church. She found she missed the upbeat music and powerful sermons Pastor Charles delivered at Hope Village, the in-depth Sunday school classes, and the camaraderie that was shared. Still, every church had its good and bad points. She'd been pleased with Lakeview before, and she would be again. *But you were just warming a pew here. There you were participating.* She squeezed her eyes tightly shut. That was true, but that could change. A large church needed even more people to minister to the congregation than a small church.

When she returned home, the light on her answering machine was blinking. She sighed, sat down, and reached a trembling hand to hit the play button.

"Rose." Her heart caught at the pain in Lucas's voice. "I know you're angry with me—and with good reason. I should have told you about the sale. I thought—well, it doesn't matter what I thought. I was wrong. I didn't know you when I signed the papers to buy the building. But I have to be honest and tell you I would have bought it anyway. I'd like to talk to you and explain." He paused. "I hate that you didn't come to church today. I hope it wasn't because of me. I think you could be happy at Hope Village. Please call me." There was a pause and then a click.

So that was that. What they'd been to one another didn't matter. He still would have kicked her into the streets. A little sob caught in her throat.

The explanation for his deception didn't matter. Trust was important to her, and she couldn't trust him. As much as it hurt, it was time to move forward.

It was a long time before she could sleep, and even then, it was a restless night. When she woke, she knew what she had to do.

Lucas stared at the words on the front window of his new restaurant: MONTGOMERY'S. Plain and simple. It should have been a proud moment, yet all he felt was a sense of loss.

It had been weeks since he'd seen Rose. He'd come to see her at the catering shop, only to discover she'd already moved out. He'd called her several times, but she didn't answer the phone or return his calls. He'd even tried calling Alex, but Rose's sister would have nothing to do with him.

Several times, he'd almost gone to her apartment, but her message was clear—stay away.

He had known he would miss Rose, but it surprised him how deeply he felt the loss. At the strangest times, he would be reminded of her by a scent or a word. He ached to see her again. She hadn't returned to Hope Village, which caused him further pain. He wanted to do something, but he didn't know what.

Rose was obviously not open to hearing his side of the matter. He knew she was hurt. He desperately needed to explain things to her, but she wouldn't give him a chance. The problem consumed him until he couldn't concentrate on anything else.

His shoulders slumped as he sighed deeply. Though he had renewed old friendships since moving back to Loudon and had family surrounding him now, he still felt alone. The word held a different meaning to him now. *Alone* meant being without Rose.

Though he longed for her, he had no idea how to make amends. Did Rose even care? Had their time together meant nothing to her? It amazed him that he could feel this way after spending only a few weeks in her company. Surely he hadn't misread her so completely.

He knew he needed to ensure this was a lasting love and not an emotional infatuation. Yet he'd never wanted to make a commitment to one woman like he wanted to make one to Rose.

What did it matter if he had a successful restaurant but no one to share the joy of his success? If it were only his decision, he'd gladly have given up the building, even with all the money they'd spent on renovations, but Nick was also owner of the building and had scoured the city to find a location perfect for their needs. Lucas hadn't known Rose then. The deal had been made before she was a part of his life.

How could he make everyone he loved happy when they were at cross-purposes? He blinked. Did everyone he loved include Rose? The thought made his heart race.

As he stood there contemplating this new piece of information, Nick walked up.

"We'll be able to open soon."

Lucas looked over at his brother. "Just another week."

"Do you think Rose will come?"

"I don't think so, Nick. Rose isn't very happy with me."

"She's a nice gal. I'm sorry things didn't work out for you two."

Lucas sighed. "She won't even talk to me."

Nick put his hand on Lucas's shoulder. "If it's the building that's the problem, why don't we just share it?"

Nick's simple statement stopped Lucas dead in his tracks. "Share?" Lucas pictured the room in his mind. "Do you think it's possible?" Without waiting for his brother's reply, Lucas strode quickly to the kitchen. He was vaguely aware of Nick behind him, close on his heels.

Lucas looked over the appliances and the counter space. "It would be a bit cozy with two cooks in here, Nick."

Nick shrugged. "I'm sure we could work it out. Most of her jobs require her to bake during the day. I work mostly at night. She could keep her business. We could even pass on some jobs to her. Our other restaurants have occasionally been contacted for catering jobs, but we haven't wanted to go in that direction. This could be another service for our customers. There's also a lot of room for expansion if we want to do that."

"Right. That would give her more business, yet keep her independent. I just don't know if she would see it that way." Again, he studied the large room. "I know we've already put a lot of money into this place with the renovations in the dining area, but maybe we could add some counter space and another oven and stove on the other end of the room. That way you wouldn't be in one another's way."

His thoughts moving at warp speed, Lucas saw the new room in his head. He remembered that Alex worked as a carpenter, and from what Rose had told him, she was good and could use the money. Being a single mother wasn't easy. Maybe she would take the job.

It was a good plan, but would it make a difference to Rose?

He sat down heavily. He didn't know if it was fair to ask her, but he had to try.

He had hurt her once. She might forgive him that, but if he hurt her again. . . He needed to be sure. Was he ready to make a commitment to her? A lifetime commitment?

His head in his hands, Lucas pushed everything else out of his mind and began to pray.

Chapter 10

His finger poised above the doorbell to Rose's apartment, Lucas shifted from one foot to the other. He'd made the decision not to call first, knowing she probably wouldn't talk to him, and if she did, she would refuse to accompany him. She might even leave the apartment if she knew he was coming. It would be harder for her to refuse if he was standing right in front of her.

He pressed a finger to the bright piece of plastic and heard the tones chime within. No sound came from inside, so he rang again. Relief poured through him when he heard the lock turning.

"Why are you here, Lucas?" Her clipped tones told him he was not a welcomed guest.

He forced a smile. "I have a surprise for you."

"A surprise? Why would you show up at my door, with no warning I might add, with a surprise? Especially since you know that I don't like surprises. You also have no business being here since any relationship we had previously is over." She moved her head to look around him, her eyes narrowed, her expression unyielding. "I don't see anything."

He grimaced. "Yes, you've made yourself perfectly clear. I didn't give you any warning because you won't take my calls." He sighed, rubbing the back of his neck to ease the aching muscles. "It wasn't possible to bring it here. I need to take you to it."

Hands on her hips, she stared at him. "I'm not going anywhere with you."

He reached for her hand and gave it a gentle squeeze. "Please, Rose. I know you have no reason to trust me, but I'm hoping you'll give me a second chance. You don't have any plans, do you? You're not catering a party tonight?"

"Nooo," she said slowly. He suspected she was tempted to lie, but to her credit, she didn't.

"So you can allow me a little of your time. I wouldn't do anything to hurt you."

"You've already hurt me."

Lucas winced and dropped her hand. "Touché. I'm sorrier about that than I've ever been about anything in my life." He shoved his hands in his pockets and forced himself to meet her eyes. "Come with me. Please. It's important."

Her head tilted and her expression softened. "Is something wrong? Is it Nick? Your parents?"

It touched him that she still cared, even if it was about his family and not himself, but he wasn't going to lie to her. "No. Nothing's wrong. In fact, I hope to make everything right."

He waited tense seconds while she thought about his request. Then she turned and went back inside. She left the door open, though she didn't invite him in. Seconds later, she returned carrying a sweater and her purse.

Stepping ahead of him, she walked slowly to his car. Lucas opened the passenger door so she could slide inside, being careful not to crowd her, and soon they were on the road.

"Where are we going?"

"You don't expect me to tell you that, right? It's a surprise."

"I think we've established I don't like surprises."

"You'll like this one." *I hope.*

A few minutes later, Lucas pulled onto a dirt road. He knew Rose would soon see his surprise. It was hard to miss.

"What?"

He knew the moment she saw it.

"A hot air balloon? That's the surprise?"

"Yep. You've never ridden in one, have you?" His heart was beating wildly as he waited for her answer. She'd spent all of her time on her schooling and then her business. He didn't imagine she'd taken time for a frivolous thing like a balloon ride.

"No. And I'm not going to today."

Lucas pulled the car to a stop. "Why not? I chartered it especially for you."

"You should have asked me first, and I'd have saved you the trouble—and the exorbitant fee I'm sure they charge. Those rides take a long time. I have work to do."

Lucas turned to face her, trying to keep his frustration from showing on his face. This was his last chance. His only chance. He was desperate to have uninterrupted time with her. "Work. That's all you think about. There's more to life than work. Are you afraid of having fun, Rose? Are you afraid you might just like it and have to think of somebody and something other than business?" He drew a hand through his thick hair. "Rose, take a chance. Take a giant leap of faith. You need to do this."

"How would you know what I need?" Rose shoved open her door and strode away from the car in the direction from which they'd come.

❧

"Rose!" Lucas's voice echoed behind her as she stomped off.

If she'd been thinking properly, she wouldn't have agreed to come. She shouldn't be here. She had a life. It just happened that work was a big part of it. She was grateful to Lucas for reminding her she needed to put God at its center, but that didn't give him the right to tell her what to do with the rest of it.

Lucas caught up with her and placed himself in front of her so she had to stop. She crossed her arms and stood still, tapping her foot in obvious irritation. When she refused to look at him, he lifted her chin with his finger.

"I'm sorry," he said. His voice was soft and quiet. "You're right. I should have asked you before setting this up. If you want to go back, you don't have to walk. I'll take you. But, Rose, I'd appreciate it if you'd give me a chance."

Rose looked into his earnest face. How could she trust him after weeks of deceit? She'd never risked her heart as much as she would today if she allowed Lucas to see how much she'd missed him.

Taking a balloon ride with him in a small confined space would risk so much. Though she wished it weren't true, she was afraid she'd already lost her heart to Lucas Montgomery.

The gift of a balloon ride was a generous one. He'd gone to a lot of trouble for her. During the annual July balloon festival they offered rides, but they were early in the morning and in the evening. He would have made special arrangements for this mid-morning ride.

"All right. I'll go, but, Lucas, don't do this again."

"Deal. No more surprise balloon rides." He took her hand and led her to the basket. Before they entered, however, he stopped. "You're not afraid of heights, are you?"

Rose studied the basket in front of her. "I never have been, but then I've never been in an open basket in the sky, either." She took a step forward with determination. "Let's go."

She allowed Lucas to help her into the sturdy basket where the pilot already waited. Lucas slipped inside, moving to stand close to her. There was nowhere to go, so she gritted her teeth and waited to see what would happen next.

❧

As they slowly gained altitude, Lucas risked a glance at Rose. She wasn't smiling, but she wasn't frowning, either. *Please, Lord, don't let her get airsick.*

"Rose?"

She turned toward him, and he once again thanked the Lord for placing this woman in his path. Her strength and courage constantly astounded him. He couldn't believe he'd ever doubted his feelings for her. Now he could only hope she felt the same way and would give him a chance to make up for the hurt he'd caused her.

"Yes?"

"I have another surprise for you." Her scowl reminded him she didn't like surprises.

"Another surprise? The first one turned out so well."

Her sarcasm didn't escape his notice, but he ignored it. With his finger he turned her head so she could see the land beneath them. "Look. All God's creation laid out before us."

She looked, and he saw the beginnings of a smile light her face.

"I've missed you, Rose."

Her gaze on the scene below, she admitted, "I've missed you, too."

"I'm sorry I wasn't honest with you about the building purchase. I thought if we got to know each other first. . .and then I thought it wasn't my place to tell you. Anyway, I was wrong, and I'm sorry. Can you forgive me?"

"Forgive you? Yes. God has forgiven me many times. But trust you? That's more difficult."

"I'd give anything to win back that trust. I had to buy that building. I'd already signed the papers when we met. I couldn't *not* buy it." He reached to take her hand and was grateful when she didn't pull it away. "I talked to Nick, and he agreed that our businesses are not in competition. We can help one another. We can share the building."

"Share the building?" She frowned as she turned to face him.

"Yes. If you agree. I've had your name added to the deed. Your copy is in the car." Swallowing hard, he lifted his gaze to meet hers. "Even more important than that, Rose, I want to share my life with you. I love you. I'm asking you to be my wife."

Her frown deepened. Lucas felt his heart lurch. "So you're saying if I agree to marry you, I become a partner with you and Nick?"

He shook his head slowly. "No. The building is one-third yours—if you want it—regardless of your answer."

"I can't afford to buy a third of a building—any building."

"I'm not worried about that. We can work out the finances."

"You would continue to work with me if I refused to marry you?"

His heart breaking, Lucas hesitated. "No. I don't think I could do that."

Her face paled, but she met his eyes. "I see."

Lucas shook his head. "I don't think you do, Rose. You'll own one-third of the building, regardless of our personal relationship. But I couldn't stay here and watch you fall in love with somebody else. I would respect your wishes, however, whatever they are."

They were quiet as the balloon passed over the area.

Having been informed by Lucas that he didn't need the tourist spiel, the pilot remained silent except when communicating with the ground crew in the chase vehicle, which kept them in sight. When he began to make landing preparations, Lucas pulled Rose to the side.

"I don't want to pressure you, Rose. Take some time to pray about what I've said. Nick will be in touch with you about the shop. If you're willing to work with him, you can move back to Arby Avenue as soon as you're ready. The restaurant is open for dinner at five. I think the business arrangement will be beneficial to everyone, but if you don't want to do it, you can opt out." He wanted to say more, but he bit his lip to stop the words.

When they landed, the chase crew drove them back to his car. Rose settled herself in the front seat, and Lucas retrieved the revised deed from his briefcase, handing it to her.

Watching her face as she read through it, he realized he needed to get her home—before he did something stupid like pull her into his arms and never let her go again.

Chapter 11

Rose sat quietly in the seat beside Lucas. He said he loved her. He'd asked her to marry him. He'd even given her part ownership of the building she wanted. He was giving her everything she could want. Yet that was the point. She didn't want it given to her. Her independence was important. Rose wanted to succeed or fail on her own. Could she accept Lucas's offer and still do that?

Her mind was awhirl with mixed emotions. On the one hand, she hated working out of her apartment. On the other, sharing the building would be an adjustment to all of them. If it didn't work out, she'd have to move again.

Since she hadn't had time to find a new building, Lucas's offer would certainly fix one problem. But if she was to share the building, then she should share the cost. At the least, she could pay him the same amount she was paying Mr. Inkman for rent.

Though the finances were important, they weren't the real issue. Could she get past her hurt feelings and her distrust? She knew she loved Lucas. There was no doubt in her mind about that. But was it enough?

Her gaze moved to him. His blue eyes remained focused on the road—the eyes that had attracted her from the first when she and Lucas had fallen into Abby's cake. Even in profile, she could see he was tense. He'd laid his heart out to her. Could she do any less?

When he drove up to her apartment, she hopped out of the car before he could walk around, hoping he'd remain in the vehicle and leave. Rather, he escorted her upstairs and stood waiting patiently while she opened the door. She turned to face him then, uncertain of what to say.

Before she had a chance to speak, he placed his finger on her lips.

"Don't answer me now," he said softly. "Think about it. I love you, but I only want you if you want to be with me. It has to be your decision. Freely made."

He leaned down and kissed her cheek gently. Then he reached for her hand and held it, looking at it solemnly. He must not have been able to find the words, because he simply squeezed it as he'd done many times before, then turned to leave.

"Lucas." His name was out of her mouth before she could stop it.

He turned, and the hopeful look on his face tore at her heart. "Yes?"

"I *will* think about it. I do love you, but I'm not sure it's enough."

He looked at her seriously, though his eyes lit up at her declaration. "Love overcomes, Rose. Jesus showed us that. Call me when you're ready."

Then he was gone.

◈

The restaurant was crowded. The grand opening of Montgomery's was a rousing success.

Nick was in his element at the stove, creating masterpieces for their opening night. Lucas wasn't worried about Nick. The menu was set. Nick would shine.

Lucas barely had time to think as he moved from place to place, checking details, greeting guests. Though he'd hired a hostess, this first night he wanted to be in view. A visible owner made people feel special.

The bell over the door would have to go. It was driving him crazy. Why had he never noticed it before? When it rang for the hundredth time that night, Lucas gritted his teeth and glanced up. His heart caught in his throat.

In a combination of moonlight from the window and soft fluorescent lighting from the fixture at the entrance stood Rose, an uncertain smile on her lips, as though unsure of her reception.

His heart pounded, but he forced himself to move slowly toward her as she stood in the line of customers waiting to be seated. He knew the moment she saw him. Her eyes lit up, and her smile grew brighter, though the hesitation was still there. Didn't she know he would have given anything to have her by his side tonight?

"Rose," he said softly. Just saying her name made his heart soar. He moved to her side and reached a hand out to her. She placed her hand in his. He drew her to him, and they moved to the side, out of the flow of traffic. "Are you here for dinner?"

He didn't want to assume anything. He'd promised her no pressure. Perhaps she just wanted to be supportive since she was listed as part owner.

She pursed her lips and fidgeted. "Yes, I suppose. Could we go somewhere and talk first? I know this is a bad time." She chuckled. "A terrible time, I guess. You must be so busy."

"I always have time for you, Rose." He said the words quietly with as much sincerity as he could muster.

He led her to the back, to the office that had recently been hers. Motioning for her to sit, he eased himself down next to her, close but not touching, waiting for her to speak.

Her eyes were shiny when she lifted her face to look at him, and his

425

heart went out to her. Was she going to refuse him?

She lifted her hand and caressed his face. Lucas closed his eyes and laid his own hand atop hers.

"I need to ask your forgiveness," she said softly. Her voice was quiet but strong. "I've been thinking of only myself and my needs."

He opened his eyes and looked at her. "You don't need my forgiveness, but you have it if you'll give me yours."

Tears made little trails along her cheeks.

"Don't cry, Sweetheart." He couldn't stand her tears. Even if it meant he would never see her again, he wouldn't have her hurt. *Lord, help me to bear it if she's going to leave me. Your will be done. Not mine.*

"I was angry with you, and then I was confused because you were giving me everything I wanted and I didn't understand why." She hesitated. "Then I found this." She reached into her handbag and withdrew the dried-up portion of the bouquet she'd caught at Abby's wedding. "It reminded me of the prayer I prayed the day I caught it. I asked God to help me find someone who would look at me with the love I saw in Stan's eyes when he looked at Abby. Someone who would understand about my business."

Lucas stared at their joined hands, resting on the sofa between them. "And did He?"

"Yes. I saw that look in your eyes the day we took the balloon ride. And when you offered to share this building, I knew you cared about my business."

Lucas nodded and lifted his head to look in her eyes. "Rose, did you mean it when you said you loved me?"

He held his breath while he waited for her answer. Her hand tensed, and she turned it over and entwined her fingers with his.

"Yes. I love you with all my heart. You reminded me that a life without God at its center is not a life at all. Your commitment to the Lord warms my heart. I've seen my own faith bloom as I watched you worship. I want to build a life, and a family, with you."

Heart soaring, he took her face in his hands. "You are God's answer to my prayers, Sweetheart." Lucas lowered his head, his lips meeting hers, sharing all the love in his heart with his kiss.

Flowers for a Friend
By Gail Sattler

Chapter 1

I 'll bet they make the playoffs, maybe even win the Stanley Cup." Geoff Manfrey opened his mouth to express his doubts when something light-weight smacked him on top of his head, then stuck in his hair. He started to raise one hand to find out what hit him when a crash resounded from the back of the banquet room. He turned to see what happened at the same time that he touched what felt like a plant on top of his head. Gales of laughter filled the room.

The closest laughing person was his friend Jason, who was also a guest at Abby and Stan's wedding. Instead of watching the action at the source of the crash—the caterer and the best man falling into the wedding cake—Jason was pointing at Geoff, laughing so hard his face had turned red.

"Look at you! You caught the bride's bouquet! You're going to be the next to get married."

"Very funny," Geoff mumbled, then winced as he tried to remove the flow-ers from his head. Some kind of tape was attached to the bundle, which made it impossible to dislodge the flowers without pulling out some hair. Since Jason wasn't offering to help, Geoff raised both hands to try to disengage the tape with a minimum of hair loss.

A camera flash glared in his face.

Geoff blinked to get rid of the spots in his eyes. "Very funny, David. Would you like to help?"

"No way. Too many great pictures are waiting to be taken."

Before Geoff could reply, David disappeared into the crowd.

Gradually, the laughter in the room died down. Since Geoff's seat at his table was next to the wall, only Jason and David had seen him. He wanted to keep it that way, because he didn't want to become the next source of amusement. However, since everyone's attention no longer remained fo-cused on the mess with the cake, his chances of no one else noticing the flowers stuck to his head were shrinking. Since he was just twenty-eight, he didn't have to worry about missing a few strands from on top; his hair would grow back. Instead of waiting for help, Geoff gritted his teeth, mentally wrote off his losses, and yanked.

While he massaged the tender spot on his head, he ignored the strands of his hair stuck to the errant piece of tape and stared at the flowers.

This was the bride's bouquet or, judging from snippets of conversation around him, a fourth of Abby's bouquet.

He had no intention of keeping the bride's bouquet or any portion of it. However, the throng of husband-hungry women from the center of the room had already dispersed.

He laid the flowers on the table in front of him. Being a Christian, he wasn't superstitious in any way, but he didn't like the idea of what keeping the bouquet implied—that he would be the next to get married. He knew, and God knew, that he would never marry.

As Geoff continued to stare blankly at the flowers, a little voice piped up behind him.

"Hi, Geoff!"

Geoff turned in the chair, then looked down. "Hi, Jenni," he said, smiling.

If David had any brains, instead of taking a picture of Geoff with the flowers in his hair, he would have been taking pictures of little Jenni.

Geoff didn't want to be biased, but he thought Jenni was the cutest and sweetest little girl he knew. Her blond hair flowed around her cherub face, and her blue eyes sparkled when she smiled. Today, wearing her little flower girl's dress, the same as the rest of the bridesmaids' dresses except in a miniature format, she looked extra special. Geoff didn't know much about ladies' clothing, but he thought that the dresses with the white tops and multicolored bottoms that were the same colors as the different flowers in Abby's bouquet—before it got all smashed up—looked just as good on six-year-old Jenni as they did on the full-grown women. Jenni had taken the responsibility of being in the bridal party very seriously.

Because he saw Jenni and her sister often, he knew that Jenni had been having a rough time over the past year after the tragic death of her parents. She was sad much of the time, even when she played with the other children. But today, she shone as the flower girl. Geoff wished there was something he could do to keep that sweet smile on her face more often.

He glanced back to the flowers on the table. Jenni had been in the throng of single women, hoping to catch the bouquet, regardless of the fact that she was only half the height of the adult women and didn't stand a chance.

Geoff picked up the flowers, rose from the chair, then hunkered down until one knee rested on the floor.

"Jenni, I think they were really meant for you."

Her face lit up like a Christmas tree as she accepted them. "Wow! You caught Abby's bouquet! That means you're going to get married soon! But if I was 'posed to get them, that means you're going to marry me!"

Geoff's smile dropped. "But—"

Before he could tell Jenni that the sequence of events wasn't necessarily related, Jenni threw her arms around him and gave him a big bear hug. "I love you, too, Geoff! I gotta tell Rissa!" She released him, turned, and skipped off into the crowd of other guests. Geoff plainly heard her animated voice announcing to anyone who would listen that she had the bouquet and she was getting married next. To him. Some of the ladies around her giggled.

"Nice one, Geoff," Jason muttered beside him.

Geoff remained in his hunkered down position. He lowered one arm to rest his hand on his knee, and the other fist he planted on his hip as he listened to Jenni showing off the flowers. "Never mind," he mumbled. "By tomorrow she'll forget all about this."

Instead of Jason's deep voice, a female pitch replied. "No, she won't."

Geoff jumped to his feet and spun around to see Clarissa, Jenni's older sister.

Like Jenni, Clarissa looked extra nice today. She was average looking— thin but not too skinny, with shoulder-length dark blond hair that flowed in gentle waves around a pleasant oval face. Clarissa and Jenni looked a lot alike, despite their age difference, except for their eyes. Jenni had big, beautiful blue eyes, yet Clarissa's eyes were a unique hazel mixture.

Lately, he'd seen her most Sundays in church, but when it wasn't winter, he saw both Clarissa and Jenni nearly every day when he was out walking his dog. He always enjoyed talking to Clarissa. Like him, she also read a lot, and they enjoyed many of the same books. She even owned a book autographed by his favorite author. In general, Clarissa was easy to talk to, and best of all, safe. Their friendship started with talking in the neighborhood when he was out with Spot and she was out with Jenni, and that was all it would ever be. No expectations, no rules, yet they could talk about anything and everything, good and bad, and then go right back to the way things were—friendly and casual.

Today, however, she was far from casual. Her pretty hazel eyes were narrowed, and her mouth had tightened into a thin line. He could almost feel the chill as she glowered at him.

Geoff cleared his throat and forced himself to smile. "Hi, Clarissa. How's it going?"

"It was going pretty well until you gave her the flowers."

"I only thought—"

"Surely you must have known that she's got a major crush on you."

"Well, I—"

"And now you're encouraging her!"

"But—" Before he could think of something worthwhile to say, Jenni's voice echoed from the crowd, telling someone else that she was going to marry him.

Clarissa waved one arm in the air in Jenni's direction, then crossed her arms again. "Look at what you've done!"

Geoff shrugged his shoulders. "She's just a little kid. She really has no idea what she's saying."

Clarissa continued to glare at him, not relaxing her stance. "That only makes it worse. Since we haven't been seeing each other as much over the winter, every time she sees you she has to recount everything you did."

Somehow, Geoff didn't think Clarissa meant to be flattering. He often saw Jenni at the living room window as he drove past their house when he arrived home from work, since Clarissa and Jenni didn't go to the park in March. He always waved to her, and she waved back.

He rammed his hands in his pockets. "I don't know what to say. She's a great little kid."

At his words, Clarissa's posture relaxed. "I'm sorry. I guess I'm probably being overprotective. She's been so happy about being flower girl, I guess all the wedding preparation has gone to her head. For the first time in a very long time, she's been happy. When reality hits that you're not going to marry her, I hope she's not going to be too hurt."

The murmur of low voices buzzed around him. Slightly above the volume of the rest of the crowd, Jenni's excited voice once again carried to him as she continued to show off the flowers to everyone in her immediate vicinity. He didn't want to give Jenni false hopes, but he didn't want to break her heart, either.

Geoff remembered the day he'd heard the couple a few doors down had been killed in a car accident. Jenni had only been spared because she had been properly secured in her safety-approved child seat. Rather than sell the house, Clarissa moved back in to raise Jenni, and that's when he first met her.

Geoff cleared his throat and forced himself to smile. "I'll admit I don't know much about little kids, but I'm sure she doesn't expect that I'm going to jump up and marry her tomorrow. By the time the flowers are dead, so will this little thing she's got for me. Just give her some time."

"I don't know. . . ." Clarissa's voice trailed off.

"Besides, now that I know what she's thinking, I can steer her away from the topic if it ever comes up and let her down gently. Soon she'll forget all about it. Little kids have short memories."

"You just told me you didn't know much about little kids."

He shrugged his shoulders and forced himself to smile, although he knew he probably looked pretty lame. "That's just what I heard."

"I don't know about that." Clarissa turned to the crowd. "Stan and Abby are leaving now. I should take Jenni and go say good-bye."

"I've already talked to them, so I'm staying right here. I guess I'll see you and Jenni at church tomorrow."

She nodded and walked away without saying a word, which Geoff didn't think was a bad thing.

Chapter 2

Clarissa Reynolds pulled up her collar when a blast of wind caught her hair. For now, the temperature was below freezing, but by the time church got out, the day would be warmer and the snow would be melting. Still, it wasn't quite spring temperatures.

She looked down to her right. "Are you warm enough, Jenni? Did you remember to wrap your scarf up tight?"

"Yes, Rissa. I'm warm. I even gots my ears covered."

Clarissa cringed inwardly at her little sister's diction, then reminded herself that Jenni was still only in first grade. "Let's hurry. We don't want to be late."

They hustled along side by side on the three-block journey to church.

Twenty-three years ago, when she was Jenni's age, Clarissa remembered walking to church with her parents, swinging between them, all three of them laughing as they tossed her into the snow so she could make angels without making footprints to get there.

There could be no such memories for Jenni. There was no one else to hold Jenni from the other side. It made Clarissa's reminiscences bittersweet.

Pushing those thoughts aside, Clarissa watched as Jenni started to skip. It warmed her from the inside out to see Jenni so happy. However, knowing the reason for Jenni's mood was only because they would see Geoff at church set the chill back, right down to her bones. She didn't want to think of what would happen when Jenni realized that Geoff wasn't going to marry her.

Geoff.

She couldn't help but like him. While she wouldn't have called him handsome, he was by no means ugly. His dirty blond hair was a nice, fashionable length. Some days his eyes were a dull green, other days a smoky gray, but he had the nicest, longest eyelashes she'd ever seen on a man. She didn't know why that fascinated her, but it did.

When they were together, they never lacked for conversation. Many days she didn't have the time or energy to take Jenni out, but she did anyway because she knew she would see Geoff. Since he only lived three houses away, he was easy to catch.

He'd been so nice to Jenni to give her the flowers, Clarissa had found it difficult to stay angry with him; after all, he'd meant well.

"Look, Rissa! I see Geoff's car!" Jenni started to run.

Clarissa cleared her thoughts, ran a few steps to catch up, and grabbed Jenni by the shoulder. "Don't run away from me. You hold my hand while we cross the street."

For once, Jenni didn't complain that she wasn't a baby.

Clarissa didn't know if that was good or bad.

They stomped the snow off their boots, ascended the stairs, and walked inside the foyer of the large church building. Just her luck, Geoff stood in a circle of people about their age, talking and laughing.

Before Clarissa could stop her, Jenni bolted forward, waving her arms as she ran. "Geoff! Hi, Geoff!"

He flinched at the sound of her voice, then excused himself from his group of friends. He turned around and hunkered down so he was at eye level with her when he spoke. "Hi, Jenni. It's good to see you. It's almost time for Sunday school."

"Will you walk me to my class?"

Before he could reply, Jenni grabbed his hand and pulled him away from his friends.

Together Clarissa and Geoff dropped Jenni off at her classroom, then turned in the direction of the adult classrooms.

Clarissa didn't want to be nervous about Jenni's "relationship" with Geoff, but she had to be both cautious and realistic. Jenni had never acted so infatuated with anyone of the male species before: not with a boy her own age and certainly not with a grown man. Just as Geoff had said, hopefully Jenni would soon forget about wanting to marry him. However, if Jenni didn't, she had to have a Plan B, which probably would have to involve Geoff.

The trouble was, she couldn't see getting any time alone with Geoff to talk about it. During the winter, pretty much the only time she saw him was in the foyer at church. However, she had to talk to him without her sister present.

She faced forward as she walked, hoping to appear casual as she spoke. "I think I'm going to try out another class on Sunday mornings. Do you mind if I go in the same one as you?"

She could see him turn his head in her peripheral vision. "Not at all. You probably already know most of the people, and there's always room for one more." He stepped aside to allow her to go in before him, then took a seat beside David. Since the seat on Geoff's other side was vacant, Clarissa sat there.

Right as she opened her mouth to see if Geoff had any ideas, the leader began the session. Just her luck, the discussion went overtime, which didn't give her the time she needed to talk to Geoff since she had to run back to collect Jenni from her classroom.

She led Jenni to their usual seats near the front of the sanctuary.

"Rissa? Where's Geoff?"

Clarissa gave her sister's hand a little squeeze. "I don't know. I guess he's gone to sit with his friends. Now let's enjoy the service."

All through the service, Jenni continuously and not-so-discreetly kept glancing behind them. It was all Clarissa could do to keep herself from also looking behind to see where he was.

When the service ended, Jenni didn't give Clarissa any time to chat with the people nearby. She grabbed Clarissa's hand and nearly dragged her into the foyer. Jenni's disappointment at being unable to find Geoff was so vivid, it was almost tangible.

Again, Clarissa gave her sister's hand an encouraging squeeze. "It's okay, Jenni. We'll see him again next Sunday. Now let's go home."

"But next Sunday is so long."

"The week will go by faster if you keep busy. There are cookies to bake this afternoon. We can make a nice casserole for supper, and then tomorrow is school. You'll see how fast it will be next Sunday. Now let's go home and make lunch."

Judging from Jenni's pouty-lipped frown, Clarissa could tell she wasn't convinced. However, not seeing Geoff for a week would do Jenni a world of good to help put some distance between them. The next step would be to remove the partial bouquet from Jenni's bedroom so she wouldn't think of Geoff when she couldn't see him.

⌖

Jenni's words as the cookies came out of the oven caught Clarissa completely off guard.

"Can I take some to Geoff? I bet he's home now."

"He may be home, but he's probably busy." At least she hoped he was busy.

"Please?" Jenni's eyes opened wide.

"But that means we have to get all dressed in our coats and boots again."

"That's okay. I think Geoff would really like some cookies. They're my favorite."

Clarissa opened her mouth to protest but changed her mind. While she didn't want to actively encourage Jenni, she didn't want it to look like she was trying to discourage her, either. She wanted her sister's emotional attachment to Geoff to die a natural death.

"Okay, let's get dressed."

Clarissa squeezed her eyes shut as Jenni squealed with glee and ran out of the kitchen. To the sounds of the closet door banging and of boots thumping against the wall, Clarissa filled a small container with fresh, warm cookies. By the time she reached the closet, Jenni already had her boots on and was slipping into her coat.

Jenni chattered brightly while they walked to Geoff's house, three doors down.

The second their feet touched the step, Geoff's dog started barking. Even though it would have been obvious there was someone at the door, Jenni knocked loudly, then immediately turned to Clarissa, her expression very serious for a little girl. "It's a good thing Geoff lives on the same side of the street as us."

Before Clarissa could think of an appropriate response, the door opened.

Geoff stood in the doorway, still wearing the same clothes he'd worn to church, with his little dog cradled in his arms. "Uh. . .hi, Clarissa, Jenni." His gaze lowered to the container in Jenni's hand. "Uh. . .come in."

The door had barely closed behind them when Jenni held the container at arm's length in front of her toward Geoff. "I made these for you!"

He tucked the dog under one arm, then accepted the container with a smile. "Cookies! Thank you."

"If you already ate lunch, you can have one now."

He fumbled between the container and the dog until he managed to pick out one cookie. He grinned as he bit into the still-warm treat. "Would you like to sit down or something? I think I can find some juice for Jenni, and I happen to have a pot of coffee made. If you're interested."

"No, I think we'd better not. I—"

"Oh, boy!" Jenni chirped as she kicked off her boots. "Can I hold Spot?"

He squatted down, still holding the container of cookies in one hand, the dog in the other. "My hands are kind of full. You're going to have to take him."

Jenni grabbed the dog far too quickly. Spot, however, took the innocent manhandling in stride. Not only did he go without protest, he immediately started licking Jenni's face once she managed to get a decent grip on him.

Geoff grinned. "Spot obviously has missed you over the winter."

Jenni giggled.

Clarissa mumbled, "That name must have taken a lot of forethought."

Geoff's grin widened as he rose. "He really does have a spot on his back. Do you know any other dogs named Spot?"

"Well, no."

" 'Nuff said. Let's go into the living room. What do you take in your coffee?"

"Just milk or cream or whatever you have that's white, so long as it's a real liquid and not that powdered stuff."

"I agree. I'll be right back."

While Geoff poured the coffee, Clarissa took a seat and glanced around Geoff's living room. For a man's home, she supposed it was fairly tidy, perhaps even tidier than her own living room, but he didn't have a six-year-old to pick up after. A large-screen television sat surrounded by a set of very impressive speakers. In the stand below the unit sat a VCR, a DVD player, a CD player, and some kind of video game set, along with four different-colored controllers. On the coffee table, besides a half-finished mug of coffee and a small stack of magazines, were a stack of remote controls and a digital camera.

His furniture consisted of a couch and love seat in a mixed pattern of shades of blue, and a recliner in a solid shade of the base blue of the couch, where Jenni sat playing with Spot, tugging on a colorful rope toy. The walls were an off-white color, and the carpet was a dark gray that probably shouldn't have gone with the fabric of the couch, yet it did.

The decorating was sparse. The only thing of any note on any of the living room walls was a watercolor painting of a car, a classic Mustang if she wasn't mistaken. Both the car and the frame just happened to be the exact same shade and color as the recliner.

The place had possibilities, and she liked it.

"Sorry I took so long. Jenni, I'll put your juice right here."

Since Jenni was busy playing with Geoff's dog, Clarissa stood and spoke to Geoff as softly as she could without whispering. "I think I need more milk in my coffee. Can you show me to your kitchen?"

He stood immediately. "I'm sorry; let me take that."

Instead, she cradled the mug in both palms. "I can do it." She motioned her head toward the opening to the kitchen as discreetly as she could. "Please show me where to go."

One of Geoff's eyebrows quirked. "This way."

Once they were in the kitchen and out of Jenni's earshot, Clarissa turned to Geoff. "I don't know what to do about this crush she's got on you. Do you think maybe we can distract her with Spot?"

He turned and glanced to the doorway leading to the living room. "Maybe. Dogs are good therapy. In fact, most pets are. Even lizards, although you can't play with a lizard like you can with a dog."

"Are you suggesting I get my sister a lizard?"

He shook his head. "Not at all. I'm just saying pets are good therapy for people of all ages. I know you work all day, so getting a puppy may not be a good idea, but maybe a kitten?"

Just what she needed. More responsibility. "I'll pass. We both know who would get stuck looking after it. Me."

"You're probably right. Sorry. I should just mind my own business."

Without thinking, Clarissa rested her palm on his forearm. "No, I'm the one who should be sorry. I had no idea she would invite herself in. You're being so nice to go along with this."

He stiffened momentarily at her touch, glanced down at her fingers on his arm, then raised his head. "No problem. I wasn't doing anything anyway."

They returned to the living room and chatted while Jenni continued to play with Spot. Clarissa had to stop Jenni from throwing a tennis ball in Geoff's house, even though he said he didn't mind. He obviously had no idea how bad a six-year-old girl's aim could be.

While Jenni and Spot played, Clarissa talked to Geoff. As the afternoon wore on, being with him reminded her of how much she missed spending time with him. Now that winter was almost over, she anticipated seeing him more, which in the summer would be nearly every day

However, seeing him more didn't fit into the trend she wanted. Jenni wouldn't lose interest in Geoff if they saw more of him instead of less.

Clarissa realized how much time had passed when the phone rang. So as not to completely monopolize Geoff's day, Clarissa convinced Jenni they had to start making supper. They thanked Geoff for his hospitality and made their way home.

Thankfully, tomorrow was back to school for Jenni. Hopefully, once she got busy, Jenni would forget about Geoff.

Chapter 3

Geoff! Hi, Geoff!" Jenni ran toward him, waving her arms, her scarf flapping behind her.

Only two steps beyond his driveway, Geoff shuffled to a halt. Faithful to his training, Spot stopped when Geoff stopped and sat beside him.

"What are you doing here?" He glanced down the deserted sidewalk. "Where is your sister?"

"She had to get the phone. She told me to wait at the door, but I saw you. Can I come with you and Spot? Rissa will say it's okay."

Geoff frowned. He wasn't as sure as Jenni about Clarissa's reaction. He also wasn't positive that Clarissa would assume his house was the first place Jenni would go if she wasn't where she was supposed to be. Worse, her presence proved the situation wasn't fixing itself. "I'd feel better if I asked Clarissa myself. We'd better go back to your house."

"We can still take Spot for a walk, can't we?"

"That depends on Clarissa. Would you like to hold him?"

"Yes!"

He handed Jenni the leash, and they walked in silence to her house. Just as he started to go up the first stair, the door opened and Clarissa stepped outside.

"Geoff? What are you doing here?"

"I was taking Spot for a walk, and Jenni joined me. I thought maybe we should come back and ask if that's okay."

Clarissa's eyebrows knotted, and she planted her hands on her hips. "Jenni, what did we discuss about Geoff?"

Instead of learning what had been said about him in his absence, all he heard was a rather subservient "I know" from Jenni.

He looked down at Spot. Spot's tail wagged even though the dog was sitting. His back legs quivered, not from cold, but from the excitement of wanting to continue on his walk. Beside Spot, Jenni shuffled from one foot to the other as she waited for her sister's reaction.

Watching both dog and child, Geoff tried to tamp down a smile. People often teased him about the small size of his dog until they knew how demanding a Jack Russell terrier could be. However, when Spot's enthusiasm for life in general was properly controlled, his small size and willing affection was a good match for a lonely little girl.

"I don't mind if Jenni walks Spot with me. You can come, too, if you'd like."

Clarissa checked her watch. "We were going to the bakery for some fresh bread for supper."

Jenni was nearly dancing where she stood. "But Geoff is letting me walk Spot."

At the sound of his name, Spot's rear end wiggled more than ever.

"He's really reaching his level of endurance, Clarissa. I'm torturing him by making him sit there. We can detour to the bakery instead of the park. We should go now."

When Spot heard the word *go,* it was all the little dog could take. He leapt up, whined, and paced back and forth in front of Jenni.

Jenni giggled. "Please, Rissa?"

Clarissa sighed. "I suppose we could walk instead of taking the car."

Jenni clapped her hands, making only muffled thuds since she was wearing mittens. "Yippee!"

Clarissa locked the house, and they began their journey to the bakery.

The rows of wet snow piled at the sides of the sidewalk had expanded into blobs during the spring melt, narrowing the width of the sidewalk so the four of them couldn't walk side by side. Jenni walked ahead with Spot, and Geoff and Clarissa walked together behind her.

Out of the corner of his eye, Geoff could see Clarissa smiling as they sauntered along. "Spot is such a sweet little dog."

Geoff made a halfhearted laugh. "Not always. Jack Russell terriers can be very headstrong. He's also very sneaky. Especially if he figures there's food involved."

As they walked, Geoff continued to chat with Clarissa while Jenni fixed all her attention on Spot, making sure he remained at heel on her left side, just as Geoff had shown her. He felt strangely disappointed when they arrived back at Clarissa's house, because he wasn't ready to part ways.

Geoff took Spot's leash from Jenni while Clarissa inserted the key into the lock. "I guess I'll see both of you at church on Sunday."

Jenni stepped closer to him, reached up, and tugged on the corner of his jacket. "Geoff?"

"Yes, Jenni?" Geoff looked down and smiled. He couldn't help himself. Despite Jenni's misguided feelings for him, the extra time he'd spent with her made him like her now more than ever.

While being fond of a little girl was fine and acceptable, it was his growing feelings for Clarissa he struggled with. A casual friendship as had been previously established he could handle, but the more time he spent with her, the more time he wanted to spend together. He didn't know if that was an upward or downward spiral. While he enjoyed their time together, the potential for it to develop into more existed. He couldn't allow a deeper relationship, but he didn't know how to stop it.

"Will you eat supper at our house?" Without releasing his hem, Jenni turned to Clarissa. "It's okay, isn't it, Rissa? Spot can stay, too, can't he?"

Geoff raised his head to see Clarissa's face. Her cheeks suddenly turned pink, but not from the crisp spring breeze. "I suppose so. I was going to hollow out the French loaves we just bought and put stew inside. So it's nothing fancy."

Geoff's stomach grumbled at the mental picture. He hadn't thought he was hungry, but he was now.

"I obviously don't have dog food, but I don't mind giving Spot some stew, if it's okay with you."

Geoff stood. He should have run for the hills, but instead, he told himself that he was doing this for Jenni.

He cleared his throat. "As much as Spot would enjoy the stew, I don't give him people food. He can wait for his dog food when I get home. If you don't mind that I can't stay too long afterward, I'd be delighted."

Jenni started to skip in place and clap her hands until Clarissa gave her a quelling glance, which stilled her. Clarissa opened the door, and Geoff followed Jenni into the living room while Clarissa disappeared into the kitchen. Spot followed Clarissa, hopeful beyond reason for a handout, leaving Geoff alone with Jenni.

He didn't know what to say, so he was relieved when Jenni did most of the talking. She told him about her teacher, her friends, how she was learning to print real words in first grade and even read them.

All he could do was smile and say he was proud of her accomplishments until, to his relief, Clarissa called them to come into the kitchen for supper.

Jenni led with a simple prayer of thanks, then continued to chatter freely while they ate. Clarissa responded in all the right ways, which encouraged Jenni to keep yakking, sparing Geoff from having to add to the conversation. He didn't know if Clarissa caught the reference, but during Jenni's ramblings, she mentioned that when they got married, she planned to make the same kind of delicious stew that 'Rissa' made.

After supper, Clarissa sent Jenni into the living room with Spot, telling her to select a good movie from their collection, leaving Geoff alone with

Clarissa in the kitchen. When she began to tidy up the kitchen, Geoff naturally began to help.

"I'm so sorry, Geoff. I really thought she'd be over this by now. I hope she didn't embarrass you. Quite frankly, though, it's good to see her like this. I haven't seen her talk so much since Mom and Dad died."

He shrugged his shoulders as he gathered the plates from the table. "I don't mind. I'll admit she caught me off guard, inviting me like that. Supper was great, by the way. Thank you."

Clarissa turned her head from him, but not quickly enough. Her cheeks darkened, which Geoff thought quite endearing. "This is getting so out of hand. She runs to you every chance she gets. When she gave you half the batch of her favorite cookies last weekend, I nearly fainted. She's got it bad, and I don't know what to do."

While Clarissa filled the sink with water, Geoff turned his head to the doorway and listened to Jenni discussing the choice of movies with Spot, who was apparently paying attention. "I have an idea. What if I let her take some time and play with Spot every day or two? She obviously likes him, and he likes her, too. She'll soon forget all about me."

Clarissa shook her head. "You don't listen to her when you're not here. Yes, she likes Spot, but the main thing is that Spot is with you. The way you let her walk Spot and play with him makes you even better in her eyes. She told me this morning she loves you now more than ever. I almost wasn't surprised to find you on our doorstep when I came outside today."

Geoff pressed his lips together while Clarissa lowered the plates into the soapy water. Of course he was flattered, but it wasn't right. He was technically old enough to be Jenni's father, even though Jenni's father had been much older. Not knowing them well, Geoff didn't know if Jenni's mother was the father's second and much younger wife, or if both Jenni and Clarissa had the same mother, and Jenni was an "afterthought."

Geoff shook his head. The age difference between the two sisters wasn't his concern, or any of his business. What was his concern was that whatever Jenni felt for him seemed to be getting worse instead of better.

Again, he turned his head and listened to Jenni talking to Spot in the living room. Instead of loving him in the "marriage" kind of way, he suspected that because she lacked a male authority figure in her life, with neither a father nor a brother in these formative years, she considered him the next best thing. What she felt for him wasn't love at all but a desire to simply reach out for another person.

As Geoff picked up a plate and dried it, he studied Clarissa, who remained silent while she concentrated on scrubbing the pot very clean.

He knew she didn't date much. Over the last year she'd told him about some of the losers she'd gone out with. Even if she hadn't told him, he would have known. Not that he paid attention to what his neighbors did, but he walked Spot every day. He knew the cars of all his neighbors, and all his neighbors' friends and relatives. Clarissa's driveway seldom housed anything but her own car and Jenni's bike. Old Mrs. Jenkins, the widow in one of the houses between them, got more company than Clarissa.

"Isn't there anyone else you can introduce her to? Maybe a boy in school?"

Clarissa shook her head. "I've already thought of that. She has no interest in any of the boys in her class. She only wants you. She thinks she's in love with you because you're so nice to her every time you see her."

"That's not difficult. She's a darling little girl. But I don't treat her different from any other children I know."

Clarissa pulled the other towel off the oven door handle and began to dry her hands. "That's exactly why she thinks she loves you so much. For someone who claims not to know anything about small children, you're doing everything right. I saw you when you gave her the flowers."

Geoff blinked a few times. "I didn't want them. It's not like I made some big sacrifice."

"It's not that. You didn't stand up and bend down, towering above her, or hand them to her from the chair. You lowered yourself to the floor so you could see her eye to eye when you talked to her, without any part of you being above her. You also don't talk down to her or use baby words or change your voice. You talk to her as an equal. You do that kind of thing all the time. I've seen you in church, too. You're a natural with children. They all probably adore you, just like Jenni."

Something inside Geoff went stiff. He didn't want children to like him. More significant than never getting married, he was never having children. Never.

"I didn't do it on purpose."

"That only proves my point."

Geoff didn't know any other way to act toward children. It didn't take a genius child psychologist to know that if he gave children the brush-off there would be hurt feelings, and he couldn't be that way. Especially to Jenni.

This time, both of them stopped their movements and listened to Jenni, who was now trying to convince Spot to give back a sock he'd found under the couch. She was explaining to him that she would get in trouble with 'Rissa' for having it there in the first place, and she had to quickly put it in the hamper.

Geoff sighed and began to dry the pot Clarissa had scrubbed so diligently.

"I wonder if I'm going about this all wrong. Maybe she's chasing me like this because I've been trying to avoid her. I'm not seeing anybody. I could pretend to be Jenni's boyfriend for a while. She's just a kid, but she isn't stupid. It shouldn't take too long before she sees that I'm not her Mr. Right. Who knows, maybe she'll even split up with me instead of the other way around. I think I could handle the day when she breaks my heart."

Clarissa stared at him blankly, glanced to the doorway where Jenni's voice was coming from, then back to him. "My first response is to say no, but I don't have a better suggestion. Maybe giving her what she wants will be the only thing that will work. I hope you're prepared for what you're getting yourself into."

Quite frankly, Geoff didn't see it as any big sacrifice. By his own choice, he didn't have much of a social life. He wasn't sure what little kids liked to do, but he figured for starters he could take her out with him when he took Spot out for his walk every day. In just over a week the snow would be gone and the weather would be even warmer. He could take her to the park to play with other children if the ground dried fast enough. Even if he spent most of his off-work hours at the park with Jenni all summer long, it wasn't like he had anything better to do.

However, he didn't know if it would be good or bad, because that also meant seeing much more of Clarissa.

He shrugged his shoulders. "I suppose tomorrow is as good a time as any to start. I get home from work at four-thirty. When would be a good time for me to pick her up?"

"That's about the time we get home, too."

"Can I pick her up at 4:45 then? I doubt the restaurant will be crowded so early on a weeknight."

"You're going to take Jenni out for dinner?"

Geoff felt his blush. "Most people go out to dinner for a first date, so I thought that was a good start. I'll probably take her for a burger, and then she'll want to go to the play center with the other kids. It might be a good idea for you to come, too. You can help me make more plans while she's busy."

Clarissa smiled and nodded. "I can tell her it's a date, and that as her sister, it's my job to chaperone."

Geoff hung up the towel on the oven door. "That sounds like a good plan. Now, if you don't mind, I should take Spot home and feed him. I'll see you both tomorrow."

Chapter 4

Clarissa sucked her bottom lip between her teeth to keep herself from laughing. Since this was Jenni's first official "date," Jenni made it more than clear that she would be sitting in the front seat with Geoff, and Clarissa was to sit in the back. Fortunately, Jenni didn't think it at all strange for her big sister to accompany her.

From the back seat, Clarissa watched Geoff interact with Jenni. She couldn't help but be impressed.

While Geoff positioned Jenni's booster car seat and made sure she was properly buckled in, he asked about her day at school. As they traveled, Jenni eagerly recounted how well she could print the letter *J*, not only for her own name, but so she could print Geoff's name. Clarissa bit her bottom lip at how Geoff gently informed Jenni that he spelled his name the other way, with a *G*, and then offered to show her how to print it.

She could see why Jenni liked Geoff so much. He had a way with children one didn't often see with people who weren't parents themselves. He was patient and kind and sensitive to young children, making her think that when the time came, Geoff would make an excellent father. Likewise, he would also make some lucky woman a wonderful husband. Not only was he a strong Christian, he was fun to talk to, interesting, and considerate. She'd been very impressed when he had helped with the dishes without being asked. He could just as easily have gone into the living room with Jenni.

Geoff nodded in understanding as Jenni explained the intricacies of how to sort and fit all her school supplies into her cubby at the end of her last class. Everything that was important to Jenni for today also appeared equally important to Geoff.

Clarissa wondered if he would be equally attentive and caring to an adult. Something told her he would.

Once they arrived at the fast-food restaurant, Geoff insisted on paying for everyone's burger and fries. They found a table near the play center, bowed their heads, and, ignoring the din around them, waited while Jenni said a short prayer of thanks for their food.

"This is such fun, Geoff! Look what I got!" Jenni held up the toy that came with the kid's meal.

He nodded, listening to Jenni as she chattered away about the other toys that came in the set and then elaborated on the movie that featured the characters. Before long, just as she had every other time Clarissa had taken her to the restaurant, Jenni politely asked permission to go to the play center.

Geoff smiled as Jenni ran to the enclosed area. Together, Clarissa and Geoff watched Jenni through the large glass window that soundproofed the play center from the restaurant area, not looking at each other as they spoke.

She could hear the grin in Geoff's voice. "It looks like Jenni is enjoying our date, although I've never had a date bolt on me like that."

"You're doing great. She's going to talk about this for a long time."

"While she's occupied, we should talk about other places I can take her. She's probably too small to go bowling."

"You'd be surprised. They have glo-bowling for the kids. The music is so loud you can't hear anyone talking, it's quite dark, and they have black lights that make stuff glow in the dark. They have rubber bumpers on the sides of the lanes, so instead of gutter balls, the bowling balls bounce off and every ball makes it down to the end."

"That sounds like cheating."

"Maybe, but the kids love it, and Jenni is no exception. It's fun, and that's all that matters when you're six years old."

"Then if you don't think it will be too much for her, I'll take her bowling later this week. Unless you have other plans."

Suddenly, Clarissa didn't feel like smiling anymore. Now more than ever, Clarissa could understand why Jenni had attached herself to Geoff. Clarissa was an adult, not an impressionable young girl, and she could feel herself also falling for his charm. He wasn't doing this begrudgingly; he seemed intent on everyone enjoying himself or herself. His attention to Jenni was bringing back the perky personality she'd had before the death of their parents, something Clarissa hadn't been able to do, no matter how hard she tried.

"No," she muttered, pointedly keeping all her attention on Jenni while she spoke. "I don't have other plans. I just don't want her to get too tired by going out too often."

"I'll take all my cues from you. How about if you give me some secret, prearranged signal so I'll know when it's time to go home? If you suggest it's time to go, Jenni might resent you, but if I say it, I have a feeling everything will be fine. After all, at least for now, I can do no wrong."

He wasn't doing too badly in doing no wrong for Clarissa, either. Going along with Jenni's boyfriend fantasy was surely a sacrifice, yet Geoff was doing it gladly and willingly so he wouldn't hurt Jenni's feelings. At the same time, he was also spending some quality time with her.

Clarissa turned to face him, knowing Jenni was safe and really didn't have to be watched intently every second in the enclosed kid-zone environment. "Are you sure you really want to do this? You know it could go on for a long time."

He shrugged his shoulders. "I don't mind. Really. Besides, I'm curious about glo-bowling. This gives me an excuse to try it. You know. Like when you want to see a movie made for kids, and you're too embarrassed to go as an adult, so you have to wait until it comes out as a rental. Actually, there's one that starts this weekend, a computer-animated flick I'd love to see. Now I won't look like a wimp, because I'll have a little kid with me."

Clarissa immediately knew which movie he meant. "Every time she sees the commercial, she makes me come watch it with her."

He leaned closer, grinning as he spoke. "You wanna come, too? Just promise me you won't cry if it's a sappy ending."

Clarissa's heart stopped beating, then started up in double time. Geoff's eyes sparkled beneath his gorgeous long lashes, almost daring her to challenge him.

She couldn't. All she could do was stare back. More than ever, she could see how Geoff had become the man of Jenni's dreams. If she wasn't careful, Geoff could easily become the man of her own dreams.

"I won't cry," she mumbled. "I promise."

"Great. What else do you think I can do to take Jenni out on dates until she tires of me? I've got Spot entered in a flyball tournament in July. The weekly practices end past her bedtime, but I could take her a few times and leave early. That might be sufficiently boring for a small child to sit through and might hasten her decision to find a man who's more likely to join her in the sandbox on a summer day."

"I don't allow Jenni to play in sandboxes. You never know what's in there. What's a flyball tournament?"

"It's kind of like a relay race for dogs. A team of four dogs runs one dog at a time over a set of hurdles, grabs a tennis ball, and takes the ball back to the starting point; then the next dog goes. The teams race against each other."

"But Spot is so small. How could he possibly win a race?"

Geoff grinned, once again sending Clarissa's heart into a flutter. "Teams consist of three big dogs and one small dog. The hurdles are set four inches below the shoulder height of the smallest dog, so the large dogs literally fly over the low hurdles. The smaller the last dog, the more advantageous to the other dogs. For a small dog, Spot's pretty fast, especially when there's a tennis ball involved. I think he really understands the game, and he really does try to win. They also have an agility competition. That's when the dogs run through hoops and tunnels and climb things. I haven't decided if I'm going to enter him this year because we haven't practiced as much as we should have. The deadline is in a couple of days; I guess I'd better make up my mind."

"That sounds interesting. I think Jenni would like to go."

His voice lowered, but this time he wasn't smiling. "And what about you? Would you like to go?"

She opened her mouth, but no sound came out. Most of the men she knew considered team sports to be hockey, football, and baseball, and most of the time, their only activity with those sports was to move from the couch to the kitchen when they were hungry. She'd never known anyone who participated in a team activity with his dog. Jenni would probably want to go to such a thing to watch the dogs. Clarissa wanted to go so she could watch Geoff.

Finally, her vocal chords decided to function. "Yes. I think I'd like that."

Before Clarissa could collect her thoughts to think of something else to say, Jenni returned, huffing and puffing, to have a long sip of her drink while she stood beside their table.

Geoff shuffled until he was sitting sideways in the seat, then leaned forward until his elbows rested on his knees. "Are you having fun, Jenni?"

She nodded rapidly. "Mmmm hmmm!" she muttered without her lips leaving the straw. In a flash, the drink was back on the table. "This is the bestest date ever!" Before either of them could respond, Jenni was back inside the play area.

Geoff made a lopsided grin as he repositioned himself to sit properly once again. "Considering her big sister came, and Jenni doesn't mind that I've spent more time with you than I have with her, it's obvious she doesn't date much."

Clarissa nodded. "Guess not."

Once again, they both turned their heads to watch Jenni playing with the other children.

Naturally, this was Jenni's first "date," if one could call it a date, but the truth was that Clarissa didn't date much, either, at least not much in the last year since she'd taken the responsibility to raise her little sister.

She'd been going steady with Kyle for nearly two years, and he'd even hinted at marriage before her parents' accident. She'd always thought he liked Jenni the few times he'd seen her. But when suddenly Clarissa became responsible for Jenni's care, everything changed. Kyle didn't want to be Jenni's quasi-father, as he so bluntly described the position. What had hurt the most was when he accused Clarissa of being unfair to him, to suddenly bring a child into their relationship. He wanted children, but he only wanted his own. When Kyle told Clarissa to make up her mind, whether it was him or Jenni, the choice had not been difficult. From that day on, she hadn't seen Kyle again. When she gave up her apartment, he hadn't even joined the rest of their friends to help her move back into her parents' house to raise her sister.

She discovered the hard way that Kyle was not unique. Most of the men who already knew her suddenly shied away, knowing that if a serious relationship developed, Jenni was part of the package.

More shocking was the reaction of men whom she didn't already know when her parents died. Because she was so much older than Jenni, most people assumed Jenni was her daughter, not her sister. When they discovered Clarissa was neither widowed nor divorced, yet came with a child, many wrongly assumed that she was easy on a date. Between the men who didn't want to become an instant father and those who had something else in mind when they went out, Clarissa didn't date much, either.

She tried not to let her pride be bruised, knowing the only reason she was with a man now was because he was allegedly dating her little sister.

The next time Jenni appeared for a drink, Geoff and Clarissa stopped her from going back to the play area. They spent a little time at the table talking and decided it was time to go home—after all, it was a school night.

Like a gentleman, Geoff parked his car in the driveway and saw them both safely inside.

Before he left, Jenni turned to him and looked up, her eyes open wide. "Thank you for taking us, Geoff. That was lots of fun."

He squatted down to talk eye to eye with her. "I had fun, too."

"Are we going out tomorrow?"

"I'm sorry, Jenni, no. Tomorrow is Bible study night, and the next day is when I go to practice with Spot. How would you like to go glo-bowling on Friday?"

"Yes!" she squealed, throwing her arms around Geoff. "I love glo-bowling! We went for Matthew's birthday party. It's so fun!"

Very slowly, Geoff returned Jenni's hug. As he gave her a gentle squeeze, his eyes closed, and for a split second, his whole face tightened, as if Jenni had somehow hurt him.

The second Jenni released him, he stood. "Then I guess I'll see you Friday." He turned toward Clarissa. "How's five-thirty? I hope you don't have anything else to do. If not, we can reschedule."

She shook her head. "That's fine." She reached down and rested one hand on Jenni's shoulder. "We had better let Geoff go home, Jenni. You've got to take a bath tonight and get to bed early. Tomorrow is school."

Jenni nodded solemnly. "Bye, Geoff."

Geoff nodded, turned, and let himself out.

Clarissa stared for a few seconds at the closed door. Even though they were together for Jenni's sake, she had wanted him to stay and have coffee. She wanted to talk some more about things that had nothing to do with Jenni. She was already starting to fear that when Jenni's crush on him ended, they would go back to only seeing each other in the park, and she didn't want that to happen.

Like Jenni, Clarissa also found herself looking forward to Friday.

Chapter 5

Geoff stared at the calendar on the wall of his kitchen. Never in his life had he lived with such a schedule. Of course, he went to Bible study meetings every Wednesday and flyball and agility practice with Spot on Thursdays, but somehow, almost every other day of the month had something penciled in, and the same with the previous month.

Every date had something to do with Jenni and Clarissa. They went to movies together; they went glo-bowling once a month. As a unit, they were on a first-name basis with many of the staff at the hamburger restaurant. On Sundays they naturally attended church together, and after the service, they stayed together for lunch and supper, too. He spent so much time at their house, they'd bought a bag of dog food.

With the arrival of summer, they were able to do more outdoor activities, and Jenni wanted to do them all. In the time since Stan and Abby's wedding, when Geoff first started "dating" Jenni, both he and Clarissa had noticed a big difference in the little girl. There were times Clarissa still heard Jenni crying at night, but those times were happening less often. When they were together, Jenni's laughter happened more spontaneously, and she was starting to reach out to the other children, participating instead of waiting to be asked to join in.

After Jenni was in bed, Geoff often stayed with Clarissa. They prayed together, they talked, and they watched television together. They shared their joys and their sorrows, or at least, most of them. There were still things he hadn't told Clarissa, things he didn't ever intend to tell her.

He didn't want to ruin what was there, but being with them so much forced him to think about things he didn't want to deal with.

Family life.

Just to put some noise in the house, Geoff turned on the television and flipped to a popular blow-'em-up space series, pointedly ignoring anything remotely related to a family setting. It didn't quell the sensation of restlessness.

Leaving the television on, he picked up his Bible and flipped through, trying to find verses telling him to be happy with what he had and not to want what God didn't want him to have.

He seldom dated because he couldn't risk opening any doors he couldn't close. He only went out with a woman as a friend, when they both knew nothing would develop from it. He'd never regretted when the time came to say good-bye.

But Clarissa was different. He didn't want to see his time with Clarissa end, but it had to. They both knew that when Jenni's puppy-love crush on him faded, their lives would go back to normal—for Clarissa it would be again just her and Jenni, and for Geoff it would be just him and Spot. It wasn't ideal, but it was the way it had to be.

He continued to flip through the pages in his Bible. He wanted to pray for God's will, but he didn't know what God's will was in this situation. He knew God didn't want him to have a family of his own—he'd been told that in more ways and more times than he could count. One day Clarissa would meet the man who would be the perfect husband for her, and he could never be that man.

Even though it wasn't realistic, he wanted to keep seeing Clarissa, regardless of when Jenni experienced a change of heart toward him. He knew he was being selfish and that was wrong, but he couldn't help himself. He thought about Clarissa at the oddest times during the day, including while he was at work. She even found her way into his dreams. He didn't find it annoying—he enjoyed thinking about her. Her warm smile. Her generous spirit. Her patience. Her kindness. He didn't know why he had thought she was only average looking before, because now that he'd been with her almost daily, he realized she was absolutely beautiful. She had the most gorgeous hazel eyes he'd ever seen.

He'd even thought about what it would be like to kiss her.

Geoff wondered if this was what it was like to be falling in love. Even though he knew it was wrong, he didn't want to stop seeing her. It made him want to pray that Jenni would be "in love" with him forever to give him an excuse to keep seeing Clarissa. Of course, he knew that was neither realistic nor fair.

He tried to let the verses he read comfort him, but they didn't completely dull the ache. Instead, Geoff called Spot for a walk, hoping the night air would clear his head.

He was sinking into a hole, and every time he saw them again, he sucked himself down deeper.

Geoff walked into the Sunday school classroom and sat in his usual place beside David.

David turned to him as soon as he finished his conversation. "I saw an ad in the paper for that dog thing you've got Spot entered in. I meant to ask, did you ever decide if you were going to do the obstacle course thing?"

"It's called agility trials. And yes, I did enter him."

David shrugged his shoulders. "Do you think you stand a chance of winning? He's kind of small."

"We're entering because it's fun. It's not about winning or losing. Are you going to be there to take pictures for the paper?"

"Wouldn't miss it. I got some great pictures last year. Do you remember that big black dog that went in the tunnel and wouldn't come out?"

Before Geoff answered, Clarissa walked in, halting his thought processes. She smiled and made a beeline for the empty seat beside him. Geoff tried not to let it show that he was happy to see her. When David saw her approaching, he turned and continued the conversation he was involved in before Geoff sat down.

Clarissa slid into the seat, tucked her purse under her chair, and turned to him. "Long time, no see," she said, grinning as she spoke.

Geoff lifted his wrist and checked his watch. "Yeah. It's been a whole eleven hours. Did Jenni sleep okay?"

"Yes. I checked on her after you left, and she didn't move."

He was about to ask if she kept her promise to get ready for church with no problem since they let her stay up late, but the leader directed everyone's attention to the front, and the lesson began.

After the class ended, when they went to pick up Jenni from her classroom, they found Jenni pacing in the back. When she looked up at them, her eyes were glassy.

Clarissa knelt down in front of her and rested one hand on Jenni's arm. "What's wrong? Did someone hurt you?"

Jenni shook her head so fast her blond curls flipped back and forth. "No. Mrs. Morgan says she's gotta have a operation. So she can't be our teacher anymore until school starts again. She said we gotta have another teacher, but no one is good like Mrs. Morgan."

Geoff frowned. Two of the prayer requests this morning had centered around Julia Morgan. First was for a quick recovery after her unexpected surgery, which would be Monday. Second was that a suitable teacher could be found for the primary-level class on short notice.

Clarissa smiled and stroked Jenni's hair. "I'm sure someone nice will come and teach while Mrs. Morgan gets better. Would you like it if I was your teacher until Mrs. Morgan can come back?"

Jenni's eyes widened. "Really?"

Clarissa nodded. "I've never taught Sunday school before, but I might like to try."

Jenni glanced at Geoff, then turned back to her sister. "Mrs. Morgan sometimes gets a helper. Can Geoff be your helper? Or maybe since you didn't do Sunday school before, Geoff can be the teacher, and you can be the helper."

Geoff tried not to choke. "But, Jenni, I've never taught Sunday school, either."

"But Rissa says you know the Bible real good."

Geoff felt his cheeks heat up. It both flattered him and made him nervous that the two of them talked about him at such length. "I like to read my Bible, but that doesn't mean I know enough to be a good teacher."

Geoff wouldn't have thought it possible, but Jenni's big blue eyes widened even more. Her lower lip quivered. "Please?"

He knew he was a goner. "I'll ask the Sunday school superintendent, but I'm not making any promises."

Before he could move, Jenni lunged forward and threw her arms around his legs. "Thank you, Geoff!" she mumbled against his thigh. "You're the best!"

Beside him, Clarissa made a strangled cough.

Geoff pried Jenni's arms off him and stepped back. "Let's go in for the service now. I think I have some praying to do."

Chapter 6

Clarissa kissed Jenni on the forehead as she tucked her sister into bed. By the time she tiptoed out of the room, she was sure Jenni was already asleep. It had been a long day.

Clarissa sighed as she sank into the couch. It might have been a long day, but it had been a short week. Or if not a short one, definitely a busy one. Monday they'd again gone out for burgers with Geoff. Tuesday he took them to the mall, where they walked and walked and didn't buy a single thing. Wednesday she got a sitter for Jenni and went with Geoff to his home group for Bible study. After the class they sat with the Sunday school superintendent and talked about taking over the primary class on a temporary basis. Thursday Jenni played with Spot in the living room while Clarissa and Geoff brainstormed in the kitchen about the lesson they would do on Sunday. Clarissa couldn't believe how disappointed she was when Geoff and Spot had to run off to their flyball and agility practice.

Friday they'd rented a movie, and the four of them huddled together on the couch to watch it, although Spot got kicked off when he started stealing Jenni's popcorn.

Then today, Saturday, Geoff had taken them to an environmental awareness event. They'd built bird feeders and then gone into wooded areas of the park to hang them. Clarissa didn't know who was more tired, herself or Jenni, but it was a good tired. She knew she would be stiff tomorrow, but she didn't care. Being with Geoff had made it all worthwhile. She'd be seeing him again tomorrow when he picked them up earlier than usual so they'd be ready to teach their first Sunday school class together.

She smiled through her exhaustion, mentally kicking herself for not noticing Geoff before Jenni fell in "love" with him.

They both knew whatever was happening was temporary, that they were only together until Jenni fell out of "love" with him. But Geoff being the man he was, Clarissa thought it very possible that would never happen. Just like Jenni, she felt herself falling in love with him, but in a different and very adult way.

It was a given that she found him attractive, but more important than that, they shared anything and everything. The only thing they hadn't talked much about was his family. She'd told him so much about her parents, including why there was such a large age difference between herself and Jenni. Yet she knew almost nothing of Geoff's parents or his family—she only knew that his family lived across town, and he had one older brother who was married. She assumed there was some kind of problem in the family. One day, she hoped he would confide in her, but that hadn't happened yet.

Clarissa yawned and stared at the remote control for the television, lying just out of reach in her current position. She lifted her arm, knowing the remote was too far away, then let her arm drop.

She smiled at herself. If she was too tired to reach the remote, she should just go to bed. Besides, the sooner she fell asleep, the sooner it would be morning.

And the sooner she would see Geoff.

❧

"Rissa! Rissa! Where are you?"

"I'm in the bathroom," Clarissa mumbled around her toothbrush, her head over the sink. "What do you want?"

"You gotta come!" Jenni yelled from down the hall.

With her toothbrush still in her mouth, Clarissa rushed out of the bathroom. She took exactly one step and skidded to a halt.

Instead of little Jenni, a much taller person stood in the hallway. "Hi, Rissa," he said.

Clarissa yanked the toothbrush out of her mouth, then swallowed the sudsy water, trying to ignore the momentary queasy feeling. Hastily she swiped her arm over her mouth. "You're early. I didn't hear you come in." She looked down at the toothbrush in her hand, then quickly swished her arm behind her back.

Geoff made no effort to hide his grin. "Jenni opened the door before I had a chance to knock. She asked me to put the craft stuff in the car, but I didn't know where it was."

"It's on the kitchen table. She knew that."

Clarissa narrowed her eyes and glared at Jenni, who didn't seem to notice her displeasure. Clarissa knew she probably shouldn't have been annoyed with Jenni. Jenni still wasn't old enough to be embarrassed when caught doing personal things, but Clarissa was. Now, not only had Geoff seen her with toothpaste dripping down her face, but her hair wasn't combed, and she hadn't yet applied her makeup. The only positive was that she was properly dressed, even if she didn't have her shoes on.

When Geoff turned around and disappeared into the kitchen to get the box, she couldn't see if he was laughing at her indignation.

She finished getting ready as quickly as she could while Geoff sat in the kitchen with Jenni. Before too long, they were at the church setting up their classroom.

Clarissa stacked the supplies they brought into neat piles while Jenni helped Geoff get the felts, scissors, and glue from the bins in the closet, since Jenni knew where everything was.

Geoff's voice echoed from within the closet. "Look at this. I never had colored glue when I was a kid. The stuff in here is amazing."

Clarissa checked her watch. "Never mind the supplies. We only have a few minutes until people start dropping their kids off. I'm too new at this to be playing with craft supplies while I'm supposed to be watching kids."

The shuffling in the closet stopped, which caused her to look up. Geoff stood in the opening to the closet, grinning. "What's the matter? You nervous?"

"Maybe just a little. Are you?"

"A little. But between the two of us, we'll do fine."

Jenni's voice piped up from the back of the storage closet. "What about me? Can't I be the helper today?"

Geoff turned around. "Of course you're the helper today. Are you nervous?"

Jenni shook her head, her effort to appear grown-up almost laughable. "No. I been the helper before."

Clarissa cleared her throat. "*I've been* the helper before," she echoed.

Jenni stepped all the way out of the closet, her eyes wide. "You were? I don't 'member when you been the helper."

Geoff bit his lower lip and didn't say a word.

"No, Jenni, I was just trying to help you say it right. Now let's get busy so we can be ready."

The first student arrived at the classroom as the last box of felt pens made it to the teacher's desk.

Not only did the class and craft time go better than anticipated, Geoff was not at all what Clarissa expected, although in retrospect, she should have known. They had previously agreed that Geoff would teach the lesson and Clarissa would lead the craft time. Geoff was a computer programmer, but he would have made a wonderful teacher. He was entertaining, yet serious enough on the key points to drive the lesson home. He could see when their attention spans waned, and he then changed his presentation accordingly.

The craft time went quickly, as she knew it would. They finished just as the first parent arrived.

As usual, Geoff, Clarissa, and Jenni sat together for the main service, and also as usual, they went to the same fast-food restaurant for lunch. The same as every other time, Jenni gobbled down her lunch and ran to the play center before either Geoff or Clarissa had halfway finished theirs.

"After all this time, I still must not be a very interesting date," Geoff said as the glass door closed behind Jenni. "She keeps running off on me."

"Then I must not be a very good big sister, because she does the same thing to me when I bring her here."

He grinned. "I guess we're even then."

"Now that she's gone, what did you think of our Sunday school lesson? I think we did pretty well, don't you?"

Geoff nodded. "We made a pretty good team. Do you want to take turns between teaching the lesson and the craft? Although I have to warn you, I don't think I'd do any better at cutting and gluing than any of the kids."

Clarissa could almost picture Geoff struggling to cut shapes with the awkward child's safety scissors and glue the pieces together using the colored glue he was so enamored with. "Maybe we should stick to the way we did it today. My father always used to say, 'If it ain't broke, don't fix it.' I think that's good advice."

Geoff's expression turned serious. "I'm sorry to say that I didn't really talk much to your father. Your parents sound like they were good Christian people."

"Yes, they were. I still miss them; I probably always will. Do you see your parents often?"

He started absently swirling one fry in the blob of ketchup on the corner of the wrapper. "I see them about once a month or so, sometimes less. I know that sounds bad, but we don't always see eye to eye on things, so I don't go as often as I should."

She wanted to ask him more, but the silence that hung after his words told her he didn't want to elaborate. Moreover, sitting in the middle of the loud and crowded fast-food restaurant wasn't the ideal place to discuss personal issues. However, Clarissa had learned the hard way that often opportunities had to be forced or they were lost forever.

She reached over the table and wrapped her fingers around Geoff's wrist. He stopped moving but didn't pull away.

"Sometimes it helps to talk. I'm a pretty good listener."

"There's nothing to talk about. I keep praying God will open their hearts to see my point, and they're probably doing the same thing about me."

"Is there a middle ground? Can't you meet halfway?"

"Not in this case."

Again, he let his words hang without explaining or letting her know what kind of dispute had no room for middle ground. Clarissa wanted to ask more questions, but Jenni's reappearance closed the window of opportunity.

They ended up back at Geoff's house, where they played video games all afternoon, then nearly destroyed Geoff's kitchen trying to make a gourmet dinner to celebrate the success of their first Sunday school lesson.

By the time Clarissa and Jenni left, it was dark. This time, Geoff walked them home, which Clarissa thought very romantic.

After she unlocked the door and sent Jenni inside to get ready for bed, Clarissa stood on the doorstep beneath the starry sky to say goodnight to Geoff.

It would have been a perfect ending to a perfect day if he kissed her goodnight beneath the starry sky.

She even thought about asking if he'd like to kiss her, but before she could get a word out, he mumbled a quick "Goodnight" and left.

Clarissa crossed her arms and watched him walk the short distance between their homes until he disappeared inside his own front door.

If only. . .

Chapter 7

Geoff sucked in a deep breath as he stood behind the line with the rest of Spot's team, the Flying Fuzzbuttons. He stiffened and looked into the bleachers, where Clarissa and Jenni sat, their attention locked on Spot and the other three dogs on the team.

The weather was warm, although not hot. The sky was overcast, but it didn't feel like it was going to rain. A perfect spring day for an outdoor event.

He almost turned away when Clarissa turned her head slightly and looked straight at him. She smiled, made an exaggerated wink, and gave him a big thumbs-up.

Something funny happened in the pit of Geoff's stomach, only he knew he wasn't hungry.

He hadn't been sure that Spot's team was ready for the big competition, but with Clarissa behind him, he felt like he could do anything, which was ridiculous. She'd never even been to a practice, although he'd taken Jenni a few times. Jenni had been totally enamored with all the dogs, and she'd even jumped the hurdles herself the first time she'd gone.

Fortunately, no one present had asked why he'd brought a little girl with him, because he didn't have an answer.

He didn't know when it happened, but in the time since he'd started "dating" Jenni, his whole life had shifted on its axis. He didn't know if it would ever be right again.

He didn't want a relationship, and he didn't want a family, yet not only was he spending most of his time with a woman and a girl young enough to be his daughter, but he missed them whenever they weren't together.

It was wrong. Very wrong. God wasn't supposed to let this happen, but it was happening, and there was nothing he could do about it.

Geoff's mental meanderings were interrupted by the applause as the scores of the teams before them were shown. The heat between the Flying Fuzzbuttons and the Racing Rovers was next.

Both teams took their positions, and at the signal, the lead dogs were off. Geoff positioned Spot, then released him as soon as Buddy returned and crossed the line.

Spot ran for all he was worth. For a dog with such short legs, he cleared all four hurdles in excellent time, activated the flyball box, caught the ball, and made the return trip even faster than the outgoing run. The split second Spot crossed the line, Shesha bounded forward.

Spot jumped into Geoff's arms, and Geoff praised him for a good run. As the team's height dog, Spot had done well, but the speed needed to win had to be made by the other, bigger dogs. So he wouldn't distract the other team members, Geoff whispered to Spot to tell him how good he'd done, and in so doing, he looked up to Clarissa and Jenni.

Jenni was watching the other dogs racing, but Clarissa was watching him. When she saw him looking back, she smiled and waved. Hesitantly, Geoff waved back, then turned as Bonkers, their fourth dog, crossed the line a full second before the other team's last dog, scoring them at 23.41 seconds. Almost in unison, both teams of four dog handlers turned to see their scores for the heat. The fastest team was not always the winner, the final score being dependent on errors and how many hurdles the dogs knocked down. So far today, none of the dogs had been red-flagged for starting too soon.

"We did it!" A cheer raised for the Flying Fuzzbuttons winning the heat. Geoff could hear Jenni cheering loudest of all.

The Flying Fuzzbuttons placed third in the competition, earning them a ribbon. All handlers praised their dogs fully, since this was the best they'd ever done.

The group broke up for lunch, during which time the flyball equipment would be taken down and the agility equipment set up for the afternoon's events.

Clarissa had packed a picnic lunch. Like most participants, they found a location as private as possible with so many people and dogs sharing the park. They ate quickly, and Geoff returned to the competitors' area with Spot.

The ten-inch division was the first to start. Since Spot was a relative newcomer to Agility, his level, Starters, was first, and unfortunately, his group, the Regulars, began the competition, which didn't give him much time to get used to the setting. Geoff did the preliminary walk through the course, said a short prayer for speed and strength, and took his place.

At the signal they began their run. First Geoff directed Spot over two hurdles and through a chute. He directed Spot to make a slight left and pointed him to the dog walk, giving him the signal to slow down so his feet touched the yellow contact zone, to avoid having points deducted for a fault. When his paws were back on the grass, they turned, and Spot ran through the "L" tunnel, which ended up back under the dog walk.

As Geoff ran beside Spot, directing him over another hurdle, Geoff turned for a split second to see David wave at him, giving Geoff a bad feeling he was going to be in Monday's newspaper. Spot was the smallest dog to be entered in the agility trial competition this year, making him somewhat of a point of interest.

Geoff gritted his teeth and tensed, ready to run again, while he waited for the judge's count at the pause table. At the word "Go," Geoff directed Spot through the weave poles and then into the collapsed chute tunnel. He ran forward and called to Spot as he appeared through the opening, then waved him to the hardest obstacle, the teeter-totter. Unfortunately, Spot's feet didn't touch the contact zone before he jumped off, but Geoff pushed the thought from his mind as he directed Spot over another couple of hurdles, then over the A-frame. In a last burst of energy, they ran at top speed, and Spot flew through the tire jump. By the time Spot made it to the final platform, Geoff was panting as hard as the dog. At the signal that they were done, Spot leapt into Geoff's arms, and Geoff gave him a big hug. Their score was good, but not good enough to win a prize.

Since there were many dogs after them, Geoff headed for the bleachers to sit with Clarissa and Jenni to watch the rest of the competition.

As he approached them, Clarissa and Jenni jumped to their feet. Jenni immediately dropped to the ground to hug Spot, but to Geoff's surprise, Clarissa stepped forward and hugged him.

With her arms over his shoulders and around the back of his neck, they were so close their noses were almost touching. "You both were wonderful! I know you'll get a good score! Congratulations!"

"We don't do it for the score, we do it beca—"

The sudden pressure of Clarissa's lips on his cut off Geoff's words. At first he stiffened, but it only took a split second for the shock to turn to pleasure as he rested his hands on Clarissa's shoulders and kissed her right back.

Her lips were soft and warm and wonderful against his. She started to pull back before he was ready to stop, so he raised his hands and cupped her chin, angled his head a little to the right, and then kissed her again, this time with every bit of his heart and soul involved. He was kissing the woman he loved.

"Ewww!!! You're kissing on the lips! That's yucky!"

Jenni's voice was as effective as dumping a pail of cold water on his head. They separated in a split second.

Clarissa wouldn't look at him, but he looked at her. Her cheeks flamed, and her lips looked as soft as they had just felt.

His gut clenched. What they had done was wrong. Not only had he kissed Clarissa in front of Jenni, he'd kissed her in front of everyone at the park.

Clarissa cleared her throat, but her voice still sounded choked. "Jenni, I think we should go get something to drink. Let's go to the concession stand."

Without giving Jenni a chance to respond, Clarissa rested her hands on Jenni's shoulders, turned her around, and walked away.

Geoff sank to the wooden seat and opened the cooler to get a drink for Spot without thinking about what he was doing.

He'd kissed Clarissa. And he wanted to kiss her again. In private. Where they wouldn't be interrupted.

While Spot slopped at the water, Geoff slumped and buried his face in his hands. He'd known that whatever was happening between himself and Clarissa had been spiraling out of control, but today proved it. He'd fallen in love. That wasn't supposed to happen; yet it had.

Geoff shook his head, then let his arms drop so his elbows rested on his knees. For lack of something better to do, he stared at Spot, who had nothing better in the world to think of than sniffing the corner of the bleacher stand.

Geoff had to do something to extricate himself from this disaster, but he didn't know how. The only thing he did know was that it was going to hurt.

Jenni's voice indicated their imminent return. Geoff stood and watched their approach, drinks in hand.

Clarissa's smile made him feel like he was being poleaxed. His stomach churned, and his heart pounded. He wanted to kiss her again, and he didn't care that Jenni was watching.

But he couldn't. Things had gone too far.

Tonight when he drove them home, he would have to tell them he couldn't see them anymore.

But until then, he didn't want to spoil the day for them, or for himself, either. Like Cinderella, he would wait until the end of the day. At midnight, the dream would be over.

Clarissa reached forward with one of the drinks. "It's grape soda. I remembered you saying you haven't had this since you were a kid, and I couldn't resist."

Their hands brushed as he accepted the drink. Geoff's chest tightened, which he knew was stupid, but he couldn't control it.

"Thanks," he muttered.

Clarissa beamed ear to ear, apparently unaffected. Geoff felt like an idiot.

"I think we should celebrate how good Spot did, but since Spot can't go into a restaurant, I'll order pizza for dinner."

"That sounds nice," he mumbled.

He reminded himself that midnight was many hours way. Until then, he would enjoy the evening, because after tonight, it was over.

Tomorrow, life would be back to normal, and he'd never felt so depressed.

Chapter 8

Clarissa closed her eyes while Jenni prayed over their pizza. She almost had to bite her lip not to interrupt Jenni and shout out praises to God.

Today had been the best day of her life.

After they all chorused a big "Amen" together, they dug in. Clarissa remained silent while Jenni chattered about the dogs she'd seen. It gave her time to think.

Even though she'd been thinking about what it would be like to be kissed by Geoff, she could barely believe what she'd done.

But now that it had happened, she didn't regret it. Not only had he kissed her back, he'd kissed her a second time.

She didn't know why it had taken so long—maybe it was because the last year had been difficult—but she felt like suddenly her eyes had been opened.

Ever since Kyle had left her, she'd been incredibly lonely yet too busy to make the effort to get back into the dating scene. The few times she'd tried to meet someone with whom she might be able to share her life, she'd been terribly disappointed. She'd even told Geoff about a few of her misadventures with men, and he'd gently reminded her that God was in control, and when the right man came along, she'd know it.

Geoff had been half right. God had placed that right man under her nose, but she hadn't known it. At least not until today.

For the last year, Geoff had been the one person she could talk to when she needed someone. He'd always been there when she needed a friend. She knew his schedule. Unless he was sick, he always took Spot out as soon as he got home from work. They'd spent countless hours talking while Jenni and the other children played with Spot.

Even during moments when there was nothing to say, they simply enjoyed each other's company. She'd go home feeling like all was right with the world after spending time with him. She'd never met a man like Geoff, and she knew she never would again. Today, she finally realized that Geoff was the man God had set aside for her to marry and love until her dying day.

Clarissa lowered her head so neither Geoff nor Jenni could see the smile she couldn't wipe off her face. At first he'd been surprised when she kissed him, and she couldn't blame him for that. Geoff was never one to demonstrate strong emotions, especially in public. For him to kiss her in the way he had, openly, in front of all those people, could only indicate that he felt the same way.

If she wasn't sure before, she was positive now. Not only had she fallen in love, she was pretty sure he loved her back.

Spot barking at the back door interrupted her thoughts.

"I'll do it!" Jenni chirped as she dropped her half-eaten piece of pizza onto the plate and ran from the room.

Clarissa found herself staring across the table at Geoff, no doubt with stars in her eyes.

She cleared her throat. "I had no idea you could do that kind of stuff with dogs. It's like a team sport, except it's the dogs that do all the action. But that's not true, either. All the owners run through the course with their dogs."

He nodded, smiling hesitantly. "We have to be in good shape to keep up that pace, that's for sure." His smile widened, making Clarissa's heart pound. "You wouldn't believe what it takes to get some of those dogs to properly trigger the flyball box. If they just take the ball out with their teeth, it's considered cheating."

Before Clarissa could think of anything to say that didn't include dogs, Jenni returned. Having heard talk of flyball, Jenni bombarded Geoff with more questions until they were finished eating and the pizza boxes were cleared.

Once in the living room, they watched a movie Jenni had borrowed from a friend. As usual, Geoff positioned himself in the middle of the couch, Clarissa sat on one side of him, Jenni on the other, and Spot climbed onto Jenni's lap.

Clarissa dearly wished that Geoff would put his arm around her, but he didn't. She tried to convince herself that the reason was because he was supposed to be dating Jenni. However, Jenni had seen them kissing, and Jenni's biggest concern was not that Geoff was kissing the "wrong" woman. It was that they were kissing on the mouth.

By the time the movie was over, Jenni was yawning, which gave Clarissa the opportunity she needed. Before Geoff stood, she tapped him on the arm. "How would you like to carry Jenny to bed? I think we should, you know. . .talk."

Because Geoff was, after all, a man, she expected him to make some kind of comment that it wasn't talking they would do, but more kissing, which would have been fine with Clarissa. Instead, his face paled, and he jumped off the couch. The quick movement startled Jenni, and Jenni's movement startled Spot. Spot sprang out of her arms, Jenni shuffled to the floor, and Spot ran around in small circles, barking at her feet.

"Actually, I think I should leave."

"Leave?" Clarissa sputtered. "But—"

Jenni ran to Geoff and wrapped her arms around his legs. "You can't go yet! I promise I'll be good when it's time to get up for church tomorrow!"

He bent down and gently disengaged Jenni. "I really have to go."

Clarissa, who was the only person left sitting, looked up at Geoff. "What time are you going to pick us up for Sunday school? Same as usual?"

"Maybe it would be best if we met there."

A queasy sensation rolled through the pit of her stomach. She didn't think he meant just for one day. It sounded like the separation was meant to be permanent. Clarissa rose, stepped forward, and rested one hand on Geoff's arm. "What's wrong?"

He stepped back, and she withdrew her touch. "This isn't working out. I think we're seeing too much of each other."

Her stomach turned to lead. "I don't understand. What have I done wrong?" The thought that he was bolting because she'd kissed him confused her. He had seemed to enjoy it as much as she had.

"You've done nothing wrong. It's me. I can't do this." He bent down toward Jenni. "I'll take Spot, please."

Jenni started to sniffle as she passed Spot into Geoff's hands.

Clarissa was too much in shock to cry, but she knew that if they didn't deal with whatever was wrong now, the second the door closed behind him, she would never know. She had to go for broke and be completely honest.

When Kyle left her, she'd demanded to know why, and she was glad she had pushed the issue. He'd left her because Jenni had been added to their relationship. However, she hadn't been that upset. While she certainly liked Kyle, she had still been waiting for love to happen, and it hadn't—even after two years of steady dating. Kyle was no significant loss.

If Geoff left her, she would never recover.

Clarissa forced herself to speak through the tightness in her throat. "Please tell me why you're going. . ." Her eyes burned, but she blinked the tears back. Her voice constricted to barely above a squeak. "Because I love you."

All Geoff's movements froze. His voice cracked when he spoke. "You can't. Love isn't an option for me." He blinked a few times, then shuffled backward. With his hesitation, Spot bolted from his arms.

Clarissa regained her senses in time to scoop Spot up. She backed up a step, holding the dog close to her heart. Geoff couldn't leave without explaining if she held his dog hostage. "Why not? I think you're a very lovable person. You've been a good friend since Mom and Dad died." Jenni chose that moment to wrap her arms around Clarissa's legs. She didn't have to look down. The sniffles told her Jenni was already crying enough for both of them.

"Being friends was fine. But we can't be just friends anymore, so it's over."

"But isn't that the way it's supposed to work? Friendship first, then falling in love?" The ditty she learned as a child playing jump rope sang in her head. *First comes love, then comes marriage, then comes Clarissa with the baby carriage.* Only in this case, she didn't want the baby carriage. But she definitely wanted the love and marriage part.

"Not for me. Give me back my dog."

Pangs of desperation stabbed through her. Common sense deserted her. She made her fingers into the shape of a gun and pressed the tip of her index finger to Spot's head. "Tell me why, or the dog gets it."

"That's not funny, Clarissa. Quit fooling around."

She shuffled back as much as she could with Jenni still attached to her legs. "I'm not trying to be funny. I'm not giving him back until you tell me."

She could see by the tightening of his cheeks and the narrowing of his eyes that he was gritting his teeth.

Clarissa cleared her throat. "I have to know what I did. This afternoon, I thought things were going. . .well."

He dragged one hand down his face, then ran his fingers through his hair. "That shouldn't have happened. If you're looking for anything more than friendship, and I know now you are, then you're going to have to find that elsewhere. I can't be anymore than a casual friend with you."

"How can you say that? What's between us has gone on for over a year."

"Suddenly things have changed. I know you want more." He rammed one hand in his pocket and waved the other in the air. "Love. Marriage. Babies. That's not for me."

"I don't understand. When you kissed me. . ." She let her voice trail off until the room was silent, except for Jenni's sniffling.

Clarissa lightly touched Jenni's shoulder with her free hand. "Geoff and I have to talk alone now. Go get your pajamas on, brush your teeth, and I'll be up to say prayers in a few minutes."

Fortunately, Jenni disappeared without argument.

Geoff crossed his arms over his chest. "Why do you want to drag this out? Isn't it enough for you to hear that I'm not interested in a relationship?"

"No, it's not. I don't believe you. Everything about you says that's not true. You've stuck with me and helped me with Jenni. You're dependable and trustworthy. You're wonderful with children. You're a good Christian man."

"Yeah. With a definite message from God. God doesn't want me to have kids, and that means I'm not getting married."

Images of Geoff and Jenni together cascaded through her mind. She'd heard many excuses from many different men about not wanting to be involved with children, or not being "ready." Everything Geoff did with Jenni denied his words, which only made her angry. "How dare you! I thought you, of all people, could be honest with me."

He stepped closer. His eyes narrowed, and his whole face became tight. "You want honesty? How's this then? I'm a hemophiliac. My grandfather was a hemophiliac, and he passed it on to my mother, who passed it on to both my brother and me. I've been in the hospital so many times I've lost count. It's no fun for me, and it's no fun for my parents to worry. A male carrier can't pass it on to a son, but I would definitely pass it on to a daughter. My brother and his wife decided to take a chance with a family. They had a daughter, and she died. My parents keep pushing me to get married and have kids, even after everything that's happened. It may be more treatable now than when I was a kid, but there's still no cure."

He stepped closer and grabbed Spot from her limp arms. "You don't know what it's like to grow up with everyone treating you like some freak made of glass. I don't think God would fault me for not wanting to put another innocent child through what happened to me. I'm not willing to take the chance that I wouldn't have a girl, so I went out and made sure I would never be able to pass it on. Just like Spot on his last trip to the vet."

He backed up until he was close enough to twist slightly and grab the doorknob with one hand. "Every woman who gets married deserves to have kids, but no one is having kids with me, and that means you, too."

In a split second, he turned fully and opened the door wide.

"Geoff! Wait! This doesn't change anything! I'm not interested in having children. I have Jenni, and she's enough for me."

"You say that now, but in a couple of years your biological clock will be ticking, and you'll change your mind. Go fall in love with someone else, because having kids is no longer an option for me."

Before she could say another word, the door slammed shut behind him.

Everything remained silent while his words slowly sank in. She continued to stare at the back of the closed door until Jenni appeared in her pajamas, clutching her big brown teddy bear. "Where's Geoff? Isn't he going to kiss me goodnight? Just not on the mouth."

Clarissa squatted and pulled Jenni and the bear in for a big hug. "I'm sorry, sweetie, he had to go. Geoff, uh, isn't feeling very good."

"Is he sick?"

Clarissa didn't know enough about hemophilia to give her sister an answer. "In a way, but not really. Tell you what. How would you like to stay up and look it up on the Internet with me?"

Jenni nodded so fast her hair bounced. "Yes! I don't want Geoff to be sick."

"Some things are beyond our control. But that doesn't mean there's nothing we can do. Let's say a prayer, and we'll see what we can find."

Chapter 9

Geoff sat at the kitchen table and stared blankly at the wall. If he were a drinking man, and if he had any alcohol in the house, this would have been the time to tie one on. But the Bible spoke clearly against drunkenness, proving God really did know best—he couldn't take the chance of hurting himself if things got out of control.

He crossed his arms on the table and let his head sink between them.

Against all his better judgment, he'd fallen in love with both Clarissa and Jenni, and it hurt.

Again, he asked God why he was so afflicted, but he didn't receive an answer. More than anything he'd ever wanted in his life, he wanted Clarissa. But he couldn't have her, because he couldn't give her what she deserved.

He ventured into the living room, where he mindlessly flipped channels until he gave up and turned the television off. Finally, he did what he should have done in the first place, what he usually did when life tormented him, and that was to read God's Word. In the silence of his empty house, he picked up the devotional book he'd been following for that year and read the page for the day. The verse it referred to, 1 Peter 4:19, somehow perfectly fit his day: "So then, those who suffer according to God's will should commit themselves to their faithful Creator and continue to do good."

He closed his Bible and squeezed his eyes shut. He indeed was suffering, because he did want children and he did want to marry Clarissa. However, in his actions today, he hadn't been faithful to his Creator. He'd abandoned Jenni, and she still needed him. Despite his own struggles, he had to continue to do the good God was asking him to do, and that was to help Jenni until she didn't need him anymore.

With that thought, Geoff went to bed. Tomorrow he was teaching Sunday school. He would never have seen himself as a Sunday school teacher, yet not only did he enjoy teaching, but the children responded to him. Therefore, he would continue, despite his pain. God's will was more important than his own.

Geoff flexed his sore fingers, then continued on his mission to pick up every piece of scrap yarn and snip of paper. He almost felt like writing a letter to the manufacturer, but none of the children had difficulty managing the safety scissors, only him.

With perfect timing, he picked up the last scrap as Clarissa directed the last child out with her parents. However, before he could dash out, Jenni dropped the box of felts into the bin and rushed to him.

"We looked up what you gots on the computer. We also is getting a book from the lieberry."

"That's library," Clarissa whispered behind Jenni, then looked up at him. "We did a little research last night, and we also reserved a book online. We want to learn all we can."

His heart pounded. "Why are you doing this? Don't you understand what I told you?"

"I understand. But you don't seem to understand what I told you. I have Jenni, and she's all I need. Besides you, of course. We both love you too much to let this go."

He backed up until the corner of one of the tables dug into the back of his legs. "I told you yesterday. Let it go, Clarissa."

"No. I won't. Jenni won't, either. You're the one who has to let it go. We can handle this together."

"Drop it, Clarissa. This isn't the time to argue. We're in God's house."

"Jenni and I aren't arguing. It's you who's doing all the arguing."

Geoff knew differently, but to say so would only make the discussion continue. He stared first at Clarissa's expectant face and then Jenni's. He knew anything Jenni thought or did was out of pure innocence, but Clarissa should have known better. "I'm not arguing. That's just the way it is," he muttered, then grabbed his Bible and dashed out of the room.

He hurried to the sanctuary, for the first time not stopping to chat with any of his friends. He sat in his usual seat near the front, starting to think how strange, even depressing it felt to be sitting alone once again, when Clarissa and Jenni shuffled in, one on either side of him.

He lowered his voice to a harsh whisper. "What are you two doing here?"

Clarissa smiled so sweetly his stomach did a flip. "This is God's house. We're here to worship with friends. One friend actually."

He gritted his teeth. She knew he wouldn't cause a scene by moving. Besides, he had a feeling that if he got up and chose another seat, they would only follow him again. If there was anything he'd learned about Clarissa in the last year and a half, it was that she was tenacious.

"You win, for now. But you're not going to change my mind."

He noticed he was getting somewhere when she didn't respond or smile. Fortunately, the lights dimmed and the worship leader came on to begin the service, giving Geoff something else to concentrate on, which was worshiping God, the reason he was there in the first place.

Unfortunately, he kept getting distracted, not from Jenni misbehaving, but because she sat perfectly still and participated in the worship. She even listened to the pastor's sermon between trying to read the bulletin notes and playing quietly with a toy in her lap.

Part of him was so proud of her he thought he would burst, but before he could get too carried away, the more sensible and realistic part of him was reminded that he was cutting off all ties with Jenni.

As the service closed, he took advantage of being in God's house to pray extra hard for an answer. He didn't want to lose either Clarissa or Jenni, but to allow them to keep their hopes up was being very unfair, especially to Clarissa. When it came time for her to get married, she deserved someone with whom she could have a real marriage, which included a real family.

The pastor's "Amen" and closing benediction signaled the congregation to stand, but before Geoff could move, Jenni scrambled onto his lap. Before he realized what she was doing, she threw her arms around his neck and gave him a big hug. "I still love you, Geoff. Don't you love me anymore?"

His eyes burned, and his throat constricted. "Of course I still love you, Jenni," he finally managed to choke out, hopefully not sounding like an emotional basket case. But more than loving Jenni as a sweet little girl, he loved Clarissa as a woman. Against all logic, the annoying way she wouldn't leave him alone made him love her even more.

At his words, Jenni slipped her hands around the back of his neck, ready to hug him again, when suddenly, she froze. Very slowly, she ran her fingers along the chain of the Medic Alert tag he always wore around his neck. Without speaking, she pulled it out. "What's this?" she asked as she ran her fingers on the punched-in lettering.

His fingers shook as he slowly turned it over for her to see the universal logo. "It's a tag that says what's wrong with me, in case I'm in an accident and can't talk."

Before he could remove the medallion from Jenni's small fingers and tuck it back under his shirt, Clarissa snatched it from them both. "It says you're B positive."

Geoff grabbed the medallion out of Clarissa's hand and dropped it back into his shirt. He set Jenni back into the chair and stood.

Their concern for him only reminded him once again of what he couldn't have. "So now you know my blood type. I hope you found that interesting. Now if you'll excuse me, I'm going home for lunch. Alone."

He heard Clarissa's sharp gasp as he turned around and walked out.

He didn't want it to end this way, but to keep going and to keep her hopes up would only make it hurt worse, although Geoff didn't know if that was possible.

Chapter 10

Clarissa watched Jenni squeeze her eyes shut and grit her teeth to shut out the hurt.

She'd never been so proud of her little sister as she was right now.

The nurse smiled as she wrapped a label around the vial containing Jenni's blood sample and tucked it into the holder beside Clarissa's vial. "We should have the results later today. We'll give you a call."

The second the door closed, Jenni squirmed off Clarissa's lap. "Do you think this will make Geoff feel better? Do you think he'll want to see us again?"

Clarissa gave her sister a hug. "I don't know. Do you remember when Melissa's mom stepped on their puppy's tail and it growled and hid from everyone? That's kind of how Geoff feels right now."

Jenni nodded thoughtfully, making Clarissa hope that Jenni wouldn't minimize Geoff's pain by thinking of him as an injured puppy, but it was the best analogy she could think of.

She'd never seen such pain in his face as yesterday when he walked out of the church. Her heart ached for him, but this was the best she could think of that they could do for him.

The whole drive home, they talked more about Geoff and what they could possibly do to make him feel better. Of course, there were no answers. All she could do was try to convince Jenni that if Geoff still closed the door to their love and friendship, it wasn't her fault.

She continued to think more about him after she tucked Jenni into bed. She could understand Geoff's conviction about not wanting to get married because he refused to pass on a genetic disorder. She even found his sacrifice noble.

If only she could find a way to convince him that she meant what she said. Not every woman wanted to be a mother, and she was one of those women. She loved her sister more than life itself and held no resentment or bitterness that she had to be as a parent to Jenni. But that situation aside, she very seriously had no desire to have children of her own.

Clarissa closed her eyes and prayed. Even though Geoff thought he wasn't a candidate for marriage, Clarissa still thought that God had dropped him into her lap for that very reason. She knew Geoff loved her the same way she loved him. He only needed to open his heart and admit it. Together, they could work around his medical condition.

Instead of turning on the television and mindlessly flipping channels, Clarissa went to bed to pray. Hopefully, she would have some answers soon.

Clarissa had just touched the door handle on her car after dropping Jenni off at the sitter for the Wednesday night Bible study meeting when her cell phone rang. As quickly as she could, she fumbled with the zipper and mumbled a quick hello.

"Hi, Clarissa. It's Geoff. I need a favor."

Clarissa's heart pounded. Ever since the weekend, Geoff had tried to avoid her, but she'd been diligent in not letting him push her away. Monday when she and Jenni arrived back from the clinic, they had knocked on his door, bringing Chinese food for dinner. She could see that part of him still wanted to be with her, but part of him wanted to push her away. Fortunately, the part of him that she knew loved her won, and he invited them in.

Tuesday she and Jenni had waited behind the bush in the front yard and then pounced on Geoff when he took Spot for their daily walk. Again, she could tell he was having a hard time pushing her away. So they made his decision for him. Jenni lured Spot inside with a treat and a tennis ball, knowing Geoff would have to follow, and he did.

Since Clarissa planned on seeing him at the Bible study meeting, they had left him alone today, for a few hours, anyway.

That he was phoning her could only mean that he was finally starting to weaken, and that he could finally see how God had put them together.

She tried to sound serious and dignified, when what she really wanted to do was dance. "Sure, anything you want, just ask."

"I need you to go get Spot for me. I was in a car accident on the way home from work today. I'm fine, but they want to keep me in the hospital for twenty-four hours as a precaution. Spot probably needs to be let out real bad, but this is the first chance I had to use the phone."

Clarissa's heart nearly stopped beating. Like most people, she'd assumed that a hemophiliac's greatest danger was of bleeding to death, even from a minor cut. However, she'd learned that instead the greatest danger was what couldn't be seen. The greatest risk was of internal bleeding, because that was something that often wasn't noticed until too late. He also was at greater risk of complications from a concussion because of the failure of his blood to clot like everyone else's.

"Don't worry; I'll take him to my place overnight. How are you, really?"

"I'm fine. It's not like this has never happened to me before. I guess I'll see you tomorrow when I pick up Spot. Thanks, Clarissa. Bye."

Clarissa tucked the phone in her purse and ran to Geoff's house.

Her hands shook as she unlocked his front door. He'd given her the key to his house, but he refused to give her the key to his heart.

As soon as she saw to Spot's needs, Clarissa drove to the hospital as fast as she could without getting a ticket. She found Geoff with the back of the bed raised to a seating position, reading. When she stepped into the room, he flinched and fumbled the book.

Clarissa walked to his side, pulled up a chair, and sat. "Jenni and I both got our blood typed a couple of days ago. I'm O positive, so I can donate if you need. Jenni's B positive like you, so she can donate when she's older."

He inhaled sharply and set the book aside. "I don't know what to say. After the accident they gave me a number of drugs that make my blood clot. Things have changed a lot over the years. I'd only need a donation if I had surgery or if I had been bleeding already. But I'm touched that you both would go to all that trouble just for me."

"I'd do anything for you. I love you, Geoff. I know you think you're doing what's best for me, but you're wrong. How can I convince you that I don't want any more children besides Jenni? No one seems to understand. I love Jenni, but she's really all I will ever need or want."

Taking her chances, she wrapped her fingers around Geoff's hand. Her voice dropped to barely above a hoarse croak. "I need you, Geoff, but you won't take me. Why? I know you love me, too."

Beneath her fingers, Geoff's pulse raced. His voice cracked when he finally spoke. "I can't impose all my problems on you. The stress and worry every time something like this happens would get to you eventually. You're better off without me."

She gave his hand a gentle squeeze. "No. We're better off together. It feels good to know I can donate to you in case of an emergency. I'll do that whether you marry me or not. But I do want us to get married. Try and put aside your preconceived notions and think about what it could be like. Please."

He squeezed his eyes shut. "Dear God. . . ," he mumbled, and she could tell that he wasn't using their Lord's name in vain. He was praying from the depths of his soul for an answer.

Clarissa squeezed her eyes shut and did the same.

For a few minutes, the only noise was that of the usual traffic in the hall.

Geoff cleared his throat and spoke very softly "Are you really sure of this? I don't do typical 'guy' things like team sports, but I have to always keep exercising. That's why I do agility with Spot. We go for a long walk every day, regardless of the weather. I'm very diligent with my diet. Still, there are going to be some scary moments in the future. I consider marriage a lifetime commitment. I have no intention of just trying it to see if it works. "

She squeezed his hand. Beneath her fingers, she could feel him trembling. Clarissa gave him a shaky smile. "I still think you're a keeper."

He slid his hands out from hers, reached over, and embraced her as best he could from his position on the hospital bed. "I love you so much, Clarissa. If you'll have a pathetic specimen like me, I'll be honored if you'll marry me."

A nurse's voice echoed over the PA system that visiting hours were over. Clarissa stood and leaned over the bed toward him.

She brushed a short kiss across his lips and backed up just as a nurse stepped in and reminded her that it was time to leave.

Clarissa waved and blew him a kiss on her way out the door. "Jenni's with a sitter; I have to run. See you tomorrow when you get home."

Epilogue

S o if you don't mind, Jenni, with your permission, I would like to marry your sister. I know we originally thought I was going to marry you, but it didn't work out that way." Geoff held his breath, waiting for either tears or an argument.

Jenni looked up at him, her eyes wide. "That's okay. I been talking to Bradley, and he says you're too old for me. But Bradley says you'd make a good big brother."

Geoff let go a relieved sigh. "Bradley sounds like a smart person. Who is Bradley?"

Jenni grinned ear to ear. "Bradley is in my class at school. He's very smart. I think one day I'm going to marry Bradley! I was too 'fraid to tell you because I didn't want to make you sad. But you're going to marry Rissa, so that's okay."

Geoff tried to hold back a groan as Jenni skipped off.

Clarissa's fingers intertwined with his. "She wouldn't have been like this six months ago. God really did put you with us to protect Jenni's heart."

Geoff nodded. "I guess. But now who is going to protect the world from Jenni?"

Before Clarissa could answer, Jenni reappeared. "Do I gets to be flower girl again?"

Geoff hunkered down to be at eye level with her. "Yes, I guess you do."

She clapped her hands. "Yippee! Then Spot can carry the rings like Cody did for Stan and Abby! And this time, I'll catch the bouquet all by myself!"

Geoff and Clarissa looked at each other. "Uh-oh. . ."

About the Authors

Lena Nelson Dooley lives in Hurst, Texas, with her husband, James, and enjoys her children, grandchildren, and great-grandchildren. Aside from writing, Lena has been a speaker to women's groups and retreats, as well as writing seminars and conferences. Lena appreciates any opportunity to spread the Gospel through missions work and writing.

Nancy J. Farrier is an award-winning author of numerous books, articles, short stories, and devotions living in Southern California. She is married and the mother of five children and one grandson. Nancy feels called to share her faith with others through her writing.

Pamela Griffin lives in Texas with her family. She fully gave her life to Christ in 1988 after a rebellious young adulthood and owes the fact that she's still alive today to an all-loving and forgiving God and to a mother who steadfastly prayed and had faith that God could bring her wayward daughter "home." Pamela's main goal in writing Christian romance is to help and encourage those who do know the Lord and to plant a seed of hope in those who don't.

Multi-published author of numerous award-winning books, Loree Lough is also a frequent guest speaker who encourages other writers. She lives in Maryland with her husband of (mumble-mumble) years, where she's determined to stay until she succeeds in prying the secret Old Bay Seasoning recipe from McCormick employees.

Tracie Peterson, bestselling, award-winning author of over ninety fiction titles and three non-fiction books, lives and writes in Belgrade, Montana. As a Christian, wife, mother, writer, editor, and speaker (in that order), Tracie finds her slate quite full.

Janet Lee Barton has lived all over the southern United States, but she and her husband plan to now stay put in Oklahoma. With three daughters and six grandchildren between them, they feel blessed to have at least one daughter and her family living in the same town. Janet loves being able to share her faith through her writing. Happily married to her very own hero, she is ever thankful that the Lord brought Dan into her life, and she wants to write stories that show that the love between a man and a woman is at its best when the relationship is built with God at the center.

In 1997, when Diann Hunt and her husband, Jim, started on their three-mile trek through Amish country, she had no idea she was taking her first steps toward a new career. Inspired by their walk, she wrote an article, which was published a year later. In 2001, her first novella hit the shelves, with other novellas and novels following thereafter. Diann, an accomplished writer and a beloved wife, mother, grandmother, and friend, passed away to her heavenly reward in late 2013.

Sandra Petit is the author of several captivating romance novels, including *Rose in Bloom*. She is a retired homeschool mom who now focuses her attention on spoiling her sweet grandson and managing her instructional website, Crochet Cabana. She lives in the New Orleans area with her family.

Gail Sattler lives in Vancouver, BC, where you don't have to shovel rain, with her husband, three sons, two dogs, and a lizard who is quite cuddly for a reptile. When she's not writing, Gail is making music, playing electric bass for a local jazz band, and acoustic bass for a community orchestra. When she's not writing or making music, Gail likes to sit back with a hot coffee and a good book.